W9-CBI-502

Praise for Sheila Curran and *Everyone She Loved*

"Sheila Curran has amazing insight into the love-hate relationship that women have with each other and their own bodies. . . . I was up way past my bedtime, unable to stop turning pages. I had to know what happened to this family. Read this book, then pass it on to your dearest friend. She'll thank you."

—Joshilyn Jackson, nationally bestselling author

"Sheila Curran writes novels that readers love—full of emotional complexity and rich plot twists, novels that echo our own deep desires and greatest fears. In her second novel, she takes on themes that touch us all—love, loss, motherhood, wifehood, and the sisterhood of friendship."

—Julianna Baggott, nationally bestselling author

"Brilliant. . . . For everyone who knows that love works, even when it's complicated, for everyone who screws up, and can still do the right thing after all, and for everyone who enjoys a great novel, with friendship and forgiveness at its heart."

—Paul Shepherd, award-winning author

Diana Lively Is Falling Down

"Beautifully detailed and rich in exceptional characterization. . . . Curran's novel gently reminds readers that fantasy has a place in everyone's life, and dreams can come true. Uniquely uplifting and never didactic, this is a gem."

—*Booklist* (starred review)

"A terrific pick-me-up. . . . Filled with characters who make you laugh out loud even as they break your heart, this is a funny, warm, inventive, original book."

—Jodi Picoult, #1 *New York Times* bestselling author

"Brilliant, touching, and funny as hell, *Diana Lively Is Falling Down* packs a powerful punch. A poignant and biting satire of contemporary family life, American business, ivory tower academics, and trans-Atlantic cultural differences. . . . Wry, engaging, and wise beyond words, Diana is bound to delight and amaze."

—Carlos Eire, National Book Award–winning author

Everyone She Loved is also available as an ebook.

ALSO BY SHEILA CURRAN

Diana Lively Is Falling Down

Everyone
She Loved

◆ A NOVEL ◆

Sheila Curran

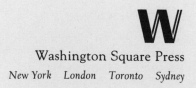

Washington Square Press
New York   London   Toronto   Sydney

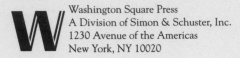

Washington Square Press
A Division of Simon & Schuster, Inc.
1230 Avenue of the Americas
New York, NY 10020

This book is a work of fiction. Names, characters, places, and incidents either are products of the author's imagination or are used fictitiously. Any resemblance to actual events or locales or persons, living or dead, is entirely coincidental.

Copyright © 2009 by Sheila Curran

All rights reserved, including the right to reproduce this book or portions thereof in any form whatsoever. For information address Atria Books Subsidiary Rights Department, 1230 Avenue of the Americas, New York, NY 10020.

First Washington Square Press trade paperback edition March 2010

WASHINGTON SQUARE PRESS and colophon are registered trademarks of Simon & Schuster, Inc.

For information about special discounts for bulk purchases, please contact Simon & Schuster Special Sales at 1-866-506-1949 or business@simonandschuster.com.

The Simon & Schuster Speakers Bureau can bring authors to your live event. For more information or to book an event, contact the Simon & Schuster Speakers Bureau at 1-866-248-3049 or visit our website at www.simonspeakers.com.

Designed by Kyoko Watanabe

Manufactured in the United States of America

10 9 8 7 6 5 4 3 2 1

The Library of Congress has cataloged the hardcover edition as follows:

Curran, Sheila.
Everyone she loved : a novel / by Sheila Curran.—1st Atria Books hardcover ed.
p. cm.
1. Love—Fiction. 2. Friendship—Fiction. 3. Domestic fiction. 4. Psychological fiction.
I. Title.

PS3603.U768E84 2009
813'.6—dc22   2008049770

ISBN 978-1-4165-9066-8
ISBN 978-1-4165-9067-5 (pbk)
ISBN 978-1-4391-0071-4 (ebook)

For John Corrigan, my favorite pirate, without whom
most of life's adventures would have passed me by.
Thank you for all these years as a kept woman, for being
such a wonderful father, and for keeping me on my toes.
You are my love.

CODICIL

I, Joseph Adorno, do hereby agree:

if my wife, Penelope Cameron May,

should die before our daughters have reached eighteen years of age,

I will not remarry or cohabitate

without the written approval of a majority of the persons listed below:[1]

Signed: Joseph Adorno   Date: _____ Signature _____

We, friends and family of Penelope Cameron May, do hereby agree to give genuine and rigorous consideration to the suitability of Joseph Adorno's spousal choices as they would affect the health and happiness of his daughters, Tessa and June Cameron Adorno.[2]

Signed: Lucy Vargas   Date: _____ Signature _____

Signed: Martha Templeton   Date: _____ Signature _____

Signed: Susannah Newsome Date: _____ Signature _____

Signed: Clover Lindstrom   Date: _____ Signature _____

_____

1. Breach of this agreement will require Mr. Adorno's immediate resignation from all executive duties at the Cameron Foundation as well as forfeiture of further annual disbursements and/or marital allotments.

2. Parties will oversee the annual disbursements of funds to Mr. Adorno and approve payment of marital allotment of fifteen million dollars in the event of unanimous approval by said signatories.

Prologue

Penelope Cameron May had more money than God, which may have explained her need to play the deity from time to time. This impulse took on even greater urgency once Penelope's daughters were born. She added a codicil to her will, appointing her stepsister and three best friends from college to make certain that in the event of her own untimely death, her husband didn't marry the wrong woman.

Joey had initially laughed at his wife's legal device, calling it a "postmortem remote control." Penelope said she preferred to think of it as a safety belt.

You could tender all kinds of explanations for Penelope's codicil, but the most obvious was the fact that after her mother died of ovarian cancer, her grief-maddened father had married a deep-fried Southern bimbo, big of breast and small of soul. The marriage hadn't lasted very long, but on the other hand, two years can seem an eternity to a six-year-old reeling from her mother's death. When the second wife ran off with another man, leaving behind her own birth daughter to be raised by Penelope's daddy, Penelope's protective mind-set was only reinforced. This was an imprint that all the happiness of her own marriage could not erase.

In Penelope's estimation, romantic attraction endangered a parent's ability to make sound judgments, its effects somewhere between the false exhilaration induced by crack cocaine and the hallucinatory optimism of Ecstasy.

It didn't help that her husband, Joey Adorno, was the quintessential *catch*. Smart, funny and true to his word, the man also happened to look like he'd just walked off an underwear ad shoot. Add to this the small fortune he would inherit and it wasn't hard to imagine Cinderella's stepmother setting up shop in their small beach town and waiting patiently for the ripe fruit to fall from the tree.

It wasn't that Joey was stupid, but then again, Penelope would have told you, neither was her own father. Marcus had loved his daughter like nobody's business but still had gone off the deep end and married the worst possible substitute for her mother. When it came to women, men could easily be deceived. End of story. This was a postmodern, politically incorrect and nevertheless profoundly obvious *truth*. It wasn't just Penelope's childhood trauma that taught her this. No. There was something else, a closely held secret, a cause for shame. Unlike her other character flaws, which Penelope would dissect to great effect at the drop of a hat, there existed a galling, awful, stupid *thing* she'd done that wasn't ever trotted out with port and cheese at the end of a marvelous meal. That mistake was something Penelope had tried to bury just as deep as she could, not only for herself, but for the benefit of everyone she loved, or so she felt at the time.

For now, lest we complicate an already intricate tale, let's just say that Penelope had several reasons for making sure her family would be safe if she died. As for Joey, he never really believed the document he'd signed along with Lucy and the others would ever be anything more than a sop to his wife's overactive imagination.

After all, everyone knew Penelope was a little histrionic when it came to those things she couldn't control. She cultivated a sense of doom you could not help but laugh with her about. She knew just how hilarious she was, poor little rich girl haunted by her neurotic imagination, dangling sarcomas and car wrecks where sugar plum fairies and Swiss boarding schools should have been.

It was just part of her *shtick*, as her best friend, Lucy Vargas, called it, this wink and a nod toward a premature death. They'd all laughed it off, her husband, her friends, ganging up on her delusions of doom until she'd worn them down, one suitably dark and liquid evening when they'd finally agreed to sign the codicil. After all, that particular year had been a spectacularly bad one for Penelope. Not only had her father died of a heart attack at sixty years old, but a plane she'd been on a few weeks later had come very close to crashing when its landing gear wouldn't descend.

Years after, when everything began to fall apart, even Joey would have to admit that he'd surrendered first. Something had overcome him, a momentary weakness. Or was it instead a strength of imagination? However silly it was, this ridiculous fear, surely it wasn't worth keeping his wife awake at night. She must have known he was humoring her, signing off on that ridiculous contract. At the time, however, it just seemed like a kindness.

By the time Joey and her friends each trooped into the second lawyer's office to sign the official documents, Joey had already taken to calling his wife's committee the Gang of Four. This was a name he'd originally handed Penelope and her dorm suite mates back in college, when China's notorious political junta had been all over the news and so many of the decisions Penelope delivered appeared to have been vetted by her three best friends but not her lovesick boyfriend.

"I hope you'll let me know when you decide we're getting married," he'd remarked in their fourth year of college, after she'd submitted his senior thesis for the university prize without asking. "I might want to get myself a suit."

"Don't worry, I know your size," Penelope had laughed.

The year they'd met, she'd replaced most of his clothes with catalog items that looked pretty identical to what he'd worn before except for the telltale softness of the cloth and the labels he'd only seen in magazines. If he'd been the only recipient of her generosity, he might have taken offense, but she'd done the same for her girlfriends and even some of her favorite teaching assistants. Joey knew it was just Penelope's *way*.

After they'd graduated, it was only a matter of time before Penelope would manage to tempt each and every member of the Gang of Four to move south with her to Omega, Florida, the town where she'd grown up. With its charming central square, sea breezes and low-country architecture, Omega was within spitting distance of the Atlantic Ocean and the Georgia border. Unlike so many benighted beach towns, this one hadn't been overrun with tourists or paved within an inch of its life. No, Omega's fortunes relied on the cleanest industry of all, philanthropy, otherwise known as the Cameron Foundation. The area's picturesque qualities had been preserved by generations of foundation lawyers who took their charity's environmental and economic mission a mite seriously. Best of all, the village was a haven for artists, with its reasonable cost of living and a series of grants restricted to local creative talent. "Hell, it's so cheap to live here, you can't afford not to," Penelope had laughed. In Lucy's case, as the recipient of several years of resident artist grants, this was true enough, though Lucy hadn't needed much inducement. After all, Omega was close to Charleston, where she'd grown up. Penelope's presence there was certainly icing on the cake, made even sweeter with the addition of Susannah and Martha to the Cameron Foundation's staff.

Envious onlookers might have argued with Penelope's hiring of her own husband and dear friends, but it was also true that all her job candidates brought with them certain attributes that met the foundation's particular needs. Joey had graduated with a double major in political science and sociology, Susannah would take top honors in finance and accounting, and Martha, the last recruit, had made the *Law Review* at UVA. No one could argue with their qualifications, quibble as they might over the suspicion that each applicant had been groomed by Penelope for the work of running a major international foundation from the time they'd all met in college.

Certainly her friends weren't balking. Who in their right mind would have passed up a chance to work for the legendary Cameron Foundation? Getting paid to give away money? To any number of worthwhile causes? Jetting across the world to witness firsthand the effects of projects on the poor, the sick, the weary? It was another form of playing God, except this time, it came with benefits.

Lucy was the only exception to this mass hiring campaign, exempted by her artistic talent, which would have been wasted at the foundation. Instead, Penelope had made it her business to grow Lucy's painting career, connecting her with galleries, museum curators and other useful contacts. When Lucy had finally exhausted the foundation's quota of one-year grants, Penelope had presented her with a large bed-and-breakfast that had been in her father's family for generations. "You need a reliable source of income," Penelope had explained offhandedly. She made it seem like the gift she'd given Lucy was a small but functional item, a coffeemaker or alarm clock, not the sort of present that took legal counsel, batches of paperwork and weeks of persuasion to execute.

Lucy had been embarrassed by the offer, even as she knew how well it would suit her needs. "No way. I'd feel like a kept woman or something."

"Oh, hush, Lucy. You know I've got more than I can spend in twenty lifetimes. Why can't I support your art?"

For Penelope, such largesse wasn't exactly *noblesse oblige*, more like *easy come, easy go*, though as fate would have it, such a turn of phrase would one day come to have the most unfortunate ring of truth.

Chapter One

Eight years after signing the codicil to her best friend's will, Lucy Vargas was celebrating her fortieth birthday with her closest companions and one perfect stranger. The stranger, a dance instructor and nutritionist who worked at the town's newest fitness franchise, had been picked up along with the gift Lucy was opening, a small bracelet-size box wrapped in gold foil and festooned with white organza ribbon.

The present had been wrapped by Penelope's stepsister, Clover Lindstrom, who was proud of her creativity, and of the guest she'd brought to Lucy's gathering. Who else would have thought of a Kick the Pounds! certificate for a fortieth-birthday gift?

Who else indeed? Lucy was thinking, the color rising in her cheeks, prompting the stranger to wonder if the birthday girl was embarrassed at Clover's generosity.

This question, like so many that the newcomer would raise about Lucy, was completely off the mark.

First of all, Lucy was *not* a blusher. Her skin, unlike the vast majority of the world's redheads, was the same unruffled bronze as countless generations of Spanish ancestors. It wasn't the sort of tender-headed mood-ring complexion that broadcast its bearer's emotions far and near. Besides, a meticulous observer would have noticed that the color change began with Lucy's narrow nose, pinking up from her delicately curved nostrils and blossoming out to her wide cheekbones before rising to those unnaturally dark Sephardic eyebrows, plucked within an inch of their Mediterranean lives for this very occasion.

No, Lucy was not a blusher. Nor was she an ungrateful wretch. She knew precisely how lucky she was, the owner of this beautiful rambling house on the ocean, surrounded by friends from college, a painter who'd established herself in the world of fine art. Nothing to sneeze at, her good fortune.

Why then, instead, would Lucy have been trying so hard not to cry?

Was she sensitive about her generous figure, about turning forty without a husband, much less children? This might have been the unexpected guest's next speculation, were she to ponder the slight hiccup in Lucy's manner, the lack of conviction in the way she had lifted her glass to her friends.

No, none of these complaints explained the sadness, which revealed itself only in the sudden tilt of Lucy's shot glass, the way she winced at the Jack Daniel's pouring down her lovely throat.

It still happened, going on two years, no matter how often she found herself ambushed by the very same impossible desire. Lucy's first thought, opening the intricately wrapped box from Clover, had been a gleeful impulse to call Penelope and share the latest Clover Moment, over which the two would *howl*.

"You are such a bitch!" Lucy's unspoken admonition was aimed at herself, a private term of endearment, admiration even, that Lucy and Penelope had begun using in college and had tossed affectionately at each other ever since. "You bitch!" they'd crow, hugging each other, loving the way the words sounded so opposite from what they'd meant.

Lately, Lucy had found herself repeating the words as a form of self-comfort and, simultaneously, a form of self-reproach. It was not the time to make a spectacle of herself, not in front of Penelope's family, who were trying their best to make her happy on this special day.

Tessa, fourteen, had painted a card of Lucy's childhood home in Charleston, copied painstakingly from one of her family albums. June, ten, had tricked out the dining room with crepe paper and balloons. Joey, his voice ragged from a nasty cold, had marked the auspicious occasion with a poignant anecdote about how he'd met Lucy and Penelope at the University of Virginia.

Around the table, other celebrants had joined in with their own tales of yore. Martha and Susannah had gone to UVA too, had participated in the same revelries about which Joey was waxing so nostalgic, and Sateesh, Martha's husband, had heard these stories so many times he felt he might as well have been an alumnus too.

Clover, Penelope's stepsister, hated it when people brought up the university, for she'd not gotten in, in spite of her adoptive father's intercessions on her behalf. Perhaps that was why, after Lucy opened her present, Clover had stood up and cleared her throat. She opened a large purple scroll she'd lettered in silver verse. "Lucy, I wrote you a poem," she said. "I was going to set it to music but I ran out of time."

Clover placed her manicured hand on her heart.

> If Penny were here, I know she'd say,
> We'll go to Paris, I promise, someday,
> Until then, let's lose that weight,
> Just like your French sophisticate.
> I'll go too,
> We'll do it together,
> And be best pals through nasty weather.

Clover stood, her trim figure enshrined in a pair of tan gingham capris with matching bustier. Her hands were clasped, her eyes shining with the emotion of the moment, grateful to have been able to give Lucy such a useful present.

"I don't know how to thank you," Lucy had said gravely, pinching the skin at the inside of her elbow. She could not look at Martha or Susannah, or she would start laughing. Then they'd all be forced to spend the rest of the night comforting Clover, whose neediness outstripped even her cluelessness, at least when it came to pressing Lucy's buttons.

This was not something Lucy would ever say out loud. Still, the thought crept in from time to time, ever since that famous night eight years earlier, when Penelope had finally talked each of them into signing her contract. Initially, instead of quieting her fears as the signatories had expected, their capitulation only seemed to confirm the urgency of Penelope's pessimism. She had spent the evening spelling out ever more precisely the things they must attend to in the event of her death. This included a complete catechism about taking care of poor Clover as well as Tessa and June. By night's end, Penelope had extracted numerous promises from each of them, promises not one of them expected to have to keep.

Even Penelope, whose imagination had been formidable, couldn't have known how things would turn out; she was just being herself, her lovably worried self. Nothing pleased her more than to talk about her impending death from a plane crash, a car wreck, killer bees or a brain tumor masquerading as a migraine, unless it was, of course, her epitaph or her funeral. "Let Clover sing. She'll be the center of attention."

"Well, no better time than a funeral for the voice of an angel."

Lucy was alluding to a compliment Clover had gotten in her teenage pageant days and couldn't help but introduce into conversation at the oddest times, no matter how far-flung, no matter how off topic.

"Don't be mean, now," Penelope had scolded, overcome with guilt at having laughed at Lucy's sentimental swoon, her faux reverence, her dainty elocution.

If there was one thing Lucy knew, it was how much they all loved Clover, even when she was driving them completely crazy. For that, Penelope deserved a huge amount of credit. "Oh, stop feeling guilty, you've been great to her. Nicer than her own mother, for goodness sake."

"Hard to be meaner, hon," Penelope had murmured.

❖ ❖ ❖

For Penelope, playing God had certain spillover effects, for her view of human nature was almost supernaturally forgiving. Clover might have seemed shallow, even silly, to most people, but Penelope had observed the damage inflicted on her stepsister at an early age. There was the fact that Clover's mother had eventually abandoned her, and then there were the two years before that, when Tabitha had been married to Penelope's father. This was a period that Penelope liked to call the "reign of terror, poise and cosmetics," when Mommy Dearest had either ignored the children completely or relentlessly prepared them for regional competitions of Tiny Confederate Dames of the South. By the time they attended that last contest in Savannah, Tabitha had already met her next husband, a bass boat magnate from Montgomery. The man apparently didn't care for children, but such conclusions were way beyond Clover's six-year-old ken. No, for Clover, the explanation was obvious. Having failed to place in the semifinals, she would just have to try harder to become the sort of person who pleased her mother enough to bring her back.

"You have to take care of her," Penelope had insisted the night they'd agreed to the contract, holding the champagne bottle over Lucy's glass without pouring, a quid pro quo in the making.

"Stop it," Lucy had laughed. "We're all going to be little old ladies together."

"I mean it."

"I know you do. That's the saddest part."

Lucy often thought back to this conversation, the way they'd all laughed, even Penelope, though some prescient inkling must have been telling her otherwise. *How could we have known?* Lucy asked herself regularly, a mantra against the guilt she felt for dismissing her friend's fears.

Up to the very moment your life changed, it was impossible to abandon the survival tactic some people called optimism, others denial. Lucy would come to see it as the naïveté of youth. Disasters were something that happened to other unfortunate souls, a conviction she'd gripped tight up to the very last moment, when a ringing phone delivered incomprehensible news.

Their particular cataclysm had hit on Thanksgiving morning, nearly two years before Lucy's fortieth birthday. Joey's plane had been delayed, and so Penelope had gone by herself to deliver a carload of food to an impoverished family. She'd left Tessa and June at home with Rocky, their golden retriever, and rushed along a country road, almost certainly rushing, knowing her girls were alone.

As it turned out, the recipient of her philanthropy, a woman named Cassie, was being held at gunpoint by her estranged husband. When Penelope arrived, honking festively in the driveway, she'd been invited inside to join the party.

They all took comfort in knowing it couldn't have lasted too long, medical examiners' estimates being what they were, confirmed by neighbors' testimony about the timing of the horn honking and the shotgun going off. And whatever else she'd suffered, there must have been a flicker, at least, of something else, an imp in Penelope that would appear even in the darkest moment to say, *See, I told you so.*

After the murder, Joey and the girls had moved out to Lucy's beach house. Staying home had been too hard. Everything in the family's house shouted Penelope's name, and every corner seemed like she'd be coming around it, rescuing them all from this terrible dream they'd been living. It was dysfunctional, or so most people said, but in the midst of shock, Lucy and Joey had blindly grasped at anything at all that could make the girls feel better. Joey had continued to work in the foundation offices, which adjoined the family's large gray Victorian house near the town square. Over the second summer, the girls had begun spending small chunks of time there, between day camps and classes. They'd even started to reinhabit their former bedrooms during the day, as a place to entertain friends or catch a nap, but at night, the family always slept at Lucy's.

It wasn't anything anyone had planned, but with Joey's travel schedule, it had just seemed easier and less disruptive for the girls to live in one place. Without really discussing it, the three of them had drifted into the habit of staying at Lucy's more or less permanently, without ever making a formal decision.

A similar inertia had emptied the guest rooms of Lucy's bed-and-breakfast, which she'd closed as soon as the last Thanksgiving guest had checked out two years earlier. Its clientele, many of whom were loyal regulars, moved on after their reservations were refused a second year. Eventually calls simply stopped coming in. Every now and then Lucy would tell herself it was time to think about reopening her doors, a thought that was quickly followed by the crushing sense that none of them, least of all Tessa and June, were prepared to go back to business as usual.

Chapter Two

On the morning after her party, Lucy was righting the wrongs of the world through an age-old practice. She'd sponged and repapered a narrow drawer with new Crabtree & Evelyn liner paper and was carefully laying white socks along the western border, blacks to the east, and in the middle, a spectrum of color from light to dark.

Proper sock-folding was a skill acquired over time, though, truth be told, raw talent could never be fully disregarded. Even as a toddler, Lucy had discovered what many housewives waited their whole lives to apprehend. Better yet, she did it intuitively, astonishing her mother, who'd adopted a careless balling technique in which the anklets were folded over one another to encase the foot's shapeless mound, a method that stressed the elastic's staying power, condemning its wearer to eventual ankle droop.

Of course, Lucy, at the age of three, couldn't have foreseen such dire consequences. No, she had been motivated by something else entirely.

In fact, had her mother not been equal parts nostalgic and optimist, Lucy's childhood might have included untold hours with specialists eager to dig out obsessive-compulsive tendencies before they'd taken deeper root.

To Lucy's rigorous eye, the perfect triangular outline of the sock was marred by the asymmetric curve of the toe.

Children play. At the age of three, Lucy poked at the bulb until it disappeared neatly into the ball of the foot, creating a straight end, which, when brought to meet the ankle band, created a pleasing angular trapezoid that only incidentally prevented elastile dysfunction.

Lucy's mother, presented with a daughter who insisted on folding and refolding all of her parents' socks, chose to interpret Lucy's attention to detail as a sign of visual genius. The bedsheets were left to mildew in the washer while mother and daughter rushed out to procure art supplies: a tiny easel, masses of paper, and finger paints in every possible hue.

Even when Lucy insisted on rubber gloves to keep her hands clean, her mother didn't fret. After all, Lucy was descended from a long line of Spanish Jews, including the great nineteenth-century painter Fernando Luria, whose fetish for order had been legendary. Indeed, as her mother saw things, obsessive stubbornness was not a character trait to re-engineer, for it had certainly helped the Luria family survive the Moors, the Inquisition, the Diaspora and eventual relocation to the wilds of South Carolina.

Lucy's mother had endless confidence in her own judgment. This translated to daily maternal praise for the beauty her daughter created in her paintings, encouraging an otherwise modest child to accept her talent matter-of-factly. Lucy's paintings were a gift from God, not unlike her features: heart-shaped face, pointed chin, high cheekbones, and deep-set green eyes fringed by lashes so unnaturally dark she appeared to be wearing mascara, even as an infant. Her artistry, as rare in Charleston as her combination of red hair with warm copper complexion, was just there, like the heavy antique furniture, the humid climate, and the sea, saving Lucy from the twin-headed beast that plagued most artists, the nagging worry about being *good* enough and the paralyzing fear of appearing foolishly taken with one's own talent.

Lucy painted as many people cooked, on a daily basis, without fanfare or analysis. Practice may not have always made perfect but it was pretty damn close.

Lucy's latest work, *The Three Graces*, was a wall-size close-up of her three best friends. Penelope, Martha and Susannah were waist-deep in the ocean, their arms lifted to the sky in that natural worshipful attitude common to body surfers, touchdown receivers and disciples of Isadora Duncan. The painting was only half done, maybe less, a fact that made Lucy's sudden procrastination with the sock drawer all the more dispiriting. On the other hand, now that Joey had returned from an intensive schedule of back-to-back project visits, he would be able to take over some of the driving and tending, freeing Lucy to spend more time in her studio.

It was partly that event, however, Joey's homecoming after three weeks away, that had brought Lucy to her psychological knees, counting out socks instead of worry beads. Much as she had craved the freedom to work she'd enjoyed before Joey and the girls had moved to her house on the beach, Lucy was lately finding herself unable to concentrate on much of anything, even her old reliable, the practice of making art.

Maybe, she told herself, it was turning forty. Try as she might to avoid it, scolding herself for being shallow enough to even think about something as trivial as aging when her best friend hadn't lived past her thirty-seventh year, Lucy had come down with midlife influenza. This, despite the fact that she missed Penelope with a kicked-in-the-stomach emptiness, despite the fact that midlife crises were, she knew, an embarrassing cultural cliché. In every respect except her work (and even that was feeling uncertain this postbirthday morning), Lucy had come up short from where she'd have thought she would be by now. It was as though she were being ambushed by her age, something she'd insisted was unimportant. Unannounced, uninvited, the iconic forty had crept in under the door, infecting Lucy's imagination with all sorts of unpleasant messages, not the least of which was her sense that she was being judged in some cosmic way for her shortcomings.

Lucy sighed, reverting to what had become an obsessive pattern of magical thinking. If only Penelope were there, every single thing would have been different.

The force of Penelope's charisma would have swept Lucy along, not simply to Paris, where they'd always planned to celebrate, but to a different way of looking at things. Penelope, for all her fabulous neuroses, could lift her friend out of whatever funk she felt, make her laugh, poke fun at social expectations (marriage, family, investment portfolios) in such a way that neither derided the people who had them nor allowed Lucy to conceive of herself in their terms. There was a shielding quality to the way Penelope viewed the people she loved, allowing them to escape certain bourgeois categories that might otherwise drag them down from the Olympian heights of her esteem. The meaning of Lucy's life, Penelope would tell her, had told her, over and over, was to create beauty in the world. Nothing else mattered. She'd made Lucy believe it, helped her achieve it, and perhaps that fact was the real source of Lucy's distress. It was as if, in letting herself get bogged down in her malaise, Lucy was letting her old friend down. She was losing her grip on the World According to Penelope, just at a time when she needed her confidence the most.

A therapist might have suggested that what Lucy was feeling was something all survivors underwent, perfectly normal twinges of conscience at the mere fact that they were still enjoying life while their loved one could not.

However, there was more to it than that. Not only was Lucy alive while her friend was not, but she was, to all appearances, living the dead Penelope's life. Again, this shouldn't have caused Lucy to feel the slightest remorse. She had always cared for the girls when their parents went out of town. Penelope would have wanted her to continue in her absence, especially when Joey was away doing the work that, prior to her death, they'd done together, visiting Cameron Foundation projects and monitoring their progress.

Still, much as she loved Penelope's daughters, Lucy worried she might be failing them. She'd been warned about the unpredictable trajectory of behaviors attending grief, but Lucy had certainly hoped to see some improvement in the children almost two years after they'd lost their mother. Instead, in the latter half of their second year of mourning, both girls appeared to be getting worse, not better. Tessa's eating, or lack thereof, appeared to be spiraling into something bordering on anorexia. The more Lucy tried to tempt her with food, the more the fourteen-year-old resisted. She devoted a great deal of time to cutting her food into smaller and smaller pieces, arranging them on her plate and thinking of reasons why she wasn't hungry while, at the same time, eyeing everything that her tablemates put in their mouths with a panicked, obsessive fascination. Even ten-year-old June had been drawn into the un-declared but nevertheless constant conspiracy to win back Tessa's appetite.

In fact, June dined with such gusto that she appeared to have gained a pound for each one her sister lost. The younger girl's anxiety and the nightmares she'd had since her mother's murder had snowballed. Lucy couldn't remember a night in the last six months that June hadn't crept in to sleep with her, her chubby arm wrapped around the bow of Lucy's waist, her elbow raised like an arrow against the intruders she feared.

Even beyond these concerns about the girls, there was some-thing else bothering Lucy. She was embarrassed, preoccupied (dare we say obsessed?) with a possible misunderstanding from the night before her birthday. She'd driven to pick Joey up at the Jackson-ville airport, where he'd flown from Mexico, having visited the last international project on his fall calendar. Lucy's car had been one of many circling the terminal in the October rain. It wasn't until her fourth full circle, a period of imagining the worst—crashed planes, Mexican bandits, pulmonary embolisms—that she'd spot-ted him standing at the curb.

Joey was wearing a trench coat despite the warm weather. His shaggy brown hair needed cutting, there were deep shadows under his hooded eyes and he was pinching the bridge of his slightly beaked nose in such a way as to suggest a desire to cut off sensation altogether. Lucy had pulled into the pickup lane and hopped out to open the trunk. She'd reached out to help him with his bag.

This, despite the fact that Joey was strong, built like a gladiator from before warriors wore raincoats and flew on great metal chariots to faraway lands. Still, there'd been something in his stance that had taken Lucy by surprise, some enormous vulnerability that disrupted her habitual reserve and pulled her mouth toward his as their fingers met on the black handle of the suitcase. This movement had felt so natural to her, like something she'd done her whole life. In the flash of the headlights, she'd lost sight of Joey's eyes, seeing only the quick movement of his chin away from hers. In the amount of time it took the jet-lagged passenger to say he'd picked up a terrible cold, Lucy had persuaded herself that the intimacy of her approach had been all but imperceptible. As quickly as she could, she'd fallen back into the middle distance of a hug that was as brisk as it was awkward, setting her soul back on track to its former safe remove.

Internal protestations of deniability could only go so far to assuage Lucy's dread that she might have stepped over an invisible line. She had put Joey on the spot, endangered their friendship. After all these years of knowing him, of turning off any attraction to the man, she'd simply given in to an impulse she wasn't even sure was anything more than a desire to have things change.

For as long as Lucy had known him, Joey had belonged to Penelope. The three of them had met their first year at Virginia, a place Lucy had gone to escape the Deep South, only to find its extended vowels flowing from the mouth of her affable roommate. Penelope had played up the Southern thing with a wink and a nod, drawing out her syllables and fluttering her eyelashes. "Penelope Cameron May. You're gorgeous, sweetheart. Call me Penny, though, and prepare to die."

One night that fall, the two roommates had been sitting in the central quadrangle known as the Lawn, after a night of drinking, sharing a joint. Penelope had pointed at Joey in a ragged flannel shirt, throwing a phosphorescent Frisbee to a friend.

"I call Heathcliff," she'd murmured, settling back on her elbows into a mock swoon.

Lucy, having smoked too much pot, had laughed helplessly,

both at the idea of "calling" a boy and at the perfect accuracy of the Heathcliff label for the brooding hulk moving gracefully before them.

Lucy could have argued that she "called" him too, she supposed, were she blessed with a clear head, but from her perspective, it wouldn't have made a bit of difference. Joey and his friends, who joined the girls at Penelope's invitation, had clearly been enchanted by Penelope's winning trifecta: careless beauty, smoky voice and the sort of moneyed confidence that announced itself in everything from the sheen of her hair to the subtlety of her clothes, right down to the telltale crust of salt on her Top-Siders, residue of a summer spent crewing off Nantucket. Not only was Penelope rich and good looking, but she had the sort of sensuality that Martha would later label "sex on a stick."

It wasn't anything you could put your finger on, for if you took apart her features, they weren't the stuff of legend. It was more an almost catlike slowness in the way she carried herself, a torpor that would make men imagine rumpled afternoon sheets and women fear their boyfriends' sudden irrepressible fantasies of rumpled afternoon sheets.

That very Thursday night, Joey and Penelope had started their love affair, and Lucy had begun the lifelong habit of convincing herself that what she'd initially felt for Joey had been nothing more than the flare of imagination lit by too much marijuana, the heady adventure of going off to college and Penelope's chance allusion to Heathcliff. Add to that the fact that Joey had instantaneously become forbidden fruit, which as every girl knows will make a man look ten times prettier, and it was easy to explain the attraction away.

Repressing such feelings had become second nature to Lucy. In fact, when she'd lost her virginity later that year, Lucy didn't let herself recall that when she closed her eyes and let herself go, all sorts of images crossed the screen, including Heathcliff and his brooding, tormented soul.

Over time, Lucy had become skilled at divorcing herself from any attraction she felt, pigeonholing it into the drawer marked "Impossible," while she threw herself into her work, which was always a more reliable source of gratification than romance. Over time, she'd come to view Joey in the more platonic light of friendship, property of her friend and patron Penelope, whose minor complaints about Joey and the hassles of family life had provided Lucy with just enough of a shield against the treachery of wondering what it might have been like if she had "called" Joey first.

Lately, though, Lucy's categories were falling apart. While Joey was away visiting sites for three weeks, she'd relaxed into the rhythm of caring for the girls without having to steel herself against her rising attraction to their father. His return had snuck up on her, resulting in the botched kiss at the airport, the rejection rubbing salt into the wound of losing her best friend, even as it seemed a betrayal of that same friend. For these reasons, Lucy felt distressed and anxious, hoping to find solace in the sorting of socks.

By the time she pushed shut the heavy wood of the drawer, Lucy had come to a decision that was part plea, part bargain. If the God who helped her paint would only continue to do so, if the images frightening June would only disappear, if Tessa's appetite would return, then Lucy would vow to stop being such a baby about turning forty, stop dreaming about Joey. She'd make plans to pay off her debts and get back on track. *Get a life, girl*, she told herself, *just get a life*.

By noon, Susannah and Martha had arrived at Lucy's for a post-mortem of the party. Their rocking chairs were lined up on the lowest of the inn's deep wraparound porches, facing the driveway, where Joey and the girls were buckling themselves into a vintage Mustang convertible. The house, built in the 1900s and restored by Penelope's father in the late nineties, was a solid brick, painted white. Each of its three stories was encircled by a large porch with sturdy wooden railings, painted the same white as the house. Floor-to-ceiling windows and doors were protected by massive forest-green shutters that drew tight to protect against storms and opened wide to let in sunlight. The front porch, with its anachronistic ceiling fan and its protection from the eastern sun, was peaceful, save the lull of waves out back and the sound of Joey's engine disappearing down the road toward town.

As soon as the car was out of sight, Susannah sighed over her iced chai. "What a fabulous party!"

Martha, who was trying her best not to throw up from running six miles with a kick-ass hangover, turned her head slowly, incredulously, until it hurt too much to do so. She settled for tipping her Gatorade bottle at Susannah and tossed a sarcastic look at Lucy. "And which party did Pollyanna attend?"

Susannah, agreeable and open-minded to a fault, was nevertheless not letting down her guard. Not quite yet. Her self-appointed role as resident optimist was an occupation she'd taken to heart, especially after Penelope's death. "It could have been worse."

"Yeah. No one brought Lucy Botox."

"Or threw up in the bushes," Lucy added, remembering a tequila-drinking contest in college between the four friends, where Penelope had ended up doing just that.

"Oops, can't say that, actually," Martha said. "Well, I think it was just one bush. A hydrangea, maybe?"

"You puked!" Lucy's voice was a mixture of disbelief and something bordering on pleasure. Martha had, for years, proclaimed that no matter how much she drank, she never, ever vomited. "Me too!"

"Maybe it was something in the bouillabaisse." Martha's tone sounded suddenly hopeful, for the lawyer was far more concerned about her consumption of festive beverages than anyone knew.

"No, it wasn't that," Lucy confessed. "I drank too much, and to make matters worse, I stuck my finger down my throat."

"That's disgusting, Lulu," Martha muttered approvingly. "Did you have the spins?"

Lucy nodded. "My bed did. And I ate about half that pecan pie."

"What if Tessa had heard you?" Susannah's tone was uncharacteristically sharp, carrying with it her worry for the teen.

"I know, I know," Lucy said somewhat mournfully. She'd had the same thought the night before, hunched above the pristine porcelain toilet that adjoined her bedroom. She'd raised her chin on her circled arms and eyed the black and white marble floor tiles, laid out before her like a chessboard upon which she had just made an astonishingly stupid move.

"Tessa's room is too far away from Lucy's to hear anything, Susannah." Martha tipped her Gatorade back toward Lucy again like a microphone. "Look, don't blame yourself. Blame Clover."

Lucy, who couldn't understand why she found Martha's bleak humor so deeply and profoundly satisfying, snorted out her last gulp of Diet Coke.

Susannah, devoted fan of New Age psychology, shook her head. "Clover can't help herself, Martha. She's still caught up in trying to win her father's approval—"

"Stepfather," Martha said.

"Exactly! Just think," Susannah mused. "First her mother abandons her. Then Marcus takes over and can't find it in himself, for whatever reasons, to give her the affection she needs. Sometimes I think Clover's still trying to replace Penelope in her daddy's heart, despite the fact that they've both gone to the other side."

It was Martha's turn to snort her neon blue drink out onto her tanned knees and the rough gray floor of the porch. "They're dead, Susannah, not in Europe."

"Oh, please, can't we just pretend she's in Europe?" Lucy pleaded, slumping against the back of her chair.

For a minute, Penelope's three friends remained silent, caught up in the wistful remedy of what-ifs. *What if Joey had gone with her to deliver the food that Thanksgiving morning like he planned? What if Penelope had brought her dog, Rocky, along, like she normally did? What if she'd gotten there later?* This was a litany of the grieving, a constant ache of uncertainty for which there came no heavenly response. For Lucy, especially, whom Penelope had invited along at the last minute, the question of what might have happened if she'd chosen to go instead of begging off to finish a painting, this line of questioning was especially unsettling.

Susannah broke the silence. "I wish Paris had been possible. I looked at tickets but they were so expensive. The Camerons would never have approved it—"

The idea of celebrating Lucy's fortieth birthday in Paris had been Penelope's idea, hatched in their twenties and embroidered over two decades. It had been almost like children playing house, except they'd all believed it would happen, given Penelope's resources. No one had reckoned on what would happen if she died, except maybe Martha, who knew the terms of the Cameron ancestors' will inside and out. Even if she had thought of it, she'd have dismissed such thinking as apocalyptic.

"No, it would have been worse to be there without her," Lucy said.

"I truly don't see how it could have been worse than it was last night," Martha whispered dramatically. They'd all wanted to make Lucy happy, but Penelope's absence had hung over her survivors like a shroud. The promise of Paris on Lucy's fortieth would not be separated from the sad fact that not only was Penelope gone, so too were the days when anyone's wish was her command. Now, most of the Cameron money was tied up in a probate dispute and what was left was scrutinized extremely closely by the new executors, a pair of Oxbridge-trained Cameron cousins who'd swooped in to micromanage the trust shortly after the funeral.

"But then again, things can always be worse," Martha said. "Clover could have *sung* her little birthday verse."

Clover Lindstrom was, at that very moment, applying eyeliner and trilling her way through Tony Orlando's "Knock Three Times on the Ceiling If You Want Me." Her husband, Brett, who'd come to hate the way she messed up the lyrics to his favorite songs, stuck his head inside the master bathroom door and interrupted. "Your cell."

"Who is it?"

"Last name's Fitzpatrick."

"Siobhan!" Clover's tone conveyed the urgency with which she wanted to dish with her New Best Friend. She reached for the phone without putting down her eyeliner pencil, jabbing Brett in the fleshy apex between his thumb and his forefinger.

"Ow!" he said, but Clover had already turned back to the mirror.

"Hey, girl!" she started, smiling broadly, winking at herself.

Clover knew the importance of facial expressions in animating a phone call. Though she'd known Siobhan less than twenty-four hours, Clover had felt an immediate affinity for the delicate dancer, who'd been working the Kicks! front desk when Clover wandered in the morning before. Clover had apologized for mispronouncing the letters printed in Copperplate Gothic font on the assistant manager's employee name tag.

"No worries," Siobhan had offered, writing "CHEVONNE" on the top of the Kicks! brochure. "That's the American spelling. Leave it to the Irish to make it difficult."

"Oh my God, are you Irish? And are you a dancer?"

This had been only the start of Clover's ejaculations, all uttered at a pitch just below the threshold at which they might be over-heard, imparting to her inquiries a sense of confidentiality and reverence they might not otherwise have attained. By the time they had finished their conversation, Clover had not only purchased several gift certificates; she'd discerned that Siobhan Fitzpatrick wasn't just a dance teacher, she was also a trained nutritionist. There had been a reserve in Siobhan, a withholding of approval as she withstood Clover's inquiries, that called up Clover's Inner Terrier.

In fact, it was almost an afterthought, or maybe even a subtle form of payback, when Clover invited Siobhan to join her at Lucy's fortieth-birthday party. "Oh come on, you'll meet the crème de la crème of Omega." Clover said, intending to show this girl *who was who* and *what was what* in this tiny town of theirs.

"I wanted to thank you for having me," Siobhan explained the morning after such lessons had presumably been absorbed.

"Well? What did you think?" Clover pressed her chin up to the mirror, the better to inspect a blackhead skirting her lower lip.

"It wasn't at all what I expected," Siobhan admitted. Having recently moved to Omega from San Francisco to help open the Kicks! franchise, Siobhan had thought the party would be something like *Steel Magnolias*, which she'd rented the night before she'd moved. Instead, there were Lucy and her friends with their offbeat banter, not a Southern accent in sight, unless you counted Clover and her husband, who didn't really seem to be part of the clique. "With your gift certificate, I thought the birthday girl would be . . . I guess I didn't expect she'd be quite so attractive. She surely doesn't look forty," Siobhan added.

"Lucy could lose five or ten pounds, though. Don't you think? And wear more makeup."

"Her complexion's amazing. You don't usually see redheads with that skin tone."

"Well, that's sweet of you to notice. Lucy's a peach, but sometimes I just want to put her in a makeover contest."

"So, is it true your sister gave her that house as a present?"

"Who told you that?"

"That gorgeous man at my end of the table. Where's he from?"

"Sateesh? He's Indian. Like from over near Pakistan, or is it Palestine? I can never keep those places straight."

"Is he married?"

"Very. He's Martha's husband. Did you meet her, my sister's lawyer? Stick-straight platinum-blond hair cut like a flapper? Ralph Lauren navy sheath?"

"To tell you the truth, all the women kind of blurred together for me," Siobhan confessed. "I didn't really get a chance to get to know anyone, except for Sateesh. Is that how you say it? Anyway, he mentioned the bed-and-breakfast once belonged to your father?"

"Penelope gave the beach house to Lucy a few years ago."

"Well, if you don't mind my asking this, Clover, how did that make *you* feel?" Siobhan's voice was gentle, therapeutic even.

Clover took a breath before she answered. "I knew why she did it."

"That's so big of you, considering it could have been yours."

"No, see—Lucy wasn't making any money from her painting then and the foundation could only give so many artist's grants to the same person before the IRS started poking into things. I was already married and had already gotten the farm property when Daddy died, so Penny knew I was all set. She wanted Lucy to have a way to support herself."

"Your sister sounds like a generous spirit."

"To a fault," Clover said proudly.

"And her daughters? How're they getting along?"

"Did you not notice how skinny Tessa is?"

"The teenager with dark hair? She *is* thin."

"And then poor June's gone in the other direction. If we don't do something soon, she'll be the size of Nebraska. The other kids already notice her weight. Do you think they'd make fun of her if she took dance?"

"No. There are plenty in my classes fighting weight problems."

"And she really could use some diet tips. Lucy lets her eat whatever and whenever she wants!"

"But I don't understand. Why would Lucy be taking care of them at all?"

"Long, long story. Basically my sister was a woman of strong opinions."

"But their father's sitting right there too?"

"He's on the road a lot with foundation business. Penny—you had to know her—she was always solving everyone's problems. Lucy loves my nieces and didn't have any kids of her own, so whenever Penny and Joey would go out of town for a visit to one of their projects, the girls would stay with Lucy. Then, after Penny died, it just seemed easier for them not to be reminded of their mom every time they turned around. Joey makes noises about how they're gonna move back into town, but they don't ever seem to get around to it."

"That's cozy, isn't it now?"

"That's exactly what *I* said. But does anyone pay a bit of attention? They don't hear a word I say."

"Your daughter's so pretty," Siobhan offered, as though trying to console her new friend for having her opinions disregarded.

"Thank you!"

"You know, if she and her cousins want to try out for the dance team, I've still got some slots—"

"I don't think Joey would let Tessa dance right now, not with how thin she's gotten."

"Well, it might be a means to an end. Get her in the door so I can evaluate her. You know, I wrote my master's thesis on eating disorders. Spent a bit of time working in a treatment setting. Often, these girls with eating problems are drawn to exercise. What I do is use the carrot of dance to get them in the door and slowly get the idea across that they need to eat to stay strong and beautiful."

"Wow. I never thought of it like that. Let me talk to Joey. For a man who looks like he cuts his hair with a mower blade, he's got some ridiculous rules."

"But rules are important!" Here, just for a moment, Siobhan's voice grew heated.

"Yeah, but I'm talking *stupid* things. Like, say, trying to get Tessa's foot in the door by telling her it was a dance class. Joey won't tell a lie to save his life, even to his own kids! I remember when Tessa was seven, she asked him if Santa Claus was real and he told her!"

Siobhan was quiet as she absorbed this information. "Is he— can he afford to send her to treatment?"

Clover snorted. "Don't let those Gap khakis fool you. He's got a great salary and once the court case is settled, he'll get a couple million a year until he remarries. Then he'll get a huge lump settlement. Besides, the foundation has an excellent health plan."

"Has he thought of putting—what's her name—"

"Tessa."

"Into treatment?"

"I don't think she's *that* bad. Besides, I hear girls pick up even worse habits from those places."

"You do have to keep your eyes out for the peer group. But still—shall I call their father then?"

"No, don't do that. Let me talk to him. You know, this might be just what the doctor ordered for both of the girls. They've been just—I don't know—sort of drifting since my sister passed."

"That's so sad."

"Sometimes I wonder if they're okay with Lucy. She lets them walk all over her. Course she never had children or a husband, so she just doesn't get it."

"Is she—if you don't mind my asking—is she gay then?"

"I don't know. I asked Penelope one time and she said no, that Lucy just hadn't met the right guy. But Lucy's—" Clover racked her brain for the words. "Lucy's from this . . . weird Jewish family up in Charleston. I've tried to fix her up before but she never would go out with anyone I sent her way. It's like she's—I don't know— too good for the men in this town or something. Penelope always said the right guy would come along and when he did, Lucy would know it. Who knows? Maybe she *is* gay. I usually figure a woman who never gets married, if she's not a complete bow-wow, she's got to be a lesbian."

Siobhan's gasp was barely audible. When Clover didn't explain herself, Siobhan did it for her. "This is a really small town, isn't it?" she observed, as much to excuse Clover's provincial logic as to absolve Lucy of having failed to procure a husband.

"Oh, don't you worry, Brett's in Rotary. We'll get you fixed up," Clover promised. With that somewhat idle reassurance, she created, both in her own mind and that of her new best friend, a set of circumstances that would overcome the inertia of bodies previously at rest. Whether it was Clover's promise of Rotary beaus or the cautionary tale of Lucy's indeterminate sexless state, Siobhan couldn't say, but her center of gravity—a dancer's first and last resort—was jarred by the distant tremble of fear, both familiar and uncomfortably real.

Later that morning, in a burst of inspiration, Clover realized something very important. The quickest way to a man's heart, at least when it came to her late sister's husband, was not always through his stomach. No, Joey had a much more dependable weak spot, though the precise location of Catholic guilt wasn't anatomically apparent.

"Joey Adorno, shame on you!" Clover cried after pulling into Lucy's driveway and catching sight of him kneeling, like the altar boy he'd once been, in front of his 1972 Mustang, holding a toothbrush and metal polish. "You snuck up to bed Friday night without saying good-bye to any of us."

"Sorry," Joey said. "My head was killing me."

"Oh!" Clover smacked her forehead. "I wish I'd thought of that—I told Siobhan you weren't upset I'd brought her to the party."

"Why would I be upset with that? I don't even know her." Joey dug his brush deeper, into the crevices of the wheel well. His biceps were bunched with the tension he'd been carrying all morning. Clover's sudden appearance had created in him a fight-or-flight response that he was taking out on the blackened tire spokes.

"I knew you weren't being a snob, but she didn't," Clover added, inspecting her brother-in-law's dumbfounded eyes to see if she was getting through to him. "I wish you could have gotten to know her a little. She's—you wouldn't believe the kind of poverty the girl grew up in. Talk about a tough rope to tow! The girl's—I bet she can't be used to that kind of dinner party, Joey."

Joey shook his dark head, loosening the tendrils that had caught at the frayed neck of his T-shirt. He pressed his five o'clock shadow with his palms. "She?" he asked, having already lost track of the conversation.

"Siobhan. The girl I brought to the party? Did you know she lived in foster care when she was a kid?"

"Clover, what are you getting at? Hand me that chamois, will you?"

"Will you listen to me for one second? Put down that toothbrush and just listen."

Sweat was running down Joey's left temple. He wiped it away with the hand that was still holding the toothbrush and dug back into his tire well. "Listen, I've got to run June to Willow's."

"You want me to take her?" Clover asked lightly.

It was a subject of ongoing distress to Clover that June preferred Susannah's daughter, Willow, to her own cousin, Clover's little girl, Brittany. This, despite the fact that Willow was a tomboy who dressed like a street gangster, while Brittany was normal and pretty and had American Girl dolls up the wazoo. "Siobhan Fitzpatrick, that girl I brought to Lucy's? She's got a dance program over at Kicks! that'd be great for Tessa and June. I hoped you'd get a chance to talk to her about it. Instead, you and the rest of the inner circle acted like the girl was invisible. I'm sorry she's not a country-club rich kid. She grew up practically on the streets and raised herself up by standing on her own two bootstraps. I think she deserves a lot of respect for going to college and getting a master's degree, but everyone completely ignored her last night."

"Clover, it was Lucy's party."

"I know, but can we not branch out and be nice to a stranger? I mean, if you knew her story and what she's been through! Penelope would have liked her, Joey. I don't think anyone but Sateesh even said hey to her."

Joey wiped his brow with his forearm. "Clover. I just got back from Mexico, my head was killing me, and I was worried about Tessa. You know that."

"I do! That's how come I brought Siobhan in the first place. You're not the only one who's noticed Tessa's appetite's gone to H-E double hockey socks."

"Come again?"

"Well, see, I went in to pick up the gift certificate for Lucy. And by the way, will you please encourage her to work out, Joey?

Anyhow, Siobhan was working the front desk. Here's the icing on the cupcake, Joey. Not only is she a dance teacher, but she's got a master's degree in nutrition! I told her some about Tessa. She wrote her thesis on eating disorders and said she'd be happy to help her!" Joey's head tilted back just slightly, which Clover took as an indication that she was being listened to. "I'm not saying Tessa's got a disorder, but still. The thing is, if you got her working with Siobhan, maybe she'd be able to do some good. Head her off at the pass. See, the good thing is Siobhan's not like most dancers, where everyone has to be slim and trim. I went by there today. Some of the girls she teaches could use a little eating disorder if you ask me."

Joey held his palm up to Clover. He shook his head and turned back to his work, rinsing the polished area and wiping it clean. "Clover, do you hear yourself sometimes? Please," Joey added. He knew Clover didn't mean any harm. "Look, I've got to go. I need to get June ready."

"I'll run her over to Susannah's if you want! I was gonna see if she wanted to head off to the mall after school tomorrow. While I'm gone, will you think at least think about this dance class? At least for June if not for Tessa?"

Clover handed Joey his chamois and turned up the driveway, belting out the lyrics to a song by Donovan, or was it Burt Bacharach? Originally titled "Jean," the song was a throaty exhortation to live life to its fullest, its subject being both youthful and still breathing. Clover had amended "Jean" to "June," this small improvisation one among the many liberties the singer took with the English language. No one ever really knew whether Clover truly misunderstood the words to commonly known songs, or whether she felt a certain poetic license was called for when it came to her own personal musical theater. In this case, the song was meant to convey to June that her aunt Clover's affection was boundless, a cup that would forever runneth over.

When June peeked out Lucy's bedroom window and saw her aunt heading up the driveway, she took the route of least resistance. "Lucy?!" she cried. "Can you say I'm asleep?"

"Ooh, can't we all be asleep?" Tessa echoed, bracing herself for her aunt's attentions.

Tessa and June had been helping Lucy decide which slides to send to the gallery for her upcoming show in New York. They were in Lucy's bedroom instead of her studio because it was the darkest room in the house and provided the best contrast for the light table they'd set up on the floor. They were looking at twenty photos of paintings Lucy had completed in the past year. Every single one was of their mother.

Clover didn't bother to knock, having swept open the downstairs screen door with the graceful élan of a conquering hero. "June!" Clover was singing up the stairs.

"Tessa!" she was crooning in time. "Lucy! What are you doing inside on a beautiful day like this?" she lilted. The scent of Clover's perfume in and of itself would have announced her arrival to any inhabitant deprived of the pleasure of hearing the voice of an angel singing her own personal ballad. As Martha was fond of pointing out, Clover's was a love that knew no bounds, or boundaries, whichever came first.

"Hey, Clover!" Lucy called out. "We're in here."

Lucy's bedroom was her haven. The walls were blue, the sheets were white. A single vase of flowers provided the only decoration. The furniture, inherited from her ancestors, was heavy, dark, ornate. The contrast between it and the austerity of the room was a satisfying one.

Chests of drawers on either side of the bed provided more than enough room to stow clutter, but even behind closed drawer fronts, Lucy had ordered her belongings into tidy arrangements sorted into categories by color, size and function. Cursed by a visual acuity that took up the lion's share of space in her psyche, Lucy found that ordering her environment allowed her the sort of peace that other people might find through yoga or prayer. Penelope's daughters, whose habits were not nearly as fastidious, found themselves nevertheless drawn to Lucy's room as well, for its peaceful, almost conventlike sparseness.

Clover too found Lucy's bedroom soothing. At the same time, it disturbed her. Lucy didn't fit anyone's stereotype of the bohemian artist. Indeed, the tidiness of Lucy's nest was a constant thorn in Clover's more conventional side. Sometimes she found it easier to suspect that Lucy's talent was a sham, or, on alternate days, that the painter might be hiding a secret trove of messy habits behind closed doors, like a bigamist's second family.

"What are ya'll doing in the dark? What is that?" Clover was on her knees and folding herself over the light table before Lucy could explain, and then there was no need. It was clear from the pictures of Penelope, if not the hushed mood of the girls, that this was a sacred moment. "Oh, Lucy!" Clover cried, putting one arm around Tessa's frail shoulders, the other on June's pudgy knee. "These are so beautiful, I could cry!"

Chapter Three

Joey and the girls were sitting at Lucy's dining room table, eating without Lucy, who'd gone to Susannah's for the evening. Joey and June were on one side of the table, facing Tessa over a large platter of pasta, three pork chops and a bowl of cantaloupe. Tessa looked even thinner sitting there alone as her father tried to appear nonchalant about what she'd put on her plate.

"Sweetie?" Joey asked. "A pork chop?"

"Dad, I told you. I don't eat meat."

"I'll have one," June offered, proffering her plate, on which a huge mound of pasta demonstrated her understanding that her father was trying to get her sister to eat.

"It's not meat. It's lamb!" Joey cried. This favorite family joke from *My Big Fat Greek Wedding* was an attempt to get through to his child, who was suddenly so withdrawn. Tessa's eyes darted back and forth from her father's plate to her sister's. The look on her face was that of someone who was pained at the attention she was getting at the same time as she was distractedly worrying about something very far away. A tear fell onto the cantaloupe she had sliced into very thin pieces and arranged into transparent petals on the white of the plate. "Sweetie!" Joey pleaded. "What's wrong?"

Tessa shook her head and pressed the heel of her wrist into the socket of the offending eye.

"Tessa got all A's on her progress report, Daddy," June said.

"Sweetie! That's really great!" Joey's enthusiasm carried with it the momentum of his concern. Even as he said it, he knew it would sound over-the-top, especially to the waif sitting across from him picking at her wrist. "I'm so proud of you!"

Tessa shrugged. Straight A's were nothing to write home about, not for Miss Perfect, as June used to call her. At least, in the olden days, June did. Now everyone treated Tessa like she was made of some kind of flammable material. No wonder she couldn't relax.

Tessa covered her irritability by scolding her father. "June got most improved on the writing assessment, Dad. Did you even know that?"

"Aunt Lucy made me a cake!" June said, adopting the part of a child much younger than she was, trying to comfort her father and distract him from Tessa's plight.

"Your favorite?" Joey asked. He turned in his seat to beam at June, which, unfortunately, confirmed Tessa's glum conviction that she could not do anything right. Otherwise he'd have looked at her like he did her sister.

"Daddy, can I go to that lady's dance class?" June asked.

"Which lady's that?"

"The only one at the party we didn't know, Dad," Tessa explained, rolling her eyes. "Aunt Clover's new loser."

"Tessa!"

"I don't like her. She looks sneaky."

"Tessa," Joey scolded. "Imagine how she felt, the only person outside the family at Lucy's party. Think about how it must feel to come in and be an outsider."

"Aunt Clover shouldn't have brought her. It was Lucy's party and Lucy hates strangers."

"She doesn't hate them. She's just shy."

"That's what I'm saying."

"That was something Mommy would have done," June argued. "Included somebody new."

"Aunt Clover's not Mom!" Tessa said, her voice low but vehement.

Joey wanted so badly to take her into his lap, almost as badly as he wanted to cut up a pork chop and feed it to her like she was the baby she'd once been. "No," Joey agreed. "No one will ever come close."

"Mommy would have wanted us to be nice to strangers," June insisted.

"That's true. What was her name again?" Joey asked.

"I don't know. But Aunt Clover says she's got a dance team at that new gym, Dad. And she said we could take a class for free."

"I don't know, hon. We don't know anything at all about this woman." Joey was careful not to express his worry, that June would be mocked if she tried to join a group of girls who were athletically inclined, whose toned bodies would make his daughter's plump figure stand out as the "Don't Bee" of the leotard set.

"It's after school, Daddy."

"How would you get there? When I'm out of town?"

"Aunt Lucy."

"Sweetie, I can't presume Lucy has the time to take you two—"

"Wait, I didn't say *I* was going," Tessa murmured.

"And I wouldn't let you, Tessa, not until you get your weight up—"

"Dad! Would you stop nagging me? You just make it harder!" With that, Tessa rose from the table and began clearing plates.

The weird thing was that despite her recent weight loss, Tessa was not unaware of culinary pleasures. Strangely enough, food was all she thought about, when she went to sleep at night, when she woke in the morning. The trouble came when she had to choose what she wanted. It was like a divine quest. The hungrier she got, the harder it was to concentrate. Like tonight, she'd sat down thinking how much she wanted something delicious to eat, but when she looked at the pasta, it was too hard to decide what she could and couldn't stomach. Everything was all mixed up together, the basil, the mushrooms, the roasted red peppers. The ingredients crowded her brain in a way that was jarring.

It had started over the summer and gotten worse when she'd gone back to school, the cafeteria being the worst place of all, the crowded colors and smells making her dizzy. Moving helped distract Tessa. Even doing dishes, something she'd avoided before, was better than having to sit at the table and not be able to do the one thing she spent all her time obsessing about.

By the time Tessa opened the door to her bedroom, nearly an hour had passed. She had finished the dishes, ten Our Fathers, ten Hail Marys, and then a hundred times, though it wasn't part of the Rosary or any penance she'd ever heard of, "Bless us O Lord for these thy gifts, which we are about to receive, from thy bounty, through Christ our Lord Amen. May God provide for the wants of others and for the souls of the faithful departed, *especially Mommy*, through the Mercy of God, rest in peace, Amen."

Tessa hadn't let herself come upstairs until she'd finished the last prayer, even on a night like tonight, when she'd had to pee so badly her belly knifed up like a cramp she couldn't reach.

Each of the bedrooms in Lucy's house had its own bathroom, decorated in a similar style as the room itself. Tessa's room, between her dad's and June's, was yellow with white trim. The small bathroom was papered in buttery stripes. A claw-foot tub was spanned by a chrome basket holding soaps and lotions that Tessa had saved over the years. Every time her mom and dad had returned from a trip, she'd added another hotel's logo to her collection. Now Tessa reached for a box to smell, each one holding in it some piece of time, untouched by trouble.

When she was finished, Tessa carefully returned the box to its nest.

These were for keeps. Her dad tried to bring her more but none of those—which Tessa insisted he give to June instead—carried the same magic.

This was just as well. June didn't hold on to anything for long. She'd tear at the cardboard, twist off the tops and slather herself with their contents in a slapdash happiness that got on Tessa's last nerve. Tessa loved her little sister desperately, but it didn't mean she couldn't see right through her phony cheerfulness, like a one-man band for the hunky-dory. It was like she thought if she was just chirpy enough, she could make everyone forget.

Tessa rinsed her face with the coldest water October had to offer and dried her hands on a square of scratchy fabric she kept hidden on the knob beneath the sink. Then she folded herself into bed without taking off her clothes, shivering as she counted to one hundred and back again, using her prayers to soothe her to sleep.

On the morning their mother was killed, the girls were watching a documentary about Elizabeth Smart, the Mormon girl kidnapped by a homeless man out in Utah. They'd been in their pajamas still, and June had snuggled progressively closer to Tessa as the story spun out, with the middle-of-the-night break-in, the little sister hiding for two hours before telling her parents that Elizabeth had been taken, the search of the neighboring wilderness.

When she saw how upset June was, Tessa had shut off the television and insisted they go upstairs to get dressed. "Don't tell Mom and Dad we watched this," she'd added. "And don't worry, it all turned out okay. They found her."

Tessa knew she'd be in deep trouble for watching this channel, much less a show about child kidnapping, but the subject had fascinated her. The fact that Elizabeth Smart was from a family of wealth and privilege, was her age, even had a little sister—all of it was kind of thrilling. Besides, it was a great distraction from the boredom she'd been feeling since her best friend, Amber, had left town with her dad for the holidays. It also gave her a reason to call the boy she had a crush on real quick, just to enjoy the delicious sense of being alone and afraid, someone he might want to protect.

On their way toward the stairs, Tessa had dug her fingers into the marshmallow–brown sugar topping of a sweet potato casserole her mom had made that morning. She offered some to her sister. "Don't be such a scaredy-cat. I told you they ended up finding the girl a little while later." Even that did no good: June had still clung to Tessa like static electricity, except maybe a thousand times more annoying.

The way Tessa saw it, Elizabeth Smart hadn't been killed, and besides, she'd come out of the deal famous. "Listen, go get dressed in your room," Tessa had told her. "Be a big girl for once."

June had dressed in two minutes flat and rushed back to Tessa's room, only to find the door locked. "Tessa!" June had shouted. "I think the phone's ringing."

This excuse was the only one she could think of to get Tessa to open the door, though it was kind of true that if June closed her eyes and listened extra hard, it did sound like something was ringing.

"No it's not! I'll be out in a minute. I'm getting dressed," Tessa had responded, her voice strangled by the extreme modesty of a twelve-year-old combined with the adolescent exasperation of a sister too close in age to be tolerant of her sibling's fear. Tessa knew the phone couldn't be ringing because she was using it right that minute to call Hunter, the boy from school she liked.

When they got downstairs again, after what seemed to June like a few aeons later, Tessa had checked for messages that might have come in while she was on with Hunter. Even though there weren't any, she'd immediately dialed her mom's cell phone to see if she had tried to call.

"Nope, not me, sweetie. Everything okay?" Penelope had asked, a hitch in her voice that Tessa would later analyze over and over and over again.

These were her mother's last words, at least the last to Tessa. Was her mom already sitting in the driveway at the house in the country? Was she so distracted by Tessa's call that she'd not been able to detect the man's craziness or see his gun? Or had the hitch in her tone been a secret signal to Tessa, some code she should have been able to read? Should she have known her mom was in trouble? Called the police?

June had never tattled on Tessa, never said they'd watched the show or that Tessa had ignored the ringing phone. June knew full well she'd invented the ringing phone to get her sister out of her room in the first place.

In some ways, both girls would have been better served if June had tattled, for if they'd had to discuss their worries with a grown-up they might have been persuaded that the dreadful punishment they'd received had not been brought on by any disobedience of their own.

Instead, they'd suffered in silence, Tessa most particularly. She had struggled unsuccessfully to forget that documentary and the shameful vicarious thrills she'd been courting at the very moment her mother was dying. She'd vowed to be better, to make it up to her mother by being the best girl she could be, emulating her mom's altruism through small daily sacrifices.

Chapter Four

Siobhan Fitzpatrick was a little bit of a thing with glossy curls, a twinkling manner and just the faintest suggestion of a brogue in her gentle soft-spokenness. The funny thing about Siobhan, a fact she held close to the vest, was that she wasn't actually Irish. No, Siobhan had once spelled her name just the way it sounded, Chevonne, as it was spelled by her hippie parents, until she received a dance fellowship to Dublin, where she picked up an attractive accent that clung to her like the Danskin wraps she favored.

Siobhan was extremely private, relishing the comfort of knowing that whatever people might think about her, they knew less than nothing, really. Information was power, a currency she'd be a fool to offer potential rivals. Instead, she carried her secrets like a droll riddle to which only she knew the answer, surveying the world from a distance that put her at no one's mercy. It was a remove she was only too happy to occupy, a tiny tigress prowling the topmost ledge on the mountain, alert to the constant danger of being displaced.

This was not to say Siobhan didn't have her charms. She was pretty, she was graceful, she was deferential. Most of all, Siobhan had developed the kind of empathy that skewed toward hurt. Indeed, perhaps her best quality when it came to making people like her was a telepathic detection system that coaxed pain from hiding. She offered comfort by teasing out narratives of persecution, directing blame onto a reliable set of archetypal villains. Though Siobhan alluded only vaguely to the details of her upbringing, she had discovered a satisfying ritual. Those characteristics she most hated in her parents could be, with minor changes, spotted in the lives of friends, all of them common victims of a paradise that wasn't so much lost as tossed aside in the careless rush for personal liberation. There were no half measures for Siobhan, no looking back at her parents' neglect and parsing out what it was that caused them to fail her, namely drugs and more drugs. Instead, she blamed the era and its hallmarks: open-mindedness, enlightenment, the questioning of authority. Indeed, in leaving the Bay Area for Omega, she'd yearned for a quintessential Southern town, something with a fixed set of rules, a code of behavior that could be understood and rigidly observed. Instead, the place disappointed her. The town seemed overrun by outsiders, disappointingly fluid, its social order invisible to the naked eye, as if all the social gatekeepers had gone to ground.

There remained a rightness about the young dancer, a graveness with which she carried herself, a fear of letting go, that could inspire either pity or apprehension, depending on the power differential of the beholder. Her frailty presented itself as a near-desperate reliance on rules. This rigidity was expressed by her body language as well as by the words she clipped with a lilting Celtic inflection. Siobhan, all five foot two and one hundred five pounds of her, was self-possessed for a woman in her late twenties, partly because she'd confined her worldly exposure to those arenas in which the rules were clear and straightforward.

Because her parents had never found a substance they couldn't abuse, Siobhan didn't drink, much less do drugs, not even coffee, which she regarded as a form of speed. She measured her food the same way she did everything else, with utter precision.

This fetish for measurement might have been Siobhan's only excessive trait, one she'd successfully channeled into her career as a nutritionist-slash-wellness-expert-slash-movement-instructor.

At the Kicks! corporate office Siobhan was also regarded as an organizational genius. Even she would allow herself to take exquisite pleasure in the fact that she was a dab hand with ledgers.

Siobhan's degrees hung above her desk in the studio. She held an associate's in accounting, a bachelor's in physical education and a master's in nutrition sciences. This education had honed her extraordinary talent for calculating, to the nano-calorie, the formula for maintaining a perfect balance between metabolic input and output. Add to that impressive skill a body sculpted with the same depth of attention some people lavished on their children's college funds, and it was no surprise that Siobhan had risen quickly as a circuit-rider in the rapidly growing corporate empire devoted to rectifying Americans' ill-fated addictions to the couch and an ever-expanding double-arched horn of plenty.

On the day of June's first lesson, Siobhan was moving through a set of forms she'd choreographed, a cross between tai chi and ballet. Siobhan never tired of performing in the mirror, repeating her steps with strict attention to detail. The image gliding through the space was all the more gratifying in that her disciplined efforts symbolized the natural harmony of muscles held perfectly in check.

When Joey and June entered the studio, Siobhan was bent into an attitude of anguish—or was it adoration? Her right leg, pointed at the ceiling, was flush with the wall. Her spine curved slightly, chin meeting thigh, and her hair fell in a honey-colored scroll to the left side of her frame.

Joey squeezed his daughter's shoulder, noticing her sudden attention, almost rapture, in the presence of perfection. June took her father's hand, content to wait.

The child was wearing a pair of black leggings that came to just below her knees and one of her dad's T-shirts from work. The emblem of the Cameron Foundation was a wreath that looked a little like wings. If June squinted her eyes just right in the mirror, she could imagine herself as a dancer, defying her heaviness, flying through space, a skill she'd have appreciated earlier that afternoon.

She and Lucy had been in the food co-op after school, picking out tomatoes, when June spotted the man. He acted like he was looking at lemons, but June knew he was sneaking looks at them. She'd moved in closer to Lucy, grasped her shirttail and hidden behind it. It had felt like she couldn't speak, was frozen. "Lucy? Can we go?" she'd managed to whisper, almost crying with her panic.

Lucy had turned her body so that it blocked the man from June's view. "You bet." She'd hurried them toward the exit, leaving their cart of food behind. "I'll come back later."

Shortly after the murder, June had happened upon a newspaper photo of the man who killed her mother. Now that vague image—something she thought of as *stranger danger*—had mutated in her brain, pasting that set of bleary derelict features onto anyone who looked at all indigent. Lately it seemed she saw more and more scary men out there, faces that made her clench with fear, despite repeated reassurances that the man who killed her mom was dead and gone. From June's point of view, if there was one crazy person out there, there had to be more. Someone, somewhere, getting ready to take the next chunk from their lives.

Now, in the Kicks! studio, Siobhan crossed the floor so quickly it was almost like she was skating, her feet pointing out from extended, perfectly muscled legs until she stood there with her hand out to introduce herself again.

"Hello there. I'm so glad you came," Siobhan said gravely, taking the measure of June's body even as she was distracted by Joey's physical aura.

His stance was that of a boxer, with a readiness to spring into action, even as he stood perfectly still with his hands in his pockets, brooding and protective. His hair was overgrown, there were dark circles under his eyes, but he hadn't let his body go. Quite the contrary, Siobhan thought. It looked as if he'd poured his emotions into working out. This gave them something in common, though now was not the time or place for such observations.

"Hi, Ms. Fitzpatrick. June wants to try your class," Joey explained, holding the brochure out to Siobhan. "What do you suggest?"

"Have you danced before, June?"

June nodded quickly. It was impossible to grow up female in Omega without having been tutored in the art of synchronizing one's steps with those of other little girls. She'd done ballet in pre-school, though all she could remember was a pink tutu that Willow had turned into a Lion King mane. "I took hip-hop last year with my friend Willow but then she broke her leg."

"How about something easy to start with?" Joey asked, wondering why he'd let June quit hip-hop just because Willow did. Sometimes, brought to his heels at a moment like this, Joey felt like he'd been woken from a very long sleep, or lost in a fog, with no recall of ordinary time or events.

Siobhan reached out to June and pulled her toward the middle of the floor. "Just walk with me, June. See? It's that easy. I can see you've got a great sense of rhythm. There, see? Just watch me in the mirror, and try to move along with me. Hear the beat? A one, and a two, and so on, and so forth, but you're hearing the steps in the sound."

June was clearly entranced by the lovely Siobhan, whose sculpted arms guided her toward the mirror, pressing gently at the small of her back. June caught sight of herself, and for just one minute the leaves turning to wings on the wreath of her shirt didn't seem so very far-fetched.

"You can leave her here," Siobhan said, crouching to press some controls on a boom box. "The other girls will be here at four fifteen. She'll be fine. I'll get her accustomed to some of the movements."

Joey looked at June to see if she was okay, then asked what time he should return. When he left the studio, though, he found himself staying to watch. Perched on a high stool behind the observation window, resting his chin onto his bent forearm, Joey leaned into the one-sided glass and tried to recall what it was about this image that made him so very, very nostalgic.

◆ ◆ ◆

"Hello?"

"Yes, may I speak with Lucy Vargas? This is Margaret Pelham, on behalf of Century Financial."

Because Lucy's mortgage had been sold and resold several times in the past two years, she could never remember the name of the company presently servicing her loans. Thus she was hesitant about hanging up on phone calls from any companies with the word *financial* in the name, in the event they needed to talk about her existing bills.

Of course, the question of why she might wish to receive *these* calls could have been up for grabs as well. The fact of the matter was that Lucy's financial obligations were well beyond arrears, and there was little she could do to change that. Even so, with a somewhat superstitious respect for the belly of the beast, Lucy asked, "Do I have an account with you?"

"Ma'am, we'd like to offer you a home equity line of credit, up to eighty percent of the value of your home."

"Sorry, I'm not eligible," Lucy said, squatting to wipe away a piece of dust that clung to the brass hinge of her Chinese red beadboard cabinets. While she waited, she knelt and extended her sponge to reach a tiny dull water splotch on the otherwise shiny black floor of the kitchen.

"Ma'am, how do you know that if you don't apply? There's all kinds of new products out there. If you'd just answer a few simple questions—"

"Miss, I'm not interested. Or eligible," Lucy added crankily.

"I'm showing you as prequalified, ma'am."

Lucy found herself being drawn in by the note of confidence in the woman's voice. "I've got three minutes."

Lucy's Lean Cuisine was already turning on the microwave carousel, the timer counting down. Rocky, the girls' golden retriever, and Precious and Bijou, Lucy's two oversize poodles, were standing out on the deck, waiting to be let back inside. Lucy opened the glass doors and told the telemarketer that she hadn't earned income for almost two years.

After two and three quarters minutes of scripted questions, Miss Pelham was sounding a bit cranky herself. "Ma'am, have you tried getting a job?"

The microwave beeped. Lucy opened the door, releasing a cloud of steam. She was very hungry, having foregone lunch. "Ma'am, I have a job and I have a show coming up that should give me some income, but there's no way I can predict what will sell. Maybe you should call back then."

"Miss Vargas, you need to pay down that balloon! The bank could foreclose. I know it seems far away, but December's just around the bend."

Lucy shook her head. "Look, do you think I don't know all this? If you want to help me out, talk your bank into giving me a new loan. I've got lots of equity in the property."

"If it was up to me, I would, ma'am, but the pendulum has swung the other way now with the subprime mess. If you don't have an income history . . . well, you know."

"That's what I was trying to tell you," Lucy said softly. "Look, I have to go."

"Ma'am, even if you only owe ten percent, you've got to pay on time. They could take everything."

"Look, sorry, time's up. Gotta scoot." Lucy pressed the Off button to hang up and tried to erase the woman's last sentence from her memory bank.

By the time Lucy finished her very late lunch, the dogs had settled down around Rocky, who held a tennis ball between his front paws while the poodles crouched to either side, their lean bodies perpendicular to his stocky chest.

Tessa entered the kitchen and flopped down on the floor, laying her head on Rocky's back. "Who was on the phone?"

Lucy hesitated just a second too long. She licked her lips. "Nobody."

"It wasn't my dad?"

"Nope. You already done with homework?"

"Finished it at school. You talked a long time."

"I did?" Now Lucy wondered if Tessa had overheard her. The last thing the child needed to do was get involved in Lucy's money problems. Should she try to make up a cover story or let it alone? "Want to help me make dinner?" Lucy asked.

"What are we having?"

"Thai stir-fry with tofu."

Since Tessa had declared herself meat-free, Lucy had gotten on close speaking terms with the Hare Krishnas at the Blessings Food Co-op, who'd explained the many-splendored life of bean curd. Actually, Lucy wasn't even sure they were Hare Krishnas, but they wore saffron robes and had shaven heads. Maybe they were Tibetan monks.

Maybe, Lucy told herself, Tessa's flirtation with deprivation was a passing thing, like joining a cult. Maybe it would be something they'd all laugh about later when they looked back on it.

Tessa had already begun her intense readings in fine print, starting with the bottle of red chili garlic sauce that Lucy had left on the counter. It was the sort of scrutiny a first-year resident might give the *Physicians' Desk Reference* the first time she prescribed a new drug, or the sort of anxiety a cheapskate would devote to a bill he was trying to get out of paying.

This intense monitoring of the fats and carbohydrates in dinner ingredients could not be healthy, Lucy knew, but there wasn't a whole lot she could do about it. Banishing Tessa from the kitchen went against every instinct with which Lucy was trying to understand the problem at hand.

"Where's Daddy?"

"He took June in to try out that dance class. They should be home soon."

"So you *were* talking to him?"

"No, but the class started around four. I can't imagine it will go on too much longer."

Tessa watched Lucy's eyes carefully. Earlier, when asked about the phone call, there'd been no doubt in Tessa's mind that Lucy was lying. Now, though, she seemed completely relaxed.

"Lucy, did you and my mom ever fight about anything?"

"Oh, sure."

"Like what?"

"I don't know. Money. How she was always taking care of me."

"What else?"

"Not much, hon. Your mom and I, we thought a lot alike. What's on your mind? You look worried."

"Nothing, no reason," Tessa said, trying not to think.

When Tessa was nine, she'd been infatuated with spying. She and Amber, Susannah's older daughter, had crept and hovered behind sofas and doorjambs, just waiting for a prize to drop into their nets. It had been astoundingly easy to hear things, most of which were forgettable, but every now and then they heard something meaty enough to warrant hours of analysis by the prepubescent secret agents.

Though Penelope was never the sort of mother who saw information as dangerous and would have told Tessa most of what she wanted to hear, such openness wouldn't have been half as delicious to her daughter as the stealthy piracy of capturing secrets. It was much more fun to creep about and experience the thrill of the chase.

Tessa had learned quite a bit in these sessions. For example, Lucy's parents had been killed by a drunk driver, Martha hated flying, Mommy hated Susannah's herbal teas, Susannah didn't believe in hate. Daddy took too long to find a parking space, Amber's daddy Darryl had won a contest at Hooters, Sateesh bet money on football and Aunt Clover once saw her fifth-grade teacher kissing the principal.

Tessa had been savvy enough to keep mum about her growing store of intelligence, which she and Amber spent hours translating into code and documenting in spy logs.

By the time the girls turned twelve, they had stopped playing the game, discarding the notebooks they kept and advancing to obsessively clipping from magazines photos with outfits they thought were cute or It boys they imagined were hot. Still, certain habits of vigilance remained in good standing. Tessa had learned that a certain tone of voice preceded good gossip, and though much of what she heard was confusing to sort through, there were still occasional secrets that dropped into her lap.

One such nugget had been revealed long after she'd given up the game and shortly before her mother's death. Tessa tried to tell herself it was this association that caused her such discomfort, though she'd been unsettled by it even before the murder, refraining from mentioning it to anyone, even Amber.

Her parents had been in the kitchen, eating olives. Tessa had come down to ask for help with mathematical orders of operation and gotten swept up in the way Mommy was saying Lucy's name. It wasn't the normal way Penelope talked about her best friend, being neither offhand nor full of affection. The tone in her voice was accusatory, and Lucy wasn't even there. This made no sense to Tessa, nor did her dad's pained, embarrassed tone when he'd said something Tessa couldn't understand. She'd leaned in closer, holding the doorjamb for support.

"You know you want to," Mommy was saying. "Be a man. Admit it." Then Daddy had whispered, "That's ridiculous. She's your best friend and you know how much she needs you. She'd be the last person I'd fool around with."

"You're attracted to her. Admit it."

"And whose fault is that?" Daddy had said.

Then Mommy had started crying, saying, "I'm so afraid of losing you. I don't know why."

"Oh, honey." Daddy's voice had sounded like it did when Tessa had fallen on her bike and skinned her knees. "You're crazy, you know that, right?"

By the time Joey and June returned from the studio, each was flushed with the sort of happiness that came from overcoming a small obstacle: in June's case, the new dance class, in Joey's, letting his youngest try something he feared might be humiliating to her. Contrary to his worry, the teacher had been enthusiastic about June's sense of rhythm and had encouraged her to come back and try out for the competitive dance team with her cousin.

"Can I bring my friend Willow?" June had asked. Brittany, Clover's daughter, had been steadily distancing herself from her pudgy cousin, while Willow, who was every bit as athletic as Brittany, was too much of a nonconformist to ever worry about what the other kids might think.

"Sure," Siobhan had said. "The more the merrier."

In terms of Kicks!'s bottom line, this was most certainly true. Any girl who signed up was automatically entered into the three-year mandatory contract their FIRST MONTH FREE! was predicated on. Indeed, Clover, who'd put four certificates on her Visa card, had unwittingly committed herself to subsidizing Lucy's training for the next three years, the cost of which would be deducted on a monthly basis.

So convenient! was the Kicks! marketing department's view of fine-print clauses such as these, though Brett, Clover's husband, wouldn't see it that way when he ran his quarterly review of his wife's finances and discovered that she was on the hook for Lucy as well as three other recipients of Clover's can-do-if-you'd-just-make-the-time sensibility.

Clover wasn't really a "detail person." This was how she explained her budget overruns to her husband, though truth be told, she had an extraordinary—if extremely selective—mind for some details. Just not, as she would put it, the boring ones. Clover could spot a new piece of jewelry on a friend at fifty feet, she could decipher the most microscopic flaws in a fake Louis Vuitton in fifty seconds and she could remember each and every Keepsake Ornament, Beanie Baby and Franklin Mint commemorative plate that had ever been issued, from time immemorial.

"I have a photogenic memory," Clover would say. This was, in her case, entirely true. If something looked good, it was. End of story. Whereas the legalese buried in infelicitous fonts at the bottom of the last page of a thirteen-page contract? Life was just way too short, Clover would say to Brett, with that look she got. This was something Brett was helpless to resist, having spent too many nights walking the hall with his wife after her sister had been killed, praying to the Lord Jesus for relief, to spend much time bemoaning the fact that she spent money like it was going out of style. Clover would have been the first to point out that money had been put on this earth by the Almighty to be spent. Otherwise, why would He have said you couldn't take it with you? Furthermore, Clover was blessed with the conviction that her shopping largesse made her the Johnny Appleseed of her family's prosperity. Of course, the exact link between outlet malls and Brett's business as an insurance salesman was one of life's other boring details, the proof of which would simply have to remain in the pudding, as far as Clover was concerned.

Another aspect of Clover's genius for minutiae was her enormous aptitude for hurt feelings. Her sensitivity was deeply attuned to slights of the smallest order. For this reason, when Lucy called Kicks! to ask about returning her gift certificate, she didn't dare identify herself to Siobhan Fitzpatrick. In fact, though the chances of her recent dinner guest recognizing Lucy's voice were extremely slim, she covered the mouthpiece with her hand and switched into a deep Charleston accent her mother had spent Lucy's formative years trying to eradicate. "I don't know what my friend paid, but I'm not able to use it," Lucy said. "Do you think I could just return it without her finding out? I don't want to hurt her feelings."

"Well, first, even if you were to tell her, you couldn't return it," Siobhan said, her voice regretful, though the only regret she really had was that somehow the call came through to her when she'd asked the front desk staff to take these sorts of complaints, especially when she was busy getting ready for class. "It's company policy."

"Well, do you think I could transfer it to someone else, then?" Lucy asked, thinking of June.

"I'm so sorry. No transfers. If you look at the contract, it's very clear. If we did it for you, we'd have to do it for everyone. The only way we can offer such competitive prices is to do exactly what's offered in the contract. We have to ask our customers to keep their end of the bargain."

"Well, I'd like to, but I live too far out of town," Lucy stammered.

"Why don't you leave me your name and one of our trainers can explain the benefit of what we do here. You might just find yourself changing your mind. What did you say your name was?"

"I didn't. Thanks anyway." Lucy quickly hung up the phone. She pressed her certificate into a special mesh envelope she kept in her purse, home to any number of forgotten coupons and expired gift cards, the existence of which was a very trivial but nonetheless constant thorn in her side. For some reason, tossing them out would have been an admission of defeat. Keeping them allowed Lucy the harmless fantasy that should she really need the cash value they represented, she'd find a kinder, gentler keeper at the gate of whatever fine establishment she'd neglected to patronize as promptly as she should have. In this utopian future of her need, the gods of fair play might have deducted a small charge for the passage of time, they might have shaken their heads at Lucy's forgetfulness, but surely they wouldn't have pretended the donors had never existed, taken their money for nothing, and claimed victory on a field so tilted to the left side of the brain it might as well have been an unscalable castle wall.

Chapter Five

Susannah Newsome was dreadfully out of step with her fellow accountants. First to raise eyebrows was her wardrobe, full of odd vintage dresses, frilly peasant shirts and luridly colorful prints from places like Kathmandu and Uzbekistan. Next were Susannah's inflections, resulting in a gentle lilting interrogative, the final syllables of which tended to end on the upswing, so as not to give offense by having her seem too certain of anything. Everything about Susannah was soft around the edges, from her curly blond hair to her forgiving gaze to the wisps of cloth that sailed behind her when she walked. Most damning of all, at least to her critics, was Susannah's chaotic personal style, which attached itself to everything she did *except* her pristine balance sheets, which were regularly praised by the foundation's auditors for their clarity, precision and rigorous attention to detail.

This sort of compliment, made in writing, year after year, had thus far protected Susannah from the housecleaning that the new executors, the Cameron cousins, Peter and Nigel, would have dearly liked to undertake. Their sorting out would have started with the accountant's office (where towers of paper were anchored by widowed shoes and cans of organic tomatoes) and ended with her title as the Cameron Foundation's comptroller, a job description so at odds with her pliant personality and cluttered psyche that it made the twins' teeth hurt to hear the title said out loud.

Susannah's facility with numbers was a gift about which she had long been apologetic, particularly in college, when, as the only female in most of her upper-level math classes, she'd been the reluctant captain of the college math bowl team. The trophy they'd taken in regionals was now entombed in the back of her daughters' toy chest, having been festooned, beribboned and bestickered beyond recognition.

Darryl Newsome, who had divorced Susannah when Willow, their youngest daughter, was four, tended to shower his daughters with insignia celebrating his own world of higher abstraction. In this case, the adhesive logos of college football teams, race car drivers and motorcycle clubs were stuck like bandages around the trophy of Rodin's *Thinker* peering knowingly off into the middle distance.

The irreconcilable differences over which Darryl had finally left Susannah were, when each was considered on its own merits, fairly trivial. Trivial or not, when added up, they did appear to comprise a whole existence. Susannah listened to NPR, Darryl to Howard Stern. She loved Vivaldi, he Metallica. Her hero: Gandhi; his: Chuck Norris. The night they'd met, at a barbecue fund-raiser for the volunteer fire department, Susannah had been wearing a tight fifties dress with four-inch spike heels. This attire may have led Darryl to assume his wife would be more traditional, may have made him hope for things she couldn't provide, despite her eagerness to make her husband happy. It wasn't as if Susannah didn't try, but for all her strengths, she was a terrible liar. It was hard to fake an interest in motocross biking, even harder to pretend she couldn't understand amortization algorithms, even though her husband, who prided himself on his smarts, didn't. Darryl couldn't help being hurt when she outshone him, and she couldn't help but look sheepish when she tried to perform the Seminole fight song or Gator Chop in public. The one thing both agreed upon, besides their love of their children, was their spectacular, phenomenal, even miraculous sex life. It had been a grand chemistry of differences, one that might have kept them married a lot longer had

Darryl not discovered that his wife would continue to have sex with him whether they lived together or not. She knew their arguments were bothering the children; she knew they couldn't live together without friction. Still, Susannah saw no reason to throw the baby out with the bathwater. Her only requirement was that they keep their ongoing liaison a secret. This suited Darryl just fine and introduced the thrill of the illicit to their meetings. Even Martha, who'd figured out her best friend was having an affair, didn't know the mystery lover was none other than Susannah's ex-husband. Pliant as she could be, the accountant wouldn't budge on this question, no matter how often Martha pressed her. Of course, the fact that Martha would have disapproved made Susannah's secret a whole lot easier to keep.

Twelve days after Lucy's party, Susannah was working at home, ostensibly because she wanted to get away from interruptions at the office. She had just kissed Darryl good-bye at the door that led from the kitchen to the garage, where he kept his car protected from the sun and prying eyes, when the phone rang, startling her out of her postorgasm lull. Susannah checked the revolving digital marquee of a Brookstone crystal ball. The gadget, which Darryl had given her for Mother's Day, magnified each incoming caller's name and number. Susannah ran to grab the cordless phone from her unmade bed.

"Hey, Martha," she said, catching her breath. "What's up?"

"Listen, tell me honestly. In that meeting with Nigel yesterday, did I lose it?"

"No. You were fine. You're so fast on your feet. Which was fortunate, since I just sat there with my mouth hanging open."

"It wasn't your problem."

"Oh, hon. To tell you the truth, I'd completely forgotten."

"I wish I could."

"You're too hard on yourself. It's ancient history."

"Not to me!" Martha insisted.

"Look, Martha, everyone makes mistakes."

"But I was the attorney drafting the agreement."

"Which you were *asked* to do, my friend. Most importantly, Penelope wanted *you* to be her attorney. At which you've done a very fine job. More than fine."

"But, Susannah, Penelope wasn't a lawyer. I should have recused myself. It could invalidate the agreement if anyone found out."

"But how would they?"

"I keep having that dream where Nigel is wearing one of those barrister wigs and the girls are sitting in the victim's docket, looking at me like I just shot somebody."

"Martha," Susannah murmured, trying to shake off the sense of foreboding that had been incubating since Nigel Cameron had asked about a set of canceled checks at a meeting the day before. Martha's recurrent dream about the Cameron brothers was starting to work its way into Susannah's subconscious, despite her evolved understanding of visualization and other lucid-dreaming techniques. "Deep breathing," Susannah whispered, as much for herself as her friend. "Serenity. That which we cannot control we must accept. And so on and so forth."

"Oh please!" Martha moaned. "I prefer artificial avenues for inner peace. Sex, drugs, rock and roll. Maybe the occasional vat or two of wine."

"Hey, hold on. Someone's at the door." Susannah cradled the phone between her neck and head and pulled her swollen front door free of its warped frame. She grinned happily at Lucy, waving her in. "Don't worry. What you said made perfect sense. I promise."

Susannah led Lucy into her kitchen, pointed at the fridge so Lucy would help herself to a drink, then stirred a pot of black beans and leaned across the kitchen counter to inspect the screen of her laptop. "Hold on a sec," she said, pressing a button to pull the machine out of hibernation and scroll to the page Martha was calling about. "I have no idea what they're after. They can ask all they want, but remember, the rich are capricious. And we've got documentation the money was used for charitable purposes in the end. Don't let Tweedledum and Tweedledee ruin your day. They've made a vocation of trying to unsettle the two of us.

They've nothing to lose, and the more time they can waste, the longer they'll get their executor's cut. Just put them out of your mind."

Tweedledum and Tweedledee's real names were Nigel and Peter Cameron, but even kindhearted Susannah had no use for polite formalities when it came to the newest members of the Cameron Foundation's board of trustees. Beyond their physical resemblance to the Alice in Wonderland characters, the brothers' interference and scattershot inquiries into every nook and cranny of the foundation's accounts reminded Susannah of the surreal mischief wrought by Alice's interlocutors.

Antipathies were mutual, for the English twins found it impossible to believe a woman who was so blurry around the edges might be capable of managing the trust's money without letting some of it go missing. Thus, despite independent Pricewaterhouse audits each year, the Cameron cousins had brought in their own financial teams, requested records for the past twenty years and managed to convince a probate court to freeze the bulk of the Barclays bank assets left in Penelope's name until the Camerons' lawsuit questioning the legitimacy of the Cameron Foundation's operations had been settled.

At issue was a fine-print clause left over from the will of Penelope's great-grandparents, who'd created the foundation in the first place. Contemporaries of the Bloomsbury set and ardent suffragists, the couple had left their money exclusively to their female descendants without exorcising the more traditional legal boilerplate clauses aimed at the "protection" of the weaker sex. While Penelope was alive, she'd had sole discretion over the principal, but once she'd died, the Cameron cousins, who'd already been disputing the terms of the estate on the basis of discrimination against males, had unearthed language that appeared to grant them, as the children's closest male relatives on their mother's side, certain oversight powers in the case of "death in which foul play" had been proven. The fact that Joey had had nothing to do with Penelope's murder didn't matter. Such "extraordinary circumstances" had led to a situation in which all the assets had to be placed in trust until such time as the court had concluded decisively that such protection was or was not necessary. Until then, as Martha put it, all expenditures had to go through "more procedural hoops than Kafka's cockroach on one of his good days."

Even the simplest transactions of regular foundation business came into the purview of the Cameron cousins, who'd been granted temporary representation on the board and now shared executive authority with its members.

"Look, Martha, Lucy's just dropped by. Let me just email you what I've got so you can take a look at it."

The accountant's laptop was balanced on a pile of papers, which was more of a *concept* of a pile than an actual one. *Heaps* by any other name, Susannah's accumulations married alarmingly disparate objects. On this occasion her laptop-bearing mound included several oversize newspapers, animé books still opened to their traced-over pages, a wet washcloth tinged with grape jelly, and a Goofy T-shirt that Willow had discarded along with her soccer knee pads, one of which had stuck fast to a neon green tube sock.

With the phone cradled in her bent neck, Susannah typed into the computer while continuing to talk to Martha. This task took enough of her attention away that Lucy was able to embark on disassembling the contents of the refrigerator.

"That's just what Lucy does," Susannah had explained to Darryl when he'd taken umbrage at how Lucy would sweep in and start cleaning. By the time Susannah had cut and pasted three columns of numbers and emailed them to Martha, Lucy had emptied much of the contents of the refrigerator shelves, dumping jars and plastic containers into a large plastic trash bag she'd brought from home for that very purpose.

Lucy worked quickly. She knew that once Susannah was off the phone she'd be begging her to "please stop." This would morph at some point into a determined campaign to scrape this wealth of fungal colonies into the composting bin, which had already reached the end of its useful life as a cat biscuit holder and was now being used to wrest the last bit of methane from legumes and other foodstuffs that Susannah couldn't bear to waste.

"What was that about?" Lucy asked when Susannah pressed the End button. Susannah held up one finger, her eyes still on the computer screen. This gave Lucy enough time to quickly stow the garbage bag outside the kitchen door and return to the second phase of her mission, the wiping of shelves with a solution of vinegar and baking soda that she'd heated in the microwave.

Sometimes Lucy's sorties targeted the kitchen, others the bathrooms. Sometimes she'd arrive and make quick work of the living room before even greeting her host. That room was easiest: just pillows and blankets to fold, dirty socks and shirts to put with the laundry, and dirty plates and cups to return to the kitchen. Other times, usually when she had a problem to work out with one of her paintings, Lucy would call Susannah at the office and ask to be allowed to tackle a bedroom closet. Lucy's cleaning was almost a hobby, one that Darryl had deemed insulting and various other friends felt abused either Lucy's goodwill (Clover) or Susannah's privacy (Martha).

From the outside, this symbiotic dance, in which Lucy cleaned and Susannah accepted the intrusion by blithely pretending not to notice, swiftly followed by feeble protestations and weakly delivered reproaches that Lucy *shouldn't have*, may have seemed a bizarre variation of the normal reciprocities of friendship. Nevertheless, like many forms of consensual adult relations, the arrangement fulfilled mutual needs. Susannah, who lived too far from her New Mexican parents for cosseting, was comforted by what seemed to her to be Lucy's miraculous organizational powers. Lucy found it soothing to bring such dramatic improvements to the inner landscape of Susannah's house and it satisfied her need for action that was simultaneously consequential and yet not.

By the time Susannah's fingers had stopped their mad tapping on the keyboard, Lucy was already returning the remaining food to designated shelves. She knew her categories of dairy, condiments, and imitation meat products wouldn't last the night, but still, it felt good just the same. "Was that Martha?"

"I worry about her chakras. She's not sleeping."

Lucy could never remember what a chakra was. If she asked, however, she would be in for a New Age dissertation, one that would inevitably connect the limited ventilation in Lucy's painting studio to her consumption of too few cruciferous vegetables and somehow culminate with deep-breathing techniques guaranteed to increase blood flow to the lower erogenous zones. Solely as a means of distraction, Lucy asked, "Where are the girls? They're so quiet."

"What girls?"

"Willow and June."

"Willow's at trombone, Lucy."

"Wha—" Lucy's face flickered from confusion to panic. She stared at the kitchen clock. "I was picking June up!"

"It's Wednesday," Susannah said gently. "Dance."

"Oh, damn it! It's Wednesday! I am such a loser!" Lucy sprinted toward the front door. "Call that teacher for me and tell her I'm on the way!"

By the time Lucy had reached Kicks! neither June nor the teacher was there, nor did the teenagers at the front desk know where they'd gone. Traffic was backed up around the rotary of the town square. Lucy's worry thrummed through her like the oversize bass notes blaring from the pickup truck behind her. Images of that poor Florida girl abducted on her way home from school competed with crosses on the side of the road from Lucy's childhood in Charleston, a shrine to the spot where five children died after being hit by a senile Impala driver. Lucy honked her horn at the car in front of her, which was driven by a woman talking on her cell phone.

Lucy hated cell phones with an all-or-nothing passion, although at times like this she was brought to heel by their apparent necessity. She veered out around the conversing driver and raced across

Garden Street toward Joey's office, chiding herself. "You are such a loser! How could you be so stupid! Where is she? What the hell is the damn dance teacher doing leaving in the middle of the day?"

Joey's office was in the house where the girls were born, where they'd lived with their mother and father until Penelope's death. A huge, dove-gray, three-story Victorian mansion with white wood trim, the building sat at the heart of the historic district, with the family home facing forward, and the Foundation's suite of rooms opening to a small alley in the rear.

Lucy assumed that June would have called her father if Lucy hadn't shown up, but just in case the child had taken it in her head to walk home, Lucy drove slowly, scanning the sidewalks and trying not to panic.

The house Joey and the girls had abandoned was on a wide boulevard called High Street, divided by a median strip lush with flower-beds and sheltered by huge live oaks draped with Spanish moss. A canopy of shade extended across the road and connected one ample lawn with the next. The neighborhood made Lucy think of a grove, with its carpet of deep green Saint Augustine grass that flowed from tree to tree. All traces of underbrush were eradicated by crews of landscapers, or in some cases by homeowners whose Protestant ancestry mandated they manicure their own yards and shun valet parking, suitcases on wheels and other forms of laziness infecting modern prosperity.

Lucy pulled into the driveway of Joey's house just in time to see Siobhan's leotard-clad figure embraced in the yawn of the open screen door. Joey and June were behind her, crowding the frame of the entry. Siobhan, wearing a soft violet miniskirt around her navy catsuit, was balanced on a pair of open-toed spike-heeled sandals.

Siobhan's hair was swept up in a hasty French twist, pinned by chopsticks. The parabola of her graceful shoulders, the full swell of her barely contained sweep of hair, her perfect calves tapering prettily into delicate high-heeled ankles—each of these features captured Lucy's painterly imagination. At the very same time, she felt a sudden constriction of dread that had nothing at all to do with her worry about June.

Lucy opened her car door and rushed up the steps of the porch. "I'm so sorry!"

"It's okay, Lucy," Joey said. "Siobhan brought her."

"Thank you so much! I really do apologize," Lucy added, reaching out to shake Siobhan's graceful hand.

"No problem. My mom was a musician. I know how you artists can get lost in your work. I didn't mind, really. Besides, driving June over here gave us time to talk. She's talented, you know." Siobhan offered this compliment to Joey, to whom she'd turned. She placed a small manicured hand on his forearm, just above his wrist.

A muscle in Joey's cheek twitched, which Lucy attributed to either anger at herself for not remembering to pick up June or a profound desire to jump Siobhan's bones. Maybe, Lucy thought, considering how the day was going, both.

June tugged at her father's shirt where it billowed slightly above his belt. "Daddy, there's a dance competition in Atlanta next weekend."

Joey peered at Lucy and back at his daughter. "Lucy, what do you think?"

"Let me think," Lucy stalled. She was remembering the many times June had begged to stay the night at Willow's, only to call at midnight to say that she was afraid and wanted to come home. She may have appeared eager then and would stay that way up until the very night in question, but this optimistic bravado was something Lucy had come to think of as June's daylight chutzpah.

"Actually, Mr. Adorno," Siobhan said, moving her fingers down to land on Joey's palm. "Why don't you come along? Having a dad come with us would be great."

"Lucy?" Joey asked, turning to look at his daughter's delighted upturned face.

Lucy pinched the inside of her elbow. "I could go if you're busy."

"That's okay, Lucy. I know you hate hotels."

Siobhan cocked her head toward Lucy, who explained herself. "It's kind of a busman's holiday."

"That's like when the bus driver takes his vacation on a Greyhound," June offered eagerly, having only recently asked Lucy to explain the phrase. "Boring. 'Cause she used to run a bed-and-breakfast hotel."

Siobhan turned her attention back to Joey. "I was planning to rent a van. Then we could all drive together."

"We have one," Joey said. "The foundation does. We could use that."

"I've been meaning to ask you about your foundation," Siobhan observed shyly, moving slightly away from Joey and turning her gaze on June. "There're some poor children I'd love to include into our program if you ever fund that sort of thing."

"Poor kids are what we're all about," Joey said, smiling. "Maybe we can talk about it on the trip."

Siobhan assured him that once the children were tucked into their beds at night, they'd have plenty of time to talk. As she crossed the porch in front of Lucy, she waved at June. "Don't forget to practice your new steps, June. You did very well today. And I'll see you in two days."

At this, Siobhan waved to Joey and June and tiptoed toward her car, only to turn on her heels once she'd opened the car door. "Oh, Miss Lucy? Why don't you come in and try the adult ballet? It's really good for your circulation and flexibility. They're even saying it might prevent memory loss as you age. Kind of like a stitch in time saves nine. You don't have to wear the ballerina kit. No one cares what your body looks like, we just want you to get out there and *move*."

Chapter Six

L et's eat at the Paki's today, Peter," Nigel Cameron was saying.
"Yes!" his brother Peter replied, as though this wasn't
where the two had lunched nearly every day of the past twenty-
two months.

Sateesh, Martha's tall, dark and exorbitantly handsome better
half, was the proprietor of a small, elegant restaurant on the town
square. The menu at Sapphire changed each day, offering enough
variety to the Cameron twins that they never tired of the food, nor
the joy of treating Martha's husband like a servant.

The pleasure of calling Sateesh a Paki (though they were well
aware the man was from India, not Pakistan) was only the first
of many rituals the twins had developed to celebrate the delight
of being handsomely paid to do what they'd have done for free:
disrupt the operations of an organization they felt had personally
discriminated against them solely on the basis of gender. Indeed,
for several years before their cousin's death, the brothers had nat-
tered away at their British solicitors, grousing about the unfairness
of a will that benefited only women. This had been an exercise
in futility until the circumstances of Penelope's death and Nigel's
obsessive knowledge of every detail of his ancestors' will had finally
provided the brothers with an unexpected opportunity to exert
actual, rather than imaginary, control.

Within a month of the funeral, the Camerons had arrived

bearing legal documents entitling them to take a seat on the Cameron Foundation board to protect the interests of the trust.

"Your Honor," Martha had argued in court a few weeks later. "This is the wolf guarding the chicken coop. These are the very cousins who've been suing the estate for years."

Martha's pleas had not endeared her to the pair, who'd prevailed in the local courts, at least until such time as the judge had reviewed the probate documents, heard arguments on both sides and decided the merits of their case. The language empowering the closest male relatives to swoop in and oversee things in the event of any Cameron female's violent death may not have made much sense given the spirit of the original will, a suffragist document if ever there was one. It was nevertheless crystal clear, having been legal boilerplate for several generations, and thus couldn't be dismissed out of hand.

As the twins saw it, if they'd been provided a legal windfall, it was about bloody time. Neither of the two had distinguished himself at Cambridge, nor was either possessed of the physical beauty presently marching toward them in the person of Sateesh Vigram. The man's plummy Oxford accent and Balliol oar would have been reason enough to hate him, even if he weren't married to their nemesis, otherwise known as That Wicked Bitch Martha. Most irritating of all his traits, Sateesh acted serenely immune to the twins' subtle, but nonetheless daily, dishing out of contempt.

"Hullo," he murmured cheerfully once he'd gotten to their table. "Shall I set aside some trifle for you?"

"What else have you got?" Nigel asked, scrutinizing the menu while Peter rested his elbow on the table and leaned his right temple into two fingers with the thoughtful sobriety of a confessor.

"I've one slice of quince pie with vanilla custard and one almond napoleon."

"I'll take the napoleon," Peter and Nigel found themselves crying out in unison. Despite their resolution not to let the Paki see them squabbling over pudding, the brothers could not overcome a lifelong habit of rivalry when it came to sweets.

"Do you think he does it on purpose?" Nigel whispered as soon as Sateesh was out of earshot.

"I don't know." Peter's tone was brusque at having lost the coin toss. He wasn't having any of Nigel's conciliatory conversations right at the moment, thank you very much. "Now what was it you were trying so badly to pantomime in the office?"

Nigel looked around him as though hidden cameras might be operating from the portrait of Chief Osceola hanging behind his head. "I had a most interesting conversation with dear Cousin Clover this morning."

"And?"

"She's worried about the eldest child. Thinks she's getting too thin. Thinks perhaps the situation at Lucy's is too—what was that term she used?—*laid-back*."

"Is she willing to tell a judge that?"

"I doubt it. Not yet. However, she does think the child should see an eating disorders consultant. I'm cautiously optimistic."

"About what?"

"Don't you see? If Tessa continues to lose weight, *ipso facto*, her father's obviously not capable of caring for her on his own. Who better than the child's uncles to make sure her welfare is their highest concern? And there's more good news I'd forgot to mention. Remember those checks the auditors found last week? When I asked Sloppy Susannah about them in Tuesday's meeting, she seemed very flustered. Even Wicked Bitch Martha jumped through hoops trying to explain why it was nothing."

"And?"

"It clearly upset them. Martha spouted a bit of rubbish about Penelope not wanting foundation money to be associated with the animal rights movement, but that didn't explain why she wrote such large personal checks. Their skittishness spoke volumes. I do think we need to fly our chap to Phoenix as soon as possible."

"Oh, Nigel, the man's found nothing. Why throw good money after bad?"

Peter was referring to the private investigator they'd retained to uncover flaws in the personal and professional lives of Joey and the other members of the board of trustees. The twins' first hopes had been pinned on speculations of some sort of long-standing adulterous affair between Joey and Lucy, or at least some indication that the two had fallen into bed shortly after Penelope's death. Either scenario might, the Camerons had imagined, convince a provincial judge that their well-paid roles as fiduciary guardians of the Cameron children should be continued indefinitely. Instead, their hired detective had spent countless hours on a wild-goose chase. For lack of anything more incriminating, the brothers were then confined to looking through bank statements and casting about for irregularities in accounting practices. It was grasping at straws, of course, but thus far, they'd been handsomely rewarded for all the time they'd managed to drag out the court battle. Besides, if it weren't for straws grasped, they'd not be in Omega right now, enjoying this lovely food, a healthy salary and a chance to reinvent themselves as posh aristocrats. The longer they could delay before having to return to England, the better.

"Can we not find a detective who charges less, Nigel? At two hundred quid an hour, I'm starting to—"

"I'm afraid you get what you pay for, as the Americans are so fond of saying. Besides, I've found a brilliant new investment scheme. Do you remember that chap we met in the hotel lounge last week?"

"Why do I feel like you're making no sense at all, Nigel?"

"Because you're put out over the napoleon."

"That's silly. But you did take the petit four last week!"

"It's not my fault the Paki doesn't make enough pudding. I really am beginning to think he does it on purpose. But never you mind, dear brother. If my plan comes full circle, we'll not only put Wicked Bitch out of a job, but we'll have her bloody Paki wishing he'd never left his Bombay hovel."

Lucy wasn't thinking clearly. She hadn't for some time. When she carried the paint to the counter, she was trying not to let the

Galbreath Prize, the art world's equivalent of a Pulitzer, fill her every waking thought. It made no sense to bank on such unreliable prospects, but it beat her other obsession, the image of her being evicted from her house, a point at which the whole fantasy broke down into panicked oblivion.

How she'd come to this, Lucy wasn't sure. To reckon with her financial disarray would have entailed replaying the past two years in some sort of sequential and logical fashion, an impossible task. She had gotten through each day by telling herself that her grief for Penelope was nothing compared to that of Joey and the girls, by reminding herself that she'd never earned what she'd had anyhow and by praying for deliverance. Having to go through any of it a second time would have been an exercise in masochism.

Lucy handed the clerk her MasterCard and counted the sec-onds it took for the high-pitched whine of the register to signal the purchase was complete. She was eager to get back home, she was starving, she was trying not to think about Joey's impending trip to Atlanta. When the teenage sales clerk winced and said, "Ma'am, it's not going through," Lucy's first reaction was to blame the technology. She shook her head, patted the counter reassur-ingly and said she'd go to a cash machine. "I'll stop back after lunch, okay?"

For weeks at a time, Lucy would give up red meat, only to fall prey to temptation at a moment like this, when she'd skipped breakfast and was hurtling across town toward Wendy's with a huge monkey on her back: the need for a cheeseburger with everything and a large Diet Coke. "I'm starving!" kept playing in Lucy's head as she lowered her window to accept the first part of her con-traband, a large cantilevered plastic cup, the chilled contents of which would tantalize her in the absence of the straw, which the franchise insisted on withholding until her purchase was complete. She was urging her worst self to keep quiet. It wasn't fair to in-flict her hypoglycemic mood on the poor kid looking off into the middle distance while listening to another customer's order on his headphone. Lucy was telling herself the straw would arrive soon enough. Complaining about corporate practices would only slow things down. "Ma'am? Do you have another card?"

"Not with me," Lucy moaned. Her debit card was limited to ATMs. "I'll be back."

At her bank, there was a line of people waiting for the tellers. Lucy pulled around to the ATM, which, in the noonday sun, was nearly impossible to read. That would be her alibi later, when she had to explain herself. Lucy had no idea how much money was in her account, for the less she had, the more distressed she got. Ergo, denial, otherwise known as putting one's head directly in the sand until the missing nest egg presented itself.

The facts were bleak but not unsurpassable. Were it not for the sleight of hand of the bank's newest financial "services" department, Lucy would have faced the fact that she had only fifty dollars left until the end of the week. With a bit of creativity and lots of legumes, she'd make ends meet without disclosing to Joey the fact that the amount they'd agreed upon for the running of the household was no longer sufficient to cover the spiraling costs of keeping the house cool, of cooking for Tessa with only organic ingredients and of driving her 1966 Volvo sedan back and forth between the beach and the girls' schools. These factors, if Lucy could only have relaxed enough about her financial predicament to sit down and analyze them, would have provided exculpatory evidence against the shame that clouded her thinking to the point of obscuring rationality altogether. It was a self-fulfilling prophecy, Lucy's blind panic when it came to all things monetary, a neurosis she'd managed to keep well hidden, even from those who thought they knew her well.

The ironies were—like the interest she would incur on the sums she withdrew from a list of available funds that the marketing department was calling Powerdraft but that weren't technically hers—exorbitant. They were also—like the vines that threw themselves across the canopy roads without benefit of human agency—preternatural, interwoven and extraordinary.

The Cameron Foundation had, only eight years earlier, divested itself of all stock in Payday Lending Pals, of which Powerdraft was only the latest demonic incarnation to reappear in the predatory lending market. This same company, in its Title Shares heyday, had once actually repossessed the vehicle of the man holding his wife hostage that horrific Thanksgiving morning.

That his second victim may have at one time been enriched by the same company that took him down might have given the man pause, had he known. He might have thanked God for small favors, but he didn't know who Penelope was, only that she drove a Mercedes station wagon. That was, it appeared, enough to set him off in and of itself.

Lucy's visual acuity was a force of nature, but though she registered a change in the cash machine's on-screen menu, it meant nothing to her. Perhaps she was blinded by the light, or by the god of cheeseburgers, or the pulse thrumming in her chest that dared to hope for Galbreath Prize rescue from on high. Ten twenties fluttered their wings in the money slot, and Lucy pinched them in one fell swoop, enough for gas and food and one large tube of titanium white.

For this moment of blindness, this lapse in caution, Lucy would pay. The money she had borrowed under an "insurance" plan to protect customers against the "humiliation" of bouncing a check came dear: five dollars a day in overdraft charges, thirty in nonsufficiency fees and a late-payment penalty of twenty-nine when the bill from the bank would go unopened for weeks on end, mistaken for a simple statement and left to founder in a basket of nonurgent mail.

Usury by any other name, such practices were cloaked in terms like *convenience* and *protection* and braided into language so deafeningly dense, so small of font, it defied understanding.

Even if Lucy were to notice the new Powerdraft symbol added to the list of available funds, there was nothing on-screen to tell her that she was actually borrowing one hundred and fifty dollars, upon which she would owe, by the time she opened the bank statement some weeks later, two hundred and eighty dollars more in fees, late-payment penalties and interest.

Were this the only debt upon which interest accumulated so rapidly, were she not so stricken by grief and guilt that she was unable to truly reckon her accounts, then this egregious charge wouldn't have constituted the straw that broke Lucy's financial back. Later, though, when she was forced to look back and understand what had become of her life, Lucy would be drawn to this transaction as the one that pushed her over the top and down the crown of the hill, with no one tumbling after.

Chapter Seven

A week later, Joey was driving Tessa to Lucy's before he and June left for the dance competition in Atlanta. "We'll be back on Sunday," he said, reaching across to pat his elder daughter's shoulder.

"Whatever." Tessa was studying the Heifer International catalog intently. Some old guy named Walter Cronkite was smiling down at a small goat, whose purchase would offer a third world mother the means of producing milk for her family. On the opposite page, another celebrity was petting a spotted calf. "Why don't we do this?" she asked.

"Do what?"

"Give people ways to feed their family?"

"We do, sweetie. Heifer concentrates on the livestock idea, that's all."

"If I save fifty dollars out of my allowance, can I do this?"

"Why not?" Joey said. "Let's talk about it when I get back, okay?"

"Daddy?" June was tapping him on the shoulder from the back seat. "We're going to be late!"

Joey tossed his head back affectionately toward June, whose excitement was contagious. "They won't leave without us."

"How do you know that!"

"You're driving the van, moron," Tessa snapped. She wished

her sister could let her talk to her dad, just once, without inter-
rupting.

Joey said sternly, "Tessa. Apologize."

"Sorry." Tessa's voice quavered just slightly.

"I'll call you, sweetie," Joey said gently, pulling into Lucy's
driveway. He reached over for Tessa's backpack and escorted her
up the walk. "Speaking of phones, I meant to ask you. I called your
cell at lunch today to see if I could bring you some pizza and Amber
couldn't find you—why did she have your phone?"

"Hers was dead."

"Well, sweetie, she sounded really—I don't know, nervous. Is
she okay? She's not hiding something from her mom, is she?"

"Why would you say that?"

"I don't know. She sounded so guilty. She's not into drugs
or—"

"Oh, geez, Dad!" Tessa began to laugh, almost giddy with relief.

"She just didn't sound right. Where were you, anyhow?"

"Makeup quiz," Tessa said smoothly, having had time to pull
her thoughts together.

"You do okay?"

"Yeah. Listen, Dad?" Tessa asked, when they'd reached the
front door. Suddenly she was filled with an urgent flash of panic,
a need to keep her father and sister right where they were. "Can't
you just stay in town? June's only gonna make a fool of herself at
the competition anyhow."

Joey's "Tessa!" had a strangled sound to it. June was still in the
car, well out of earshot, but Tessa's comment was still unaccept-
able. He shook his head. "Siobhan says she's got a lot of talent."

Tessa dropped her backpack in the front hall before turning
back quietly to her father. She shook her head at him. "Dad, she
is playing you."

"She's ten years old, Tessa."

"Not June, Dad. Think! Like Mom used to say, whose bread's
getting buttered in this transaction?"

"I don't want to hear another word—" Joey whispered, fiercely protective of June's confidence. He looked up to see Lucy trotting down the stairs, wiping her hands on the tail of her work shirt.

Her eyes were lit with both pleasure and worry, flickering from Tessa's face to Joey's.

"Be careful!" Lucy said, despite her resolution not to let Tessa witness her anxiety about the trip.

"I will," Joey said, handing her a piece of paper with the Atlanta hotel numbers. "You know I'm a good driver."

"I do," Lucy sighed, wrapping an arm around Tessa's shoulders. "You have a good time, now," she urged, even as she recognized the immense evil of her profound hope that when Joey returned home from Atlanta, he'd be safe, sound and bored beyond tears, in that order.

"She called you Miss Lucy?"

Martha's indignation was a joy to behold. As often happened, Martha's volatile reaction lowered Lucy's own level of chagrin simply by giving it voice. Lucy was also calmed by an endorphin rush, the product of trying to keep pace with Martha and Susannah as they race-walked down the beach.

"Siobhan wouldn't know," Susannah offered. "That's a Southern expression."

"My point precisely. It's not like it just slipped out from habit. She knew what she was doing," Martha replied.

"Whatever; it sure made me feel ancient."

"What a bitch!" Martha muttered. "Who the hell does she think she is?"

"She can't help how cute she is," Susannah said.

"I know," Lucy sighed. "I'd love to be that tiny."

"Lucy, you're not fat," Susannah scolded. "I love your body. It's the sacred feminine in its purest form."

Lucy laughed. "More like Buddha, hon. If only my waistline would change places with my bottom line, everything would be perfect."

Martha, who had been trotting along ahead of her friends, did a little circle around Lucy, stopping her in her tracks. "Lucy, do you need money? I can give you some."

"No, you can't."

"Can too. Susannah, tell her," Martha insisted, pulling Lucy's arm to get her to move faster.

Susannah looked pained, having recently examined Martha's last bank statement. "Did you come into something I'm unaware of, Martha?"

"No, but I make good money and I can afford to—"

Susannah shook her head. "I told you not to get a flexible interest rate, Martha. I do remember telling you that."

"Susannah, what is wrong with you! Of course we can help Lucy." Martha shot her former college roommate a warning glance and strode forward, pressing her body through an invisible wall of resistance.

Sateesh had opened his restaurant when interest rates were low. With the increased cost of gas, people were eating out less, a fact that Sateesh wouldn't let compromise his resolve to use fresh, organic ingredients. On top of that, the monthly note had blossomed into almost 11 percent per year. This, on the two hundred thousand they'd borrowed, came to a chunk of change, without even factoring in the restaurant's overhead or payroll. "What do you need, Lucy?"

"I'm fine. I was just kvetching. As soon as I have my show next month, I'll be fine."

"How's your work going?" Susannah asked Lucy, distracted by the annoyance she felt toward Martha, whose cavalier attitude about money was at least partially responsible for their present inability to rescue Lucy from her financial woes. Not only had the attorney taken out an adjustable-rate loan against Susannah's advice, but she'd also supported Penelope's abrupt decision—eight years earlier—to dump all her Payday Lending Pals shares in one fell swoop. Susannah had pleaded with Penelope, whose father had always handled their investments until his unexpected death from a heart attack, to put the shares up for sale in batches instead of flooding the market and caus-ing the price to plummet. Martha could have sided with Susannah. She should have known Penelope was still mourning her father. She could have helped Susannah talk Penelope out of doing anything too hastily. Instead, the lawyer had fanned the flames of Penelope's outrage, insisting that the foundation must make an ethical stand. After all, Martha argued, the endowment could more easily weather financial pain than the victims of predatory lending. Further, she warned, losses in the Cameron Foundation's moral credibility would be far more damaging than reverses in its bottom line.

This impulsive decision to sell at any cost had been applauded in the philanthropic community and by the media, but not on Wall Street, where the market dump had caused severe ripples throughout the financial services industry. Even nearly a decade after the sale, though Susannah had managed to recoup much of the money the foundation and Penelope's personal estate had lost, the Payday debacle raised questions about the comptroller's com-petence. It was, in Susannah's opinion, the main reason a probate judge had agreed to hear the Cameron cousins' claim for protective injunction, the reason he'd given them auditing authority and vot-ing power on the board of trustees.

Now Susannah's every move was scrutinized and questioned. On top of that, the less careful Martha was with money, the greater the burden Susannah felt to be vigilant, forcing her to act like the counter of beans she'd sworn never to become.

"Do you need supplies?" Susannah pressed Lucy. "I could put them on my Visa."

"No—" Lucy said, but Martha interrupted, leaning in and tug-ging on Lucy's shoulder.

"Why aren't you putting your paints on the girls' charge, Lucy? You do teach Tessa art, do you not?"

"No. I won't do that."

"You are so pigheaded, Lucy!"

"She's right to be, Martha," Susannah scolded. "Peter and Nigel would have a field day with that."

"Oh, please. I don't think they're going to argue over art sup-plies when Tessa's clearly working on a painting for the art fair at her school."

"The truth is that she's used next to nothing on her project and she used watercolors, not acrylics. I won't charge my paints to her!"

"Jesus, Lucy, why the hell not?"

"Because it's not right."

"Why not? Are you not taking care of them night and day without pay?"

"Martha, for one thing, I was given a very nice house by their parents. Two, I am fine, I promise. I was just having a good moan, as your beautiful husband would say."

"Are you really alright, Lucy?" Susannah asked, appraising Lucy carefully.

"I'm fine. I can't believe we're even talking about this when Tessa's the one we should be thinking about." Lucy tucked her chin down slightly, picked up speed and pressed her body into the strong wind that was coming off the ocean. "I don't know what to do with her."

"Amber told me something," Susannah found herself blurting out despite her resolve to keep her daughter's secret. "In confidence."

"About Tessa?"

"She's disappearing at lunch. Amber thinks she's not eating."

Lucy stopped and turned to face her friends. She gripped their wrists. "What are we going to do?"

"What's Joey saying?" Martha asked.

"I think he's hoping maybe this is just a phase," Lucy replied. "Aren't we all?"

"God, this whole thing makes me want to return to the days where you made kids sit at the table till they cleaned their plate," Martha sighed. "I just want to force her to get something into her system!"

"I know," Lucy said, pausing. "I'm beginning to think Clover's right. She needs to see that nutritionist."

"I don't trust that woman as far as I can throw her," Martha said. "And I hear Tessa doesn't either."

Lucy persisted. "Tessa's going to resist changing anything at this point. Especially because that first one was *such* a disaster."

The only nutritionist in Omega was a woman in her sixties who'd cut her therapeutic teeth on helping obese patients understand the negative impacts of deep-fried cuisine. After one counterproductive "knowledge-based" session with the older woman, Tessa's ascetic tendencies had only gained some very serious informational clout.

"Susannah, you need to tell Joey."

"But I promised Amber I wouldn't. It's so difficult in these teen years to keep the lines of communication open—"

"You know what?" Lucy interrupted. "I'll drop by school at lunchtime. Then I can be the one to tell Joey without anyone knowing Amber was involved."

"That's brilliant!" Susannah said gratefully.

"For a freaking mathematical genius, you sure can't lie your way out of a paper bag, can you, girl? You won't lie, and Lucy won't cheat. I swear, I think I need to send you both to law school," Martha laughed. With that, the three friends turned back toward Lucy's house, ready for cocktails and the faux crab cakes Sateesh had lovingly constructed out of squash blossoms and tofu in hopes of tempting Tessa back from the brink.

Later that evening, Sateesh was rubbing Martha's feet with lavender oil. She sighed and snuck a peek at the man she couldn't believe was hers. Doing so for too long, like staring at the sun, might have been dangerous.

Sateesh still provoked predictable questions from strangers. "Who is he?" they'd ask, assuming he was a celebrity they couldn't put their finger on, though they'd like to, they really would. "Is he straight? Is he for real?"

Answers in the affirmative were roundly dismissed, for, as Martha herself put it, the man was too pretty by half, and that was his homely side.

The two had met when Martha was finishing her third year at law school. Sateesh had come into legal aid for help with his visa. Martha had been the reluctant recipient of his inquiries, delivered in a posh British accent that made her immediately wary. This wasn't the sort of needy immigrant who made her heart bleed. His cashmere V-neck and Brooks Brothers pants had told her as much, even if his accent wasn't enough of a clue. Combine that with the fact that the man was drop-dead gorgeous, and she didn't need a government label declaring him a hazard to her health. As brusquely as she could, Martha had interrogated him as to pertinent facts, filled out his form and kissed his pretty little ass good-bye.

Two days later though, she'd run into him at a bar near campus, where he insisted on buying her a drink. Given that he was actually tending the bar, it was easy enough to accept, since his job punctured the image of a pampered rich Punjabi she'd so abruptly constructed against even an inkling of attraction. By drink three, which she later insisted must have been laced with something, she'd invited Sateesh Vigram home to her apartment.

That first night together, remembered through the kaleidoscopic lens of an altered state, Martha had been set upon by a man who prayerfully undressed her and whispered his adoration of her revealed flesh in a set of lush vowels marked by urgent, clipped consonants that, had he done nothing else at all, would certainly have made her come, despite her terror that all of this was just *way* too good to be true.

In their early courtship, every time she had sex with Sateesh, she felt it would surely be the last. This provided those first interludes with a melancholy abandon, each lovemaking an elegy for the impossible illusion of someone like him being interested in someone like her.

It wasn't that Martha was hideous. She knew she was attractive, but in a fresh-faced, farm-girl kind of way. Her skin had that ruddy appearance of having been scrubbed too often, and her eyelashes and brows were so blond they appeared invisible. Worst of all, as far as previous suitors went, was the sense of extraordinary intelligence Martha could not help but radiate. This aura was an involuntary, autonomic force against any beau looking for the weaker sex. In the movies, Martha would have been cast as the inspiring teacher or capable nurse. She would most certainly not have been the siren, vixen or femme fatale.

Therefore, in her defense, being courted by the male equivalent thereof had been an entirely new and not quite believable experience for her.

Sateesh was classically handsome, with a bottomless black gaze and dark exoticism. Even before 9/11, his looks had seemed synonymous with danger, if only because of Martha's experience clerking for an immigration attorney in Northern Virginia, where the family court landscape was littered with American women who'd found themselves duped by charming foreign men seeking green cards.

The lithe angularity of his graceful body repeated itself in Sateesh's delicate features, saved from perfection by a scar on his right cheekbone and brows that hung a bit too far over his soulful eyes.

"You're wasted on me," Martha was prone to sigh. "A gift from the gods should be shared."

"I'm not sharing you," he'd snap back. In Sateesh's world, handsome was as handsome did. He may have had that rarefied British cadence that sounded sophisticated, but when it came to romantic codes of conduct, he was deeply old-fashioned. Having found the woman of his dreams, he was holding on tight.

In fact, what Sateesh adored about Martha was exactly what had kept the college boys away. Her intelligence, her straightforward competence, even the white eyebrows and lashes she hated— all of these were balm to his soul. Sateesh's parents were dead, but when they were alive, his mother had never stood up to his tyrannical father, who'd bullied and beaten his children until they were old enough to leave home.

When he'd met Martha that day in legal aid, Sateesh had felt a tug of recognition, almost like déjà vu. When she'd come to his bar two days later, he found himself questioning his prior skepticism about reincarnation. No other explanation made sense of Sateesh's overwhelming certainty that, of all God's creatures, here was a woman he'd known forever.

"I hope she's alright," Martha sighed, pressing her elegantly narrow foot into Sateesh's ribs.

"Tessa?"

"No, June. She's never done a real sleep-away, much less gone out of town by herself."

"But Joey's with her."

"Yeah, but the dancers are staying in one room, with each other. The dance Nazi says they need to bond."

"So why is Joey going along?"

"I think the teacher'd like to bring more than a trophy home from this competition, dear husband. And she doesn't mind using June to get it."

Sateesh ignored Martha's insinuation. "Doing something like this is good for June. Clover's after Joey to let Tessa dance as well."

"How can one person be so stupid?"

Sateesh shook his head at this rhetorical question, something Martha had uttered so often it had become meaningless. Clover *had* had her share of harebrained notions over time. That much Sateesh would admit. In the present case, however, he disagreed mightily with his wife. "I think it would be good for them. You know she's a nutritionist."

"That's completely beside the point. For what it's worth, Chevron, or whatever her name is, seems like the worst influence in the world."

"How can you say that? You don't even know her."

"Sateesh. Dancers are famously anorectic. Besides, she's not old enough to drive, as far as I can tell. I wouldn't put Tessa's hairdo in her hands, much less her health."

"Martha Templeton, you are a snob."

"And you, Sateesh Vigram, you are a helpless man turned to jelly by a sweet young thing in spandex."

"*You* are my sweet young thing in spandex."

Sateesh's nervous grin was an old habit, or curse, more precisely, a throwback to his adolescence, when his father would interrogate the children at the dinner table. The problem with its reemergence at times like the present was that Martha, who'd won best moot court cross-examiner three years running, would interpret it to mean her husband wasn't telling the truth.

"Look, let's please not put me and spandex in the same sentence."

"Would you stop thinking of yourself like that? You're absolutely splendid."

"Right." Martha shook her head, dismissing her husband's compliments in a preemptive strike. "Joey's not going to let Tessa dance, is he?"

"Not until she gains weight. Unfortunately, though, I think Tessa now sees dance as something she's being denied. Ergo, she's half-annoyed she's not being allowed to do it. At least that's the impression I got from her while you three were out on your walk."

"It's so nice she talks to you."

"I think it's because I'm the only one not constantly urging her to eat."

"That's because you can't imagine such a thing as not being hungry."

"True." Sateesh pulled Martha up into his lap and licked her upper lip. "I'm hungry right now."

Martha kissed her husband back before pressing his chest with the heels of her hands. "Seriously, Sateesh, you should talk to Joey. How could he not see that anything he denies Tessa is the very thing she'd be certain to want?"

Sateesh pushed himself up abruptly, away from his wife. He strode into the kitchen and opened the door of the SubZero. He was accustomed to Martha's very American belief in the power of persuasion, as if knowing something and being able to act upon it were the same thing. "He's too wrapped up in worry to hear what I might say. I think he's operating at an instinctual, primal level."

"Which is why we need to help him."

"Martha, for a sophisticated woman, you've got far too much faith in reason. There are times when people are so distressed they can't think clearly. And being reminded of that will only compound his nervousness."

"Fair enough," Martha admitted, brought up short by an unwelcome, intrusive memory. She too had made her own share of mistakes in the grip of anxiety, things she'd never want to admit to anyone, not even her adoring husband. Especially not her adoring husband. "All I can say is, if those children end up twirling batons and wearing sequined beauty-queen swimsuits, Penelope will be turning over in her grave so fast the cemetery won't need rototilling for the next three hundred years."

When Joey heard the knock at his hotel room door, he assumed it was June, saying good night before she scrambled back to the double room she was sharing with three other small dancers.

"Want me to rub your back?" he asked, struggling with the latch. Having squatted down to meet his daughter's eyes, Joey found himself spitting distance from Siobhan's wasp-waisted peasant dress. "Sorry!" Joey stood back up. "I thought you were June."

Siobhan was holding a bottle of ginger tea and a glass filled with ice. "I just tucked them in. I thought I'd check to see how you were." She lifted the glass. "Some tea?"

"I'm having a scotch. Come on in."

"Sure you weren't lying down?" Siobhan asked, eyeing Joey's bare chest and loose flannel pants.

"No, I was just hot."

Siobhan gulped a quick sip of her cold drink and settled into a chair across from the couch.

"So, how are you?" she asked. Something about her eyes, their obsidian intensity, her brow crumpling slightly, communicated the way in which she intended this as a question of the man's deepest self, the one no one reached anymore, the one she'd often seen in her clients. Most people had centers of tension they held to themselves, knots of worry they were afraid to reveal. Men like Joey, roaming the planet to save it; they were worst of all. They saw pain as selfish and told themselves how lucky they were not to have suffered more. Add fatherhood to the mix and the recipe for self-denial created its own punishing momentum.

Joey took a swallow of his scotch, its bitter warmth scorching his throat. He nodded his head, as if to push the liquid past his sternum, where it appeared to have settled and begun to sear. "I'm fine, thanks."

Joey's automatic response came naturally, a defense against the pity he was accustomed to inspiring in strangers.

"How could you be? You've just spent hours listening to Kidz Bop and affronted by the smell of nail polish remover," Siobhan said. "You've got to have a saint's patience to put up with that."

Joey laughed dismissively. "Patience has never been something anyone could accuse me of."

"You have no idea how great a father you are. The way I grew up . . . I never knew fathers could—oh, ignore my blather."

Siobhan's kewpie lips, painted a glossy coral, pulled across the tiny pearls of her teeth into an embarrassed grimace. A smudge of lipstick on the cusp of her incisor caught Joey's attention.

This unexpected flaw relaxed Joey's reflexive restraint, an ingrained habit from monogamy that had become second nature by now. Rather than disappearing when Penelope died, Joey's reserve had been hardened by grief into a shield. It wasn't that he felt Penelope watching, nor that he thought he must remain celibate in her honor, but only that opening himself up to a woman was too dangerous, for it would remind him of all the parts of his life that had been destroyed, places he could not allow himself to revisit.

There was something, though, about the smudge of color on Siobhan's tooth that snuck past his emotional sentries. Maybe it was because Penelope hadn't worn lipstick, hadn't liked the taste.

Joey's eyes flickered briefly to catch Siobhan's inquiring gaze. By the time she rephrased her question about how Joey was doing, *really,* he found himself letting go. In a halting interrogative, sprinkled with questions about nutrition, Joey described Tessa's recent vegetarianism, her dramatic weight loss, her lack of interest in things she once enjoyed.

"So that's how I am," he apologized, after he'd gone on for several minutes. "Worried sick."

"So, is Lucy trained to work with teens?" Siobhan asked, after a slight hesitation.

"No," Joey said. "But she's known my kids forever."

"What about structure? Would you say your girls feel safe?"

"What do you mean?"

"Children need a certain degree of order and predictability in their lives. Do you eat at the same time every day, together? Have you set expectations for them in terms of what they may and may not do?"

Joey shrugged. "We talk about how they're not allowed to waste food when people in other places don't have enough to eat. We want them to eat a balanced diet. My wife never believed in making the dinner table a battlefield. Lucy's on the same wavelength."

"Is it possible they might feel things are chaotic? Out of control?"

"Everything's changed for them. For all of us."

"Well, that alone could explain your daughter's recent slide. She might be trying to control her eating because she is terrified by a universe in which she doesn't feel there are safe boundaries."

"We have rules."

"How about eating everything on their plate?"

"No," Joey said mildly. "Like I said, we don't fight with the kids over food."

Siobhan nodded impassively. "Why don't you have Tessa come in and talk with me? Unless she's seeing a nutritionist already."

"No, we tried the only one in town. She was a nightmare. Gave Tessa dieting advice. Jesus."

"Let me guess. Was she . . . of a certain age?"

"I'd say somewhere between fifty and seventy, it's hard to tell."

"So she knows next to nothing about anorexia." Siobhan tucked an errant curl behind her ear. "You know, you could have Tessa come in for a dance class. I could build a relationship with her that way."

"I think she'd see right through that. But I will try and get her to come in and talk to you. If I can get her to listen to me."

Siobhan shook her head gently. "You're her father, Mr. Adorno. She's fourteen years of age. Don't underestimate your power. She needs you to be certain, when so few other people around her are."

With this, Siobhan rose to leave, but not before she offered Joey a reprieve from his guilt. "Unless you've been there, you just can't imagine what it is she needs. We'll sort her out, don't worry."

At home, Lucy was doing her best to ignore a set of stimuli intended for Tessa. There was a gorgeously gooey chocolate cake arranged on a tiered glass plate that Sateesh had brought from his restaurant. Next to the cake, a stack of dessert plates and a shiny knife vied with an ice cream scoop and a note Martha had written, in the event that Sateesh's merchandizing wasn't tempting enough.

> **Don't forget to top with**
> **vanilla Swiss almond**
> **Häagen-Dazs in freezer!**

This had to be Martha's first gratuitous exclamation mark in decades, a symbol of just how worried the attorney was about Tessa's weight loss.

We're all twisting ourselves around her not eating. Who knew that when we grew up we wouldn't know what to do about something like this? Lucy thought, reaching for the phone and trying to pull her jaw apart around a sodden mass of Mary Jane she'd settled on as a substitute for the cake and ice cream she'd really wanted. *We're going to be the size of this house trying to inspire Tessa to remember what it felt like to enjoy food.*

When the phone rang, Lucy dashed for it, forgetting her lock-jawed predicament until she tried to say hello to whatever friend of Tessa's must have been calling at this hour.

The operator's voice, asking if she'd accept a collect call from Atlanta, was a shock to her system, allowing the adrenaline to kick in enough to yank her back teeth apart so hard they actually clicked.

"Lucy?" June's voice was tiny, sounding much smaller than when she was running through the house with Willow, shouting the words to Michelle Branch's latest hit.

"What's wrong!" Lucy asked. "Are you okay?"

"There's a phone in the bathroom!" June whispered. "Can you say good night?"

"Oh, sweetie, of course I can. Are you okay?"

"Fine," June squeaked. "I just wanted to say good night."

"Where's your dad?"

"We're not allowed to bother them after lights out."

"You aren't bothering me a bit. You can always call me, any-time."

"Don't tell my dad, okay?"

"Sweetie, he so wouldn't mind."

"No, Miss Siobhan says we're s'posed to let the parents relax. The other kids'll think I'm a baby."

"You know, June, I still feel like I want to be tucked in by my mom sometimes. That's not being a baby."

"Lucy?"

"Sweetie?"

"Is Rocky okay? I think I forgot to put my spelling worksheets away."

"I got to them before he did, but just barely. You were lucky."

Keeping Rocky away from paper products had become second nature for Lucy, his obsessive foraging an unfortunate outgrowth of June's attempt to train him to fetch *The Omega Times* by coating it in bacon grease. Rather than returning to drop the newspaper in June's lap, as she'd assumed any retriever worth his salt should do, Rocky had loped down the beach with his prize. Because the scent of bacon had adhered to the plastic newspaper box, Rocky had become adept at fetching but ever more cagey about hiding the local paper in various bushes between Lucy's front door and driveway. Rocky's love of "reading" had become a family joke. The more they tried to outwit the dog, the greater his desire to capture any item resembling that first "kill." They'd suspended their subscription to the paper, at which time he'd gravitated to the mail, and when they'd developed a lock for the mailbox, he'd transferred his attentions to anything that crackled. More than once Rocky had chewed his way into the children's backpacks and forced Lucy to write notes to teachers in which she tried to make them believe that in this one case, the old excuse was actually true: the dog really had eaten the children's homework. Joey had finally installed cubbies with doors on them to protect the children's backpacks and books. Lucy had had to banish Rocky from her studio and find shelves for books and magazines that were well above the six feet the dog had shown himself capable of jumping.

"Was Rocky upset?"

"What, at not getting to your stuff? No, I told him 'Down' and gave him a treat. He misses you and so do I but we'll be fine. Want to say good night?"

"No, I'm okay. I love you."

"I don't love *you*," Lucy murmured against the sound of June's rising giggle on the other end of the line. "I totally, completely and absolutely love you."

June yawned.

"Good night, Juniper. Good luck tomorrow."

"Okay. Love you."

"Love you too," Lucy whispered, waiting for the sound of the click before hanging up. She turned off the overhead bulbs but left the range light shining like a beacon on Sateesh's cake plate, in case Tessa decided to venture downstairs for a midnight snack.

Chapter Eight

Siobhan was the sort of person who was marvelously efficient, having modeled herself on a foster mother whose ordered household had felt like heaven after the decrepit chaos of her parents' rent controlled apartment in the Haight. Mrs. Leiffert, German born, had taught the young Chevonne how to save steps. "If you are leaving the bedroom, you take wit' you the glass of water from the night before, you bring it to the kitchen sink and you wash it and put it back in the cupboard. When you take your bath, use your washclot' to wipe the bathtub dirt."

The sheer miracle of having a clean glass from which to drink, to say nothing of a washcloth of her very own, had been so momentous that Chevonne became an immediate convert, following Mrs. Leiffert around the house and absorbing her habits with every fiber of her being. As Chevonne saw it, the alternative to these routines was the place she'd come from, layered with grime and soot and cockroaches, a place that smelled of bong water and spoiled garbage, and rang with the constant shriek of stoned laughter from visitors who came and went at all hours of the night without considering the four children trying to sleep in the curtained alcove off the kitchen.

Siobhan was performing her first choreography of the day, a five-minute run-through of her apartment. She made her bed, dust-mopped the floors, wiped down the bathroom and kitchen and hung the cloth to dry over the faucet. By the front door were video discs to return to the library and a sticky note reminding her to drop her grant application at the foundation on the way to the studio.

Siobhan threw the note into the trash can and tried not to mind the waste of a perfectly good Post-it on something she'd not have forgotten anyhow.

Seeing Joey was the reason she'd woken an hour earlier than normal, shaved her legs and underarms, ironed her immaculate halter dress and rubbed cocoa butter from stem to stern of her nubile frame. She'd repainted her lips a glossy lavender pink while waiting for the lotion to be absorbed, sitting patiently in a lacy pink and white thong and matching strapless demi bra from Victoria's Secret.

It wasn't that Siobhan's breasts needed much assistance keeping upright, having been "restored" to a grandeur they'd never before experienced. The plastic surgeon had traded a year's membership at the San Francisco Kicks! for Siobhan's original surgery. Dr. Kling still sent her 10 percent of every patient she'd referred, funding the cosmetic dentistry she'd completed last year and the Lasik she'd gotten in February. Siobhan's breasts, just under a C but slightly over a B, were a testimonial in themselves to Kling's talents, for the doctor had pioneered a new silicone/saline hybrid that felt much more natural than other breast implants.

Each time she had undressed in the California locker room, the young Siobhan had graphically promoted the benefits of nipping and tucking to untold legions bearing falling collagen and failing elasticity. Between the Marin County trophy wives and the Palo Alto entrepreneurs, Siobhan had socked away plenty in her investment account and still had plenty left for the occasional manicure or bikini wax.

She also allowed herself the luxury of expensive undergarments, her reward for hard work and culinary discipline. Siobhan wore bras not as much because they were needed for support but because they were part of a uniform she'd adopted to convince herself she'd joined the ranks of the successful. These were the people she aspired to become, put together as a lifestyle montage from the magazines that she pored over as if they were urban survival manuals, glinting with truths by which to shape her every move.

Though the glossies weren't exactly pertinent to Omega, Florida, their airbrushed pages still allowed Siobhan to view herself as a powerful young woman. The way Siobhan felt as she exited her apartment building clutching her proposal in one hand and an understated Marc Jacobs briefcase in the other was a happy combination of prepared and excited.

It was a perfect fall day, sunny but not too hot. Siobhan drove with her windows down, barely noticing as she passed Kicks! in the town square, and searched for the unmarked access road Joey had told her ran behind High Street and would lead her to the parking area for the foundation. She rounded the corner carefully, slowing down, searching next for a narrow trellis-covered driveway and then a small bricked-in parking area, still deserted in the early morning. Siobhan opened a small gate in the hedge of box woods, traversed a small octagonal garden framed by brick walls and knocked at the massive mahogany door. Its creviced surface and arched metal lintel looked like something out of a cathedral from *Travel + Leisure*. The print on the tiny brass nameplate was so small that Siobhan was almost upon it before she could read THE CAMERON FOUNDATION, 1919.

When Joey opened the door, Siobhan asked nervously, "Is that the address?"

"What's that?"

"The number on the door?"

Joey laughed. "Oh, that. That's the date we were founded."

"Oh, right. Of course. How dumb of me."

"No, how would you know? Come on back, I'll show you around."

The reception area was dominated by a large stained glass window that faced northeast, translating the morning sun into watery rays of blue and green. It took a minute for Siobhan's eyes to adjust to the darkness of the room, its soft heart-pine floors collecting pools of color that echoed the glass outlines above. An emerald sofa faced two lapis velvet love seats. Between them, a Victorian checkerboard coffee table was covered with oversize marble chess pieces, laid out midgame. "Wow," Siobhan breathed. Despite her care to appear nonchalant, she clenched her fists so tightly that her manila envelope crackled noisily.

Joey smiled at Siobhan and gestured for her to sit down. "I know. Pretty intimidating. I remember the first time I saw Penelope's father's house, I didn't know whether to shit or wind my watch. Sorry."

"No, I'm—I feel the same. Like I'm in the—I don't know—some fancy palace in Europe or somewhere."

"Yeah. My wife found this stained glass window in Provence and had it flown in. The walls had to be reinforced before they could bear it. I think the bill of lading cost more than my family's house in Ohio."

"I brought the proposal." Siobhan had remained standing, teetering nearly, on her strappy sandals as she moved across the distance between them and pressed the envelope into Joey's hand.

"Thanks. You got time to sit and talk about it?"

"Ah. No. Sorry! I've got to get to work."

"Okay. I'll read it over and get back to you."

"Okay, thanks," Siobhan said hesitantly. "My cell number's in there."

Joey opened the heavy door for Siobhan and stepped aside. "I'll call."

Joey couldn't help noticing that not only was the envelope's metal clasp fastened, but its flap was glued into place with evenly cut, precisely laid transparent tape.

This caution struck Joey the same way Siobhan's earlier awkwardness had, as a sign of social insecurity. He found himself feeling maternal, protective, remembering how nervous he'd been when he'd met Penelope's father for the first time. It had taken years for Joey to overcome his intimidation, despite his educated apprehension of class consciousness, of status and its various referents.

What must it feel like for Siobhan? She'd not even had the benefit of Penelope's patronage or any network of nearby friends. Clover had mentioned something about a foster mother in San Francisco, saying Siobhan had come from nothing and pulled herself up by her own bootstraps. She must, Joey assumed, have felt isolated as hell in Omega, yet she'd still taken the time to put together a proposal for scholarships for kids from the wrong side of the tracks. For that he had to give her credit, and even as he reached for a letter opener, Joey was finding himself feeling sorry for her, a disposition that would only grow as he read her proposal.

Siobhan's description of latchkey kids and the sense of peril they endured was clearly based on personal experience. Meanwhile her belief in the order dance could provide them was both naïve and affecting.

Though Joey's mother had been home when he arrived from school, his family had been poor enough to drink powdered milk, ration orange juice, collect Green Stamps. When Joey had gotten a scholarship to the University of Virginia, no one in his extended family had ever heard of the place. His dad had worried Joey would be lost in some Appalachian backwater until the nun in Guidance set him straight. By that time, all the mills in Youngstown were closing and most of the auto plants had been laying people off, including Joey's dad. It didn't take much for Sister Catherine to convince Joey's parents to let him leave home and try his way in a new place. Every year Joey went back home to visit his parents, sent them money and made sure his siblings were okay. Still, there was a part of him that felt guilty for having left that world behind, especially since he'd done nothing to earn the money. He'd fallen in love with Penelope; how hard was that? It had been like winning the lottery. Not a day went by that he didn't tell himself how lucky he was, and not a day went by that he didn't measure his worth by the difference he was able to make in other people's lives, given the huge resources at his disposal.

There were holes in Siobhan's logic, her goals weren't phrased according to the foundation's guidelines, her syntax was choppy, but Joey could see past that. Siobhan could be shown how to fix her writing. She deserved a chance to show what she could do. After all, he reminded himself, there for but the grace of God, a scholarship and marriage went he. Joey knew better than anyone just how far he'd come and how fickle a pal his old friend luck could be.

Tessa's high school was a large redbrick building with four-cornered wings bisecting the soft green of playing fields and tennis courts. The entrance was rather grandiose, with Doric columns and Palladian windows set over three huge painted metal doors.

Lucy had called ahead to find out what period Tessa had lunch. She was carrying a soft blue sweater, the morning's slight drop in temperature a pretext for dropping by. After stopping at the front office for a visitor badge and directions to the cafeteria, Lucy pressed open the windowed doors of the lunchroom and tried to look nonchalant, strolling between tables of students. When she finally spotted Amber Newsome handing a long-haired boy a cupcake, she headed toward Susannah's daughter and tapped her lightly on the shoulder.

"Lucy?" Amber had turned in her seat, peered over Lucy's shoulder and hopped up, as though fearing an alien apparition, or worse still, her own mother, tagging along. "S'up?"

"I dropped by to see Tessa. Where is she?"

Amber shrugged, swiped a lock of hair behind her ear and looked miserable. "Bathroom maybe?"

"She's on the track," the long-haired boy interrupted. He gave Amber a reproachful tilt of the head. "Like every day."

Amber stood up and pressed herself toward Lucy, as though trying to wipe out the young man's remarks with a sudden groundswell of over-the-top friendliness. "I'll tell her you came by! Is my mom with you? Do you want some Kashi?"

"No, thanks, Amber. Where's the track?"

Amber hesitated just long enough to realize she could not prevent Lucy from discovering Tessa's whereabouts. When she gave Lucy her response, there was an unmistakable sense of relief in her tone. "Behind the tennis court. I don't know if she's there or not," she added, consulting her large pink vinyl watch.

Lucy hurried across the lot, trying not to panic at the idea that Tessa was not only *not* eating, she was apparently exercising too. By the time she reached the track, Lucy was running to catch up with the small figure moving away from her around the spongy black and white oval. Tessa's back was to her. Lucy noticed her hands were held stiffly at her sides, fingers splayed into counting formation. As Tessa passed the starter's mark, she released her clenched forefinger to calculate another lap. By the time Lucy got close enough to be heard, she felt out of breath. "Tessa! Wait!"

"Lucy? Why—what are you doing here?"

"I brought you this." Lucy pushed the sweater out toward the teen. "It got chilly since you left for school. Honey, I looked for you at lunch. What are you doing out here?"

"Thinking."

"Thinking? On the track? Why aren't you eating in the cafeteria with all your friends?"

"I can't relax in there."

"Tessa, honey, we need to talk." Lucy put her arm around Tessa and guided her over to the bleachers. "Let's sit for a minute. Sweetheart, you can't afford to skip lunch."

"I ate."

"When?"

"Before. On my way out here."

"Tessa."

"I did."

"Okay, tell me what you ate."

Tessa's lips clamped shut. She shook her head. "What is this, the Inquisition?"

"Tessa, what is wrong with you? Why are you not eating lunch? Look at you! You're too thin as it is!"

"Lucy, I'm fine. I just hate the lunchroom. It smells like dirty socks."

"Tessa, what did you eat for lunch today? Tell me what I packed you."

"No! I can't believe you don't trust me."

"I trust you. But I love you too and you are too thin, Tessa. I'm really, really worried. So if you're eating, please! Tell me! I'll feel a lot better."

Tessa looked down at her outstretched fingers. Her nails were bitten down to the point where blood was raised behind the beds. "A sandwich."

"What kind?"

"I don't know what kind. I was hungry. I don't remember."

"Tessa, tell me."

"A portobello?"

"Wrong. Tessa, you threw your lunch away, didn't you? That cheese was nineteen dollars a pound!"

"Since when are you cheap?"

"Tessa, since when do you waste perfectly good food by throwing it away? Look at your arms! Honey, this is serious."

"I'm fine."

"No, you're not. Give me your phone."

"Why!"

"Give it to me. We're calling your dad and he's calling the doctor and we're going there now."

"Lucy! Don't tell Dad! Don't tell him! Please!" Tessa leaned over, her face pressed between her knees, in the position a person would take trying to prevent herself from fainting. Lucy began to rub the girl's back, causing Tessa to pitch herself forward, out of Lucy's reach. In her rush to get away, the girl teetered slightly before kneeling on the track, her arms stretched out in front of her. She tucked her head down and began to pant with quick, short breaths. Lucy squatted on the ground next to Tessa and laid the back of her hand against the girl's neck. "Look at you, Tessa. Your blood pressure is so low you can't stand up."

Tessa jumped up unsteadily, trying to prove Lucy wrong. She turned to face her and said, pulling her wrist out of Lucy's grasp, "Stop pretending you care, Lucy."

"What in the world are you saying, Tessa? How could you think I don't care about you?"

"If you cared—look, forget it."

"No, tell me."

"Don't you think I don't already know everything you're gonna say? Do you think I'm stupid? Don't you think I feel horrible enough? My mom got killed trying to give food to poor people and here I am throwing my lunch in the trash? You said it yourself!"

"Oh, Tessa. Look. I don't know what I'm saying half the time."

"Yes, you do. It's so freaking twisted. Don't you think I know all that? Plus lying to my dad? I don't have to look too hard to see who's ruining everything in this family."

"Sweetheart, you've got it all wrong. No one expects you to be perfect."

"Yeah? Perfect's one thing. I'm everything my mom didn't want me to be. Everything."

"That's so not true!"

"I try to eat, Lucy. But everything gets all—I don't know. I just can't. If I tell my dad, trust me, it's—it'll mean I'm going to feel ten times worse for making him feel worried about me. Why would you want to freak him out, anyway?"

"Come here," Lucy said, pulling Tessa back over to the bleachers. Tessa's skin had taken on an unhealthy color and Lucy didn't like the sound of her breathing. "We need to get you help. Give me the phone."

"Lucy. Please! I can't stand it if he knows!" Tessa began to weep soundlessly.

Lucy pulled her into her arms and said, "Ssssh. It's okay. It's okay."

Tessa was quiet for a minute before she raised herself up by pulling on Lucy's wrist. Her eyes were pleading, her tone desperate. "Lucy, please, don't tell him any of this. It's not like he's not worried already! I know he is. I'm such a freak!"

"Sweetheart, where would you get that idea?" Lucy's question, she realized, would sound to Tessa like further criticism. "Sweet pea, you're holding yourself to too high a standard."

"Don't tell me how to feel," Tessa protested. "You don't know. I promised my mom over and over. No matter what, I'd talk to her and my dad about what was on my mind. But I can't."

"Everyone makes mistakes. But do you see? If I don't tell your dad what's been going on, I'd be doing the same thing to him that you're upset about already. Not telling him the truth."

"See? See? I'm so messed up!" Tessa moved away from Lucy and started trudging away between the elliptical white lines. "Please, Lucy! You don't know what went on in our house. You don't know everything."

Lucy ran to catch up with her. "Tessa, what are you saying?"

"Lucy, I heard my parents fighting. Maybe—I don't know." The girl took a deep breath. "Maybe my dad didn't come home on purpose."

"What do you mean?"

"He should have been with us. He should have been there. It was Thanksgiving, Lucy! Why wasn't he with his family?"

Lucy shook her head and pressed two fingers against Tessa's temple. "Oh, honey, no one knew what was going to happen that day. If any of us had known, we'd have—everything would have been different. It wasn't anyone's fault."

"Don't tell me that!"

"Look, we need to talk about this. It's normal to try and find someone to blame. It's part of the mourning—"

Tessa was already dismissing Lucy's words, caught up in a different anxiety. "Oh, God, don't tell my dad I said anything! I didn't mean it!"

"I know." Lucy tried to take Tessa's chin in her hand, but the teen buried her head between her knees, flinching away from Lucy's touch. She coughed unproductively and began to retch. Lucy put a tentative hand on Tessa's shoulder and held her breath until Tessa turned toward her. She clung to Lucy's arm needfully, like a much younger child. "Please," Tessa moaned. "I'll go to the doctor. Just please don't tell my dad about not eating lunch! And the other stuff I said. I hate myself."

"Sweetie, he loves you so much."

"He'll send me away!"

"Where did you get that idea?"

"That's what they did to Sally Baker when she lost all that weight."

"Your dad is not going to send you away, Tessa."

"Lucy, I'll do anything. I'll go to the doctor. But please—he'll totally freak out! The more nervous he gets, the more I feel responsible! I can't relax already! I—I almost can't breathe from being so nervous, I can't sleep, I can't eat. Please. I'll do anything, just—don't freak him out. He'll be so disappointed in me. I already feel guilty enough."

Tessa's eyes were her mother's, almond shaped, the color of amber, haloed in black. They curled up slightly toward the temples, giving to Tessa's demeanor a merriness that was made a mockery of by her tears.

What would you have me do here? Lucy pleaded, summoning the soul she couldn't help but beckon back at times like this. The result was invariably the same, a staggering silence, leaving Lucy with only a vague sense that she'd become the object of a certain cosmic pity.

"Honey, he loves you. He's your dad."

At this, Tessa began to cry, her lips moving soundlessly around the notion that her father had been forced to bear such a thing as a daughter who was so selfish. The lies she'd told her father, his easy acceptance, his belief that she'd never deceive him—all these would kill him when he found out she'd been lying to his face. And what she'd said about what happened to her mom? How could she even think such an awful thing?

The more Tessa tried to calm herself, the harder it became to breathe, especially since she was coughing again.

Lucy gathered her body behind Tessa, supporting her and rock-ing slightly back and forth. "Shssh, it's okay, don't worry—"

Lucy didn't reflect on what she was saying, she only wanted to calm the child down, wanted this frantic, panicked fearfulness to dissipate. Besides, what good would it do Joey to hear that his daughter blamed him, even partially, for her mother's death? "How about this?" Lucy countered. "I'll make an appointment with the doctor. You call your dad and say it was your idea. You can tell him you're worried about your weight. How's that? Can you do that?"

Tessa nodded blearily, pulling a breath deep into her chest.

"You have to see the nutritionist too," Lucy insisted.

"I will," Tessa said, her shoulders settling back into place. "I'll tell him I want to go to the doctor 'cause I'm worried . . . about . . . my health. That way, he knows—without—without getting all upset over—I'll tell him I'm worried. 'Cause I kind of am."

"You are, honey?" Lucy couldn't believe how much it relieved her to hear Tessa say these words out loud, finally.

Tessa nodded. "I want to eat, Lucy. I just, nothing seems— when I get ready to put it in my mouth, I just have trouble—I can't decide. And then it's hard to—I can't relax. But I'll go see my doctor. I will."

"And Siobhan Fitzpatrick," Lucy added.

"I liked the other lady better."

"No. You'll see Siobhan. And right away."

With that uncharacteristically blunt command, Lucy told herself the secrets she had agreed to keep weren't all that important in the scale of things. After all, once Tessa had agreed to get help, what difference would it make if Joey knew all the details of his daugh-ter's suffering? If Lucy's own rising panic was any indication, the knowledge would only make him feel that much more worried about a sickness whose cure would ultimately rely on factors outside his control. Besides, anything that helped calm Tessa would be better for everyone, at least for the time being. Lucy could tell Joey later, or better yet, she could talk Tessa into telling him how she felt. That's what she'd do, she vowed, just as soon as the dust began to settle or Tessa started to get a little stronger, whichever came first.

Later though, when there were opportunities to tell him, Lucy would continually err on the side of discretion. So little time, so many mistakes to make. At least that is how Lucy would later come to view her failure to disclose this conversation to Joey. At the time, she only wanted to help Tessa calm down, get to a doctor, get well. Why upset Joey with the news that his daughter had been lying to him about eating lunch, or graver still, that Tessa might hold him responsible, however subconsciously, for her mother's murder? Learning these things would serve no one's interest, especially Joey's, if it meant putting Tessa into even more distress when she was already so unstable.

Lucy found herself walking very slowly with Tessa, holding her hand. They remained silent for a full circle. Without prompting from Lucy, Tessa reached into her back pocket, retrieved her phone and dialed her father's work number.

Later that afternoon, Joey met them at the pediatrician's. After Dr. Beecham examined Tessa and ordered labs, she herded them into her office, Joey, Tessa, Lucy.

Peering up over her charts at Tessa, who was shivering despite her sweater, the doctor didn't mince words. "At five three, a healthy body weight is somewhere between a hundred and four and a hundred and forty. Eighty-nine pounds moves you off the charts, Tessa. You've lost twelve pounds since we saw you for your high school physical. And twenty since July. Can you talk to us about why you think this might be happening?"

Tessa looked down at her fingers, crossed over each other like the church and the steeple, but backward. Her knuckles were showing white with the pressure she was applying.

"Tessa?" Joey said. "The doctor's asking you a question."

Tessa shrugged.

"Is she eating?" the doctor asked, looking at Joey.

"Not enough," Joey admitted. "Not when I'm there. She says she eats her big meal at lunch. How about when she's with you, Lucy?"

Lucy gulped, knowing this was a chance to explain what she'd learned. It was also a surefire way to break Tessa's trust. "I think Tessa would admit she's having trouble eating," Lucy stammered, avoiding Joey's eyes. She reached out and covered Tessa's gripped fists with one of her hands. "Honey? Can you talk?"

The sound of Lucy's voice, or maybe it was her touch, coincided with the release of a single tear, which dropped onto Lucy's knuckle, a soundless plea. Lucy forced herself to ask again. "Tessa?"

Tessa shook her head. Lucy looked up at Joey before they both turned their attention to the doctor, broadcasting their shared helplessness across the large plane of the desk.

"Tessa, are you still seeing the counselor we referred you to after your mother's death?" Dr. Beecham asked.

Tessa shook her head. The doctor looked at Joey and said, "I think she needs to start therapy again. Did you like Tracey Satterfield, Tessa?"

Tessa shrugged. She stared down at her hands.

"Tessa, you are obviously having a difficult time making the decision to take in the nutrition you need to grow. That's why you're shivering right now even though it's warm in here. You've lost too much body fat. Do you understand? I can show you pictures of what you can expect if you keep this up. You'll grow hair on your face and back. Meanwhile, the hair on your head will continue to split and thin and eventually fall out. Your heart rate will slow down even more; your muscles will begin to deteriorate. Your bones will weaken and thin out."

Tessa's chest heaved with a breath she'd been holding. The doctor softened her tone. "Tessa, I know this is upsetting to you, but you've got to understand how dangerous this is. We're here to help you. Do you understand that?"

The doctor turned to Joey without waiting for Tessa to reply. "Mr. Adorno, you've already tried the only nutritionist in Omega, so you know we're short on local treatment options. Here's a list of inpatient treatment facilities in the Southeast. I'd be happy to go over the offerings and help you find—"

Tessa pinched Lucy's arm so hard she couldn't keep from yelping. Lucy's cry of pain, however, was nothing against the pitch of Tessa's wounded fury. "I told you, Lucy!"

"What are you talking about, Tessa?" Joey asked. "Calm down, now. It's okay."

"You can't make me go. I'll run away!"

"Wait a minute, I still—" Lucy interrupted, raising a panicky hand in the air as though fielding an attack. "Dr. Beecham is suggesting—Doctor, what are you saying?"

"There's no outpatient program within driving distance. And Tessa's already lost twenty pounds since her summer visit."

"I told you, Lucy! I told you!" Tessa was sobbing. "You promised!"

"Honey! Look—"

Joey crossed to his daughter's chair and knelt beside her, stroking her back. He addressed the doctor. "We're not ready for that. Let's think of other alternatives."

"What if she starts seeing Dr. Satterfield again? What if she promises to start eating? And we supervise her?" Lucy asked. "I could make sure she eats."

Dr. Beecham pulled her glasses off her face, back over her hair, and rubbed her forehead with the weariness of someone who's already had to make this explanation too many times. "It never works. I'm sorry, but family can't treat this disease. You're too close to the patient. I wish it weren't true. No one wants Tessa to go through this, but this is a life-threatening illness. I would be remiss if I didn't make it clear to you that unless we respond dramatically, the outcomes aren't promising."

"Listen, doctor, I've got an idea." There was something in Joey's tone, a ring of desperation, that caused Lucy to turn her attention from Tessa back to her father. "Do you know Siobhan Fitzpatrick, by any chance?"

The doctor shook her head.

"She works at that new gym on Green Street. Turns out she has a master's in nutrition. She just moved here from San Francisco. What if we got her to move in with us and duplicate what they do at the hospitals, but we do it at home?"

"It sounds dicey to me. For one thing, if she's not licensed to practice in the state, your insurance won't cover it."

"That's not a deal-breaker," Joey said. "I'm pretty sure I can get the money. It's talking her into taking a leave of absence from her job that'll be the hard part."

It was only accidental that when Joey found Siobhan in the performance studio, she was dressed as a fairy, waving a wand and perched on a stepladder. She was posing for the Kicks! Christmas card. A photographer was crouched beneath her, all the better to capture a certain tone of afternoon light that fractured itself through the crystal prisms of her rhinestone headband.

Joey waited quietly, thinking of all the things he needed to do. He'd already researched the costs of treatment programs, which ranged between seven and ten grand a week. He'd called Martha to get her started on paperwork requesting a lump sum from the girls' trust. Now all he had to do was get Siobhan to agree to something he wasn't even sure she'd think was possible.

Joey stood with his hands behind his back, waiting, trying not to make Siobhan uncomfortable as she struck several beneficent poses for the camera.

"Is everything all right?" Siobhan asked, pulling off her gossamer wings, waving the photographer away.

"Well, no. It's not. Can we talk?" Joey was nine inches taller than Siobhan, who compensated by lifting her heels into an unsupported élevé, second position. This put them on a more equal footing. Siobhan led him into her office and pointed to the client's chair in front of her desk. "What is it?" she asked.

Instead of taking her chair, Siobhan leaned against the front of the desk and gently rested her fingers on his shoulder.

When Joey explained what he was he wanted, it wasn't the leave of absence that Siobhan objected to. She seemed more than willing to ask San Francisco to send a replacement, more than willing to create a customized treatment program for Tessa. What she couldn't wrap her brain around was moving to Lucy's. First, she pointed out, almost apologetically, it was too far from the studio. A leave of absence was one thing, but she couldn't abandon her dance teams in midseason. "Second, and more importantly," Siobhan added, lowering her voice, "Lucy's house is where Tessa's sickness developed. There'd be way too many cues, or triggers for unhealthy behaviors. She needs to start fresh. We might consider having you move back to your old house with both the girls. I could even drive June to dance when her team's practicing. The rest of the time, I could administer the treatment for Tessa. But I have to warn you. The doctor was right when she said family can't treat this illness. Your every instinct will be to soothe your daughter when the going gets rough, to let her revert back to the sick behaviors. You have to promise to let me use my professional expertise. It will be hard for you not to interfere. If you don't think you can do that, we might as well send Tessa off to inpatient treatment right now."

"No, I hear you. I can—we'll do anything to make this work. I've already talked to Martha about requisitioning the money. So, what's your experience with treatment?"

"I interned at Ridge Mountain, which is the best place in California. It's not rocket science, really. It's simply the application of a highly structured program in which we start from the assumption that the patient has lost her way and needs help doing what she'd normally do. Right now, Tessa's gotten herself into a biofeedback loop that rewards her for not eating. She feels alert, altered. It's a high. By not eating she's getting control. These good feelings reinforce her not eating, and at some point in this spiral, her brain loses enough nutrition that her thinking gets muddled. That's why, at the beginning, we take away all choices. The patient can't and won't decide what's best for her, and if we're going to help her, we have to impose a very structured regimen that surrounds her intake."

"Okay, so help me understand. We'd move back into town?"

"And I'd prepare all the meals. The family would sit down together. I would concentrate on making sure Tessa eats three meals plus two snacks a day. When you and June have eaten, you'd leave us alone at the table until Tessa's eaten everything on her plate. We might be able to make it work if you're willing to hold the line with me. But I'll warn you, Tessa will act as if she hates you, and she will most definitely hate me. On the other hand, if she thinks of it as the only alternative to going into a hospital, she might cooperate."

"Look, if you could—I'd—it'd be a lifesaver. I'll do whatever I have to. I'm asking the trust to give you as much as we'd pay a treatment center."

"It's not just the money I've got to think of." Siobhan blinked, hoping Joey didn't see her surprise. She knew what it cost to hospitalize a patient, far more than her salary at Kicks! "You see, I'm very active in the online fitness community. I supervise a chat room—"

"We've got high-speed Internet. And if you don't have a computer—"

"Just the one at work—"

"You know what? You could use my wife's laptop. It had all the bells and whistles a little over two years ago, so it should be fine—"

"I don't need anything fancy. As long as you've got wireless."

"We've got all that. And we've got plenty of space, so you could have an office."

"Mr. Adorno—"

"Joey."

"Joey, you should know—I'm not high-maintenance. I didn't grow up with much of anything. I know the circles you move in aren't that way, but I am used to working for what I earn."

Joey nodded, saying, "I hear you. I didn't grow up with money either, believe me. Listen, thanks for being willing to consider doing this. If there's anything you need, anything at all—"

"I appreciate that. It won't be easy. In fact, it will go against your instincts as a parent. You think you can handle that?"

Joey inhaled deeply. "I'll do whatever I have to do. And so will Lucy."

Siobhan looked at him, her head tilted to convey concern. "Are you and Lucy . . . Are you involved?"

"No, I didn't mean that. But the girls, they need her."

"You'd be surprised at the difference between what they need and what they want. The thing is, I'm sorry, but I can tell you right now that having two grown-ups in the house whose every instinct is going to be to soothe Tessa when the going gets rough, it won't work. I—there'd be no point to my asking for a leave from work if that's what you're proposing."

Joey winced. "You think?"

"Sorry, but I don't *think*. I *know*. It won't be business as usual, and you're going to have to trust me when it comes to routines. The household will have to be on a schedule. It will be very different from your life at Lucy's house. It has to be, or it won't work."

Joey nodded, telling himself that whatever any of them had to put up with, it would be worth it. They had to get Tessa to eat. "Look, if you were able to help us, when could you start?"

"I'd need a few days to tie up loose ends and get moved. Certainly not until Monday at the soonest."

"That's probably just as well. I've got to fly to Los Angeles on Wednesday. But what should we do? With Tessa for now?"

"Well, you and Lucy should try to see that she eats. But don't expect too much. I'm presuming the lab work didn't show dramatic declines in heart rate and kidney function or the doctor would have checked her into a hospital already. She should be alright for a few days. And listen, don't say anything to Tessa yet. Wait until the day before we're ready to start. Otherwise your daughter will spend all her time putting up barriers."

"Done. I don't want to leave town and have Lucy taking any heat for this. Besides, June's got big plans for the weekend."

"Oh, right. I forgot it was Halloween!"

"*And* her friend Willow's sleepover birthday party. Tessa's best friends with Willow's sister, Amber, so she's going to be there too, to help with the littler girls. You think that's okay?"

"As long as she seems physically stable."

"Listen, one other thing. I'll have to get formal permission from the trust to release the money. The board might want to interview you."

"Just let me know when."

"Thanks, Siobhan."

"You can thank me when your daughter's gained her weight back; how's that?"

Joey didn't realize he'd been holding his breath until he gave himself over to the image Siobhan had conjured up with such matter-of-fact assurances. When he let out a sigh, he found himself dizzy with relief, followed by a quick intake of fear that he could, simply by hoping too hard, jinx the cure whose mere mention made him weak in the knees.

As soon as Martha had left Nigel's office, the two Cameron brothers rose up, heaved their pendulous bellies over the top of the conference table and attempted a rather awkward high five. Such provincial American customs allowed them to celebrate without making noise. Martha mustn't know the sad news she'd brought their way was, to their minds, anything but.

Not only did they have proof that Tessa's health was suffering due to psychological stress, but they'd now been asked to subsidize a very expensive in-home treatment program. This would only bolster their case that the children weren't flourishing under their father's sole supervision. The brothers' one condition, that they interview the nutritionist privately before she began the program, would allow them to impress upon her exactly how important it was that they get full and accurate reports from her, reports that would constitute evidence their attorney could later use to cast doubts on Joey's parenting.

"Who knows what she'll discover lying about?" Nigel mused. "I do so yearn to understand everything about these fascinating creatures."

"I do believe you've come to take your role-playing seriously, Nigel."

Peter was referring to the fact that whenever the Cameron twins were with Clover, they spoke wistfully about what a shame it was they'd never known Penelope. This gave them ample opportunity to pelt the flattered stepsister with all manner of personal questions.

"Somebody has to, Peter. If it were up to you, we'd still be answering phones at that beastly bank in Suffolk and planning our two-week holiday in Malta."

"Not true. If it were up to me, we'd not have invested our entire savings in that dreadful payday loan company in the first place."

"Oh, do stop whinging, Peter. It's very tiresome, especially when we should be celebrating each victory that comes our way, small as it may be."

Chapter Nine

Lucy was in her studio forcing herself to work. She knew it would make her feel better, for it always did. Besides, she needed *product*, as her gallery guru, Sigmund Hartmann, called it. The New York show opened the Wednesday before Thanksgiving, just in time for holiday shopping—not a minute too soon for Lucy to pay off some of her more egregious debt.

For Lucy, denial functioned the same way that hermit crabs burrowed in the sand. Her worries would remain in hiding for short spans of time, but there was always the inevitable panicked moment when the last fraction of each and every relentless wave would chase them out of their hidey-holes, startled, before they scurried for cover with an amnesiac's confidence that that time, or the next, they truly would stay buried.

Lucy had managed to tuck her anxiety about Tessa into her subconscious, right along with her monetary concerns. There were several details to sort through before they knew whether Joey's idea of having Siobhan move in with them would work or not. While the prospect of having the woman move into the house was not appealing, it would be worlds better than having to send Tessa away to a treatment center.

"I bet you never thought it would come to this," Lucy whispered, looking at a photo of Penelope frolicking in the waves between Martha and Susannah.

It wasn't unusual for Lucy to talk to Penelope in her studio, even when she wasn't looking at her picture, though, truth be told, over the past two years, if Lucy was working, it meant she had an image of Penelope clipped to her easel. It just so happened that no other artistic subject had the same appeal. It was Lucy's means of keeping her friend alive, and besides, there was something about the way she felt when she worked—a reverent awe—that allowed her to feel connected to a world where spirits might just talk back if you waited long enough.

When Lucy concentrated on her work, she lost herself. A hush of calm would descend as she captured the glance of sunlight on a blade of grass, the unutterable loveliness of the inner arm, the blank, shadowed hollow in a curl of surf. Time fell away, memory intervened, and the result endowed her work with a nostalgia that was almost tangible. Her work was unfashionably pleasant to look at, too harmonious in color and form, except for the longing it ignited in viewers. As one *Art World* critic had put it, "Lucy Vargas's canvases are imbued with a sadness, not so much for an era gone by as one that is yet to come."

Lucy wouldn't have put it so sentimentally, but she felt holy when she painted. It was like worship, this being held captive to the temporary beauty she was trying to transmit into two-dimensional space. God *was* in the details, for it was in the smallest of segments that she reveled, carried away by mysterious trinities, whether it was three friends holding hands in the surf, the tapered apex of a bending knee or the hypotenuse of waist to the triangular curve of an elbow.

She was so lucky, she knew, to have these moments where she was lifted out of the everyday. So lucky, in fact, that what was left of Lucy dared not ask for more. *Yes*, Penelope had married Joey; *yes*, Penelope had had children; but Lucy was regularly blessed, transported, her exultation transferring just a fraction of itself to her paintings. This may have been what critics saw when they discussed her art, the longing she felt to imitate a form so perfect it could not be captured.

Herein lay the key to Lucy's apparent selflessness, her seeming submission to the wills of others without declaring her own needs. Her need was to create, something she could do day in and day out, something most artists would kill for. She was one in a million, this Lucy Vargas, for she happened to love her work in a way that was close to unseemly. For this she was grateful, and also superstitiously protective.

Sigi had hinted more than once that Lucy might want to consider branching out to painting subjects other than her deceased friend, advice that she had been able to neither disregard nor completely heed. Thus her current work, a triad of Martha, Susannah and Penelope cavorting in the ocean. Even here, though, Penelope had managed to take over *The Three Graces. I can't decide what I'm going to care about,* Lucy told herself.

It wasn't just grief that pulled Lucy toward Penelope. It was gratitude as well. If it hadn't been for the heiress's initial encouragement, to say nothing of the help she'd provided financially, Lucy might have been forced to give up her art long ago.

The beach property, which had belonged to Penelope's daddy and wasn't encumbered by the Cameron trust's legal constraints, was already a functional bed-and-breakfast when Penelope had given the deed to Lucy. When she'd broached the idea, Penelope had said it was a quid pro quo for taking the girls when their parents left town. The trouble was, Lucy knew her friend too well. The quid pro quo was a pretext, something Penelope had invented to make it easier for Lucy to accept her generosity. Predictably, Lucy had balked, and predictably, Penelope had pressed. The negotiation had gone on for weeks.

"Lucy, you've got it all wrong. I need *you,*" Penelope had insisted over and over. "Now that Martha won't fly and Susannah's a single mom, Joey and I are stuck doing all the site visits. I need him along; we need time alone together. But we can't do it unless the girls are happy."

"Penelope, you know I'd take them anyway. You don't have to pay me to do it!"

"No offense, sweetie, but your house is too small. Besides, how will you tend to my precious offspring if you're scrubbing other people's toilets?"

Lucy's constant entrepreneurial efforts, a housecleaning business at the time, had exasperated Penelope on two fronts. First, she ranted, Lucy needed to be painting, and second, she was deeply wounded by Lucy's refusal to ask for help.

"You're always rescuing me," Lucy had responded.

"Apparently not enough. I just wish you'd trust me."

"It's not that. I know you'd give me money if I needed it. It's just . . . it's not right!"

"Stop right there. I didn't earn my money, hon. You know that. My parents didn't either. It's a sacred trust I've been handed. It's not like I'm supporting you to eat bonbons and watch soap operas. You were meant to create beauty in the world. You were. Let me be part of that by helping you with the mechanics of living."

Still, Lucy had resisted, until Penelope had started crying.

"Why are *you* crying!" Lucy had shrieked. "I'm the supplicant here."

Lucy knew, of course, there was far more to Penelope's tears than her frustration over Lucy's not accepting the house. Not only had her beloved father, a vigorous athlete, died of an unexpected heart attack that fall, but Penelope's fears about her own mortality had been reinforced by what she and Martha referred to as their "first-class near-death experience." Getting ready to land at the Jacksonville airport, their plane's landing gear had malfunctioned, causing the pilot to circle the airport for an hour while emergency crews prepared for a tough landing.

"Figures I'd go away to grieve Daddy and nearly get killed on my way back. When that pilot told us to get into crash position, I was like, *hey!* You can't kill me! My daddy just died! That's just not fair! I just kept thinking that Joey and I had had this big fight right before I left and if I didn't get home to tell him I was sorry, I'd, well, I guess I wouldn't have had to kill myself, but you get the idea. Thank God that pilot knew what he was doing."

The flight—which Lucy and Susannah had taken home a day

earlier—had landed safely in a corridor full of fire trucks and ambulances, but the experience had profoundly affected both Martha and Penelope, though in vastly different ways.

Martha had gotten home from the airport, walked into the living room and told Sateesh she'd decided not to continue seeing the fertility specialist in Jacksonville whose office she'd dragged him to only two weeks before. She'd sworn off flying, started seeing a therapist and begun running marathons.

Penelope, on the other hand, had decided that if she was going to die, she'd better make something of her life before she did. It was during that period she dumped all her stock in the predatory Payday Lending Pals. She set about expanding the foundation's work, rededicated herself to her relationship with Joey, with her daughters and her friends. Most of all, she became ever more elaborate in her fatalism, which culminated in her insistence that they sign the codicil to her will. It was almost as if, by embroidering and sensationalizing her fear of death, she could make it implausible and therefore improbable, exerting control over the one arena in which no one, even poor little rich girls, had control.

Eight years later, as Lucy painted in the studio of the house Penelope had given her, as she waited to hear about Joey's meeting with Siobhan, she could not see past the obligation she felt to her dead friend. On top of the guilt she suffered over Tessa's health was layered an extremely shameful, petty concern. Even if they should be lucky enough to get Siobhan to agree to Joey's plan, what if her continual presence in the house caused him to fall in love with her? This was such an ungenerous, to say nothing of regressively antifeminist, sentiment that Lucy was tempted to revisit her monetary problems simply as a means of distracting herself from her own loathsomeness.

Instead, Lucy gave herself an internal slap-down, resolved to think about thorny issues some other time and wrenched herself back to the more immediate challenge of translating Martha's expression from photo to canvas.

Lucy was filling in highlights where the sun illuminated the sharp tip of Martha's nose, the peaks of her cheekbones and crest of her full upper lip, curled back in a rare moment of letting go. The three friends were romping in the waves; their hair was slicked back, their skin exposed to the salty spray. The triangular green of Martha's bikini top was shifted slightly to the right, exposing the pale foothill of her left breast, cradled softly in the dark shadow of her underarm.

So rapt was Lucy with the adrenaline of capturing just the right color and forms that when Martha tapped her on the shoulder, she dropped her palette, spattering paint across the floor.

"Damn it, Martha, you scared the shit out of me!"

"Sorry, child. I keep forgetting how you startle. Have you thought about taking something for it?"

"Nothing wrong with me. I have to concentrate is all," Lucy said, kneeling to wipe the floor.

"I swear someone could come in here and take everything you own and you wouldn't give a crap. You'd just be happy they didn't come down and interrupt you."

"Nice try, but I'm not so generous as you think. Besides, why do you think I have dogs?"

"Oh, is that why? And here I thought you liked the beasts."

"Nope. Especially since they let you waltz in without making a peep. So, have you heard anything new? Did the Camerons interview Siobhan?"

"As we speak. She's still waiting to hear whether her company will let her take the time off. The third time Joey came in to ask me if I'd heard anything, I told him if he didn't call Sateesh and go for a long run, I'd have to shoot him."

"Oh, that's where he is. I tried calling him earlier."

"Yeah, well, I tried calling you. About sixteen thousand times. Your damn phone's off the hook again."

"Oh, shoot."

"Seriously, would you please get a cell phone? Or call waiting with an answering machine? Or both?"

"Oops. One of the dogs keeps knocking it off the hook. Maybe

I *should* give them away. So you drove all the way out here just to tell me that?"

"Otherwise Joey would have. Besides, I told him if he would take off to go running, I'd be happy to come out and visit you. When the cat's away, I'm more than willing to play."

The concept of Martha as mouse to anyone's cat made Lucy giggle. "You? Play? I don't think so. What's really up?"

"I'm playing in that picture," Martha said softly, suddenly thoughtful. "Of course, that was back when I was a lazy slob. Look how spongy my tummy was."

"Please. You were, and are, Mizz Martha, gorgeous."

"Seriously, Lucy. Friends don't let pudgy friends wear two-piece bathing suits."

"Martha, are you insane?"

"I just, I don't know. I'm still worried about Tessa, I guess."

"So if you can't beat her, you'll join her in the land of anorexia? What's wrong?"

"I don't know. I just, I'm not sure I trust this woman."

Lucy shook her head, wishing she didn't feel the same way, knowing it was against her principles to judge someone on the basis of so little real knowledge. Still. She leaned forward and continued to work on the painting.

"Lucy, I hate this picture of me."

"I repeat, you're insane. In fact, all modesty aside, I think this might just be the best thing I've ever done. I'm going to send it to the Galbreath Committee."

"The what?"

"It's a long shot. Like a MacArthur grant for painters. They called Sigi last week and asked for slides."

"Wow, Lucy. That's wonderful!"

"Thanks. I'm calling it *The Three Graces*."

"What's the prize?"

"Five hundred thousand. But even more than that, once you win it, well, everyone wants your work. It's like winning the lottery. I know it's a long shot."

"Lucy, I'm begging you. If there's even a remote possibility of this painting getting known, I want out. Can you either change my face or put me in a one-piece?"

"Martha, this is *so* not like you. That sounds like something Clover might say."

"Thanks a lot. Look at me, Lucy! My face is so . . . sloppy."

Lucy squinted at the photo clipped to the top of the easel. "In my people's country, the land of the mellow, we call that relaxed."

"You? Mellow? Give me a break."

"I may not be, but I know it when I see it. I took this picture. You don't look at all sloppy. You look happy. Were we drinking that day?"

"Is a bear Catholic? Does the pope defecate in the woods?"

"Don't blaspheme."

"Where'd a nice Jewish girl learn that word?"

"CCD," Lucy said, referring to the Catholic extracurricular program Tessa had been attending since her mother's death. "I've learned a thing or two from the catechism. Besides, we Jews invented the Old Testament," Lucy added, though the truth was that her parents' style of Reform Judaism had left the local rabbi scratching his head.

Martha proffered a stemmed glass. "Wine?"

"Not yet. But help yourself."

"Done that. But I think I need a refill now that I've seen your painting."

"Okay, get me one too. We'll drink to your nascent eating disorder."

"Look, I'm serious. Can't you enter something else?"

"No. This is the one. You're just unable to *see*."

"Don't distract me with platitudes. I see just fine and I wish you'd listen to me. It's my body, in a terrible state of disrepair. You're planning to expose me to the world."

"I wish. The chance of me winning the Galbreath—you might as well hope I'll get hit by lightning."

"Well, I know I'm supposed to be your friend, but I'd rather have you hit by lightning, then. Vain as that sounds, if you win that prize, and that picture gets splashed across the papers, I might have to kill you."

Lucy laughed.

"Can I say something really bitchy?" Martha warned, clawing her fingers through the air like the cat she was about to become.

"I thought you'd given up being a bitch."

"*Moi?* Not in this lifetime."

"You've been so nice lately."

"To whom?" Martha asked, mock chagrin stamped on her wrinkled brow.

"Well, your husband, so that doesn't count. Though it should, given how you take the man for granted. I swear, you treat him like a pair of old shoes."

"Comfy old shoes," Martha corrected. "New ones are a pain. Lord Jesus, save me from the *Good Housekeeping* fairy. If it was up to you I'd be answering the door with his pipe and slippers, wearing nothing but plastic wrap. Besides, I didn't come over here to talk about the poor defenseless creature that is my husband. I came to bitch about Nurse Nightingale."

"Who?"

"This is so petty, I can't believe I'm saying it, especially now that she's hopefully going to help with Tessa. But bear with me. She shows up at the restaurant yesterday with an armload of basil for Sateesh."

"Wow! How incredibly wrong of her! Basil!"

"Wait. I'm getting to the good part. Supposedly she'd just come from the garden store and just hated to waste the extra she couldn't use."

"So?"

"Garden store, my ass. She was wearing a pair of shorts that gave her a wedgie and a see-through shirt with a black lace bra. Straight out of Frederick's of Hollywood."

"That home-wrecking witch!" Lucy laughed.

"Look, you better believe it. I know for a fact she thinks Sateesh is cute."

"Sweetie, the only people on the planet who don't are Ray Charles, Stevie Wonder and the man's wife."

"What's that supposed to mean? You know I think he's cute. So does everybody else. I'm not blind."

"No. Neither are you a musical genius. Nor are you of African-American descent. The point I'm making is that most of the time you act like Sateesh is not even there. Meanwhile he acts like you're the only person in the room. Why don't you allow yourself to enjoy his attention? Are you afraid if you adore him back he'll get bored?"

"That's so not true." Martha fended off Lucy's reassurance as though it might be dangerous, as if it might allow her to relax just at a time when she needed to be most vigilant. "He might love me, but that doesn't mean he couldn't fall out of love."

"Martha. Stop it. He's crazy about you. Who else would put up with your incredible neglect?"

Martha tried to repress a smile. "Lucy, stop. I came prepared to bitch. Don't ruin my fun."

Joey and Sateesh were running in Napoyca State Park, a three-hundred-acre forest preserve northwest of town. The trail was six miles and bent around a shallow lake known for its abundance of alligators and water moccasins, the presence of which Joey claimed helped him keep pace with Sateesh, who was four inches taller and had the lean body of a runner, despite his prodigious appetite.

For the first few miles, both men were silent. This wasn't atypical. They were accustomed enough to being together that there was no need to fill the air with sound.

"What do you think?" Joey asked without explanation after they'd passed the third mile marker.

Sateesh kicked a stone out of the way and just missed tripping on a tree root. "Not paid to, my friend. It's my day off."

"Bullshit."

"Look, you've enough people telling you what to do."

"Which is why I'm confused."

"And you think my twopence will make a pound?"

"Come on, Sateesh. Tessa talks to you. She trusts you. I want to hear what you think."

"I think you should disregard everyone else's opinion and make up your own mind."

"Look, it's not just me that's involved. You know that."

"Yes, that's the rub. The truth is, I believe in instinct when it comes to the important questions in life. So what's your prefrontal lobe telling you?"

"Not to send Tessa anywhere."

"Alright then. You've got to put up with moving into town."

"But Lucy—I don't—how can I tell her?"

"She'll understand, Joey. It's out of your hands, isn't it?"

"I feel that way. But still, I—look, don't say anything to Martha about us moving until I get a chance to tell Lucy. I might wait till I get back from L.A."

"The longer you wait, the harder it's going to be."

"I know. But the girls have a sleepover party this weekend. I'd rather come back early and explain the whole thing to Lucy when they're out of the house."

"You know, I think Lucy's concerned enough about Tessa's health that she'll go along with whatever you need to do. We've all been worried, you know."

"I know. I'm just—I hope Lucy doesn't take it as a slap in the face."

Sateesh said nothing for almost a full lap of the lake, and when he finally spoke it was to utter a question that had been brewing since the birthday party, when he'd noticed Joey's eyes following Lucy around the room. "Let me ask you. You and Lucy, did you . . . have you ever . . . ?"

"Jesus, Sateesh, that would be like sleeping with my sister!"

"She wasn't your sister when you fancied her in college."

"Having a crush on a girl in college is one thing. Wanting to screw your wife's best friend is another."

Sateesh sped up and then slowed down. When he spoke, the question was not what Joey expected. "Something occurs to me. Is that a problem for you? That she makes you think of Penelope?"

Joey shook his head. "No, it's just, it's all ancient history, that's all."

"It's not that you feel guilty?"

"Why would you say that?"

"Because I remember very well when Susannah's Darryl said he found her hot, you threatened to . . . what was the turn of phrase you used? Clean his clock? Are you sure you weren't just feeling a bit of the same yourself?"

"That asshole. He was still married to Susannah! Besides, like I said, that was a long time ago."

"Yes. I was there. I was also present another night, when you and I spoke of fantasy females. I do believe you mentioned a certain woman named Lucy."

"You did too!"

"So what's changed?"

"Everything. I can't go there, man, not with anyone." Joey shook his head again, this time so vehemently that he sprayed sweat all over Sateesh's shoulder.

"Jo-hee!" Sateesh uttered his friend's name in his uniquely attenuated British–South Asian fashion. In this case, it sounded like two separate pleas, which he repeated in disgust.

"What?"

"Do warn me the next time you're getting ready to shake your fur dry."

"Sorry," Joey said, but the memory of shaking his head and the reasons why he had done so threw his body into automatic pilot. Once again he spattered Sateesh with sweat. "I love her, man, but not that way."

Sateesh moved into a defensive crouch, arms crossed over his face in surrender. "Desist! Forget I ever mentioned such things!"

"Sorry, man. Sorry."

"No, I'm sorry. It's obviously a sore topic," Sateesh apologized, keeping to himself the observation that two years without a woman's touch was a very long time.

Joey hadn't had sex with a real woman in two years, but many nights, in his dreams, he was with a woman whose face he couldn't see. When he woke up, he was often relieved to find his sheets sticky with the evidence that he was still functioning on one level, even if the experience had been out of his conscious control.

In college, when he had met Penelope, he'd only had one long-term girlfriend and two one-night stands. Penelope had had a lot more sexual experience and wasn't shy about recounting her high school glory days in graphic detail. After years of listening to Penelope reminisce about former lovers, Joey had once made the mistake of blurting out, "I wish I'd slept around more when I had the chance."

Penelope, the fixer, thought she had a solution. "Look, we don't have to let other people tell us what marriage is. If you want to, sleep with other people. It's okay with me."

That was where Joey had stopped her. "Jesus! I don't want an open marriage. I just wish I'd had more, I don't know, more fun when I could have."

This wasn't completely accurate. What was true was that he hated the idea of her having had sex with other men, hated that she'd had more experience than he, no matter how petty he told himself this sentiment was. The way he felt when he pictured her with someone else was awful. The last thing he wanted to do was put his wife through the same agony.

So Joey had tried to pretend he hadn't really meant what he'd said and Penelope had pretended to accept it. What she did instead was surprise him when they had sex, just before he came, by tantalizing him with descriptive images of other women. At first they were strangers, people he didn't know, but then as time went on, she'd brought up Lucy as the third member of their virtual ménage à trois.

At a point in sex when he was too far gone to regain control, Penelope would describe some feature of Lucy's body in detail. Afterward, Joey felt ambushed. He'd tell his wife to stop. It wasn't fair, using her friend like this, it wasn't right.

The trouble was, even as Penelope had laughed at him for being so Catholic, even as she reminded him, "It's sex, Joey, not the Blessed Sacrament," there was some part of her that was jealous over the fact that her husband was surrendering himself to another woman. The fact that Penelope had been the one to initiate the fantasy, not him, didn't seem to matter when it came to how bad it made her feel.

"Penelope, please don't do this," Joey had asked. "Let's just—I know what you're trying to do. But it's complicated. It makes me feel guilty."

"Honestly, Joey. Don't be so hard on yourself."

"Hard on myself? It's not just me. Or haven't you noticed?"

"What?"

"I don't want your friendship with Lucy to be damaged by this. You've got to be jealous on some level. I can see it in your eyes."

"You've got a thing for her, don't you?"

"No."

"You can tell me, Joey."

"I've got nothing to tell you."

"How do I know that?"

"How do you know anything?" Joey had put a hand on Penelope's cheek. "Please, you've got to stop worrying about this. Do you think . . . Honey, maybe you need to see a shrink! Ever since your dad died, I'm—you just seem—I don't know. Different. Like you don't trust me."

"Joey, it's not that I don't trust you. It's more that I don't deserve you."

"Look, honey, these feelings you're having. Maybe they're—maybe they've got to do with grief. Maybe they're not really about you or me. I love you so much. And I'm not planning anything at all with Lucy. She's your best friend. And one of mine too."

"But you want her."

"No, I don't! First, I'm your husband. Second, I know too well what it's like to be jealous. I sure as hell am not going to inflict it on you for the momentary pleasure of having a fling with somebody else. Besides, what could come of it but grief for all of us, if you think about it?"

Later, when Joey thought back to that conversation, he'd marvel at how truly naïve he'd been, to think reason and honesty might trump all their problems or that the worst thing that could happen to their marriage would be an affair. Whether he'd wanted it to or not, Lucy's sexuality seemed to have become entwined with Penelope's and had become linked in his mind not only with his culpability for wanting another woman while his wife was alive, but for having not been there to protect her the one time she truly needed him.

Chapter Ten

Peter and Nigel were leaving Traders' and Merchants' Bank when they spotted Clover feeding coins into a parking meter. The twins' second meeting with the chap whose investment scheme had piqued Nigel's interest had gone swimmingly, so much so they were feeling especially festive. "Yoo-hoo!" Peter trilled across two lanes of asphalt. "Where are you off to looking so smashing?"

Clover was delighted to see her cousins. The two had been charming to her ever since they'd arrived in town. She understood they had nothing at all against her or poor lost Penelope. Indeed, it was apparent to Clover that the two brothers counted not having known her sister as one of the most tragic deprivations anyone could have suffered. She knew, even if no one else did, that the twins' interest in overseeing the management of the Cameron Foundation was motivated by the filial devotion of second cousins once removed, all the more so because they'd missed out on too many years of family bonding already.

"Tessa and June will thank us when they've come of age," Nigel was wont to point out at appropriately somber junctures. "And your Brittany too. I don't think it was ever our grand-ancestors' intention to disenfranchise *any* descendant, especially a female. In fact, were they alive today, I think they'd see all this exclusion as a bit over-the-top. It's quite contrary to the *spirit* of their bequests."

Nigel would tsk-tsk and shake his head wearily. "Besides, it's men who are discriminated against these days."

Clover crossed the street as fast as her Pappagallos would take her. She was dressed to impress, having scheduled two back-to-back sessions with the financial counselor Brett had insisted she see before he'd pay off her latest Visa bill. Ballet flats, navy pencil skirt, Peter Pan–collared shirt and the tiniest strand of pearls known to man, all to convince the damn adviser of her demure, modest approach to all things, including shopping.

"It's not like I buy things for myself!" Clover was saying to Peter and Nigel, explaining her errand of absolution. "It's just, well, I know what it's like to be embarrassed about my clothes and I don't want Brittany to have to suffer like that. You should have seen what Daddy Marcus made us wear! If it didn't have a duck or huntin' plaid on the cover, he didn't shop in that catalog."

Peter Cameron tsked and Nigel clucked. Together, they soothed Clover's troubled soul. "You look lovely. Very Audrey Hepburn in *Sabrina*."

"You're spot-on, Clover. Exactly the mood you want to strike."

"I think it's so unfair you've got to suffer like this for something you had nothing to do with!" Peter murmured. "Nigel and I are just now getting back on our feet."

Peter didn't need to elaborate. The October Surprise was something the twins had discussed with Clover ad infinitum.

Pre–October Surprise, the Cameron cousins, privy to the foundation's many investments over the years, had put what little money they could scrape together into any stocks that the fund's manager had signaled he intended to buy. For the most part, this strategy had been a winning one, since the cousins were able to place orders well before the general public but safely after knowing the pending volume of the endowment's purchase order would nudge the price higher in the markets. This inside information, a bone they'd been thrown by Penelope's father to keep them from taking up his time with any more frivolous lawsuits regarding their inheritance, or lack thereof, had worked like a charm until the day it backfired. This was when Penelope shocked the financial markets by impulsively and unilaterally dumping all her Payday Lending Pals stock in one hour of one October afternoon.

Until that time, she'd remained detached from the investment side of the foundation. However, the combination of having lost her father, who'd handled that side of the endowment's business, coupled with her chance attendance at a symposium on predatory lending, had been lethal, at least when it came to the foundation's stake in Payday Lending Pals, to say nothing of Nigel and Peter's much smaller nest egg, heavily invested in the same.

Perhaps Penelope might not have reacted quite so strongly were it not for the heavy footprint of Payday Lending Pals in one of the more atrocious anecdotes presented at the symposium. In a small North Carolina town, a young family had one piece of furniture, a king-size bed they'd "bought" from a rent-to-own furniture company for four hundred dollars. Each month, for the privilege of borrowing, they paid forty to the rental company, a small fraction of which was applied to the principal of four hundred dollars. When their child got sick, they fell behind on the forty-dollar payments. The father, who worked full-time at the local chicken processing plant, borrowed a hundred dollars from Payday Lending Pals. He used eighty to catch up on two months of bed payments and paid twenty in fees to Payday. Two weeks later, when he couldn't repay the loan of a hundred dollars, the man brought thirty dollars to the Payday payment window, which he hoped to apply to the hundred he owed. Instead, because he couldn't pay the amount in full, the company told him he could borrow a second hundred to pay off the first loan and pay twenty in fees for that new loan.

After a year of having to take out a new loan every two weeks because he didn't have the lump sum of one hundred to pay it off, the man had paid five hundred twenty dollars in up-front fees. However, he still owed a hundred dollars he couldn't pay, plus interest on the revolving one hundred. After four years of trying, after nearly two thousand in payments, the family fell behind again on their payments, for they still owed money to the furniture store for the bed, a piece-of-shit particleboard atrocity that was, nevertheless, a place to sleep. At this point, the rental company repossessed the family bed, and the family were shortly thereafter evicted from their apartment.

Stories like this, which illustrated the "usurious quicksand" of the predatory lending trap, were piled one on top of the other. By the time Penelope had left the symposium, she'd already made up her mind. The victims included pensioners, military families, single moms and every sort of person in between, 90 percent of whom had full-time jobs at minimum wage, and two thirds of whom had gotten into the debt trap because of a medical emergency, for which, of course, they had no health insurance.

It was Penelope's abrupt decision to dump her Payday Lending Pals stock, and her very public announcement that she would sever all ties with the company, that had caused the price to fall so precipitously. What had been worth millions at the market's opening bell had dropped by the end of the day to half its prior value. By the time of her death, Penelope's private fortune, and the foundation's investments, had recovered somewhat, but they were nevertheless diminished enough to make credible the Camerons' suggestion that the comptroller and board had been imprudent in selling so quickly. Because Peter and Nigel had lost their own money too, they had brought to their oversight of the foundation's subsequent investments no small amount of zeal.

While the chance that the English side of the family would wrest complete control was slim, their newfound proximity stateside had allowed them to unleash their anger at having been left out in the cold for so many years. Meanwhile, they were happy to be earning a comfortable living with their executor fees, so much so that they'd begun testing the waters of new investments— riskier ventures in foreclosure refinancing—that promised rewards so enormous they'd brought a new sheen to Nigel's smile.

He squeezed Clover's shoulder solicitously. "You must stay shy of those credit counselors, dear heart. They can be extremely un-scrupulous—"

Clover shook her head. "Oh, this guy's from Brett's prayer group. I've known his wife forever."

"Well *that's* humiliating," Peter offered.

"My husband just doesn't *get* that you've got to spend money to make money. He keeps me on such a tight leash, I can't get my Heavenly Angels website off the ground."

"So to speak."

"Hah! Hah! Too funny! Hey, speaking of angels, how did my friend's interview go? Isn't she a cutie?"

"Quite," Nigel admitted. "She seems amazingly sensible on top of it."

"I knew you'd like each other!" Clover said. "I just knew it. Did she, is she going to take the job, do you think? 'Cause Tessa is just, I saw her yesterday and the girl is a stick!"

"She seemed amenable to our terms," Peter said.

"The Cameron Foundation's terms," Nigel rushed to say, pinch-ing his brother's elbow with more ardor than such a minor clarifica-tion might have warranted.

"Ow! What're you pinching me for, Nigel? I didn't say a word—"

"Wait," Clover said mischievously. "Is one of you asking her out?"

"No, not that. I—we're not supposed to tell anyone."

"What?"

"It's an investment opportunity we've just been fortunate enough to suss out—"

"Peter!" Nigel scolded. "You know we're not at liberty to— Besides, you can't get blood from a stone here. Poor Clover's right. Her husband's too conservative for—"

"She's family, Nigel."

"What? Tell me! What kind of secret are you yammering on about?" Clover pressed. "Look, I'm late. Got to go, or this bean counter will tell my husband I'm not serious and remorseful enough. But when I'm done, let's talk. I could stop by the office."

"You know, Nigel's right. It's not that we don't want to help you. But the sort of cash you'd have to have for this, I'm afraid it's not—"

"Hush now. For one thing, I've got the farm. That's in my name. Daddy left it to me. So I don't have to get Brett's signature if I want to borrow money on it."

"Look, let's walk you to your meeting, Clover. Come, Peter. What sort of equity have you got in that property, darling?"

"Mind your p's and q's now, Nigel, it's none of our concern."

"Stop, both of you. I'm going to my meeting now and then we're going to get together and talk about what you're hiding. Is that clear?" Clover's expression was stern, a demeanor she tempered with a broad wink at Peter.

"Why don't you come for dinner on Friday?" Nigel asked. "Peter and I'll make curry."

Siobhan was having her nails painted at Linh One Nail Studio when the call came in—all the more reason to ignore it, but she couldn't. It might be Joey. She grimaced prettily at the Vietnamese girl and pressed one talon against the flashing green phone, another against the speaker button. "Hello?"

"Siobhan, is that you?"

"Yes, this is Siobhan. Who's calling?"

"Clover, silly. Where are you?"

"Having my nails done. You?"

"Oh, hell! I'd have gone with you! I just broke one. Darn. Listen, I was wondering—do you want to come to my cousins' for dinner on Friday?"

"The English ones?"

"Yes. They said you had a good meeting. I thought maybe you'd like to get to know them better. I don't know if you realized this, but they went to Oxford University over in England, and I swear, they're so witty. They just make me laugh. They're almost all the family I have now."

"Your husband doesn't count?"

"No, I mean blood relations."

Siobhan said nothing, though she was already quite aware that Clover wasn't, in fact, a *true* Cameron. Clover had been adopted by Marcus May when her "no-good trailer-trash momma took up with some nouveau riche sleaze bucket from Alabama." This was a bit of spite that was repeated fairly regularly by the town wags, who believed no married woman should spend as much time as Clover did singing karaoke in bars with two know-it-alls from England while her husband stayed at home with her child.

Brett's aversion to the Cameron twins may have had something to do with the same objection, though he preferred to say it was because "they ain't worth the shit they drip."

Her husband's dislike for the twins was something Clover preferred to see as simple pigheadedness. In the ongoing conversation that Clover conducted in her head, with her husband and just about everyone else in her social world, the Camerons' detractors just didn't *get* the twins' British sense of humor.

"They went to school in England?" Siobhan asked. "Isn't that where Sateesh went to university? Is that how they met?"

"Oh, Lord, no. You'd think they would be friends but Martha— Martha has no tolerance for them. I think Sateesh takes her side even if he doesn't have to."

"What's Martha got against them?"

"Well, after Penny was killed, the Camerons had to come over and, like, investigate things with how the foundation runs. It's, like, in the will—not Penny's, but the original great-great-grandparents on the Cameron side. They were kind of kooky and made it so only the girls in the family would be able to inherit."

"Except you?"

"Well, the thing is, I was adopted by Penelope's daddy. Her momma had already passed when I came into the family."

"That's so unfair."

"Oh, hey, that's just the way the cookie grumbles. Anyway, it's not Peter and Nigel's fault they had to move here. Martha just—she just takes it too personal, like they're criticizing her and Susannah."

"Well, I'd take your opinion over Martha's. I don't know why, but she is so unfriendly to me."

"Aw—she's just—she doesn't really open up with strangers. She's a Yankee and they're, like, night and daylight from how we go about things down south of the Mason-Dixon line. Plus, Penny's passing was—well, you can imagine. It just killed us all, but Martha's so like all 'stiff upper lip' about everything. I think she's just held it all in. Like I said, she doesn't open up."

"That's for certain."

"So anyhow, Peter's making curry and Nigel's rented a karaoke machine. Why don't you come with me? They're both eligible bachelors, Siobhan. If they lost some weight, they'd be cute, I think."

Siobhan nearly snorted, having observed not one kilocalorie of attractiveness in her earlier meeting with the aforesaid eligible bachelors. "Oh, I'd love to some other time but I've got so many loose ends to tie up right now."

"Loose ends. I hear you. Daddy Marcus used to say if you left enough loose ends you could make the next generation spend their whole lives knitting a sweater they'd never be able to wear."

Marcus May, Penelope and Clover's daddy, had died quietly during the Virginia–Florida State game, surrounded by his hunting buddies and fifty thousand cheering fans. Neither daughter was with him, but they took comfort in knowing Virginia had scored a field goal right before he went.

"Hell, if there's a Heaven, we know the man's there," Penelope said during her eulogy. "If not, at least he had a little slice of it on the way out."

However glib she sounded, Penelope had taken her father's

death harder than anyone expected. This was saying a lot, given her highly charged emotions and her deep attachment to the only parent she'd ever really known.

The shock was that despite having lost her mother, this was really her first death. You couldn't count her mom's. Too long ago. Whatever it had done to Penelope had seeped so deep into her pores there was no pulling it out as a blueprint for "getting over" the loss.

Penelope had girded herself against death by imagining her own in such detail that when her father keeled over just after his sixtieth birthday it was a complete and total surprise.

"I just keep thinking he's gone away on a fishing trip," she'd said. "Truly, it hasn't hit me that he's not coming back."

At the time of this comment, Penelope, Lucy, Martha and Susannah were themselves on a trip, their annual girls' weekend getaway to Phoenix, a chance to pretend they were all in college again, and to act like it too, since no one had to drive home or take care of children, dogs or husbands. They'd considered canceling, out of respect to Marcus, but Joey had insisted Penelope needed to get away, needed to have fun, when all she'd been doing for weeks was staring into space as if she'd seen a ghost.

Joey had upgraded their reservations at the Ritz to the presidential suite, where the four friends faced each other on two sofas, wearing white terry cloth robes and drinking Drambuie. This had been Marcus's favorite liqueur. Penelope had ordered a bottle brought to their room with a plate of Brie surrounded by dried Jerusalem figs.

When Penelope had said she couldn't quite believe her father was gone, Lucy, whose parents had been killed by a drunk driver three years before, nodded. "I felt like that too. It's not at all like you think it's gonna play out. You think you'll just be sad, like, bittersweet and all, but then you find—well, first it's hard to feel anything, and then *wham*, it ambushes you when you least expect it."

The room was quiet except for the sound of Enya, which

Penelope abruptly stood up and turned off. "Sorry, Susannah, that woman's keening makes me so cranky."

"That's part of it too," Lucy said. "You get so irritable. Angry even."

"Well, you had a right to be," Martha said. "They left you such a mess to clean up."

Martha was referring to the fact that Irving and Isobel had lived beyond their means, using a reverse mortgage and then a cascade of credit cards to cover their bills, which Lucy had only discovered after their death and countless hours of executing a worthless estate.

"No, that's not true at all. I'm glad they lived life *large*. They put me through college, and they gave me everything. But whether I had a right to be angry or not, I was. I felt so *deserted*."

"Seriously?" Penelope asked. "I'm so glad I'm not the only one. You wouldn't believe—I hate myself for it but I keep obsessing about how Daddy could be so *stupid*. No—make that *careless*."

"Oh, sweetheart. He didn't—he wouldn't have known his heart was in bad shape!"

Susannah's voice was gentle, her eyes beseeching her friend to forgive her father for dying.

"Hell, Susannah, I know that! I'm not talking about that. I'm talking about how he married that *bitch* after my momma died and *trusted her* with me. How could he have been so stupid?"

"Men *are* stupid." Martha's tone was matter-of-fact, low-key. She sounded like a pediatrician telling a new parent that babies cry. "They think with their penises, and the worst part is they don't even know they're doing it. Which makes that particular level of stupidity all the more dangerous."

"That's so sexist!"

"Yeah, Susannah, so what? I'm sexist. They're stupid."

"Martha, honestly, you don't know how lucky you are. Sateesh is so sensitive!" Susannah's voice trailed off. She knew that bringing Darryl's name into the conversation, so close to their upcoming divorce, would have unleashed a torrent of Drambuie-fueled opinions about how much better off she'd be without the bastard. This was a battering by the Furies, as she'd come to call her girlfriends, whose comments were so constant they were like a babbling brook, easy to ignore.

"*Too* sensitive," Martha groaned, thinking of Sateesh. "You should have seen him at the gynecologist's last week. If he hadn't been sitting down, I think he'd have fainted. I really do. The doctor was telling us about this operation men get to improve their sperm count and Sateesh—this is actually pretty funny—his hands flew up into a shield to cover his crotch, except he forgot he was holding that model of the fallopian tubes in his hand! He banged himself so hard, it brought tears to his eyes. Though I'm still not certain he wasn't crying at the thought of the scalpel."

"That *is* radical," Susannah insisted protectively. "Surgeons are knife-happy, I know that. Listen, I can check into herbs for fertility. I remember something about men wearing boxers instead of briefs. And avoiding hot tubs."

"Susannah, do you not think we've tried all that?" Martha snapped impatiently.

"Sorry. I—"

"Just because you got pregnant the first time Darryl *looked* at you doesn't mean we all can."

"What exactly did the doctor say?" Penelope interrupted. "Is it morphology or motility?"

"Both."

"So will it help?" Penelope was conversant with the medical jargon, well acquainted with the way Martha envied Susannah's fertility. She and Joey had taken a year and a half to get pregnant before Penelope's fifth month on Clomid allowed her to conceive Tessa.

"It might help if he were willing to do it. That's what I meant about men. Sateesh won't even consider anything"—here Martha curled her fingers into quotation marks—"'*artificial.*'"

"Why in the world not?"

Martha shook her head wearily. She was a woman well accustomed to argument, but her many attempts to discuss the matter with her husband had been futile. "Sateesh thinks if he's meant to have children, he will. If he's not, and pushes it, he thinks God's gonna come down and strike him dead."

"I didn't know he was religious," Susannah said.

"That's the thing. He's not." Martha's voice broke. Her anger and frustration and obsessive desire for a baby were enough to bring tears to her eyes, which she used her knuckles to press into submission. "He's just superstitious. Thinks he could end up with some horrible, mean, monstrous child. His father reincarnated."

"Well, he's got a point there. Considering he's carrying the genetic material."

"I don't think it's like that. I think he's just—*cosmically* afraid. It's hard to explain. He's a believer in destiny and he doesn't want to screw with what the universe has in store for us."

"Jesus!" Penelope muttered. "Give the man a tranquilizer or something. Tell him to *hush*. It's normal to be nervous. Everyone is."

"The thing is," Martha complained, "if I push him and we end up with a monster, it'll be my fault. I figure it'd be just my luck."

"What about adopting?" Lucy asked.

Here, Martha upended her snifter and sent her tongue into the glass to lick away the last few drops. She lowered her voice and ducked her chin into her chest before looking up at her friends beseechingly. "Sateesh would do it in a heartbeat but I, this is, I just don't know if I could love a child that's not mine. Not in the same way."

"Of course you could!" Susannah murmured.

"You don't know that. And I'm not willing to take the chance."

"It's worth a try, Martha. You've been so, you've been wanting a baby so, I just want you to be happy!" Susannah pressed her bare toes into Martha's instep.

"It's not about me, Susannah. It's not fair to take someone else's child, one other people are dying to have, and *hope* you'll love it. See, I'm calling it *it*. That's a bad sign right there."

"I promise you, I worried about the same thing with my biological children. I worried if they looked like Darryl's mean sisters I couldn't love them—"

"I hear you, though, Martha," Penelope interrupted. "Look at Daddy. He loved Clover, but she never felt like it was the same."

Susannah leaned over and took a fig from the plate on the table. "No, Penelope, that was different. The poor thing was already five years old; her mother had left without even saying good-bye. No matter who adopted her, Clover would have been needing more than they could give. Now, Martha, if you're so eager to have your own child, what about artificial insemination? Sateesh would love any baby that was yours."

Martha shook her head. "In his book, anything *artificial:* forget it. Any extraordinary means, he feels like we're interfering with what's meant to be."

Penelope sighed. "Jesus, that's so silly."

"Back to my original point. He *is* a man. And a stubborner one you haven't seen. But then again, if you'd been brought up in his family, you might have some crazy ideas too."

"Might?" Penelope said, pointing her finger at herself and turning it near her temple in a circular motion. "Have you forgotten who you're talking to?"

By the time the women had dressed and gone down to Bistro 24, they'd gotten to the point in their festivities where they'd melded consciousness and begun to talk in a shorthand that no one but the table's occupants could be expected to understand.

Because these friends had come of age together, because they'd charted these waters of conversation so many times before, they found themselves completely undaunted by unclear antecedents or indefinite pronouns.

What was important was the communal flow of togetherness they felt, a connection that soothed their troubled nerves, wrapping their individual predicaments into a single swoop of sisterly acceptance.

When Penelope leaned across Susannah's lap to pull Martha's chin toward hers and whispered her newest brainstorm, neither Lucy nor Susannah paid any attention.

Lucy and Susannah remained lost in their conversation. Not even when Penelope had to repeat herself to Martha, who was certain she couldn't have heard her friend correctly. "You're a complete idiot," the lawyer murmured affectionately when Penelope broached the same idea a second time.

"Idiot savant."

"Look, I love you, but this ain't *The Big Chill*," Martha laughed. "You'd be—I know you. You're just not that nice a person. And Sateesh? The man's a sweetheart, but he's not going to let another man father his child."

"Not even his best friend?"

"Especially not his best friend. Besides, it would still involve lab coats and turkey basters. Ever since Astrid and Kevin's baby, Sateesh thinks there's something in the plastic that leaches into the DNA. It's ridiculous, I know. Look how many kids are born absolutely perfectly through artificial insemination! But statistics won't convince my husband. It's like he's stuck on the image of that poor baby."

Penelope grimaced, remembering the funeral they'd attended the year before, the infant daughter of one of Martha's lawyer friends. "How are they doing?"

Martha sighed heavily. Astrid's baby, whose long-awaited conception had been the expensive and hard-won result of in vitro fertilization, had lived three days outside the womb before dying of a hopeless genetic malady known as trisomy 18. Within three months of the baby's death, her husband had declared himself in love with a woman he'd met on the Internet. "Astrid's screwed. Totally screwed."

Penelope picked up a piece of asparagus, dipped it in béarnaise sauce and took tiny bites, feeding it into her mouth like a tree to the wood chipper. "Do you ever wonder if Sateesh would cheat?"

"To tell you the truth, I try very hard to ignore the possibility.

But Jesus, thanks for bringing it up while I'm away and the world's hottest Indian man is presently alone for the weekend. Did you see that new hostess he hired?" Martha paused. "Look, when you're married to a man who strangers come over to, saying he's the most beautiful person they've ever seen, right as you're sitting at the same table with the guy, you have to wipe the concept out of your brain. Which I manage to do successfully. Most of the time."

"Sorry. I guess I was just really shocked at Kevin's—just what he did."

"That's a whole different ball of wax. When their baby died, the disappointment just about killed them. The man fell off into the deep end is all."

"Sometimes I think Joey is ripe for a takeover."

"How so?"

"Just something he said. How he wished he'd had fun when he could have. You know, he hardly had sex with anyone before me."

"Seriously?"

"So I told him he could—if he wanted."

"Jesus! Are you insane! What did he say?"

"No way."

"Dodged a bullet there, Pen."

"Yeah, I guess. But I don't think the issue's solved. I think he might feel more and more deprived. And when he hits his midlife crisis—"

"Honey, tamp down that imagination of yours. And repeat after me: you can't preemptively micromanage your husband's emotional development. He's thirty-three years old, for Christ's sake."

"I know. I know. But I keep thinking. His head may be saying 'Absolutely not,' but his heart might spin out on its own without asking."

"Or another part of his anatomy," Martha couldn't help but add, even as she understood she'd just reinforced Penelope's fear. "Still, that's what trust is about. It's a chance you've got to take."

"But that's the thing. Do I? What if I can find a way to . . . add a little pizzazz to his portfolio—"

"Portfolio! You are so funny, hon. Let's get our waiter. Ooh, look at the Dom Pérignon on that guy's table over there."

"Forget the Dom, look at the guy." Penelope raised her fingers to their waiter, but her eyes remained fixed on a customer sitting two tables away. "Wow, he looks like Adonis. Or Mars. Or one of those Norse gods."

"Maybe he's the god of fertility. Maybe he'd like to say a blessing in my general direction."

"Honey, maybe he'd like to do more."

"Hah! I can see me presenting Sateesh with his blond-haired, blue-eyed child."

"Why not? You're fair."

"For one, my coloring's recessive, so the father would have to be carrying a blond gene in his genetic code. Whatever else you might say about Sateesh's parents, may they rest uncomfortably in a moldering grave, they weren't hiding any Anglo-Saxons in the genealogical closet. And for another, I may be a certified bitch, but even I would *never* lay another man's child on my husband and tell him it was his."

"No. But damn, I'd be tempted. Especially when the husband in question won't let you have a baby because of some weird superstition he's got."

"Maybe, but still. Even I'm not that horrible."

"What are ya'll talking about? Lucy asked, pointing at the waiter, who was approaching the table with a bottle in his outstretched palm. "And who ordered another bottle of wine? I'm about to fall down already."

Chapter Eleven

June and Willow had been planning Willow's eleventh birthday party for weeks, with only slightly less attention to detail than a Pentagon strategist on the eve of invasion. The fact that Willow's party would be held on Halloween had only upped the ante in this extravaganza of celebration. There were the decorations, the games, the arrangement of the sleeping bags, the snacks, and most of all, the unspoken question that ran like a current between June and her best friend: would June make it through the sleepover without calling Lucy to collect her?

Susannah and Lucy had also worried this same question to death, seeing the evening as a chance for June to overcome her anxiety and make herself proud, or, alternately, as an opportunity for her to fail miserably at a time when her peers would hold it against her. As a precaution, Susannah had offered Tessa and Amber six dollars an hour to be party helpers, applying themselves to the rituals of nail painting, facial scrubs, loofahs and all other manner of feminine indulgence. She hoped if Tessa was right there with her, June would be less likely to "flip," less likely to need to go home in the middle of the night.

When the time came, Lucy dropped the girls off with a pretended nonchalance. She waved good-bye as though it was a foregone conclusion that she'd not see them until the next morning. Joey was in Los Angeles and wouldn't be back until the next day, so if there was any middle-of-the-night panic attack, it would be Lucy who'd be roused from sleep.

"Feed Rocky!" June shouted from the front porch.

Again, Lucy waved and nodded as if to say, "Of course." She forced herself to drive away before further directives could be issued as a means of delaying her departure.

It had been months since Lucy had had her house to herself for a night, a status about which she was of two minds. On the one hand, she'd envisioned the solitude as a luxury. On the other, because she wasn't accustomed to it, she felt taken out of herself enough to feel she was being watched, though by whom or what in the universe, she couldn't quite say.

This discomfort persisted until Lucy gave up her halfhearted attempt to clean her studio and instead surrendered to her restless mood. She poured herself a gin and tonic and carried the drink to her favorite chaise on the back deck.

The surf was pounding below, kicked up by the sudden unseasonable warmth of the October day and the shifting currents of the Gulf Stream.

Lucy, having swum with the girls earlier in the day, was still wearing her damp black bathing suit under a sundress so ancient its hem and straps were fraying.

By the time the phone rang, Lucy had settled into a relaxed state, all the better to greet her caller. "Joey! How's L.A.?"

"Actually I'm on my way home from the airport. I was thinking. If the girls haven't gone to the party yet, I could drop them there after I get home."

"Oh, sorry, I took them already!"

"Don't apologize, Lucy, it's okay."

"I thought you were coming back tomorrow."

"I was. I just—got antsy to see the girls."

"Why not just stop at Susannah's on your way home?"

"No. June will think I'm babying her."

"I feel terrible you missed them. June looked so cute in her costume," Lucy said.

Joey's response was lost in a rumble of static. Lucy hung up, filled her glass with ice and topped it off with tonic. She cut a piece of lime and rubbed it around the rim. She knew she should shower, brush her hair, but for some reason, it was as if all the muscle had left her body. She was incapable of doing anything but lying back down on her chaise and staring out at the light capping the incoming surf.

When Joey found her, Lucy was still there, watching the ocean.

Something about the look on her face made Joey fear that the conversation he'd been dreading, the real reason he'd come home early, was going to be harder on Lucy than he thought. He reminded himself that he needed to follow Siobhan's advice but he felt unable to summon the words. Stalling, he offered to refill Lucy's drink.

Lucy handed her glass to Joey. He mixed her drink and made a vodka martini for himself. When he returned, Lucy said, "I hope June'll be okay—"

"Tessa will be there." Joey's expression belied the assurance he was trying for. "Painting the little girls' nails."

"Can't say I'll miss that part." Lucy looked at her hands. Her nails were short and unpolished, her fingers sinewy from their constant attention to small motor movement.

Lucy was already rethinking her request for a second drink, for she felt slightly woozy. Maybe she was disoriented from the weather being so warm and the girls being out of the house at a time when Joey was not. "I should start making dinner."

"I'll make dinner," Joey offered. "You never just sit and relax."

Lucy, gave him a sideways look. "What is it?"

"Hey. Can't I be nice?"

"You're always nice, Joey, but making dinner isn't something you do."

"I can make spaghetti. Or sandwiches."

"Okay, now I know something's up. What is it?"

Joey avoided Lucy's eyes and jumped up from his seat again. "Look, let me get us something to munch on. I'll be right back."

Joey returned with a tub of cashews, lifting the lid and tipping the nuts toward Lucy.

"Thanks," she said, carefully taking a small handful. "Such a guilty pleasure—"

"Nuts are good for you."

"Fattening," Lucy replied, nibbling them slowly.

There was an awkward pause from Joey, who watched her and then said, "Lucy, you don't really think you're fat, do you?"

"Now I know you're trying to win me over, Joey Adorno. What's up?"

The truth was that Joey thought Lucy's body was just fine. Still, it was impossible to say such a thing to her without the unsaid coming across too, the hint of attraction, the implied nakedness under all those clothes, the fact that they were alone on a Friday night and the sun was setting over an ocean's lulling waves. The whole atmosphere was like something out of those commercials trying to get people to go to Aruba and reinvigorate their sex life, except for the part where he told her that he and the girls were moving back into town.

Lucy was right. He was buttering her up. How else could he break the news?

"Lucy?" he started. "We didn't get a chance to really talk about Siobhan. I told you she'd agreed to help with Tessa, but there's more . . ."

"More," Lucy said blankly, her eyes throwing off the slightest spark of alarm. Was this where he told her he was dating someone half her age? To say nothing of half her size? Was this where he told her he wanted to have a sleepover too?

"She thinks we need to move into town."

"Town?" Lucy took a large gulp of her drink.

"She says there are too many—I think she called them *cues*—here. She wants Tessa to start over, kind of. Plus, it's too far for her to live out here and train her dance teams."

"Oh."

"I guess she thinks if we moved back home, it might be drastic enough to bring Tessa to her senses. She says you and I love Tessa too much—we can't be as hard on her as she needs us to be. Something like that."

"Joey? What do we know about this woman?"

"Lucy, I'm thinking she's right."

"Whoa." Lucy looked at her glass, nodded at it and tipped it up. She took a long drink, then another. Her anxiety earlier, had it been about this?

"Living here with you. It's like the girls and I don't have to face the truth. Besides, it might be easier for Tessa to be in town too, with needing to go to therapy and the doctor's and school. It's not something I wanted, and I don't know how the hell June will get through the night without you, but, Lucy, I—the nutritionist says having two of us in the house who are so attached to Tessa, it will be too hard for us not to sabotage the treatment. Does that make any sense at all?"

"I—can see what she's saying," Lucy said, though nothing could be farther from the truth.

Between trying not to cry and mentally bitch-slapping herself for hating the adorable nutritionist so intensely, the possibility that this might be good for Tessa pressed itself front and center. All this despite an overwhelming need to hold on to what she had, to continue with the unearned blessings she'd come to enjoy, another woman's husband and children. "Will you get me another?" she asked, holding her glass out to the side without looking at Joey.

Joey looked at Lucy, willing her to look up at him, to say she wasn't as upset as she appeared to be. "You sure?" Joey asked. Lucy was not typically a heavy drinker.

"I'm sure," Lucy insisted, though she would not meet his eyes. She had turned her head the other way, staring off over the ocean, squinting, almost, in her fury to get her emotions under control at the same time as she wanted to call Penelope and tell her what was happening so she could step in and fix things.

You bitch! She wanted to weep. *Where are you when I really need you?*

In the kitchen, Joey maneuvered to put together sandwiches. He defrosted a frozen loaf of French bread, cut a piece of steak into thin slices, drizzled olive oil onto lettuce and carefully salted and peppered each square inch of food. *Lucy will like this,* he told himself. By the time he'd refilled their drinks and set all the food onto a tray, he was telling himself it wouldn't be so bad.

"Lucy," he said, using his elbow to open the door. "Look— Lucy?"

The chairs were empty. The battering of the waves below was too loud for her to hear him call. Joey set down the covered tray and descended the steps off the deck. Down below, he saw Lucy's dress folded neatly behind a stair column. She was kneeling in the surf, wearing a black tank suit, her skin copper in the rosy dusk. Her hair was wet already, flipped back on her neck like a pelt, and she was crouching over the inch-deep surf, watching something intently.

Joey was already pulling off his shirt, kicking off his shoes, eager to get cooled off. The ocean seemed like an old friend he'd run into unexpectedly.

"Lucy?" he called.

When Lucy turned her head to look up from the hermit crabs, there was something in her eyes, some astonished—almost delirious—grief that pulled his feet out from under him.

Joey crawled the distance between them, ten feet with his knees in the mucky chill of the wet sand, sucked down and under by a riptide of lost opportunities, his calves and feet digging against the tidal gravity of hunger.

He was not drunk; he was not dreaming; he was under no influence but one, the overwhelming certainty that he needed to touch her.

"Lucy?" he called one more time before he reached her, a reckless sailor in love who wanted nothing so badly as to pull off the straps of her suit and see her body, see where the bronze faded into pale. He could not say a word.

His mouth found hers and he was ripping at her straps. His hands were heavy shovels for the soft yield of her skin.

Joey could not see Lucy's breasts; it was dark already. Besides, he was too close to the skin to see anything, his fingers seeking areolas gone stiff against his own. Joey's hands were a disembodied force cupping her ass, pulling her up onto him. He had forgotten he was still wearing his shorts. He could not let go. He was too afraid to stop, shuddering with the fear that he would wake up and this would be gone.

Lucy was lost too, she was dreaming, she was pulling Joey's prick from his pants with her fingers, careful to note the satiny softness of his skin so she would remember it later. This moment. Her suit was wedged down around her thighs. The sand felt like the paper that took its name. It was indescribable, this thick cock coming into her open warmth of wanting. Her vaginal muscles constricted against him with a mind of their own, though calling it a mind might be a bridge too far. Nothing cerebral about it, this determined creature of need that was hellish in its circled fury to have and to hold, a searing contrast to the scratchy chill of her back.

Joey's waist was a thing of beauty. As she moved up with her fingers, Lucy was Michelangelo, marveling at the graceful lines of his torso, taut with tension, blooming out from his groin in a perfect triangle. Her painter's hands rounded his pecs. She was a sculptor now, reveling in the muscled flesh against her fingers. She held all this in her head but it was colliding now, the memorization of this moment with the fear of looking up, of finding him not there.

She did not remember finding her way out of the water, only kissing him in the outdoor shower with the warm water cusping their lips, his hands cupped sacramentally under her chin.

He was tender then, attentive, determined. He was teasing his tongue into the ribs of her gum line, finding his way into all the spaces of her that, in twenty years of knowing, he'd never before found.

By the time they got to her bedroom he was hard again, enough to push her down against her pillows and hold himself while he savored watching her. Joey felt proud in some deeply primitive way. "Jesus, your body might just be one of the seven wonders of the world."

She was both round and delicate. The arc of her ribs, the intake above her waist, her smooth hill of belly with its soft indentations near the pelvic knobs. Her boobs were a throwback to some other time, and it wasn't the sixties or the fifties. It seemed like BC or something, Joey thought.

All the words that people used to describe breasts sounded ridiculous, but Joey's imagination was drawn to the morbid language of oncologists. Fruit seemed the only comparison worth making, but only if you were to cross a peach with a gourd or a pear. Lucy was nectarine smooth, and yet limpid too, like ripe plums.

Who's had you? Joey desperately wanted to know, but he knew he could not ask. He had no right. He knew that.

Nevertheless, he could not keep the words from coming out. Before he could clamp shut his lips, he was saying it. "Who's had you?" The syllables came from deep in his chest. Lucy shook her head. She pulled him down to her by the wet curls he'd let grow too long. "Oh, please," she whispered, aroused by the rough edge of Joey's beard against her shoulder. "Ask me that again."

Joey's phone was ringing off the hook, or would have been if it weren't soaked in water and abandoned in his shorts' pocket in the outside shower with the rest of the wet clothes he'd brought up from the beach. The phone was incapable of registering cellular signals, something to do with connectivity—or lack thereof—in high-moisture environments.

It was 3:00 AM.

Susannah had been calling the house since two, but the landline was off the hook, where Bijou had knocked it after being ejected from Lucy's room.

Susannah assumed Lucy had gone to bed already, assumed she'd fallen asleep so soundly she couldn't hear the phone. What didn't occur to her was that Joey had fallen asleep with Lucy, head pillowed on her waist, arms circled round her legs, bent around her like a bracket holding her steady, one hand on her mons, another on her knee.

When the doorbell rang and Lucy flinched, Joey's first impulse was an irrational need to hold her, to stay inside this cocoon of sleep, even as the dogs were yelping and Lucy was reaching for the light. "It's the girls," she whispered. "You better find something to wear."

Joey reached for her hand, pressed it against his cheek and kissed her palm, stuck still inside his reluctance to leave the bed.

"Joey. Go." Lucy was already across the room, her white cotton robe trailing behind her, her hair still matted in damp clumps.

By the time she opened the door and scooped June into her arms, Joey was headed down the stairs in a pair of flannel pajama pants, pulling his hands through his hair, which had dried against the pillow and was sticking straight up in the back.

"Dad, you look electronified!" June shrieked, rescued from her own humiliation by the sight of her father looking so silly. It made her laugh out loud. "What are you doing home?" June had been calling him on his cell all night, in between dialing Lucy's house. All she could imagine by the time she finally woke Susannah was that her father had been in a plane crash and Lucy had rushed off to find his body.

Willow had tried to talk her down. "You know how the dogs knock the phone off the hook!" June could hear the words, but she also knew Willow just wanted her to stay the night.

"You don't understand," June had said. "My dad always answers his cell."

Susannah had reminded June that cell phones didn't always work so reliably, especially as far away as Los Angeles. Tessa, awake by then, had rolled her eyes and said that she wished June would just let her go back to sleep.

However, truth be told, the more they called and got no answer, the more frightened Tessa became as well. Thus she was extremely relieved to see her dad and Lucy standing there in the foyer, even if they did look like they could be spokesmodels for the dreaded perils of bed head. "Dad? You're home?"

Joey pulled each of his girls under a separate crook of his arm, beamed at Lucy and Susannah. He sighed, sounding strangely exhilarated for someone who'd just been woken in the middle of the night. "I'm home."

Chapter Twelve

When Joey told the girls they were moving back to town, Lucy was right there with him, on the beach. The weather, like that of the days before, was unseasonably warm, a cause for celebration, or perhaps for commemoration, since that weekend would be their last at Lucy's for the foreseeable future, though at that point in time, this was a fact of which the children had not yet been informed.

June and Lucy and Joey were in bathing suits, still dripping from their swim, their sand chairs surrounding Tessa, who faced directly out toward the surf. The teen was wrapped in an old UVA sweatshirt of Penelope's, her knees tucked up inside it. Her heart-shaped face was animated by the subject they'd accidentally wandered upon, the upcoming anniversary of her mother's death. This was an occasion that Tessa felt strongly about, arguing it should be spent serving Thanksgiving dinner at the homeless shelter.

June found Tessa's proposal alarming enough that she was pouring all her creative energy into panicked substitute ideas, none of which had gotten Tessa to budge from her repetitive "Whatsoever you do to the least of my brothers, that you do unto me."

This, of course, was exactly June's point, in reverse. What was done to their mother was done to them, and spending a day in the company of men who looked like the murderer's picture in the paper was not the younger child's idea of solace.

Joey and Lucy were exchanging helpless, pained looks. The children's tension was palpable even without the news the grown-ups had planned the day around breaking. So far they'd put it off twice, once at breakfast, when a piece of Tessa's toast had gotten stuck in her throat and she'd coughed relentlessly, and once, minutes ago, out on the beach.

Joey had started by saying, "There's something we need to discuss," only to have Tessa interrupt.

"I've been thinking about it too. Mom's anniversary." Before anyone could correct her assumption, Tessa had launched into an intricate and impassioned argument about sacrifice and suffering and doing good in her mother's name.

"Actually," Joey said, his eyes broadcasting his apprehension. "There's something else."

"We've made a decision," Lucy interrupted forcefully, as though having them leave her house so abruptly wasn't causing her stomach to cramp with incessant, anxious woe. Lucy knew even the slightest sign she might give of the sadness she was feeling would only make things harder on the girls. "Tessa, the treatment program—"

"I know!" Tessa said irritably. "I know!"

"Well, the thing is, honey, you don't," her father murmured gently. "We've had to make some decisions. It turns out we can't do the treatment here."

"You promised!" Tessa cried, except there were no tears, only panic.

"No! Don't worry, hon," Lucy continued. "It's just that—"

"We're going to move back home," Joey said, pressing his fists into his thighs. "It's time."

"Home?" June asked, as though her father had just said something embarrassingly stupid or so far-fetched it didn't make sense.

Lucy put her arm around Tessa's shoulders until the teen wriggled away and faced her father. "What are you saying?"

"We're moving back. Tomorrow."

"Tomorrow!" June cried, ignoring Lucy's signal, a sharp knife-like motion at the base of her throat. "Why?"

"Because that's when Miss Siobhan can start working with your sister," Joey murmured. "We're lucky she's doing this, girls. Very lucky."

"But I thought we'd stay here!" Tessa's brow was crumpled, her eyes narrowed fiercely to mask the relief she couldn't help but feel. Going into town with her family was bad, but not nearly as bad as being shipped off somewhere all by herself. Still, it wasn't in Tessa's adolescent persona to acquiesce so easily, not without a show of indignation.

"We all think it's better for you to start fresh in your old house," Lucy said quickly. "It will be easier for you to change habits—"

"Where will you sleep, Lucy?" June interrupted, already wrestling with the floor plan in her mind's eye, already tracing new steps to Lucy's relocated bed.

Here Lucy could not keep from wincing. She was too aware of June's phobia to repress her empathetic response. "S-sweetie," she stammered, seeking the words, telling herself that every child needed to get used to sleeping by herself.

"Lucy's got to stay here. She's got to keep—"

Lucy interrupted Joey's halting explanation. "I've got clients coming, and I'm way behind deadline for my show."

Lucy's remorse was obvious, so much so that it didn't occur to June to doubt her or to wonder why Lucy might suddenly be open for business again, after all that time.

"Can't we just sleep here?" June pleaded, even as her father was shaking his head and issuing "no" from the depth of his sternum. Parental responsibility and worry for Tessa had trumped his instinctive sympathy for his younger daughter. She'd feel way worse, he reminded himself, if Tessa were being sent off to a hospital, to say nothing of the unthinkable result of leaving her worsening illness untreated. Joey took a deep breath, told himself to calm down, and pulled June's hand into his own for comfort.

Chapter Thirteen

B y six thirty Monday morning, the girls' duffel bags had been loaded into the trunk of their father's Mustang. Lucy was hugging the girls good-bye, knowing what Tessa did not. She wanted to tell the older child that everything would be alright, she wanted to tell her it would be over before she knew it, she wanted to tell her any little thing that might comfort her. In the end, though, Lucy couldn't say much of anything. In the end, all she could do was whisper to Tessa that she loved her. "Take care, baby," she managed to add, squeezing the teen's bony shoulder before opening the car door. Lucy leaned over to give June one last smooch, and the car pulled away, with Joey keeping one eye on the road, the other on his daughters' tense faces. Much as he might have known this was his best chance of helping Tessa get better, it so went against his instincts that he'd had to force himself to operate at a completely detached intellectual distance, observing himself as an outsider instead of broaching the treacherous terrain of a father's empathy.

Siobhan had re-engineered Penelope's kitchen to meet her exacting standards. She'd put aside the Florentine cookie jars, the brightly colored dipping oils, the decorative pastas encased in green glass. These emotionally laden displays were replaced with measuring cups, graphing notebooks and digital scales. This was no longer a kitchen in the normal sense of the word; it was a laboratory, a treatment facility. Some might even dare to see it as Siobhan did, a platform for the renovation of the self.

Siobhan had moved her things in Saturday night, having gotten approval from San Francisco and the Cameron Foundation's board by Friday. She'd spent the time productively, familiarizing herself with the house, preparing herself for the psychological war of wills that lay ahead.

Part of the challenge was internal to Siobhan, requiring a certain transformation. Essentially, she needed to make the house her own, even as she distanced herself from its luxury and subtle comforts. All this to inhabit the powerful being that one hundred thousand and counting was paying her to become.

Like the trainer who must force her clients to do what they didn't feel they were capable of on their own, Siobhan's job would be part enforcer, part coach, except, of course, that on top of this, Tessa was sick, incapable of making good choices for herself.

Siobhan had no illusions that the process would be smooth, nor that Tessa would surrender herself without resistance, or even that she and the girl would enjoy one another's company. To a certain extent, treating Tessa involved breaking the teen's spirit, intruding into her identity and probing into areas that would almost certainly involve great discomfort.

"The truth is," Siobhan had said to Joey when he dropped off the check and house keys at Kicks! a few days earlier, "there is no free lunch. In other words, without pain, there will be no gain. And I mean that literally," she'd added gently. "I think I've told you before, you can expect her to hate me. You too, probably."

The treatment plan Siobhan would follow was an approximation of the highly structured programs adopted by many treatment hospitals. Tessa would be supervised while she consumed three meals and two snacks a day. All privileges would be contingent on cooperation with the meal program, as evidenced by weight gain.

Tessa's teachers had agreed to provide assignments she could complete at home until such time as she'd gained at least five pounds or shown enough compliance that the privilege of seeing her friends was reinstituted. "By removing her from contact with her peer group, who often tend to reinforce anorectics by saying how skinny they look, we'll nudge things along. Remember, your daughter's not thinking clearly right now, so the more influences we can remove, the better. No TV, except for videos I screen beforehand; no Internet except to communicate with teachers and do her homework. No magazines. She'll have plenty to occupy her and I don't want distractions. Twice a week she'll see the therapist and once a week the pediatrician."

The family would eat all their meals at the kitchen table, allowing Siobhan to carefully monitor Tessa's consumption and to diminish the ill effects of Lucy's overly permissive environment.

To this end, Siobhan had instituted a set of procedures and expectations that needed to be followed to the letter, including where the girls would sit in relation to the adults as well as their posture and table manners. Beyond that, Siobhan had made it clear there could be no deviations from routine. No visitors, no dinner parties, no meals eaten out. "It's important to cement the new routines without distraction," Siobhan explained to Joey in an email summarizing the rules she planned to cover in her first session with Tessa. "I look forward to seeing you bright and early on Monday morning. If June needs to be at school by eight, we'll have to eat breakfast at seven sharp."

At six fifty-five, Joey unlocked the back door to his former kitchen. He held it wide open, saying nothing, watching his daughters' faces. Tessa edged around him with excruciating slowness, feigning indifference with a heartbreaking lack of conviction. June followed, carrying her backpack like a baby and bravely trying to smile at Siobhan as if she might compensate for her sister's lack of warmth.

Siobhan hurried to usher them in, her manner that of a hostess greeting guests. The round kitchen table was set with an unfamiliar yellow tablecloth and white napkins. Tessa could not help but notice the irrelevant fact that Siobhan's wrap dress was the same yellow as the cloth, her belt the white of the napkins. Why this distressed Tessa so, she could not say, but her eyes clouded with tears before they were even seated.

"Tessa, can I get you to sit here, please?" Siobhan started, indicating the seat next to hers with a queenly wave of the fingers. "June? You're here. Dad, why don't you take the spot at the head of the table?"

Tessa couldn't decide what offended her more, the fact that Siobhan had called her father by a name she wasn't entitled to use or that the man formerly known by that title appeared to have traded souls with a robot.

Siobhan opened the oven door and pulled out four plates, each with its own perfectly portioned serving: two eggs scrambled with exactly one ounce of grated cheddar, a golf-ball mound of cheese grits (three ounces), a link of tofu sausage, and one piece of raisin toast (two triangular slices spread with two teaspoons of butter).

Siobhan continued to act like everything was hunky-dory, sweeping over to the refrigerator for four small glasses brimming with orange juice. She set the glasses six inches northwest of each plate.

Tessa rolled her eyes at June, seeking conspiratorial rebellion. Instead the younger child had already tucked into her food with enviable ardor.

Tessa shifted herself into the chair across from June, the rigid angle of her chin and forced arc of her lower back speaking volumes. She stared at the plate before her, the segments blurring together, her eyes brimming.

Siobhan took care not to reward Tessa for emotional manipulation, keeping her voice level, matter-of-fact. "Put the fork in your right hand, Tessa," she said briskly. "Dip it in the eggs and bring them to your mouth."

"I know how to eat," Tessa shot back. She used the back of her hand to wipe the tears running freely down her cheeks.

"No, you don't. If you did, you wouldn't be in this position. But I'm going to teach you, or you're going to be sent away to a treatment program. It's your choice," Siobhan said. "June, take your time, now. This isn't a race."

With that, Siobhan bent over her open ledger, entering precise checks in the boxes next to "Breakfast, Day One." Next to that square was a list of nutrients consumed. Two eggs, one ounce cheese, three ounces grits, one slice raisin bread, one tablespoon butter, four ounces orange juice. Each was itemized with its component parts, protein, fat, calories and carbohydrates, calibrated to the last molecule.

When Joey and June finished, they left for June's school. Siobhan stayed at the table with Tessa as she slowly chewed her food. Breakfast took an hour to consume, but Tessa was given no choice. She sat there, chewing and swallowing, tears spilling down her cheeks. There was nothing else but this yellow table, these white napkins, this woman she didn't trust, didn't even know, watching her every move. When it was over, a marathon of moving her jaw around progressively more disgusting textures that forced her to break her fast, Tessa was expected to sign her name in the ledger, next to "Breakfast."

It was as simple as that. Compliance was key.

Siobhan then handed Tessa her algebra textbook, a tablet of paper and two sharpened pencils. "You'll do your work in here, with me. Later, we'll take a stroll around the house and talk about the rules. Then I'll drive you to therapy."

That said, Siobhan embarked on her own version of therapy, a habit she'd kept up for more than a decade. That year's ledger, identical to the others, was an oversize book bound in forest-green vellum, dense with information. Siobhan had brought it into the kitchen from her bedroom in a leather briefcase, where it nested with an aqua marbleized pen and a pair of scissors, part of the nutritionist's specialized tool kit for personal reflection.

And reflect she did.

Indeed, on any given day, in each appropriate page and column, Siobhan's experiences were documented in stunning detail. Hours slept, foods consumed, hours exercised, muscle groups worked, money earned, money spent, pounds weighed, pages read. And so forth. And so on.

In subcategories, Siobhan annotated her numbers with descriptive titles. For example, under "Nutrients Consumed," she would list first the calories, then the fat, protein, fiber and carbs, followed by, in exquisitely small cursive, "Date bran muffin," "Carrot juice," "Albacore tuna in spring water," "Miniature dill gherkin." When it came to "Networking Contacts," Siobhan would list her clients' names as well as phone numbers, hair colors, body types, training goals and ethnic backgrounds. Under "Nightly Reading" she listed such titles as "CliffsNotes: *War and Peace* or "*US News and World Report*" or even, when she was in a lighter mood, "*Cosmopolitan* magazine: 'The You He Needs.'"

There were also entries for expenses. These were tax-deductible and could be submitted to the children's trust for reimbursement. All food costs and mileage were documented to the nearest penny. Little things added up, after all. Besides, even if Siobhan had been born with a silver spoon in her mouth, she reminded herself, it would have been insane not to document the four miles to Piggly Wiggly at forty-eight and one half cents per mile, or her number-two pencils, fourteen, at one dollar each.

The ledger also functioned as a scrapbook, featuring newspaper articles about Kicks! or photos of Siobhan and her dance teams pasted into a special section called "Celebrations!" These special sections were sorted chronologically and framed by backgrounds appropriate to the activities themselves. Siobhan had chosen pink for the ballet recitals, black for hip-hop, purple for poms, and green for the clippings regarding promotions, raises or employee awards.

For every year of Siobhan's life since she had finished college, there existed an evergreen, vellum-wrapped book, each one a treasure trove of pertinent detail. She stored these journals in a small bookcase near her bed, allowing herself the comfort of paging through them from time to time, particularly when she was discouraged or confused. Siobhan's life was capable, she felt, of passing by so quickly that it might otherwise have been forgotten. These ledgers were a bulwark against loss. Filling in the blanks served an important function, but more than anything else, the practice offered a reference point for everything she did, a proof to herself that she actually did, in point of fact, exist. Indeed, it wasn't unusual for Siobhan to find herself more excited about the documentation of certain things she did than the actual doing of the thing she'd be writing about.

All in all, Siobhan found filling in her ledgers a pleasant addiction. Certainly, in the life she'd fashioned for herself, there was nothing quite so satisfying as keeping counts, the steady accumulation of completed squares filling in the snowy void of graphing paper with evidence of human progress in the shape of her own particular alphanumerics: fleet, irrefutable, right.

Martha and Susannah had taken it upon themselves to make sure that Lucy's first night without the girls and Joey wasn't spent alone. They'd arrived at six thirty bearing gifts: two bottles of pinot grigio, a pot of filé gumbo from Sapphire and a small wrapped box, something Susannah insisted Lucy open as soon as they walked in the door.

"You don't need to charge it," Martha explained as Lucy pulled away the glossy paper to unearth a sleek silver cell phone. Her friends, knowing her, had already programmed this model with important phone numbers, already entered her name as the caller of record, already jumped through the initial hoops of ownership in Lucy's name. They'd removed all traces of its original packaging, this last a precaution they'd learned through experience.

"Now listen, you can't return it. We've already broken it in, hon. You need it. See, here—the girls can text-message you on this screen."

Martha demonstrated this to Lucy by pulling up a short missive from June composed largely of abbreviations.

4-got 2 say ur gr8 :)

Lucy smiled through a sudden blur of tears, frantic to respond in kind, while at the same time she was recoiling from the new technology with the entire upper third of her body.

"Okay, so here's how you write back," Susannah said patiently, squeezing Lucy's arm. Susannah had spent the last twenty-four hours getting a crash course from her daughters in the fundamentals of text messaging. "Trust me, it's not that hard. I know you can do it," she repeated reassuringly. Lucy's aversion to technology was, like her obsessive tidiness, a well-established fact.

Martha poured them each a glass of wine and handed Lucy hers. "Loosen up, honey."

Lucy, whose brain had frozen, could not process a word Susannah was saying. She reached out tentatively and then pressed so hard on the keypad that she knocked it out of Susannah's hands. It clattered onto the floor, causing Lucy's body to go into a full-throttle flinch. "Shit, I can't do this! Now I've broken the damn thing!"

"Calm down," Martha said. "I promise, it won't bite. Here, take a slug of this wine and we'll help you write back."

"What does Siobhan say—is this allowed?"

"It's none of her business. Who does she think she is? It's not her call to effectively cut off all contact between you and the girls. That's not good for either one of them! I still can't believe the bitch didn't even copy you on the email she sent the rest of us about Tessa's treatment."

"It's okay. Joey showed it to me," Lucy murmured, distracted by competing questions. "Look, like it or not, the way Siobhan's going about it seems to be the way treatment works. I've been looking into it. It's almost like they've got to take away Tessa's identity in order to build it back up. I'm pretty sure her phone will be turned off until she earns the right to use it."

"Tessa is one thing. But there's no reason to punish June. And she's been wanting a cell phone forever."

"Wait, how did *June* get a phone?"

Susannah's features were concentrated on the task at hand, that of seeing if the phone would work after the first of what would, given Lucy's panic at all things technological, be one of many close calls combining minimum know-how with maximum impact on unforgiving surfaces. "Willow got two for her birthday. We couldn't return it."

"She needs to have a way to reach you," Martha added.

"Joey's okay with it?"

"I haven't had a chance to mention it to him. Or Siobhan. But I will," Susannah said.

Martha snorted at the note of apology in her tone. "Why would Siobhan have any say over June anyhow?"

Lucy ignored the question. "Well, Joey needs to know," she said, feeling so lost in the ether of their changed relationship that she couldn't discuss it with anyone, not even her best friends.

"Lucy, it's not really *yours* to tell. It's Susannah's gift actually. Don't make a big deal out of it. We just want June to have contact with you right now. She needs a way to feel connected when she's lonely without having to ask permission from Nurse Ratched."

"It's not that big a deal, Lucy," Susannah said. "Willow got two of these for her birthday, one from Darryl and one from my parents. I don't think Joey was against cell phones in principle or he'd not have let Tessa have one."

"I don't know." Lucy kept her tone even. "I just—I think we need to be very straightforward and not muddy the waters."

"How does June's being able to reach you when she's scared, or call Willow, how does that compromise anything at all? I'll be happy to mention it to Joey, as soon as we get a chance to talk," Martha muttered. "While we're on the subject, where is he? Sateesh left a ton of messages and Joey didn't answer all weekend. Said he dropped his phone in the ocean or some such nonsense."

"True story," Lucy said, raising her fingers to cover her mouth, holding back a moan that moved up through her chest, warming her throat. It was quieted only through a transcendental effort at detachment on Lucy's part. She swallowed. "What did Sateesh want?"

"To see if the girls wanted to come in and make macaroons with him. Plus I'd asked him to make sure Joey knew the Tweedle twins had signed off on Siobhan's payment."

"I still can't believe they gave in so easily!" Susannah sighed. "What a relief! I never thought—"

Lucy put her fingers over the new cell phone, aligning its position on the table with the edge of her placemat. "Clover was right. She said she'd get the Cameron brothers to see the light and she did! Who knew? Maybe they're not—"

"The spawn of Satan?" Martha asked. "Don't count on it. I don't know what they've got up their sleeve but I still don't trust them. It doesn't compute they'd roll over and play dead when they have a snowball's chance in hell to yank my chain. If anything makes me even more skeptical about this dance Nazi than I already was, it's the fact that the Camerons insisted on a sit-down with her all by themselves. They didn't even include Clover."

Lucy's own sentiments were, if anything, equally wretched and ill-explained. This made her so ashamed she found herself rising to defend Siobhan. "Martha, things are bad enough without borrowing trouble we don't even know we've got. Let's try to give this woman the benefit of the doubt and stop being so . . . catty."

Martha's cheeks flushed. She poured more wine and took a long sip. "You're right. I'm a complete bitch. But there's something about this that makes me nervous."

"I think we all are," Susannah said, taking Martha's free hand, gripping it tightly with her own. "Martha, why don't you warm up the gumbo and Lucy can show me what she's accomplished on *The Three Graces?*"

Martha rose from her seat so quickly she rocked the table, tipping the wine bottle before reaching out to steady it. "Don't give me a hard time, Lucy. Remember, I'm a Yankee. I didn't get that Southern-girl memo on how you're not s'posed to say *shit* even when your mouth is full of it."

* * *

Martha wasn't sure what was more embarrassing, the fact that she'd loved *Gone with the Wind* as much as she had, or that she'd swallowed hook, line and sinker some romantic notion of the South as a bona fide *place*. By the time Penelope had finally convinced Martha to visit her in Omega, Martha had lived in Virginia long enough to quash her nostalgia for a place she come to realize had never existed, not even in the good ol' days of yore. Hell, Southern History 101, that was one myth toppled after another. Martha's unspoken assumptions were shells of their former innocence, arranged like headstones in the graveyard of her imagination, displaced by the sad grit of the true past: Celtic debtors exiled to Georgia on filthy brigs, slave ships carrying victims of what wasn't the first and wouldn't be the last mass American tragedy, the decimation of native Indian tribes, the ongoing institution of cruelty to others upon which those stunning plantations like Tara would have depended.

Still, truth be told, Martha's fantasy of the South, unspoken and unacknowledged, had only been swept under the rug of her psyche. Every now and then, when she couldn't get to sleep, Martha would find herself drifting into this mythical South as a means of escape. The town was all front porches and shady lawns and lemonade, with a steady pulse, no pressure to be perfect. Maybe there was a gazebo or two in the middle of town where the paint never chipped, the camellias never needed deadheading and dogs never shat. It was soft and blurry at the edges the way Martha's Mississippi grandmother's voice had sounded on the rare occasions she was allowed to visit, before Martha's mother had divorced her father and prevented the child from seeing him or her grandmother.

By the time she'd spent seven years in Charlottesville and had finished law school, Martha was absolutely confident she'd tamed the beast that dared not speak its name, worshipper at the church of William Faulkner, Walker Percy, Eudora Welty, Kaye Gibbons and Pat Conroy. In fact, as fate would have it, the beast was only dormant and waiting to be revived, all the more so because after nearly a decade of living in the South, Martha had fancied herself well past such sentimental journeys.

She'd already been courted by firms from Miami to Maine when Penelope called on behalf of the Cameron Foundation, offering to fly her down to visit and look around. "My dad wants to retire. You'll get to spend a weekend with your old girlfriends if nothing else. Or are you droppin' us now that Wall Street is callin'?"

When Penelope had picked her up at the airport to show her around, Martha had few expectations other than a boozy weekend with her college buddies, each of whom had already been induced, enticed or, in Joey's case, seduced into moving to Omega. There was no summoning of defensive strategies, since Martha had already decided to refuse the offer she knew Penelope was planning to tender.

Unfortunately, or fortunately, depending on which side you took, Omega ended up being a hell of a lot more charming than Martha had expected. All this despite the fact that it wasn't technically in the South but in the northernmost corner of Florida, a state she'd always equated with retired golfers and Disney World.

Saying *North* before *Florida* would become a distinction Martha would take a while to get, a difference she hadn't known to hang on to until Penelope explained, "In Florida, the further north you go, the deeper south you get. We like to call this the Real Florida."

"As opposed to the pretend?"

"Exactly. We aren't a mess of concrete and plastic and sand. Our roads aren't lined with billboards and we're not one big flat mall. Hell, as a matter of fact, the shopping here is awful, but you'll like the seafood, I promise. And hey, just look up, girl."

The street they were barreling down in Penelope's father's Carrera was one of Omega's sacred canopy roads, a quiet tunnel of gray and green that formed an overhead trellis of vines and leaves. Along the sides, nothing but more lush green, punctuated by bushes, branches and wisteria vines with blossoms that formed perfectly identical spades of purple petals. The air was fragrant with honeysuckle and permeated by a mossy, dank undercurrent. Penelope was pointing at the overgrown vines. "Other places, people plant a garden. They water it, stake and weed it. Then they pray for it to grow. Here in Omega, you plant your garden and spend the rest of your life trying to beat it back with a stick."

Try as she might, Martha had found her urban ambitions melting in the musical warmth of Penelope's voice, in the face of Omega's idiosyncratic neighborhoods, houses placed next to each other without regard for similarity of size, style, social status or zoning codes. A ranch with a Jetsons carport might perch atop a mound of hill like the crown that Jack broke, overlooking a large Victorian set too close to the curb and surrounded by every lawn statue known to man. Then, on the right, a rambling flagstone of Tudor sympathies would open its gables in the middle distance to a discreet gazebo that looked as if it were nicked from the Victorian two doors away under the noses of gnomes, fairies and a family of Bambis. These egregious clashes of style were tempered by the fact that the entire town appeared to be under a blanket of vine, whether Confederate jasmine, ivy, wisteria, honeysuckle or the million other species that climbed in where they weren't invited. These plants threw themselves across streets, rivers and paths and generally cloaked the dissonance of Omega's architectural range with a single wave of green that thickened as it traveled east and descended to dense forest before drowning itself in swampy marshes.

By the time Penelope's convertible had landed at what would eventually become Lucy's beach property, Martha was a goner. She was already formulating the words to explain her decision to her mother in Poughkeepsie, who would, she knew, be furious.

Indeed, her mother's reaction to the news, a bitter litany of the ways in which her daughter had deserted her, had provided Martha with an additional incentive for accepting Penelope's offer: the distance it would put between herself and the home she'd grown up in.

"Or *not*," as Martha was wont to add whenever a slip of her

tongue led a listener to assume Martha's upbringing might have
been somewhat normal.

From the age of eight, Martha had been sent to boarding
schools and summer camps, spending very little time at home. In
Martha's case, this may have been a kinder fate than it would or-
dinarily seem. Martha's mother battled severe depression, which
manifested itself in an obsessive quest to uncover flaws in herself,
her daughter, her husband and her extended family, in that order
and with descending levels of intensity.

After college, Martha had tried to reduce her exposure to these
fault-fests, as she called them. She'd fly home once a year, by herself. Sateesh would always volunteer to go along, but Martha knew
better. Her husband's dark skin would have provided a field day
of backhanded insults and spring-loaded inquiries, this from the
very same mother who'd proclaimed Martha's father's Mississippi
derivation reason enough to assume he and his family were too
racist to ever be allowed in his daughter's presence once the marriage imploded.

Such inconsistencies were the stuff of her mother's madness,
something Martha had given up trying to reconcile or even understand. Indeed, Martha blithely claimed that growing up in a crazy
household had put her at a real advantage for her career.

The law, she pointed out, was just one more labyrinthine system of contradictory rulings, with the advantage being that its
logic had been somewhat codified, with precedents established.
"At least in law you get to argue your case!" Martha would laugh,
as if it was no big deal to have a mother like hers, as if her upbringing were simply a slightly amusing boot camp of the brain rather
than an emotional obstacle course rigged against its sole competi-
tor from the very beginning.

Glib references to her childhood notwithstanding, Martha had
felt terribly responsible for her mother's unhappiness, all the more
so when she'd stopped flying and effectively stopped visiting her
mother. She knew she could have driven to see her but kept finding reasons why she couldn't take the trip. It wasn't until a couple

of years into therapy that Martha finally wondered whether her fear of flying had more to do with avoiding her mother than it did with her fear of a plane crash.

"I feel terrible. I know she's really lonely. She's got no one else. I'm such a wimp," Martha had said during a particularly grueling therapy session.

"Not at all," her doctor had replied. "I think this fear of yours is an emotional survival strategy. After all, if you can't fly, you can't easily visit, can you? And I have to say, you, Martha, I can help feel better. But your mother, she will never get better. You've got to decide whether you're going to spend the rest of your life taking care of her, which will probably kill *you*, or begin to take care of yourself the way you deserve."

Sateesh had agreed with Martha's doctor. Of course this was a man who'd last seen his parents when he was sixteen years old, the day his father had beaten his sister unconscious. Sateesh had cashed in his savings and bought a ticket to London, where he'd lived with a rich childhood friend of his mother. "Each time you come home from seeing her, you don't sleep for a week. Why should you force yourself to get on another plane? I know you might like to get away with your friends occasionally, but truly, Martha, I've traveled the world enough for three lifetimes. Too much. And when I think of what could have happened to you on the way home from Phoenix, well, I can only say that for me, I'm finished. Lesson learned. Thank God I wasn't at the airport or my hair would now be completely white."

Martha had told Sateesh about the man she'd met in baggage after landing, whose wife and four children had been on the plane and who was saying to anyone who'd listen how terrifying it had been to hear the announcement that the landing gear wasn't working, to watch the runway being coated with fire-retarding foam, to watch several emergency vehicles move into position. "My life would have been over," he'd repeated blankly, as if unaware that his listeners, the plane's passengers, might have felt a certain ownership of that particular phrase, at least technically speaking.

◆   ◆   ◆

Lucy's cell phone buzzed in the middle of the night, or what seemed like the middle of the night. At first, she couldn't fathom what the sound was. Lucy's reaction was much like that of the three dogs, who'd surrounded the small vibrating creature twisting on her dresser, growling back at it. "Hush, it's okay," Lucy ordered.

Her posture as she approached the phone on her dresser was so at odds with her words, however, that the dogs continued their noisy standoff. The fact was, Lucy felt just as dumb and helpless as any other living creature after being startled from a deep sleep by this new, disconcerting rumble. Lucy crouched tentatively as if facing a frog that might jump forward without warning. She opened the phone to see a large "11:00 PM" in the top left corner of the screen.

Eleven was earlier than she'd have thought it was but awfully late for June to be calling on a school night.

"Sweetie? You okay?"

"I miss you."

"I don't miss you," Lucy said in a deadpan voice. "I super-infinity miss you."

"Miss Siobhan says Rocky can come live with us."

"Oh, honey, I'm so glad! I knew she would."

"But what if he misses Precious and Bijou?"

"Oh, I think he'd miss you more. Besides, I could bring them by now and then. Maybe we could take them for walks." Lucy's voice could not help but rise at this new possibility, an excuse to see June every day.

"Miss Siobhan said old dogs don't like new tricks."

"She did?"

"That's what made me wonder—maybe Rocky wouldn't like it here."

"He'll get used to it," Lucy said, thinking that June might be projecting her own discomfort onto Rocky's future. "You will too, sweetie. Remember, this is good for Tessa."

"I know," June muttered quickly. "Lucy? If I called 911, would they be able to see where I was?"

"You bet," Lucy replied. "Besides, there's an alarm system in the house. And those security guards drive around the block in your neighborhood just making sure everything's safe. I know for a fact the bad guys avoid houses with alarm systems and roving security patrols."

"Will you bring Rocky in tomorrow if Daddy doesn't come out to get him?"

"I would love to."

"Do you really think he'll be okay? Maybe Miss Siobhan's right."

"About what, sweetie?"

"Old dogs can't do new tricks."

"If that's true, then how come you've been able to teach Rocky so many new commands? He didn't learn to fetch until he was eight years old. And you taught him that. Either he's not an old dog or maybe that saying is just a load of hooey."

"He still chews, though," June muttered.

Lucy laughed, thinking of Rocky's zest for paper products.

"Lucy, can you stay on the phone for a minute?" June asked quietly. "Will you tell me a story?"

By the time Lucy got to the part where Rocky and Precious had built a house out of pinecones, she could hear June's even breathing at the other end. Still, she kept on talking, just to make sure, until she'd finished the familiar story. "Night, Juniper," she whispered. She closed the phone with a gentle snap and vowed to mention June's new cell phone to Joey the first chance she got.

As it happened, however, when Lucy saw Joey, cell phones weren't in the realm of thoughts that crowded her brain, elbowing one another out of the way. Besides, her mouth was occupied in communicatory pursuits that were preverbal. Joey had called Lucy's landline a few minutes after she'd hung up with his daughter.

They'd agreed to meet a block from the house. Lucy would bring Rocky with her to the neighborhood's small park, where she and Joey could walk and talk.

Instead, Rocky was tied to a metal swing set and Joey had pinned Lucy against the hurricane fence. He was giving her a going-over that would shock onlookers, were they able to see in the dusky night. Lucy, meanwhile, found herself looking to the heavens for a means of not screaming, her breasts exposed in the chill, her belly wet with kisses, her body sopping with tortured relief at the mouth she'd missed as though it had been her own.

She pulled Joey up by his hair, hungry to kiss him. A thought flitted into and out of Lucy's brain, unsolicited, unwelcome, but joltingly true just the same. This sex, so seamless, no condom, no need for it, this too was, at least partly, like so many other details affecting their life, Penelope's doing. Joey's vasectomy was inextricably linked to the circumstances of his marriage. On the other hand, Lucy's insistence on condoms with previous lovers had been more a form of separating herself from them. Her many long distance love affairs had been a holding pattern that allowed her to withdraw from the universe in which what she had wanted most was forbidden her. There was a dissonance between mourning Penelope and the exquisite lift Lucy felt at that moment, a collision of logic and loyalty that defied reconciliation. All cognition had fled. The man denied her was now inside her as though he'd been there forever. His hands had wrapped hers until they hurt, pressing into the rough metal octagons of the fence until the sense memory had printed itself deep inside her. She wondered at the geometry of it, pulsing outward eightfold, over and again. "Joey," she called, causing Rocky to leap against his leash for a chance to save her.

The opposite of love is not always hate. Sometimes, the opposite of love is a certainty born of limited experience and honed by the absence of imagination. When Siobhan had made her impulsive decision to follow Joey to the park, she was motivated by the need she observed on the man's face as he'd left the house, a need she could not help but think to meet.

It would never in a million years have occurred to this pretty young sylph that the urgency she'd noticed in Joey might have something to do with Lucy. Hadn't he himself told Siobhan only days earlier that he and Lucy were not involved?

There'd been no deceit in the man's body language, no eyes floating up to cover a lie, no muscular bunching to show a boundary breached. Besides, Siobhan would have reminded you, were you to accost her as she stopped on the street and faded into the trees bordering the park, Lucy was *old*. Also, Siobhan could not help but notice—her fitness professional's eye trained to notice—that Lucy had let herself go. As far as Siobhan could see, Lucy, the artist, fit the bohemian mold Siobhan had constructed to contain her: eating, drinking and throwing herself into her painting projects while Joey's children had languished in a no-man's-land of low expectations, allowed to do whatever they wished even as it jeopardized their health.

Lucy was, in Siobhan's universe, simply not in the realm of Joey's romantic possibilities.

The park was deserted. Neighborhood preschoolers had been tucked into their beds hours before, as were June and Tessa. Siobhan had declared lights-out at nine o'clock, no ifs, ands or buts. This was all part of the family's new, improved household regimen.

At midnight, she had stood outside the door of each girl's room, looking for telltale signs, a crack of light under the door, a buzz of headphones surreptitious and blurred, a stirring of sheets, a shifting of springs. *One–one thousand, two–one thousand.* Siobhan had stood sentry, keeping silent count past the two-minute mark.

Satisfied they were truly asleep, Siobhan had run downstairs and down the hall, knocking on Joey's office door just as he was hanging up the phone.

"I'm meeting Lucy," he explained. "She's bringing Rocky."

"So late? But aren't you tired? Do you want me to go?"

"No. That's okay. It's just down the street."

"Just down the street" meant lots of things, as it happened. This insight dawned on Siobhan as she patiently waited for Joey to get rid of Lucy and take the bleeding dog for its walk. This was the point at which Siobhan planned to appear on the sidewalk, to meet him halfway home, to suggest they walk and talk. Joey's kinesthetic orientation, a phrase that had come to Siobhan out of the blue from an educational psychology course, would surely benefit from a chance to connect thought to movement.

Jesus. The man was moving, but it wasn't at all what she'd thought of when she'd blithely recaptured terminology from graduate school. By the time Siobhan had trudged slowly home, she found herself captive to an image of Joey splayed crucifixional against the fence, his brawny shoulders heaving in time to Lucy's whimpers and the dog's slow, crying whine.

Tucking herself into her sheets that night, Siobhan was struck by an odd sense of defeat, of having lost a battle she'd not even begun. *Jane Eyre* was not a book she'd read, not even in CliffsNotes. Still, the archetype of the pretty young governess, the Gothic mansion, the grieving widower and his secrets—somehow these notions must have crept into Siobhan's expectations through the collective unconscious. Lying there in the muddled darkness, Siobhan felt very alone. More than that, however, she felt almost undone by the terrific unfairness of having a golden opportunity dropped into her lap only to have it snatched back, and, worst of all, by the very woman whose influence she'd been hired to redress.

Chapter Fourteen

Two days later, Joey was visiting Phoenix. It was one o'clock Mountain time, and Joey had already wrapped up most of his work. The project he'd flown out to see had already surpassed its yearly benchmarks. The meeting had gone smoothly, preceded by a PowerPoint presentation with smiling kids, graphs with climbing arrows and a walking tour of the project's premises. Just as Joey was finishing up his formal meeting with the staff, the executive director pulled him aside and asked if they could talk privately.

The words came out of Joey's mouth before he had a chance to think. "How about the Ritz?" he'd asked. "You know it?"

"Perfect," the director had said. From the look on his face, Joey couldn't tell if he was being a wiseass about the contrast between the poverty his program ameliorated and the luxury symbolized by the hotel, or whether his surprised expression was simply due to the fact that he'd not thought Joey would be so quickly available. Whatever it was, Joey didn't really give a shit.

The drive was a quick trip up Piestewa Peak to Camelback, a route he knew so well the car just about drove itself. The Ritz-Carlton hotel, a pink diamond-shaped building near the Biltmore shopping district, was where Joey and Penelope had stayed on their first trip to Phoenix and for many years thereafter.

Joey pulled his rental convertible into the half-moon drive, handed the valet his keys and tipped his sunglasses back like a headband above his ears. Even with this automatic caution, he couldn't see in the lobby, blinded by the light.

A bellhop flashed his teeth in a smile, forgiving Joey his lack of luggage, following his progress through the lobby and toward the bar, the assorted geometry of which was slowly presenting itself to Joey as his pupils adjusted.

It was in this building that Penelope had told him she was pregnant with Tessa, here that they'd sketched the renovations to the house on High Street, here that they'd decided to have another baby. Penelope had insisted the place gave her good luck, returning time and again until that very last visit with her girlfriends, when the landing gear had malfunctioned on the flight home.

After that, she'd insisted just as vehemently that they stay at the Biltmore, just a few blocks away.

"The Ritz got old," she'd explained "Besides, Frank Lloyd Wright started his life over at seventy-two when he moved out here to build the Biltmore. I like the symbolism in that."

Joey understood the way his wife's brain worked. If she needed to displace her anxiety about flying into the body of the hotel she'd favored instead of the transportation that nearly killed her, it was a fortunate accommodation to what otherwise might have put her in Martha's shoes, leaving her constitutionally unable to board a plane.

Besides, Joey liked the Biltmore Hotel.

In fact, in some ways, he'd been grateful for the near miss on the plane. It meant that he and Penelope had subsequently done most site visits together instead of apart.

This had been one of Penelope's many first-day-of-the-rest-of-her-life resolutions. Martha's refusal to get on a plane and Susannah's divorced-mom status may have been the necessity that mothered Penelope's new invention, but Lucy's willingness to accept the beach house as a means of support, freeing her up to watch their children at a moment's notice, had been the final cog in his wife's reinvented wheel.

"I realize I can't control everything, can't control anything,

really. You gotta live your life like—Jesus Christ, I sound like a
damn Hallmark card! But when my mother died, Joey, I didn't
have anybody. Just Daddy. Now I've got you, I've got the girls. I've
got Lucy—and Clover and my friends. I want to—Here's the thing.
If I put all our daughters' eggs in one basket—me—" Penelope
had stopped talking. She'd pointed her cupped hand at her heart,
an unnecessary but nonetheless poignant directional. "Then I'm
crippling them. Do you see what I mean? It's selfish."

Giving Lucy the bed-and-breakfast had been part of creating
that extended network of support for the children. By giving Lucy
her daddy's house, Penelope had hoped to achieve a sort of as-
sociative transformation between family land and familial bonds,
a kind of adult adoption. This gift made Lucy more than a friend,
more like a sister. In Penelope's mind, if she and Joey were killed,
her girls would still be at home in the world, staying with Lucy and
surrounded by several other people who loved them, Susannah,
Martha, Sateesh, Clover. This was a bit of vaguely articulated social engineering the new-and-improved Penelope couldn't avoid,
despite her lips' moving in time to the quaint notion that there
were things in this world a parent couldn't control.

Joey hadn't been back to the Ritz in years, not since the last
time he'd stayed there with Penelope, but something about sleeping with Lucy had unleashed a perverse nostalgia for his wife and
a simultaneous sense of distance from her, a gap he hoped to close
with this trip down memory lane.

When the executive director of the Phoenix Neighborhood
Initiative arrived, he looked nervous, causing Joey to wonder just
what kind of bad news had to be discussed privately. On the other
hand, the man might just have been worried about something un-
related to their meeting.

"Gabriel is loony-tunes but he's crazy like a fox," Penelope had
said when she'd bucked the rest of the foundation board to insist
they fund Gabriel Sorensen's initial proposal, a community development center with a pragmatic and comprehensive approach
to economic and social problems. The Phoenix Neighborhood

Initiative began with a community garden, local food co-op and credit union. Over the years, it had branched out to include a free health clinic that provided medical, dental, nutrition and wellness programs; a rigorous charter school with preschool and after-school services; and a series of peer-to-peer mentoring networks.

Sorensen was wearing his signature seersucker suit with Teva sandals, looking like a Nordic Jesus as he shook three waiters' hands on his way to the table. He was a Viking Jesse Jackson figure in Phoenix, having rocked more boats than Melville's whale in the handful of years since his program had gotten started.

His accomplishments, however, were as outsized as his rebellious profile, earning spreads in the *New York Times*, the *Washington Post*, *Vanity Fair* and the L.A. *Times* as well as *Mother Jones* and the *Utne Reader*. What made his message so compelling, apart from his considerable magnetism, was his backstory. Gabriel had been a typical spoiled rich kid until the age of twenty-four, when he'd quit his father's company, a highly profitable chain of convenience stores whose business had been built upon bilking the same underclass his initiative was aimed at saving. Over the past seven years, with the help of Cameron Foundation money, Sorensen had spread his own unique form of economic democracy to anyone who'd listen, a combination of fuck-you-and-that-corporation-you-rode-in-on populism with self-sufficient grow-your-own-prospects pragmatism.

"Hey, Joey," Gabriel said, pulling his patron up for a man-hug before settling back into the banquette and taking a fistful of nuts from the plate in front of him. Before Joey had time to ask if he wanted a drink, their waiter appeared with a shot glass and a bottle of Dos Equis.

"They know you here, huh?" Joey asked.

"Yeah, back in the day when I was working for my dad's company I might as well have had a booth named after me. The money I spent on booze and drugs was enough to fund a small country. Every now and then I come back just to remind myself of what I don't ever want to turn into again."

"So what did you want to talk about, Gabriel?"

"Look, it's probably nothing, but last week I got a phone call from some guy asking about checks Penelope had written to my wife."

"Your wife?"

"Ex. See, the thing is, my ex-wife, Pasha, is crazy. Not just crazy like fun-crazy, but crazy like certifiable. She's got borderline personality disorder."

"Wait, back up. Why would Penelope write your wife checks? Was she on staff at the initiative?"

"No. See, years ago I made the mistake of introducing Pasha to Penelope. Somehow she got hold of Penelope's cell phone number and kept bugging her about funding a project that rescued lab animals. And when I say bugging her, I mean three or four calls a day."

"So we funded your wife?" Joey asked, trying to remember some detail that would jog his memory. An animal rights group would have stuck out like a sore thumb, however, since that wasn't one of the Cameron Foundation's charitable domains.

"No, at least the foundation didn't. Pasha and her friends didn't have a 501(c)(3). They were more political than charitable. The truth is, I suspect Penelope got so tired of getting phone calls she just wanted Pasha to leave her alone. So she told Pasha to use the money for her cause but not to say anything to anybody."

"Why the secrecy?"

"I suspect the last thing she'd have wanted was every kook in the universe calling her to support their projects. And besides, unless you're into animal rights in a big way, the stuff Pasha's group did was pretty extreme."

"How much money we talking about?" Joey asked, thinking it wasn't that unusual for Penelope to give a thousand here or there to get rid of somebody pestering her.

"The guy faxed me three checks. One was forty, one was thirty and one was forty."

"Who was this guy? And why would he care about small change like that?"

"He claimed to be auditing the foundation accounts."

Joey felt his whole body relax as he connected the dots. "Jesus, that's funny."

Gabriel tilted his head to one side quickly and then tried to smile. He took a sip of his drink. "I'll bite. What's funny?"

"It's a long story, man. I'm sorry they bothered you with this. Penelope's cousins are just trying to piss me off. That's all. No amount of money is too small for their magnifying glass. The pinheads." Joey took another sip of his drink. "I'm trying to remember if I ever met her. Your wife, that is."

"No," Gabriel said. "It was—Penelope told you how she and I met, right?"

"Maybe. Remind me."

"I was in here one night with my dad and she was in that booth over there with a bunch of her girlfriends."

"You met here?"

"Yeah. I'd just told my dad I couldn't work for his company anymore. He left and I stayed to drown my sorrows."

"When was this?"

"Right before I applied to the foundation for my project. That's how I knew to apply. I hadn't even been thinking along those lines but we got started talking and they helped me brainstorm. Anyhow, long story short, I'd been trying to come up with a way of undoing the things we'd done to people."

"We?"

"My dad's company. He ran a bunch of convenience stores with check-cashing and wire services down on the south side. Totally ripped people off. Everything cost twice what it would up in the nicer part of Phoenix. Gas, milk, you name it. Twice the price."

"You quit over that?"

"Sort of. I actually think I might actually have been having a nervous breakdown. But that day I'd been in one of our stores over in south Glendale. This little old lady was trying to wire money to her son in Mexico. Two hundred bucks, and we were charging a thirty-dollar fee just to get it there. I don't know. Something about the way this lady looked reminded me of the woman who took care of me when I was little. It just—I don't know—for some reason, I just flipped out."

"So you quit?"

"Yeah. I just—my dad didn't take it very well. He stormed out of the restaurant and left me sitting there with everyone just staring at me. Your wife took pity on me and asked me to come have a drink with them. One drink led to another. I told Penelope about my idea for the initiative. Just an affordable resident-run store, a community garden, loan co-op or maybe a credit union. She told me to write up a proposal and deliver it the next day. I went home, drank a pot of coffee and typed up my ideas. When I brought the concept paper over, my wife, Pasha, came with me."

"Okay, but I still don't get the connection."

"It's the crazy woman—my ex-wife. She's the connection. I don't know how the auditor got her name. I have no idea what she told him, but I don't know—I just wanted you to have a heads-up about the checks."

Joey laughed. "Look, I doubt forty dollars here and there is gonna get us in hot water. Penelope probably just felt sorry for her."

"Um, Joey, it wasn't forty dollars. It was forty thousand."

"Holy shit. What the fuck was that about?"

"I'm really sorry, man. I never knew about the money at the time, or that Pasha was calling your wife nonstop. I only discovered it, like, a week ago. My ex-wife, she's plain crazy. Who knows what she said?"

Joey shook his head. "Why didn't I know any of this?"

"I don't know." In the silence that followed, Gabriel brushed his silky hair back from his brow and continued. "Pasha was obsessed with research labs, with how they were killing poor defenseless animals. When she got hold of a topic, she wouldn't let go. I'm sorry, man."

"Back up. Tell me more about how this all shook out. When did you first meet Penelope?" Joey asked, a dry tickle coating the back of his tongue.

"I was sitting here. They were at that table right there." Gabriel pointed his finger at a big booth in the corner and made like he was aiming a gun. "When my dad dressed me down publicly and stormed out, I think they just felt sorry for me. One thing led to another. I started rambling about how I had this idea of a community-based development corporation modeled on the old settlement house concept. Before I worked for my dad I did a degree in urban planning and finance."

"How could I not know this story?"

Joey's mood, until now, had been fairly expansive, despite the thought of a hundred ten thousand dollars he hadn't known about. The fact was, and Penelope knew his thinking well, Joey had almost zero tolerance when it came to animal rights fanatics. That alone would have probably kept her from telling him, but what she'd have hated worse was that he'd have insisted she "just say no." Telling people to buzz off had never, ever, been something Penelope had been good at. This was all the more true if someone pressed her over a lost cause.

Still, for some reason, talking to Gabriel in the Ritz bar, Joey found himself bristling. Not only had Penelope failed to mention the checks, she'd never said a word about meeting Sorensen before he put in his application.

It was beyond petty to envy Gabriel Sorensen for time that was long gone. Still, like it or not, that was often the result when Joey heard a story about something Penelope had done without him. It took a scoop out of him, like the storyteller had swiped something precious. This made no sense, but like so many parts of grief that had been irrational and unexpected, this was something Joey had become accustomed to.

As it happened, things only slid from bad to worse with Gabriel's next question. "Whatever happened to that single friend of hers? I've always wondered how she ended up."

"Lucy?"

"Right. Lucy! Pretty girl. Looked damn fine in a bikini, if memory serves."

"She's doing good," Joey said.

That Lucy, a confirmed devotee of the black tank, had chosen that same night to wear a bikini only added insult to the injury of Joey's imagined invasion. His whole reaction was all the more pitiful for its utter lack of legitimacy.

Joey motioned to the waiter for another drink and stilled his Inner Caveman with a bland deflection to professional turf. "Her work is getting pretty well known in the art world."

"Really? Wow, I wouldn't have taken her for an artist. She was really argumentative. I figured she'd make her living in politics or something like that."

"Lucy argumentative?"

"After a few shots of tequila, she gave me a raft of shit about how I was privileged enough to stop feeling sorry for myself. How I needed to get a life. That girl drank me under the table. Put me through my paces."

For Joey, the thought of having lost a night of Penelope's life, one he'd not spent with her, called forward such contradictory feelings—protectiveness, nostalgia, jealousy. Most overpoweringly, he felt a dissonant clamor of guilt, complicated by enormous irritation at the way Lucy's name had rolled so familiarly off Gabriel's tongue. This was so ludicrous, and yet all the more painful because it was completely unfounded for Joey to find it offensive. Any explanation, even to himself, much less to Sorensen, would sound callow and ridiculous.

It was all water under Joey's already ramshackle bridge. In the meantime, he found himself focusing on the trivial. "Lucy was drunk?"

"Well, that was my impression, but then again, I was pretty far into a bottle of champagne by the time we met. She might not even remember me, now that I think of it."

"I can't believe I never heard about how you all met. How did I miss that story?"

Sorensen looked suddenly uncomfortable, as if he could read Joey's emotions and regretted having said anything at all. "Hey, it wasn't a big deal to any of them, I'm sure. It changed my life, so I remember it. For them, it was just what they did. Besides, I think, well, wasn't there some kind of emergency with the plane on the way home? I thought I remembered seeing it on the news. I didn't even know they were on that flight until I got an email explaining why I hadn't heard anything back on my proposal."

"Oh, *that* weekend. Our lawyer never flew again."

"They had to be all shook up. Shit. Scary. Is that why you came along after that?"

"What do you mean?"

"I don't know, to keep her safe, I guess?"

Joey nodded, even as an awkward pause had infected the space between them, as they both tried to think of something to say that could quickly distract Joey from the truth of what had happened to his wife, the truth of his not having been there to keep her safe that Thanksgiving morning.

"Shit, sorry, man," Gabriel murmured.

Joey, though, had headed off in a completely different direction, only to arrive back where he'd started. The hoops of his memory were wheeling one after the other like old tires on a rutted downhill path: the girls' weekend out west, the landing gear going bad, the end of plane travel for Martha and thus effectively the beginning of Joey and Penelope's second honeymoon as they visited project sites together and Lucy stayed home with their kids.

Lucy stayed home with their kids. Except now she was alone at her house and his kids were with a virtual stranger and Joey's impulse was to get back home again, out of that bar, out of the conversation.

It was coming back to him now, meeting Gabriel Sorensen. He and Penelope had flown out to Phoenix together, stayed at the Biltmore for the first time and visited the Neighborhood Initiative's fledgling program on the south side. Joey remembered how green Gabriel had been. Nervous, eager to please. In fact, as Joey now revisited that first meeting, Sorensen had seemed so inexperienced that Joey had again questioned the wisdom of funding such a novice. Little had he known that before Penelope's wave of her magic wand, the guy was a washed-up corporate suit drowning his sorrows in a hotel bar.

That must have been why Penelope had never seen fit to mention how she'd met Gabriel in the first place, knowing Joey would only doubt the guy's capacities even more. Joey understood this omission as something that happened in every marriage, a means of avoiding argument, nothing more.

Besides, in the long run, despite the chance she'd taken, his wife's instincts had proven right. The Phoenix Neighborhood Initiative had grown social capital like nobody's business in a part of town where Interstate 10 met Interstate 17, a dirt-poor, meth-infested, gang-strafed and godforsaken stretch of abandoned buildings.

In seven years of Cameron funding, the PNI had created a vibrant anchor of self-sustaining services, allowing residents to trade knowledge and skills in subjects as varied as personal finance, home ownership and maintenance, addiction recovery, English as a second language, nutrition, healthy cooking, computers, marketing and car repair. This neighborhood had drawn to it a whole set of mini-enterprises: restaurants, art studios, repair shops, dog groomers, hair salons and immigration attorneys. There'd been a few scrapes along the way: a scandal in the health center involving bulk prescriptions ordered from Canada, a few marijuana plants found in the greenhouse from time to time and a condom-and-needle distribution program that ruffled the feathers of the more mainstream social services. Mostly, though, PNI had done the foundation proud.

"So, anyhow, I just thought I'd better warn you, in case Pasha gets you into trouble with your auditors. She'd say pigs flew if it would give me a hard time."

Joey nodded. "Thanks for warning me. As long as the money came from Penelope's private account, it's none of their business. I'm sorry they saw fit to make your life miserable. Who approached you on this?"

"The guy I talked to claimed he was an auditor."

"English accent?"

"No. He sounded Southern to me. He faxed me copies of the canceled checks. That was the first I knew about them. Then I got a call from Pasha on my answering machine with her usual download of bullshit."

Joey shook his head sympathetically. However much he missed Penelope, he couldn't imagine being estranged from her or having to go through the bitter revisionist history that divorce could impose on a marriage. "How long you been divorced? Do you have kids?"

"Two boys. Joint custody, unfortunately. How are your little girls?"

"They're okay. Losing their mom left a few dents and scratches."

"No shit. Being a single dad sucks."

"Well, actually, I've . . . Lucy's been a lot of help."

"Nice. She ever get married, have her own kids?"

Why this question would put Joey on the defensive, he wasn't sure. Were they in court, his answer would have been termed unresponsive, but in a bar, changing the subject was easy.

"Listen—we need to deal with your problem," Joey said brusquely. "Tell me what they're asking you."

"Oh, that." Gabriel groaned. "They've subpoenaed all kinds of shit, back from the beginning. Back when we bought the first building and started digging up the empty lots."

"What's your lawyer saying?"

"He thinks it's a fishing expedition. But to tell the truth, these pro bono guys, at least half the time, you get what you pay for."

Siobhan Fitzpatrick couldn't shake off the image playing in her brain, the tableau: Lucy and Joey in the park. It stuck with the younger woman like a pie in the face. It wasn't so much the sex, it was the architecture of the couple's spines against that ghostly backdrop of fence. They'd seemed so hungry, so lost in each other, like no one else existed.

This disturbing loop began to play over and over again on a

repetitive track in Siobhan's brain. It interfered with her concentration, interrupted her sleep. On the night Joey was away in Phoenix, after two hours of lying against her pillow, rolling over in the dark, shutting out what she couldn't stop seeing, Siobhan couldn't help but wonder what would drive a man to such desperate stolen pleasures. Was he still, after all that time, so captive to his late wife's beck and call that the only person he would allow himself to love was her chosen surrogate?

By the next morning, when she'd roused herself from bed and typed the email she'd been drafting in her head for two days, Siobhan found herself flayed by the question that had finally prompted her to act. What if Tessa's eating problems were linked to her parents' marriage? Was it possible Joey's affair with Lucy had begun long ago?

Before Siobhan had time to close her screen, having done her duty and sent the report, she got a reply from Nigel Cameron on Instant Messenger.

NIGEL: Are you absolutely certain?

SIOBHAN: I've got 20/20 vision.

NIGEL: You didn't happen to get a photo?

SIOBHAN: What kind of pervert do you think I am?

NIGEL: Sorry. Do continue to keep us posted. Have you found anything yet? In the hard drive?

SIOBHAN: Not really.

NIGEL: Peter wants to know. Have you checked her deleted files?

SIOBHAN: No. I have no idea how to do that.

Nigel Cameron pulled his brother's cigarette from his mouth and took a quick hit. "This is terrible news."

"Look, if you want to smoke, buy your own fags."

"Peter, can you please pay attention to me? Do you not understand what Miss Fitzpatrick was telling us?"

"I'm not an imbecile, Nigel. But I thought this was what we were waiting for. Unsuitable behavior by the girls' father. That sort of thing."

"Except that we have no proof. Worse, what if the man's in love with her?"

"Well, all the better. Wouldn't it finally put that ridiculous codicil to the test?"

"Think, Peter."

"If he's in love, wouldn't he have to gain approval of that committee? Oh. *Merde*. But wait, wouldn't Lucy need to recuse herself? She can't very well decide on her own suitability."

"Pursue that line of reasoning a bit further, why don't you?"

"Alright. Haven't we been patiently waiting for the man to want to marry someone? Now it looks as if he might. Which means there's at least a chance that he will lose his post. And who better than a Cameron to replace him?"

"Peter, think."

"Give me my cigarette back. I can't think when you snatch things out of my mouth."

Nigel took a quick drag on the cigarette and pressed it back into his brother's outstretched hand. "Any epiphanies, Peter?"

"No. And stop being so facetious. It doesn't become you one bit. I'm not even properly awake yet. I thought this was just the kind of information we'd been waiting for. We could print out the email from the Irish and show it to the judge."

"Peter, for God's sake, what is the composition of the committee that must accept the man's new wife? Not a single one would oppose Lucy Vargas! Which would mean once Adorno's safely married, not only have we lost any chance to be rid of him, but also we'd be unlikely to find another hot-button issue to divide the trustees."

Peter's mouth opened and shut as he realized what his brother was saying. He reached across the partners' desk in their apartment and pulled a pack of Dunhill cigarettes from a carved wooden box in the middle. "I see. United they stand and so forth. Of course,"

Peter said hopefully, letting a new cigarette dangle from his lips, "the sex could have been a one-off."

"P'raps. I still don't like it."

"Chin up, now. What about the chap in Arizona? Has he found anything promising?"

Nigel shook his head. "He's done everything but bed the beast and she still refuses to fill out the affidavit. She's insisting we go there if we want to know what happened."

"Come now."

"I know. But it may be worth it."

"But I thought the detective said she was mad as a hatter."

Nigel sat up straight and extinguished his cigarette in a nearby ashtray. "Honestly, Peter, how can you be my identical twin? What if she's telling the truth? What if Cousin Penelope did shag the man as a basis for funding?"

"She's dead, Nigel."

"Precisely. But her husband is alive and well. He might be vulnerable to the persuasive powers of suggestion. Who knows what sort of tailspin his wife's infidelity might set into motion?"

"But that's simply spiteful!"

"Why, Peter, thank you so very much for noticing."

Chapter Fifteen

The next morning, after slogging through breakfast with the reluctant Tessa, Siobhan conducted two new searches on Penelope's computer. At the twins' direction, she tracked all files that had been put into the recycle bin. Peter had explained to Siobhan what most computer users didn't understand: once they'd deleted their files, they were still maintaining copies in the electronic equivalent of a wastebasket. This virtual trash can held everything they'd assumed they'd tossed out. Unless they knew to take the second step of emptying it, their discards could easily be resurrected for the discerning eye to review.

Easy was one word for it, gruelling another. Separating the wheat from the chaff didn't happen instantaneously. On the other hand, as Siobhan forced herself to read every single tedious document, she was fueled by her sense that doing so would be instrumental in her work with Tessa. She told herself that in finding out more about the dead Penelope, she would be helping a husband and his children recover from their mother's death. After all, as an impartial, unbiased observer, Siobhan was well suited to detect dysfunctional patterns in Penelope's jottings, patterns that might need to be considered in the difficult chore of retraining Tessa's brain.

While Siobhan may have initially recoiled at the surveillance assigned her by the Cameron brothers, the therapist in her could not look a gift horse in the mouth. Any counselor worth her salt, especially one who'd been paid so handsomely, would need to take family relationships into account.

The more Siobhan read the dead woman's text files, the less she doubted the correctness of her action. Among the recipes and to-do lists, Siobhan found letters from Penelope to Clover, to her friends, her husband and children. There were also journal entries that shocked Siobhan with their brutal honesty and relentless questioning. Penelope's thoughts were jumbled, often angry, confused, even bitterly critical. True, the aim of her anger most often appeared to be Penelope herself, but still, the words offended Siobhan with their messy, often illogical conclusions. As a whole, the image that emerged from these fragmented jottings punctuated by the occasional letter was a far cry from the Saint Penelope her family and friends appeared to have built up since her death. Perhaps it wasn't Siobhan's job to topple false gods, but she could not help but think that, in this particular case, a little bit of truth would go a long way toward setting the girls—to say nothing of their father—free.

One file in particular, a letter addressed only to an indeterminate "Girl," raised questions of such magnitude Siobhan could not help but think it must be relevant to Tessa's disorder. If nothing else, even if the teen was unaware of the issues raised by its contents, the letter hinted at family boundaries having been very clearly breached. Indeed, by the time she had saved this narrative smoking gun, Siobhan found herself troubled only by what she considered logistical issues. Ethical questions paled, after all, when compared to the scale of Tessa's disease, to her father's illusions about his marriage and to his clear dependence on the very person whose actions appeared to have been at the heart of his wife's unhappiness.

The fact that Penelope might have used her journal entries, or even unsent letters, as a sounding board or, more to the point, an emotional spittoon hadn't occurred to Siobhan. Nor did it trouble the young advocate (for that is how she increasingly saw herself: an investigative reporter on the side of good, representing neglected children the world over) to pull this letter free from its mitigating surroundings, the journal entries that preceded and followed its composition. Too often, and Siobhan had seen this over and over again, victims sought refuge in the most extraneous of excuses for why the people they loved had let them down. It was easier to go on pretending that nothing had really happened. Better that than to face the fact that trusting and loving that very person might have been a mistake.

Psychological progress, Siobhan knew, often required a shock to the system.

By printing copies of the letter itself and erasing everything else from the hard drive, Siobhan would accomplish two things. First, she'd cover her tracks, preventing Joey from the all-too-common trap of blaming the messenger and ignoring the message. Second, if he was faced with the remorse and self-questioning of his wife's journal entries, he might be tempted to seek solace in finding mitigating explanations for her betrayal. What Penelope had done to him had been wrong. Unless her husband came to grips with that fact, unmired by equivocation, he'd be unable to break free.

After all, in Siobhan's world, as she often reminded herself, gray was *not* the new black. There was black, there was white, and what was in the middle needed to be assigned to the side of good or of evil. End of story.

"You've a right to be happy. You know that, don't you?"

"Sateesh, I'm fine." Martha laid her hand on Sateesh's breastbone and her head on his bare shoulder. Their bedroom was illuminated only by a thin string of light that reflected off the lining of the curtains.

"What does your therapist say?"

"She says women are different from men. They need to be relaxed."

"What have you got to worry about?"

"Let me count the ways. I've got Tweedledum and his fat brother up my ass. Lucy's out of money and we can't afford to help her. Tessa's going to blow away in the next storm. Oh, and then there's the fact that I didn't get up and run this morning and the race is only two weeks away."

"I'm worried about you."

"Well, stop that, now. I'm already guilty enough."

"But that's exactly the point, Martha. You've nothing to feel guilty about."

"I do, though. I deprived you of children."

"We made that decision together."

Martha rolled over and pressed her head into the pillow, unable to meet her husband's eyes. She stretched her neck and pulled herself up onto her knees, exhaling so deeply that her flat stomach retreated even further into the cavity under her ribs. "You are so good to me," she said. "I'm sorry I'm not more of a sex kitten."

"You're purrfect," Sateesh insisted. He laughed gently, pronouncing the word slowly, with a burr in his voice. "There's no one else in the world remotely like you."

"For which I'm sure the Cameron brothers give thanks and praise on a daily basis. You should have seen them combing over the expense reports this morning! They didn't bat an eye at writing Siobhan Fitzpatrick an ungodly check before she's even started working, but they raked me over the coals about twenty bucks a month for June's and Lucy's new cell phones. Shit, they're like nine ninety-nine a month, which Frick and Frack blow out their ass every five minutes talking to their freakin' solicitor in London. They are so selfish and evil and ugly and fat."

"I wish you'd stop hiding your feelings!" Sateesh laughed, startled by his wife's invective. He sighed and said softly, "Martha Templeton, you mustn't let them get to you. That's all they live for."

Sateesh used his fist to knuckle the small of Martha's back as she rose into a downward-facing dog.

Tightness in her lower back was aggravated by running, a fact that didn't seem to have shrunk her expended miles one measurable bit. It might even, Sateesh reflected, not for the first time, actually have given his wife a perverse pleasure to suffer, much as it floated the Cameron brothers' boat to torture her over the smallest deviations in all things legal.

To change the subject, Sateesh asked how Lucy had reacted to the gift of a cell phone.

"You know Lucy. I think she and Penelope must have attended some secret society at Virginia. You know how many Southerners it takes to screw in a lightbulb? Eight. One to install the bulb and seven to sit and talk about how much better the old one was."

"Penelope wasn't such a Luddite, was she?" Sateesh asked.

"She was! It was like—I don't know—the electromagnetic field of anything with a computer chip would set off her alarm. Ask Joey. Every time he'd buy Penelope a new laptop for Christmas, she'd sneak off to Computer Tutors and get them to replace the new software with exact transfers from the one she had before."

"Well, that makes sense, actually. I hate losing everything."

"You don't have to lose data. You just back up to another drive. But she didn't want anything to *look* different, so there she'd go, throwing good money after bad to install old operating systems that overrode the new ones, just so she didn't have to see new icons, much less cope with progress. Lucy's the same way. She hasn't even learned how to use a digital camera."

"But she says slides have better quality."

"For galleries maybe. But she could do a lot marketing her paintings on the web. I keep meaning to sit her down." Martha rolled over and pulled her knees into her chest. "I worry about her. You know she mortgaged the house when Penelope died so she wouldn't have to take in clients anymore. Now she's lost touch with all the old customers. Even if she wanted to make money again, she'd be starting from scratch."

"Can't we help her?"

"That's why I love you, you beautiful man. I wish we could." Martha paused and then confessed, "Susannah's read me the riot act. The interest rate hikes are killing us, or so she says. I swear, when we took our loan out at five percent, I thought the rate was locked in."

"So did I. But that's water under the bridge."

"But you aren't a lawyer. I should have known better."

"None of us was thinking clearly."

Sateesh was referring to the fact that they'd closed on the restaurant's loan weeks after Penelope had been killed. "Death has a way of doing that, despite Shaw's claim to the contrary."

"What's that?"

"I think it was Shaw who said 'Nothing like death to concentrate the mind.' Something to that effect. Not at all true."

Martha shook her head and rolled back over to rest it on her husband's shoulder. "No, that was Samuel Johnson. 'When a man knows he is to be hanged in a fortnight, it concentrates his mind wonderfully.' Page fifty-six of my high school literature review, bottom-left of the page."

"That memory of yours is a frightful thing."

"If only it were as reliable in recollecting *useful* data," Martha said, sighing. She pressed her forehead against her husband's dark skin and closed her eyes against all those things she could not make herself forget.

At dinner, Tessa chewed her food slowly. She was waiting for the warden, as she'd come to think of her, to look the other way. June had asked for more rice, and Siobhan had gotten excited enough about portion control to allow Tessa a moment's peace. She quickly spat a mouthful of finely chewed rice into her palm and smeared it onto the underside of the table.

"When's Daddy coming back?" June asked. "When is Rocky coming home from the groomer's?"

"I don't know." The irritation in Siobhan's voice was new, something Tessa hadn't yet heard. Siobhan had kept her emotions very visibly in check, but Tessa had perceived a recent change in her manner. Tessa allowed herself a moment to rejoice. If the warden was showing her colors already, it might be just a matter of time before she slipped and fell in front of the grown-ups.

Tessa's relief, however, was quickly dog-heeled by panic. What if Siobhan's anger had something to do with her patient's rebellion at being forced to eat? Had Siobhan found the layers of food pasted under the table?

Tessa moved her knee along the subsurface until she found the hardened ridges of meals gone by. She told herself that if Siobhan had found out why her patient had been so compliant, surely she'd have scraped down the mess. Surely she'd have confronted her prisoner already.

June was trying to cheer Siobhan up. She was babbling about the sleepover at Willow's, though Tessa noticed her sister conveniently forgot to mention the part about not sleeping over. About coming home in the middle of the night.

"We had a conga line and *American Idol* contest and I did a hip-hop split without even trying. We died laughing, it was so funny! Did I say we dressed the cats up like nuns, so when they jumped down from the china cabinet it looked like they were flying? It was so cool and Beasley landed on top of Midnight. Did you know that poodles are good watchdogs? We saw it online. Did you know the worst is a sheepdog? Or maybe it's a Bernese mountain dog. I can't remember."

Siobhan nodded her head like she was really listening. Tessa could see that the warden was totally *not* paying attention. She was smiling like she was, but she was also scanning a huge reference book with numbers in it and writing them in the ledger. Every now and then she'd look over at June and do this fake sweet smile that made Tessa want to vomit, except throwing up was gross.

Tessa may have been anorectic, she may have read online about bulimia, but she couldn't understand how people could make themselves vomit. It was disgusting.

"Tessa?" Siobhan said. "Let's pick up the pace. June's got homework, so, please. Try to be considerate."

Tessa felt her nose stinging with a fresh deluge of tears as she tried to simultaneously chew faster and repress her desire to spit the food out on her plate. The idea of the warden pretending to care about June when it was clear she didn't possess *feelings* was so freaking bullshit!

Suddenly Tessa was furious at her father for being stupid enough to believe in this lady, furious enough that she allowed herself to drift off into her rage. Before she could stop herself, Tessa was struck by a realization.

It wasn't just her father she blamed, but her mom too, gone and buried. Not there to defend herself. This was a sentiment so awful it caused bile to rise in Tessa's esophageal canal. She then lost her focus long enough to actually gag on the mouthful she'd been holding on to, after waiting patiently for an opportunity to disgorge.

Siobhan forced herself to ignore Tessa's theatrics. "June, time to go do your homework," she said. Siobhan then sat working on her various ledgers until such time as the plate Tessa had made such slow progress in cleaning was respectably empty.

When the girl had cleared her plate, Siobhan handed her a pen and offered her the ledger to sign off on her intake. "Okay, why don't you get a head start on tomorrow's assignment? I'll be done in a few minutes and come in to check on you."

Tessa headed into the study, where she and June did their homework. Siobhan could not help but notice that neither child ever used her mother's desk. The nutritionist had even taken the time and trouble to clear it of papers and books, thinking maybe it was too messy for them. Still the girls avoided the convenient surface, balancing their papers on their laps or kneeling at the coffee table to draw.

Siobhan made a mental note to discuss this issue with Joey, for it was becoming ever more clear to her that the man and his daughters were stuck in a rut of denial. Their wife and mother was gone. Not the wife and mother they thought they had, either, and maybe that was the problem. They couldn't get over her loss because they'd all but sainted her. Siobhan felt the same impatient rush come over her that had struck earlier. *For heaven's sake*, she wanted to snap, *it's time to move on.* It may have sounded harsh, but Tessa's health hung in the balance, as did that of June, whose gluttony was just the other side of the anorectic coin.

This characterization of June's eating was not something Siobhan was careless enough to vocalize. Still, it was impossible not to be irritated by the younger girl's hunger, not to notice how greedy she seemed and how unattractive those added pounds looked in a leotard.

"Lucy?" Martha was asking. "Is that you? On your cell phone!"

"It's me," Lucy laughed. "Scared you, didn't I? Are you okay? You don't sound so good."

"Oh, I'm—I'm fine. Where are you?"

"At the groomer, picking up Rocky and bringing him by the house. Oh, hang on a sec."

Lucy dug in her purse and pulled out her MasterCard, which she handed to the girl behind the counter. "You know, on second thought, do you think you can bill this to Mr. Adorno?" Lucy asked. "I can give you the new address."

"Lucy, why don't you put it on the girls' charge?" Martha asked. "And why are you picking up the dog?"

"I gave their card back to Joey so Siobhan could use it."

"But why are you at the groomer, Lucy?"

"They still have my phone number in their computer. Anyway, I guess Siobhan found a tick on Rocky and brought him in."

"*She's* a tick," Martha muttered, glad to have something other than the Phoenix Neighborhood Initiative's audit to get her hot under the collar.

"Martha," Lucy scolded, grinning. "Just a sec." She turned to the clerk at the desk. "I'm sorry. I hate people who talk on their cell phones. So sorry."

"That's okay, but, ma'am, we need payment at the time of service."

"Okay," Lucy said. "Just use my card then. Martha? Let me call you back."

"Lucy! Don't you dare not get reimbursed for that!"

"Hush, Martha." Lucy signed the credit card receipt and moved toward the door with Rocky, who was taking urgent, small steps, his body twitching with what Penelope had called the "pee-pee dance." Lucy opened the door with one hand and followed Rocky outside.

"Why wouldn't Siobhan just fetch him herself?" Martha asked. "When I think of the money she's making!"

"She can't leave Tessa by herself at dinnertime. I had to come in to meet with Clover anyhow, so it's not that much trouble. I didn't want June to have to be without him tonight. Besides, I thought if I brought the dog by, I might get a chance to see the girls real quick."

"Well, come around back to the office when you're finished," Martha said. "We're working late tonight so we'll definitely be here. I'll unlock the door."

When Lucy arrived at the house, Siobhan was waiting on the front porch. She held her forefinger up to her lips. "The girls are doing their homework. Do you want to bring Rocky to the laundry room door? That's where he's sleeping."

"Oh. I thought he'd sleep with June."

"We're working on getting her to understand there's nothing to fear when she goes to sleep. Letting the dog in her room would only reverse the progress she's made and reinforce her sense that she's not perfectly safe alone." Siobhan smiled prettily.

"Do you think I can say a quick hello?"

"I'm so sorry, Miss Lucy. I can't—we really need to hold firm on the rules right now. But I do appreciate you running Rocky over to us. I'm sure the girls will too."

There was something so proprietary in Siobhan's "us" that Lucy had to turn away rather than let Siobhan see her reaction. She hadn't realized how much she'd counted on seeing June, how much missing Tessa and June was wearing away at her.

"You're welcome," Lucy finally said, facing Siobhan with her mouth held tight against any show of weakness. She straightened her spine and stood completely still while her eyes followed Rocky's progress on Siobhan's very tight leash, away from her and down the path to the laundry room door.

Around back, Martha had propped the foundation office's door open with a chair. Lucy let herself in and followed the sound of her friends' voices down the hall. Martha stood next to Susannah's desk, holding the phone to her ear, writing something down on a pad of paper. Susannah, meanwhile, was kneeling up on the seat of her chair, legs in a yogic pretzel under her. She was leaning over her laptop, squinting furiously at the screen.

"Bad time?" Lucy asked. "I just—"

Martha shook her head and pointed toward the only free chair, which Lucy had to clear of magazines before she could sit down. "Susannah?" Lucy whispered, so as not to disturb Martha's phone conversation. "What's going on?"

Susannah shook her head and said, "The Neighborhood Initiative," as though that explained anything. "In Phoenix," she added.

"Phoenix," Lucy repeated blankly, kneeling to begin sorting the magazines by size.

"Don't do that," Susannah scolded affectionately. "How are you?"

"Better than you two, I guess. I just dropped the dog off at the front but the girls were working on their homework—"

"You didn't see June?" Susannah pressed a button and looked up at Lucy. "Willow said she fell asleep in class today. I hope she's not getting sick."

"Me too. God, Susannah, I miss them! Why's Martha on your phone?" Lucy whispered.

Susannah shook her head and pressed a finger to her mouth. "I've got to go to Phoenix. She's trying to sort things out with Delta—"

Martha shot warning looks at Susannah and Lucy, whose conversation was distracting her. She raised her voice to be heard by the Delta representative. "No, that's the flight we want. Just a sec. Hold on a minute. I have to go to my office." Martha laid the phone on its side and headed for the door.

"I thought Joey was already in Phoenix," Lucy said. "Why are you—"

"Just some due diligence stuff with the project out there. Joey's coming home but I want to run out and look at their books just to make sure there isn't anything the Camerons can use against us. Hold on a second . . ."

At this, Susannah pressed several buttons on the keyboard and watched as her screen registered a new series of numeric columns. "There! Sorry, I needed to print that while I remembered. Look, sorry we're so besieged. If you can wait a minute, I can run a check for the groomer, hon. Martha said you paid. So, how are you coping with the girls being gone?"

Lucy shrugged, not trusting her voice to remain steady.

"It's got to be hard for you! Why didn't you get to see them just now?"

"Siobhan said they were doing their homework and with the new program, she—I guess I don't get to see them, at least not right now."

"Oh, hon. I'm sorry."

"I know."

"Look, as soon as this report prints out I can run a check for you."

"Don't worry about it, Susannah. Ya'll are stressed as it is. And I'm late to meet Clover."

Clover was already at the Five and Dime Coffeehouse when Lucy arrived, breathless with her apology. "Clover, I'm so sorry. I had to stop for cash and my card wouldn't work. You're going to have to treat me to a latte."

"Already did, Miss Priss!" Clover said, gesturing toward the mohawk-haired waiter standing with his back to them. The metallic whine of the cappuccino machine made it hard to hear. In the waiter's case, this was just as well. "Halloween is hanging on here I guess." Clover mugged, tilting her head conspiratorially in an overly conspicuous manner toward their Goth server. "Wait till you see what I got!"

Clover lifted three shopping bags and began demonstrating her day's haul to Lucy, who dutifully oohed and aahed at each purchase, a necessary prelude to getting down to the business with which she'd been asked to help. The more confident Clover felt, the better she'd be able to accept any suggestions Lucy might give about her new project and the less Clover would second guess every lift of the brow, twitch of the nose or involuntary coughing reflex.

Clover's idea for the Heavenly Angels website had hit some snags, including a recent Google search that produced several pornographic web pages responding to those exact terms, to say nothing of its fundamental flaw, euphemistically referred to as a "revenue streaming setback." Brett, Clover's husband, had been less tactful. "Who's going to pay to send a prayer when they could kneel by their bed and do it for free?"

When Clover pulled out her new laptop and began booting it up, Lucy whistled. "Nice."

"You should get one, Lucy. They're on sale at RadioShack this week. I could take you over there and walk you through the place. I know you don't like computers—"

"No, thanks anyway. I'm broke as broke can be," Lucy said. "Maybe if my show goes okay—"

"Hell, by then the deals will be gone, sweetie pie."

"It's okay."

"No, it's not. Why are you so broke, hon?"

"No money," Lucy said, laughing a little helplessly at the tautology she'd gotten stuck inside.

"You know—if you need money, honey, I heard about something. I'm not supposed to tell anyone, so you can't either. Not even Brett."

"What?"

"I just refinanced the farm. He wouldn't approve."

"Why, Clover?"

"You gotta spend money to make money. Brett just doesn't understand. This way if I want to make an investment, I don't have to go begging to him. Anyway, I signed the paperwork yesterday and got my cash today. Oh, just put that there." Clover pointed to an adjacent table for the waiter, who was standing with a tray of drinks and no space on their table to set anything down. "*Mucho dinero*, baby."

"That's quick," Lucy said, eyeing the new computer screen. Clover's doe-eyed angels were performing a series of ham-handed somersaults across a space Lucy recognized as the massive front lawn of Clover's farm. "Be careful, though."

"I am! How do I turn up the volume on this thing?" Clover was asking, fooling with the mouse to activate the volume icon. Clover swayed in time to her voice singing "Memory," one of her favorite Barbra Streisand songs of all time. She was grinning at Lucy with that fixed look a particular type of Southern woman got when she was concentrating on a conversation but had simultaneously gotten her features stuck on "smile." "They gave me a twenty grand, 'cash out' just for signing. And the great thing is, I'll make enough with what I borrowed to turn around and pay it all off in three months."

"How can that be?"

"Peter and Nigel told me about it. Get this. You make over a third back on your investment in a single year."

"Are you sure?" Lucy asked. "You know what they say, if it's too good to be true, maybe it is?"

"Oh, I'm sure. This company buys houses for cash. They get 'em cheap and then turn around and flip the property within a few weeks. They're geniuses at *staging*. You want, I'll introduce you to the owners."

"No. I already mortgaged my house two years ago. I can't refinance because I haven't had any income for so long."

"That's crazy. That property's gotta be worth a million-plus by now. How much did you borrow?"

Lucy groaned. "Too much. Believe me, I've tried. No bank will touch me."

"Well, hey, I'm telling you, these people I refinanced with? They were so nice and I didn't have to do anything but prove I owned the property. They just printed out the paperwork, I signed it, and I had twenty thousand in my bank account the next day."

"Wow."

"Look, I'll give you their number. A couple of cutie-pies run the place. They're working out of the Ramada Inn until their office gets built."

"I thought the real estate market sucked right now."

"Not on the coast, honey. Especially not in high-end properties."

"Clover—did you have Martha look over the contract?"

"Are you serious? You know how critical she is! I didn't want to hear it. Besides, she hates the Camerons and would just *have* to ask why I wanted the money. I'm not even s'posed to tell *you* but it sounds like you could use the help."

"But how do you know it's kosher then?"

"Because I know *people*. Here." Clover pressed a business card into Lucy's hand. "It can't hurt to try. Look at it this way. if you make thirty-six percent in a year, that's twenty-somethin' percent more than what you're paying ten percent to borrow. Do the math."

"Is it a fixed interest rate, Clover?"

"A what?"

"Will it stay at ten percent? How do you know they won't raise it later?"

"I don't know. But look at it this way, if it goes up, I'll just refinance again."

"What kind of business is it, Clover? That makes the thirty-six percent?"

"It's coastal real estate. And like Daddy Marcus used to say, God ain't making any more land."

"I don't know—maybe you should tell Brett."

"No, he's a stick-in-the-mud when it comes to money. The man sells insurance, for goodness sake."

Siobhan had barely locked the laundry room door when she heard the sound of June's feet running down the stairs. Clomping was more like it. The child was not exactly light on her feet. Nor was the dog, who had launched himself against the door and begun to whimper.

"I was just coming to tell you your faithful companion's returned from the groomer," Siobhan murmured soothingly to June. "Have you finished your assignments?"

"Rocky!" June sighed happily, opening the door and kneeling to rub Rocky's belly. "Did Daddy get back?"

The ten-year-old had collapsed into a ball on the laundry room floor. Rocky licked her face while his tail thumped against the metal side of the dryer.

"Lucy dropped him off. I thought it would be a nice surprise, since you've been so good, but you can only play with him if you're done with your math."

"Aunt Lucy was here?"

"Miss Lucy, June. Manners, please. Come now, why so glum! Your dog's back. That's good news, isn't it?"

June buried her head in Rocky's fur, which she tried to pretend was Lucy's welcoming embrace. When she looked up, her tears were barely visible, but Rocky was astute when it came to salt, licking them into history before the next pair blossomed from the corners of his mistress's eyes.

"Oh, June, grown-ups can be so *thick* sometimes. I'm so sorry Miss Lucy couldn't come in. I don't know if I mentioned, but my mum and pap were musicians. They never understood what we needed. Always off in never-never land while my brothers and I were practically wasting away. 'You're not hungry already?' my mother would ask, as if it were the worst thing in the world to be wanting supper at eight in the evening. We were just children!

Here now, that's a girl. Let's go into the kitchen and get some water for Rock."

"Rocky," June whispered, moving into the kitchen with the dog at her heels.

"Righto. Rocky, like the boxer. Did you see that movie, June? He does his best to get into shape. Did you see that?"

"Rocky, no!" June scolded. The dog was standing under the kitchen table and rubbing his nose against its underside. June pulled at his collar, but the dog was determined to loosen the hardened bits of food that Tessa had so laboriously set into a solid crust. June knelt underneath the table. "What have you got there?" She turned her head upside down to see what Rocky was trying to get. Before she could stop them, the words were out of her mouth. "Oh, gross! That's disgusting!"

"What's that?"

"There's like —it looks like boogers. Oh, Rocky, stop it! That is too gross! Sick!"

Chapter Sixteen

Sick was what Joey felt when he arrived home to hear more bad news, and sick was how Tessa acted when she was confronted with the stalactites of gunk under the table, and *sick* was the word Siobhan used to explain her patient's regression. No one noticed that June was looking pretty damn ill herself, having gotten her sister into so much trouble that Rocky's return from two days at the groomer had been completely ignored.

"You need to keep your hands in plain sight when you eat," Siobhan told Tessa when they sat down to lunch the next day.

"Daddy? Now that Rocky's groomed, do you think he can sleep in my room?" June asked, seeking to distract him. "Daddy?"

"What?" Joey asked, the knot in his stomach getting tighter with every second that Tessa took to pick up a pea with her spoon.

"Oh, June, you've done so brilliantly sleeping in your own room. Why don't we wait until you've got a couple of weeks of meeting your goal?" Siobhan's brow was crumpled; her eyes were warm with affection; her tone was brisk and cheerful. "You ought to be proud of yourself, overcoming your fear."

June swallowed hard, unable to respond without expressing how much hope she'd pinned on her dog's return to the house. She looked to her father, hoping he'd read her thoughts, save her.

Too bad; he had his eyes trained on Tessa's wobbling spoon,

the slow, slow arc up toward her mouth, the tears coursing down her cheeks.

June felt sorry for her sister. At the same time she couldn't help but blame her for every second of the last few nights she'd endured with her hands white-knuckled on her comforter, her eyes trained on the windows for signs of a stranger's hands, her ears pricked up for the clunk of a ladder, the angry whisper of a glass cutter, the malign workings of a crowbar. The truth was, June wanted Rocky as much for his special sense of smell and hearing as for his comforting bulk.

Tessa was chewing her one pea within an inch of its life. She was summoning up the spit to swallow it. At the same time she was trying to decide whether the potatoes or corn was more difficult to digest.

"Dogs are pack animals. They aren't used to sleeping by themselves," Tessa muttered finally, stabbing the mound of mashed potato with the hoe of her small teaspoon.

Siobhan was unruffled, her voice smooth as glass. She frowned sympathetically at June, as if the dog were every bit as dear to her as he was to Tessa and June. "Well, if you think it's too difficult for him to wait 'til June's met her goal, we could always send him back to Miss Lucy's. I've already mentioned there's truth in that saying about old dogs and new tricks."

"Rocky's not old!" Tessa's voice was sullen. She felt barely able to breathe, hating the Warden, wishing her father would stop looking at her like she was breaking his heart.

June was pained by the discord between Tessa and Siobhan, even as she wished desperately that Rocky could be allowed to sleep upstairs, wished that everyone could get along, wished that Tessa would just feel better. Why couldn't she see that Miss Siobhan was only trying to help her get better?

"Daddy?" June asked. "Did you see what I taught him?"

"No, honey. What?"

"Rocky!" June called, rising to open the laundry room door.

Siobhan cast Joey a quick glance, shifting her eyes toward Tessa's downcast head as if to remind him that his daughter's health was at stake. "Oh, actually, June, I'd rather you didn't bring the dog in here while we're eating. I told you this would be hard," Siobhan said, to no one in particular.

Joey took her comment in, remembering what he'd been told. Tessa would hate her, and probably hate him, and his father's instinct would recoil at how difficult this new regimen was on his daughter. "Show me after we're done, sweetie," he said to June. "We'll take him to the park and throw the ball. Tessa, you want to come?"

Tessa's head reared back on her neck as though her father had suggested she might like to watch Barney videos or take up yodeling. Then Siobhan cleared her throat. This small disapproving gesture had the power to completely transform Tessa's thinking. She nodded and chewed her food at the same time as she raised her spoon for one more bite. Such pacing amounted to warp speed compared to her prior rate of consumption.

"You two go ahead. Tessa and I have miles to go before we rest," Siobhan said briskly, trying not to mind so much that Joey had apparently forgotten the house rules. Tessa couldn't go anywhere until she gained five pounds. Such a suggestion coming from her father now that she'd relapsed was the exact sort of behavior she'd warned him about.

Tessa's eyes clouded with tears, her jaw cramped and she told herself that this too, this trouble, this too would pass.

When the phone rang at seven, Lucy had sorted her coins into small towers of dimes, nickels and pennies. "Sigi? You are so punctual. Did you get my slides?"

"It's my Inner Kraut, darling. Yes, I did finally, though I have to say I thought FedEx did a better job of making sure they made it here by ten thirty."

"I know. But they charge more."

"And your point is?"

"Money. Anyway, sorry they were late." Lucy swallowed and forced herself to ask, "What did you think?"

"They're fabulous, darling. Just gorgeous."

"Why do I feel a *but* coming on?"

"No, *I* love them. It's just—have you got anything else under way?"

"Sigi! You hate them."

"No, I don't. But I'm—you know how provincial my clients are. A lot of them run in the same circles. I'm just not sure . . . Lucy, I'll be straight with you, or as straight as *I* can pretend to be. Have you been taking your medication? I mean, these glorious paintings: they're all of your friend Penelope! Have you thought about how it might look?"

"What do you mean?"

"Is she your Beatrice, Lucy?"

"Sigi, what are you talking about. I don't—"

"Like Dante? Look, you know *I* don't care, Lucy. It's just my clients."

"Your clients."

"It just, it just is *odd*." This statement, from Sigi, was like Osama bin Laden calling Hugo Chavez a fanatic. "Were you in love with her?"

"Sigi—Penelope wasn't my lover. She was my friend. You know that."

"Lucy. I'm a tad concerned is all. I mean, all my artists are a bit nutty, as are the ever-present and imperial *we*, but truly, I don't know whether I can sell the bridge club on hanging the same woman's picture in their otherwise identical Georgian drawing rooms. Do you see the problem? I mean, who will they say it is? Not Great-Aunt Kate and her pugs. Not some attractive but nonthreatening ancestor to trot out the Mayflower links before the dinner guests. No, ladies and gentlemen, it's Penelope Cameron May, whose untimely death makes us all feel just the teeniest bit

206 • Sheila Curran

uncomfortable, especially when we mull over the fact that all that money was no real protection, when it came right down to it. On top of the suggested unsavory love affair."

Lucy's fingers grazed her neat stack of nickels, which collapsed against the raised edge of her side table. She knelt to retrieve them, the phone crooked between her head and her clenched shoulder. "That's insane, Sigi."

"No, it's not, love. It's just the way my clients think. Death and décor don't do well together. To say nothing of the whole lesbian motif."

"Sigi, why in the world would you say that? Penelope was married with children."

"Which makes the scandal all the more unnerving, darling."

"Sigi, with friends like you—"

"Lucy, look at me. Oh, you can't. Well, if you were able to see yours truly, you'd know how very swish I am today. I'm practically wearing a pashmina thong under my kilt. I'm not trying to be insulting. *Au contraire.* The woman was a goddess. She made even me think about sex, and you know how women disgust me."

"You don't have to flatter me."

"Not you, darling. I've got dispensations for my girly-friends, and you know you're one of them. Which is why I care about your show. Which is why I want you to get busy with some still lifes or landscapes or even romping puppies, for Jesus the Savior's sake. You've only got three weeks to get more work together. I don't know about *you*, but my mortgage comes due every month at the same time, Lucy. How can I be the parasite God meant me to be if you won't do yourself a favor and rethink the single-subject show?"

"There *are* other people in the paintings, Sigi."

"If you're talking about *The Three Graces*, that's still a work in progress. In fact, again, the only person you've finished in the whole shebang—no pun intended!—is Penelope. Your other two ladies look like they've faded away. Reminds me of those medieval groupings around the Madonna and Jesus. Nobody without a halo really counts."

"I should be done by the end of the week."

"Well, I'm glad to hear that. But that's the piece we're sending to the Galbreath competition. We can't sell it."

"Sigi, this is really bad timing."

"I know. But look, don't worry. We'll figure something out. By the way, my assistant Claire Ann may be able to find out who's on the Galbreath selection committee. She's just fallen into a huge lust-fest with Keven Auchincloss. Do you know him? The performance artist? Anyhow, Keven's one of the big swinging hoo-has in the art world and rumor has it he's been appointed this year."

Lucy tried to keep her spirits from sinking onto the floor along with the spare change she'd knocked over. "Tell me you didn't say performance art."

"I know. It doesn't rain but it pours. But think of it this way. Representational painting's been out so long, I think it's got to be coming back in."

"Thanks."

"Lucy, now, keep your spirits up. You've got three weeks. Do some landscapes or ocean scenes or something quick. In browns and teals and pinks. They're all the rage in sofa colors."

"Very funny."

"I kid you not! Just get busy. You know the drill. The less time it takes to paint, the more I can get for it at auction. I'm serious."

"I know you are. That's the saddest part. If only I did that . . ."

"It's never too soon to start, now, is it? So, when are you flying in, darling?"

"Haven't gotten my tickets."

"Good God, Lucy, why not? You'll miss the best fares."

"I'll do Priceline. But, Sigi, listen, your friends who wanted to rent my house for Thanksgiving last year? Do you think they might be interested still?"

Later that evening, Joey and Lucy were walking on the beach. It was dark except for the gleam of the moon on the ocean. The surf's rhythm kept time with their steps, which were slow and deliberate, a trudge through deep, moist sand several yards up from the water's edge. This difficult terrain seemed appropriate to the news of Tessa's having stuck her masticated food onto the underside of the table, to her father's sense of despair mixed with guilt. He had a fear of being hopeful and an equally awful fear of losing hope. Mostly, Joey was overcome by bewilderment that something as simple and joyful as eating had become such an imponderable challenge to his daughter.

This was not anything about which Lucy could enlighten him. She felt similarly baffled and helpless, all the more so because of the sudden separation between herself and the girls.

"I meant to tell you, Joey. The dentist called and left a reminder today about the girls' cleaning appointments. I asked the receptionist to call your house too, but it occurs to me it might be at a bad time for you. Do you want me to take them?"

"Actually, Siobhan's going to take them. She says there's a lot the dentist can tell from looking at Tessa's teeth. Something about the enamel getting worn away by stomach acid."

"I read that. But I thought it was for bulimia. Does she think—"

"She's hoping not. But since sneaking is part of this disease— we just won't know."

"Well, call me when you find something out, okay? I've missed the girls."

Joey sighed and took Lucy's hand. He'd been so caught up in himself, he hadn't thought about how hard this would be on her. The girls were part of her life. To have them out of reach so suddenly had to be difficult.

"So, tell me more about Phoenix," Lucy said, tightening her grip on Joey's hand.

"Funny you should ask. You know, all this time, I never knew how you guys met Gabriel Sorensen in the bar at the Ritz."

"Who?"

"The director of the project out there. The one whose project I went to see? Anyway, he told me how he was eating at the Ritz one night and he met you and Penelope and Martha and Susannah."

Lucy was quiet, trying to sort through her memory bank for some kind of recognition. "I'm drawing a blank."

"Well, he sure remembers you. It was that girls' weekend when Penelope and Martha's plane had trouble on the way back?"

"Oh, no wonder I'm drawing a blank. I don't think I've ever had a worse hangover in my life. I still can't bear the smell of Drambuie."

"That was Marcus's signature drink."

"Which was why we were drinking it. He'd just died—I don't know—a little while before the trip. We were toasting him. Let me tell you. That's a very bad cocktail on an empty stomach."

"I hadn't been back in years."

"But you go all the time."

"Oh, not to Phoenix. To the Ritz."

"You know, I haven't been out west since we stayed there that time. I was so sick I spent that last night on the bathroom floor. I still remember how cold the marble felt."

"Is that why you came home early?"

"It wasn't early. Remember? We were all supposed to be on the earlier flight. But Penelope and Martha—there was some kind of meeting they had to stay for. Oh wait, now I remember the guy! Really good looking and, like—the son of some big money family. He'd gone to Exeter and Dartmouth and you could just tell by the way he spoke, he'd been raised with beaucoup money. I remember being surprised when he started talking about settlement houses and community development."

"Yeah? He says you gave him a hard time about doing something with his life, and that's how he broached his idea to Penelope for what became the Phoenix Neighborhood Initiative."

"I did? I'm telling you, that whole night is such a blur."

"I think he has a crush on you."

"No way."

"Way. Talked about you in a bikini. I—How come you never wear one when I'm around?"

"Are you jealous?" Lucy asked happily. "I don't remember any-thing of the kind but if it floats your boat, maybe I'll get one. After I lose ten pounds."

"Lucy," Joey scolded. "Don't—"

"Shit. Sorry. It's so reflexive. I don't mean to do it."

Siobhan's instructions to Tessa's friends and family had been clear. Comments like Lucy's were part of the cultural petri dish that bred anorexia. Such logic was unassailable and yet difficult to integrate into practice, since the sort of thing Lucy had just said was so much a part of how she thought about herself that it seemed innate.

They walked silently for a while, but when they turned back to the house, Lucy asked, "How was it, being back at the Ritz? It must have made you miss Penelope."

Joey paused and took a deep breath. "It did. Just when I think I'm making progress I—I had this weird reaction to what Gabriel told me about meeting all of you that first night. I was . . . jealous. I just—I felt like he'd taken something that belonged to me. A night I didn't have."

It was too dark for Lucy to see Joey's expression. Her eyes fol-lowed the flashlight beam instead, their sole illumination on the path back to her house. The bed-and-breakfast was dark, its lights turned off to allow sea turtles and birds the illusion that their habi-tat was still intact. Lucy squeezed Joey's hand, not knowing what to say exactly but feeling the need to comfort him. "Well, if it makes you feel better, I might as well have missed it too, for all I remember."

"Stop it! Please! Stop it! Ow! Lucy!"

When June woke the house with her nightmare, Siobhan moved quickly, but not fast enough to make it upstairs before Joey did. She rounded the corner of the third floor just in time to hear him murmuring soothingly in June's room. Siobhan stood outside the open door, listening.

"Daddy?" Tessa called from her room across the hall. Siobhan opened June's door far enough to whisper that Joey should stay with his youngest.

"I'll tell her it's just a dream." Siobhan's feet moved gracefully across the hall, her chest swelling with sadness for the lost children of the world.

Later, when she was back in her bed, trying to get to sleep, Siobhan couldn't help but wonder at the timing, couldn't help but puzzle at the words in their sequence, playing over and over. Was June's plea meant to be a cry *to* Lucy or *about* her?

The child seemed attached to Lucy, but then again, most victims of abuse felt that way. Given the fact that so many anorectics had histories of childhood abuse, and given the outsize fears June had about going to sleep, it didn't take a rocket scientist, or even a master's in nutrition, to add two and two together.

By dawn, Siobhan's brain had calculated more than arithmetic. She'd been visited by a means of bringing this family out of their denial, doubly therapeutic in that it would separate them from certain unhealthful influences and clarify for their father certain things about the women in his life.

There was such solace in her solution, such sorting efficiency, that by the time she reckoned with her conscience, Siobhan's very soul was brimming with moral courage and not a whiff of spite.

As she would be compelled to remind herself later, it wasn't her job to sweep other people's messes under the rug. Such acts—given the stakes—might amount to enabling. She'd not be doing this family a favor by collaborating in a deception that had crippled them for too long. Besides, Siobhan told herself, she was only doing the very thing she'd been directed to as part of her paid employment. The Cameron brothers had said as much when they agreed to hire her. Let them decide what to do with the letter she'd discovered, let them decide whether Joey would benefit from the facts within. After all, they'd been the ones to insist she investigate in the first place.

By the time the family came down to breakfast, Siobhan had

already driven a copy over to the Camerons' mailbox. She'd also tucked her own copy away, in case she needed it, between the pages of one of her sacred ledgers.

Such caution was not a reflection simply of Siobhan's orderly mind but also of her need to cement her interpretation of events by documenting them in black and white. In another life, Siobhan might have been a librarian, sorting information into categories and preserving it for future generations.

It was not her desire to interfere.

Of course, some observers might have argued that retrieving a deleted letter from a dead wife's files, printing it out and handing it over to a pair of strangers bent on destruction might have constituted interference of the highest order. Those critics, though, would surely have been the blurred-boundaries types who believed in mitigating circumstances, in shades of gray or degrees of guilt. Siobhan, like the Swiss grandparents her father had ditched along with his draft card, was blessed with a rule-bound code of ethics that was blind to nuance or paradox of any sort. This allowed her to clear her mind of second-guesses or even the slightest trace of remorse. As she'd been ever fond of quipping, gray was not the new black, which was fortunate really, considering how ghastly the color could make her appear.

Chapter Seventeen

June was sitting on the front porch with Rocky, whom she was trying to teach to jump over a footstool. *Trying* was the operative word here. As in, *very* trying. The stool was tipped over on its side, and the dog was asleep, despite the Cheerios June had been proffering to lure him awake.

"Daddy! We just got back from the dentist. Tessa had three cavities. I had one."

"Ow! Sweetheart, we need to get you girls brushing better." At the look on June's face, Joey softened his tone and kissed her. "How did your filling go?"

"It made my lips totally squishy and I bit my tongue. Thee?" June stuck out her tongue with its invisible wound.

"Double ow. Where's Tessa?"

"Eating Popsicles."

"Cool."

"Ha!"

Joey hadn't meant the pun, but he smiled back as though he had. "Did you get a blue one?"

"Miss Siobhan said it would ruin my appetite," June explained. She didn't ask her father why Tessa, whose appetite was terrible and whose teeth were a lot worse than her sister's, would be allowed the sugary snack.

Joey picked up a pile of mail on the way into the kitchen, solely to slow himself down and try to think of how he might express to Siobhan his sense that restricting June's diet wasn't something he wanted her to do.

The problem was, of course, that he was so anxious to have her stay and treat Tessa, he was afraid to offend her.

On top of the stack of mail sitting on the table in the hall was an envelope he nearly threw away. For one thing, there was no return address, the label was typed and in place of any postmark, a large CONFIDENTIAL was stamped diagonally across the front. Joey was telling himself how direct-mail marketers would do anything to get people to open solicitations, and he was still thinking of Popsicles and of what he would say to Siobhan. On his first quick skim, he read on automatic pilot.

A small Post-it was written in an unfamiliar, cramped handwriting.

> *Dear Sir,*
> *I return to you this document,*
> *which appears to have been written*
> *by your wife.*
> *I trust you would wish to see it.*

It was attached to a piece of paper that appeared to be a letter. There were the words, which he read over and over, trying to make sense of them. It was so familiar, this voice from the past, and yet so unexpected, that when he explained to June that he was heading upstairs because of an upset stomach, he was being entirely truthful.

Of all the reactions Joey might have expected to the discovery that his wife had cheated on him, paralysis behind the closed doors of his master bath wouldn't have been one of them. He felt completely numb but so afraid of what he might do or say, he couldn't allow himself to move.

June had come into his room and knocked at the bathroom door. "Daddy? Are you okay?"

"Just my stomach, honey." That much was true, his body having worked its way through the meaning of the letter faster than the rest of him.

"I'll be okay," he whispered, forcing himself to say the words. "I must have eaten something."

"I could call Aunt Lucy, Daddy."

"No! Don't, sweetie! I'm—I just need privacy!" Joey said, trying not to let the panic that was brewing inside affect his tone.

He read the letter over and over until it made even less sense than it had before. Then he sat against the door and grieved anew the death of the woman he thought he'd married, the one whose affectionate generosity so permeated the words of the text, whose syntactic imprint was as distinctive as her use of *slainte* to say goodbye, whose fears of losing him had been so vocal, he'd never considered the possibility that she might leave him for someone else.

Dear Dear Sweet Girl,

I know I should have the courage to talk to you about this in person, but right now I'm just confused and upset. I don't think I could organize my thoughts right now.

I don't know what I could have been thinking, offering you what I did. In the clear light of day, I have to face the fact that I'm not as free and unconventional as I thought. Maybe also, I worry about the girls, how if they found out later, well, they might feel they were less Joey's. Human nature is strange that way.

For what it's worth, please know: you're beautiful. Anyone who's felt your skin against theirs couldn't help but want to repeat the experience, over and over.

Much as I'd like to, I feel like I can't take any more risks right now, whether it's out of fear or possessiveness, I'm just not sure.

In the meantime, of course I wish I'd had the presence of mind to lie when I got that phone call. I couldn't think. I just fell apart. Anyhow, if you can make yourself call this woman

back, tell her the same thing I already did. Just reiterate what
I said. You're not married, you're a starving artist, she might
as well stop barking up that tree. Tell the bitch it would only
enhance your reputation in the art world if people found out.

In the meantime, do not worry about me spilling to Joey.
Believe me, what happens at the Ritz stays at the Ritz. Which
is why I'm never going back.

I know I got your hopes up. For that and everything else,
I'll make it up to you somehow, I promise you that.

Slainte,
Pen

Questions crowded Joey's brain, edging out answers in their manic
scrambling for resolution. The words kept running through his
brain. *What happens at the Ritz stays at the Ritz. Which is why I'm*
never going back.

Upon that abrupt syntax Joey found himself stuck, twisting his
past to make sense of the words. The conclusions he drew were
swift and absolute. His gut cried out for resolution; his intellect
complied with a punishing analytic response. Penelope and Lucy
had slept together. At the Ritz. That must have been the real reason Penelope had changed hotels, not some near-miss on a plane as
she'd claimed. He'd been a gullible fool, ready to believe anything
she dished out. This letter, appearing now, right after he'd started
sleeping with Lucy, told him everything and nothing at the same
time.

His whole marriage had been a lie. From the tone of the letter, Penelope had at least contemplated leaving him for Lucy. It
must have been near the time her plane had almost crashed. Had
Penelope thought God was giving her one more chance? She was
egotistical enough to believe in all sorts of things, even microman-
agement by the Almighty on her behalf. The scare would have
prompted her to take away whatever it was she'd offered Lucy, to
promise to make it up to her somehow.

Of course, maybe her apparent change of heart hadn't been

about Penelope's soul or Joey's happiness. Maybe it was more about the girls. She'd written that bit about how they might feel less like a family, which they would, if their mother left their father for another woman.

How convenient that fate had provided a perfect cover for what must have broken Penelope's heart: saying no to Lucy, putting a stop to something that was clearly meaningful to both of them.

Joey had gotten Penelope's call from the Jacksonville airport before he'd seen the news coverage that night. He'd known Penelope was safe, but even then, watching the footage of the plane circling while the emergency crews foamed the runway, watching ambulance after ambulance and fire trucks end to end, listening to the tense commentary that accompanied the harrowing landing, Joey had felt his blood shrink in his veins.

Penelope had walked in the door a complete freaking mess. How much of that had been fright? The idea of Penelope and Lucy in bed with each other, that was hurtful enough, but what made it worse was how Penelope had played him. She'd been so dramatic, so convincing, drawing him into the story she'd concocted. He'd not even thought to doubt that her distress was due to a near miss on a plane.

Meanwhile, it was clear from the tone of this letter that something very serious had happened between the two women. Why would Penelope have apologized so profusely unless she was breaking Lucy's heart? This meant they'd been carrying something on for a long time. Maybe ever since they'd been roommates in college.

Once he'd begun to sort through possible interpretations, Joey saw that Penelope and Lucy had left clues. He'd just not connected the dots. Like the aftermath of an ambush, the trail of evidence— in hindsight—seemed obvious, inescapable. Joey pressed his hands into his knees and tried not to think. It was too late. The tumblers of judgment locked into place so quickly his ears rang.

Jesus, how could he have been so blind? The two women had been so physically affectionate, so easy in their demonstrative attentions to one another. And of course, Lucy had never married, much less lived with a man. She'd claimed to dislike hotels, saying they never seemed clean. Had she always felt that way or had it been around the same time Penelope developed her sudden dis-taste for the Ritz-Carlton? And when was it that Penelope had begun to describe Lucy's body in great detail in the midst of making love to him? Joey had assumed she wanted to excite him. Now, it seemed clear, Penelope had had her own stimulation in mind, felt her own need to replay a stirring memory.

The final nail in the coffin was Joey's own deep attraction to Lucy, a double-edged sword that brooked no skepticism when it came to imagining the desire she would have ignited in his wife. The same inflamed connection he'd felt with Lucy since Hallow-een—how could he bear to think that it was something she'd al-ready shared with his wife? Had he been a better person, maybe he'd have compared the two feelings, traded one for the other on some level playing field of the fucked. Not Joey. What he'd done after two years of holding himself back was entirely different from what Penelope had helped herself to all along.

And Lucy? Lucy could argue she'd never taken marriage vows, never promised to remain faithful to Joey. Still, her complicity in his betrayal hurt almost as much, maybe even more, than his wife's, if only because it came as even more of a shock. There'd always been a quality to Lucy that had struck Joey as chaste, removed, even ascetic. This despite the fact that Joey knew she'd had lovers before him. Still, God forgive his ridiculously simple male ego, Joey had actually believed there was something in the way they made love together that was new, something she'd never experi-enced before. What if what he'd felt from Lucy wasn't about him at all? What if her intensity had been more about pretending she was with Penelope, and he was just a poor substitute?

The past was a thicket he couldn't find his way completely into or out of. He was covered with scratches, stung with nettles, caught up in irrelevant concerns. The timing of his wife's gift to Lucy, the deed to the bed-and-breakfast. That had been within months of that last traumatic trip to the Ritz. Worse, instead of telling him the truth, that she'd been having an affair, or that she'd given Lucy the house to make it up to her for not leaving her husband, Penelope had lied to his face. She'd led him to believe her desolation had been caused by a near-death experience, by her father's recent passing. He'd actually felt sorry for her, worried about her, so much so that he'd signed her fucking codicil. Lucy, of all people, had been put in the position of deciding who he could marry next! Joey found himself choking on the humiliation of having been so easily fooled, his cluelessness adding insult to the injury of having ever trusted his wife in the first place.

Talk about being played. Penelope had been so damn good at manipulating him that she'd managed to make him think he was the dominant one, acting out of *noblesse oblige*, humoring her obsessive worries.

This letter, coming out of the blue, had pulled the rug out from underneath him. It made him doubt everything he'd ever known about Penelope and brought up all sorts of feelings he'd not allowed himself to experience in the wake of her death. She was so impulsive, always pushing the envelope, whether it was throwing millions into a project headed by somebody she didn't even know or setting off to deliver a basket of food when she'd promised him never to do such a thing alone. They'd talked that Thanksgiving morning; she'd told him she'd make sure she took someone with her. She'd said she'd call Lucy or Sateesh, or Martha or Susannah. She'd given him her word she wouldn't go out to that woman's house by herself. Instead, when Lucy had said she was finishing a painting, Penelope hadn't even bothered to call anybody else. She'd just decided to go it alone, telling the girls she'd be right back. She'd driven off, typically impatient with waiting, dismissing her husband's worries about her safety.

Joey stayed in his room through the evening and into the night, telling June and Tessa he'd caught a stomach bug. From time to time he would hear another knock at the door and he'd manage to groan a reply, though what he'd said he could not later remember. He was too occupied with the questions that were hammering what remained of his psyche. By the time the sun came up in the morning and Joey folded himself into bed, he'd found a peace of sorts, though the price he paid would continue to exact its toll for some time. In a bargain as confused and paranoid as it was Faustian, Joey regressed to an almost primitive reliance on absolutes. It would become a point of pride that he impose on his friends—all of whom he believed must have known about Lucy and never told him—he would impose on all of them, especially Lucy, the same dire ignorance that had obliterated several years of his life, just like that.

Chapter Eighteen

The longer Lucy waited for Joey to answer his phone, the more often she dialed his number only to find that the customer she was calling could not be found, the greater the number of catastrophes she was able to envision.

Susannah was in Phoenix and Martha might as well have been. The three times Lucy had called—hoping to catch her after work—the attorney was out running.

The more Lucy catastrophized, the less she knew, and the greater was her ability to embroider the forms of disaster that would explain Joey's not calling.

Front and center, occupying most of her imaginative energy, was the physical torment of wondering whether she'd misinterpreted Joey's sexual interest. It began to seem entirely plausible that for him, their sex had been a one-night stand, stretched out longer but meaning the same thing. Was he afraid to see her, embarrassed to admit he was no longer interested? Had he moved onto greener pastures? Closer to home? From that notion, it was just a hop, skip and jump to wondering if he might have found solace in the perfect body and nubile resilience of a twentysomething helping professional.

Lucy stumbled back and forth down these garden paths of explanation, trying to understand Joey's abrupt disappearance from her life. Was it sexual buyer's remorse? Guilt over betraying his dead wife with her best friend? Falling in love with someone else?

When she got a text message from June that her father was sick, Lucy's first reaction was relief, swiftly followed by worry. She dialed the house phone.

"Hello? Siobhan? I—may I please speak to Joey?"

"Who's calling?"

"It's Lucy. I heard he was sick and I—is—do you think he's well enough to talk?"

"I'll tell you what. Let me see. June? Here, take this and see if your father's well enough to talk to Miss Lucy."

"Lucy!" June cried. "Hi!"

"Sweetie? Hi! Your dad's sick?"

June's voice became a whisper. "Don't tell him I texted you. He told me not to call you."

"He did?"

"Don't tell Miss Siobhan I told you either."

"Oh, sweetie, are you alright?"

"Dad's been really sick."

"What's wrong with him?"

"He's, like, his stomach's all messed up. He thinks it might be food poisoning or something. Lucy, do you think it's cancer?"

"No, I'm sure it's not, honey. It doesn't come on quick like that. Don't worry. Why don't you see if he'll talk to me?"

"Dad?" June called. Lucy could hear a muffled knock. "Lucy wants to—Daddy? Lucy, he's not answering!" June banged on the door. Lucy heard Joey call something to June but his words were lost in the sound of her own heart beating. "It's Lucy, Daddy! What? Are you sure?"

When June spoke again, she was on the brink of tears. "I think he knows!"

"What, honey?"

"He told me not to call you. What's wrong with him, Lucy?"

"I don't know. But listen, didn't your mom always say your dad was a big baby when he got sick? Do you remember that?"

"No," June muttered, but she was calmer.

"I do. Remember she said if the seven dwarfs got the flu, he'd definitely be Grumpy."

June's laugh was high-pitched, a cross between hysteria and relief. "Grumpy!"

"Listen, honey, let me talk to Miss Siobhan for a second and then maybe you can call me on your cell when it's time for bed and we can chat some more."

"I'd have to whisper."

"That's okay. We won't talk long but I want to say good night. I miss tucking you in."

"You do?"

"Of course I do. You have no idea how much I miss seeing you, honey. But we've got to do what's best for Tessa. I just hope she doesn't catch what your dad has."

"No, she's okay." June's voice lowered to a whisper. "I listen for her when she's in the bathroom."

"What do you mean?"

"Miss Siobhan took the locks off the doors."

"What?"

"So Tessa doesn't try to throw up."

"Oh."

"So that's how I know she's not been sick. She's not even allowed to shut the door."

Lucy took a deep breath. "How does Tessa feel about that?"

"She cries. But Miss Siobhan says she's got to earn her right to privacy."

"Oh, June. I'm sorry. That must be hard for you. Are you downstairs again?"

"Why are you whispering?"

"I don't know, because you were?"

"You're funny," June laughed, hurrying into the kitchen. "Miss Siobhan? Aunt Lucy wants to talk to you."

"Miss Lucy," Siobhan admonished, taking the phone from June.

Lucy took a breath to calm herself but still her voice was sharp. "Look, Siobhan, June can call me Aunt Lucy! She always has. Listen, the reason I'm calling, have you seen Joey? Is he getting fluids?"

"What a bitch!" Martha said, predictably.

"That's why I love you. You have the best taste in people."

"What's not to hate? She's so fucking smug. When I stopped by to give Joey some paperwork to look at, she acted like I'd taken a huge dump on the parlor floor. Who the fuck does she think she is?"

"You saw him!" Lucy's heart dropped back into her chest. She wanted to break down and cry. "What is wrong with him?"

"I didn't see him. Nurse Ratched said he didn't want any company."

"What did you say?"

"That I wasn't there to have tea and crumpets, that I needed his signature. She actually told me to leave the papers with her, that she'd have him look them over when he was feeling better."

"You don't think she's got him locked up there against his will?"

"No. Tessa and June were sitting right there in the kitchen."

"How did Tessa seem?"

"If looks could kill, the dance Nazi would be dead meat."

"No, I mean—how did Tessa *look*? Any healthier?"

"I hate to admit it, but she did."

"I'm so glad! I've been beside myself not hearing anything. Joey usually calls and lets me know—it's been like three days now!"

"He hasn't called? Sateesh said he hadn't heard from him either. Geez, maybe she is keeping him prisoner after all."

When Joey returned to the office suite the next morning for a brief meeting with Susannah, he had morphed into a cross between an automaton and perpetual-impatience machine. His diction was clipped, tight, concise. He appeared to be holding his body in check, muscling a suit of armor out of molecular willpower that warded off questions and warned against dissent of any kind. Even Martha, who made the mistake of popping her head into the office and asking if he had called Lucy, couldn't quite find the pipes to press the question when he squinted at her and said tightly, "No."

Susannah thought valerian, hops and kava kava might assuage the negative magnetic field that boomeranged incoming overtures straight back across the hard wooden table between them. Susannah found her gentle inquiries ignored, replaced by acerbic questions about travel records going back twenty years and counting. "I—Joey, they're somewhere. We keep it all—but—"

"Just do it. I just need you to do what I ask."

"Alright. Do you want to talk about my meeting in Phoenix? Joey? Are you—are you okay?"

Joey put his head into one hand, his elbow resting on the table. He closed his eyes. "No. I'm not."

"Let me make you some peppermint tea. It's good for your stomach."

Joey shook his head vehemently, though doing so made him nauseous. "No." He stood up and weaved his way toward the door. When Susannah hurried to accompany him, she was rewarded with a look of fury. "Just get me the records," he whispered. With that, he closed the door and retreated to his house, where his first act was to lock the door, his second to take the phone off the hook and remove the cord from the wall.

Sateesh was the next of Joey's friends to try to see him, but the front door of the house was as far as he was able to get. Siobhan was pleasant, almost loquacious as she explained to Sateesh that they'd worked very hard to get a regimen developed for Tessa. It was important to maintain it. "I'll tell him you called," she trilled, waving good-bye as Sateesh loped down the front steps and wrapped his lanky frame back into the front seat of his station wagon.

◆ ◆ ◆

"I tried!" Sateesh told Lucy that night at Sapphire's bar, where he'd joined her and Martha for a glass of wine. "Siobhan says he's still sick."

"But even when he's sick as a dog, he keeps in touch with you," Martha said. "Just to complain, if nothing else."

"I know. I did try."

"When was the last time you talked?" Lucy asked, overly casual. Her eyes focused on the bottom of her wineglass.

"I don't know. Three, four days. After he came back from Phoenix. He was upset about Tessa. The stuff she'd been wiping under the table."

"He told me that too," Lucy mused.

"So it wasn't his trip to Phoenix?" Martha said, sounding uncharacteristically confused.

"No, I saw him after he got back," Sateesh said. "Besides, he goes there all the time."

"Well, whatever it is, he's apparently anxious to keep it close to the vest." Sateesh was pouring more wine from behind the bar. "He'll sort it out. P'raps it's just hit him, Tessa's illness. P'raps it's finally settling in."

"Maybe," Martha said. "It had to be a shock to find she'd been pretending to eat but was mashing it into the table."

"Right. A bit like not eating her lunch at school," Sateesh murmured.

"And he doesn't even know about that," Lucy replied.

"He doesn't?" Sateesh and Martha seemed incredulous in unison.

The floor seemed to be spinning away from Lucy. Or was it the ceiling? Her nostrils widened slightly; her voice rose with the truth that had settled into her limbs as if nesting there for centuries. "Oh, my God, I am so stupid! That's it! That's why he's not talking to us. He knows! And he knows I kept it from him!"

"Don't jump to conclusions, Lucy. Let's think. How would he

know?" Martha pressed Lucy's forearm. "Sateesh? Did you mention it? I know I haven't. Jesus, though, with the way he's acting, I'm not sure now's the right time to bring it up."

"No, that's it. Shit! I've got to explain it to him."

"What do you bet that bitch somehow got it out of Tessa and blabbed to Joey?" Martha whispered. "Oh, Lucy, why in the world didn't you tell him? You—wasn't that the plan all along?"

Chapter Nineteen

Lucy was wearing a dress her mother would have called a *schmatte*. Once sea-green and formfitting, the sheath was now a flimsy, overwashed sack drained of color. It was the sort of dress Eeyore would wear if he were disposed to ladies' clothing, and it brought out the raccoon circles under Lucy's eyes.

Standing there on the porch of the High Street house, holding her hatbox, Lucy looked like one of the orphans in *Annie,* except she was forty, pushing past the age at which that barefoot-and-Appalachian look would get you anywhere.

At least this was what Siobhan could not help but think when she answered the door, her fingers clenched on the frame like she was afraid Lucy would batter it down to kidnap the children, or at the very least contaminate the premises with her aura.

Lucy, who'd timed her visit to coincide with Joey's morning run, lifted the blue and yellow hatbox by its ribboned carrier. "This is for Tessa. She—I thought she might miss these."

"What's in there?"

"Just some stuff from her mom. Hard to explain."

"Try me."

"No offense, but ask Tessa. It's her stuff."

"Secrets aren't a healthy—"

"It's not a secret," Lucy said. "But it's sacred. Listen, do you think I could talk to Tessa for a minute? It's important."

Siobhan gave Lucy a look as full of pity as it was of reproach. "We really have to stick with the rules, Miss Lucy. Don't worry, though. I'll tell her you came by."

Lucy was swept by the defeated loneliness of having become expendable. She flushed, embarrassed, idiotic, supplicant.

"Look, could I write her a note, then? And Joey? Can you bring me a couple of envelopes?"

Siobhan opened her mouth to say something. Even this hesitation was enough to cause Lucy to apologize.

"I'm sorry. But it's important. I'll just sit on the steps and write this quickly. I just really need to."

When Siobhan returned with two envelopes, Lucy had composed a short note to Tessa and another to Joey, each of which she folded and inserted into envelopes. She scrawled Tessa's name across the front of one and Joey's on the other, then brought them to her lips to lick the seal.

"Lucy, can you hurry?" Siobhan interrupted, reaching for the first envelope with one hand and taking the other from Lucy's lap, "Sorry, but I can't leave Tessa unsupervised. You understand, I'm sure."

"Will you tell June I said hi?"

"As soon as she gets home from school and does her homework." With this, Siobhan quickly shut the door behind her, turning the deadbolt.

There were ribbons tied around the hatbox, which Siobhan quickly untied, lifting the lid of the box. It was filled with tiny boxes of soap, minuscule bottles of shampoo and lotions. Most had the names of hotels on them, boutique hotels Siobhan had never heard of, except for the Ritz and the St. Francis. Siobhan shook her head and quickly put the box on the top shelf in the coat closet. Then she moved into the dining room, the envelopes behind her back. "Tessa? Are you done?"

"Do I look done?"

"Do you think you could manage to be civil to me?"

"Sorry," Tessa said glumly. "Who was at the door?"

"No one."

"It sure sounded like someone."

"Tessa, even if it was Alicia Keys, I think you know the rules. No company until you've met your weight goal. I'll be right back." Siobhan tucked herself into the small alcove off the dining room and quickly read the notes Lucy had written.

Sweetie,

I so wanted to talk to you about this in person, but I can't. Must resist the impulse to bang down the door and beg your forgiveness. Instead, just know I love you and wouldn't be coming clean if I didn't think it was essential to your getting better.

I love you so much!
Lucy

Joey,

We need to talk. I've got a confession to make. Maybe it's something you already know, but please let me try to explain why I did what I did. I wonder if you and I and Tessa sat down together with the therapist and just talked things out, she might feel better about everything. I know I was wrong in keeping secrets, but at the time, I didn't want to hurt you, silly as that may sound now.

I miss you!
Lucy

That afternoon, while Tessa was doing homework and Joey was off running errands, Siobhan took the mysterious hatbox down from the closet and carried it in to June, who was in the media room, watching a video from the competition in Atlanta. It was Siobhan's belief that her dancers did best if they could see themselves as the camera did. Nothing quite motivated a girl like the sight of an added ten pounds. At four foot ten and one hundred six pounds, much of which was concentrated in her torso, June could ill afford photographic expansions. When the video was finished, Siobhan moved the hatbox over to an ottoman in front of the couch and opened the lid, saying, "Look what Miss Lucy dropped off for Tessa."

"Lucy?"

"She said to tell you she came by, honey. She said to say hi," Siobhan said, with no small pride at having kept her promise to Lucy.

June knelt by the box, prayerfully attentive. She breathed in the scent and breathed again, using her hands to waft the smells up to her face.

"Take one," Siobhan offered. "Your sister's got enough to share."

"That's okay."

"Miss Lucy gave me the impression Tessa is attached to those," Siobhan murmured casually.

"Yes, ma'am."

"If you don't mind my asking—why?"

"Mommy used to bring them back from trips."

"Oh my goodness! Only for Tessa? How did that make you feel?"

June shrugged. "I never—I was just little."

By the time June remembered that Mommy and Daddy had always brought her her own notions from the hotels, it was too late. Siobhan had returned the box to the shelf in the hall closet and commiserated with June for having had to be in the care of strangers while her parents went away on business. Then she was on the phone with Tessa's therapist, asking questions in a voice so low she couldn't be overheard.

When Joey arrived home, he found Siobhan elbow-deep in the makings of faux meatloaf, wearing an old apron of Penelope's. Tendrils of hair had snuck free from her topknot and her face was flushed with the exertion of kneading together soy crumble with raw egg, but beyond that, there was something in her carriage that spoke volumes about the sympathy she felt for him. This man had been so badly used, she could not help but think.

"How are you?" she asked gently when he entered the kitchen. "Can I get you some tea?"

"No. Thanks. I'm fine."

"Are you?" Siobhan cocked her head to one side, compassion vying with honest inquiry on her therapeutic bandwidth.

"You bet," Joey said distractedly.

"Look, there's something I need to discuss with you," Siobhan said. "The girls are in the study, so if you could wait two minutes, I'll meet you up in your office?"

Joey flinched as if expecting a blow, redoubling Siobhan's empathetic imagination. She scraped the sodden batter into a loaf pan and set it in the oven. While the water ran in her mixing bowl, she washed her arms to the elbows and tried to temper the indignation building inside her.

When she entered Joey's office, she began gently, tentative in her tone. "Lucy came by today. Oh, don't worry. I didn't let her talk to Tessa. But . . . I think you should know. I think it's possible certain boundaries have been crossed, which may have had something to do with why your daughter's so ill."

"What do you mean?"

"I suspect that Lucy has never really comprehended that children don't really want to be treated by the adults in their lives as if they're simply friends. They need the adults to set firm boundaries and expectations, and to protect them from inappropriate information. Much as they might act differently, they crave a strong parental authority figure. You know that, naturally, but Lucy, whether it has been giving in to June's anxieties and letting her sleep with her, or now, coming to the door and demanding to see Tessa—I just can't help wondering what else she may have let seep into their lives."

"Siobhan, I'm lost. What are you talking about?"

"Lucy came to the door today asking to speak to Tessa. When I said no, she wrote her a note. I read it, and, well, maybe you should just take a look. I just wonder about her judgment."

"What note?"

Siobhan retrieved the envelopes from her apron pocket. She handed them to Joey. "Sorry. She wrote you one too. I didn't read that one, of course."

After Joey read Lucy's notes, he was silent.

Siobhan filled in the awkward silence by continuing to hypothesize. "I just wonder what it was she felt so urgently about that she wanted to bang down a door to tell your daughter. If anything, I'd have thought she'd discuss it with you first. And if it's what I think it is, I just can't help but wonder what her motives could be. Do you see what I'm getting at?"

Joey appeared to be avoiding Siobhan's eyes, focusing all his strength on not breaking down in front of her. "No, I don't. What do you mean?"

Siobhan found herself moved by his stoic grace, his withheld grief. She was overcome suddenly with anger at the suffering he'd undergone.

"It just seems so . . . *twisted* After what Lucy's done to you, to your family, to pile insult onto injury by thinking it was fair game to suggest off-loading all that to Tessa! When she's this fragile already! I'm sorry, but I can't help but wonder. Where exactly did Lucy draw the line when they lived with her? No wonder Tessa felt things were out of control."

"What are you talking about?"

"I'm just trying to tell you I'm sorry," Siobhan said, her voice barely above a whisper.

Joey shook his head, and suddenly, when he looked up, it was almost as if he didn't recognize her. "Sorry?"

"For—never mind."

"No. Tell me. What are you sorry about?" Joey asked, rising from his chair, his voice tight, his words clipped. "Why would you say that?"

Now Siobhan felt as if all the man's pain had been turned around and was aimed at her. He crossed the room and towered above her. It was almost as if he were angry, like she'd done something to offend him. Rather than blaming Lucy or his dead wife for what he'd been going through, he almost appeared to be blaming Siobhan. The look in his eyes was half fury, half disbelief. "How would you have reason to know what Lucy has or has not done to my family?"

Siobhan rose from her chair and turned away from Joey. Overcome by concern and indignation, she'd made a terrible error. However, in the time it took the man to cross the room, she'd already arrived at a way out of her predicament.

"I've been so stupid, Joey. Please bear with me," Siobhan explained, holding a hand up defensively. "There's something I haven't told you. I'll be right back."

Siobhan left the office and walked briskly to her bedroom. When she returned, she was carrying a neatly folded piece of white paper. Thank God she'd saved it in her ledger! Though she might not have understood at the time what purpose it would serve, it was clear now that some subconscious part of her had realized that Joey might need to be jolted out of his denial. Of course he'd be tempted to believe anything Lucy told him, if only because he couldn't face the truth of what had happened between her and his wife. Not only would *his* recovery depend on circumventing that denial, but in a sense, Tessa's would too.

The stakes were high. The fact that Lucy was foolhardy enough to broach the idea of telling Tessa about her affair with her mother was proof positive that the artist posed a real danger to the child's health. Tessa was barely hanging on, psychologically speaking. That Lucy was self-absorbed enough to even consider burdening the girl with such disturbing information was, in and of itself, an indictment of her judgment, or lack thereof. It was important that Joey understand exactly what sort of woman he'd opened himself up to.

Siobhan held up the letter. "Lucy brought Tessa a box full of soaps and lotions. I found this tucked away inside. I read it before I realized what it was. I'm very sorry. I didn't mean to intrude. I certainly should have mentioned it right away; I just, well, I didn't want to distress you. That's all."

Siobhan handed him the copy of the letter she'd sent the Camerons. There was no other choice. How else to explain to him what she knew? How else to get Joey back into the all-important process of facing his pain in order to get beyond it? The paper he now held had a heft to it and was still bright white, still clean. Still, that could be explained. If Lucy was the neatnik the girls had described, she'd have kept the original in a safe place, especially if she valued it. While it wasn't technically true that Lucy had squirreled this exact piece of paper away in a box of Tessa's soaps, Siobhan's cover story held a certain symbolic accuracy. After all, Lucy had made it clear she planned to "come clean" with Tessa. Whether it was in therapy or by exposing the child to the contents of a letter, the point was that Lucy's intention was to inform Tessa of her mother's affair. Siobhan was only making certain that Joey recognized that intrinsic truth. *Honestly, Siobhan asked herself, how could Lucy be so heartless?* What child would wish to know of her late mother's infidelity with another woman, or even a man, for that matter?

Despite Siobhan's conviction that everything she was doing was completely justifiable, she couldn't help but feel a twinge of vicarious pain watching Joey read the letter in front of her. His eyes held fast to each syllable, flickering across the text.

He sank into a chair and stared out into space. He opened his fingers, letting the letter flutter to the ground.

"Honestly, Joey, I'm so sorry. I didn't mean to pry. I was just checking the box she'd brought over to make sure there were no laxatives in it. I didn't want to tattle on Lucy, but when I saw how upset you were, well, I couldn't help but think how much more upset Tessa would be if she were to come upon this. I wanted to spare you this, but now I see that Tessa's health—well, we've got to protect her from this sort of overture. Lucy's need to talk about it now, after all this time, it strikes me as pathological. She's got no appreciation of appropriate boundaries."

The timbre of Joey's voice suggested he could barely breathe, much less speculate on Lucy's motives. He looked up at Siobhan, looked right through her, actually. "Did Tessa see this? Did June?"

"No—of course not. I wanted to wait and discuss everything with you. What's wrong?" Siobhan asked.

"You found this in a box of soaps Lucy brought to Tessa? Are you sure Tessa didn't see it?"

"Oh, I'm sure. I took it out, but I also put the box away until I asked you what you wanted me to do. I didn't want to rock the boat."

Joey was already across the room, pulling on his jacket.

"Where are you going?"

"I need to find out why Lucy would do this!"

"Joey, please, wait. Sit and let yourself calm down before you go anywhere. Maybe Lucy didn't mean for Tessa to see it. It could have been sitting there, in the box, under all those soaps. Lucy might not have realized she'd left it there. She might not have done it on purpose. Please. Sit and think about this a minute."

"You sit! I'm gonna find out why she did this to me!"

Siobhan would remind herself later: this white lie she'd been forced to tell wasn't something she'd planned on. Truthfully, Siobhan had assumed that Joey would pick up naturally on the utter self-indulgence of Lucy's suggestion that they "come clean" with Tessa. She'd even dared to hope that Joey, in his wounded state, might take the opportunity to confide in Siobhan about the heartbreak he'd suffered, the letter, his wife's betrayal. It was important, after all, that Tessa's entire treatment team understood the family dynamics they were facing. The more Siobhan thought about it, the more her invention seemed almost fortuitous. For one thing, it would force Joey to see what he was up against, having let Lucy Vargas penetrate his and the children's lives at such an intimate level. Also, now that he knew that Siobhan had read the letter, if he wanted a confidant, he'd find a shoulder to lean on.

Tessa's recovery was at stake, Siobhan told herself. Besides, she would insist when the stray whisper of guilt crept in to remind her of her transgression, she hadn't written the letter, nor had she taken any part in creating the marital mess it revealed.

All Siobhan had done was to discover the words on Penelope's hard drive, words clearly written to Lucy. The fact that the painter had decided to confess the whole tawdry incident to Tessa was damning enough. Who knew how many other boundaries Lucy had crossed with those poor children in the years she'd been with them?

Joey's Mustang raced along the beach road and arrived at Lucy's house in a storm of gravel and sand. The dogs were barking as Lucy raced down her stairs. Joey met her halfway up. "Why!" he cried. "Why would you do this?"

"What, Joey?" Lucy asked.

"This!" Joey said, crumpling the letter into a ball and throwing it at her. "You know, the two of you, what you did to me, and then keeping it from me all this time, that's bad enough, but why would you bring it out now, why would you want to hurt my daughter like this?"

"Joey, I wasn't trying to hurt anyone. I thought—I assumed you'd *want* me to bring it out into the open. I know I should have told you earlier, but I allowed myself to be convinced I was protecting you."

"Oh, my God!" Joey's tone was so full of incredulity, it brought tears to Lucy's eyes. "Don't give me such bullshit. It's Tessa who should have been protected, Lucy. She's only fourteen!"

"You're right. I know! But at the time, I just allowed myself to be persuaded it didn't matter if you knew all the sordid details. Especially since Tessa was already getting help. I wanted to tell you," she whispered. "Especially after we—you and I—"

At the look on Joey's face, part repulsion, part disgust, Lucy realized how terribly she'd let him down. How could she have been so stupid? Of course she shouldn't have kept Tessa's secret, not about something so important as her health. The fact that she wasn't eating lunch at school and was exercising all that time was bad enough. Much more critical were the fears Tessa had expressed to Lucy, that her father's failure to return home on time had been purposeful, related to arguments Tessa had overheard between her parents. This information was too serious not to be dealt with in therapy, too serious not to bring to Joey's attention. How had Tessa persuaded Lucy to hide all of this torment from her father? How could Lucy have allowed herself to be convinced?

"Why didn't you tell me?" Joey demanded. "Why didn't she, for fuck's sake?"

"She didn't—she thought it would freak you out. Oh, Joey, I let myself be convinced. If you could have seen her, she was just sick about it—"

"Oh, that's good to know. I'm glad to hear she had a conscience after all."

Lucy was struck by the memory of Tessa on the track, keeping time with her hand, the sense of urgency in her walk, her obsessive fixation on being perfect. "I don't think she could help herself."

"What?"

"I think it's like an addiction. You wouldn't blame the addict, would you?"

"Oh, my God! Where the fuck do you come off telling me such horseshit? Look, what you did was bad enough, but to think a kid could process that kind of thing is just so unbelievable!"

"I don't understand, Joey! What kind of thing?"

Joey shook his head at Lucy and ignored her question. "How could you?" There were tears in his eyes; his five o'clock shadow was etched in ash. "I thought you loved Tessa!"

"Of course I love her, Joey." Lucy's whisper was bewildered. She wanted to comfort Joey, she wanted to retrieve the crumpled ball of paper that had landed at his feet, she wanted to sink to her knees and thank the god of unexpected hopes that he was finally close enough to touch.

She couldn't help what she did next. She approached Joey with her arms held open. When her palm grazed his cheek, Joey met her advance with disbelief. He ducked his head, as though avoiding a punch. When he turned away, Lucy persisted, placing her hand on his elbow. Without turning back to look at her, Joey lifted the offending hand and flung it away from his body. Such was the force of his rage that he didn't calibrate his strength, nor did he see the angle of the banister. What he'd intended as a firm rebuff ended as a crush of knuckle and cartilage into an unforgiving edge of the carved wooden handrail. This gave a snapping sound Lucy would remember, muffled though it was by her yelp of pain and the downward pound of Joey's shoes on the steps. It would be the way he looked at her next, however—so uncaring, so cold, so full of hate—that was so much harder to bear than the damage he'd done her hand. Joey had already slammed the door behind him before he thought better of it and returned to retrieve the balled letter he'd left at the bottom of the steps. He picked it up, forced it into his pocket and said, his tone deadly quiet, "Don't you ever come near my kids again, or I swear to God, I will fucking kill you."

Calling Susannah was harder than Lucy would have thought, for she was unaccustomed to using her right hand for anything, much less pressing numbers into a cordless phone through a veil of tears. She'd pinned the handset with her left elbow, pressing down on its plastic antenna. Her injured hand pulsed with the sort of radiant throb that brought to her nerves a peculiar frenzy of displaced panic.

It was welcome, this pain, a sensory distraction from the stinging beat of Joey's words, which played over and over in her head.

When Susannah arrived, Lucy was kneeling in the kitchen, her left hand in a bowl of ice, her right on Bijou's neck. Both dogs had taken this crisis as an opportunity to pitch a tarantella of nervous twitching and whimpering, which Lucy could only match by repeatedly murmuring. "You're okay, you're alright!" The words were meant to soothe, but they were inflected like questions and aimed as much at herself as they were at the dogs.

Susannah took Lucy's right elbow and said, "Let me look at your hand, sweetheart." Precious and Bijou, reassured by the sweet mothering in Susannah's tone, calmed themselves by pacing in a circle around the two women and the kitchen island.

"Where're your Baggies, Lucy?" Susannah asked, following the tilt of her friend's head to find them in the drawer next to the fridge and filling one with ice. She was brisk, efficient. Susannah had always been good in a crisis, dropping her normal air of uncertainty as though she'd never ever had moment's pause about anything.

Susannah whisked her friend out the door and into her Honda Element, sweeping the passenger seat free of its kid dreck: empty orange juice boxes, Fig Newton wrappers, Sierra Club coloring books and promotional flyers for the semifinals of World Wrestling Entertainment.

"Keep it on the ice if you can, Lucy-loo," she said. "I'll try to keep things smooth but you might want to brace it with your other arm when we go over the rough spots."

Lucy murmured her assent, leaned back and closed her eyes. Each time they hit a bump she was startled by the sound of her own voice rising in her sinuses to top the octaves at which a sound could emerge from tightly clenched lips. Each time this happened, the sound was met by an equal and opposite sigh of sympathy from Susannah. She was driving carefully but couldn't see all of the frost heaves, in the road, places where the asphalt had collapsed and swollen again with extremes of temperature.

"How did this happen?" the ER doc asked, after the fentanyl kicked in and Lucy's eyes flickered open and shut with the drunken glimmer of lights gone haywire.

"I fell," Lucy whispered, but that was all she'd say, or rather, it was all she *could* say before she fell asleep against the raised back of the examining table.

The doctor looked at Susannah. "Did she tell you how it happened? Is it possible someone did this to her?"

"She lives by herself. Maybe the dogs tripped her, though."

The doctor shook her head. "We're gonna need X-rays. She's not pregnant, is she?"

By the time Susannah left Lucy's house, it was ten thirty, late enough to have missed saying good night to Willow but not too late to dial Martha's number and tell her what had happened.

"Which hand did the son of a bitch break?"

"Her left, the fourth metacarpal. The doctor says it'll be at least six weeks, maybe eight."

"But that's her painting hand! Why would he? It's not like Joey to—"

"Lucy said he didn't do it. She said it was an accident. They were having a big fight over the fact that she hadn't told him Tessa wasn't eating lunch. I feel so terrible. I should have told him as soon as Amber told *me*."

"Why would he be so pissed about that? It's not like Tessa's not getting treatment. So what's the big deal?"

"I don't know. Lucy said it was complicated, that Tessa had told her some pretty upsetting stuff and she should have told him about it. She wouldn't go into it, but I guess she'd gone to the house this morning to try to tell Tessa she was going to tell Joey. Siobhan wouldn't let her in but Lucy left a note for Joey and one for Tessa. Apparently, that set him off."

"Are you sure she's telling the truth? If he was pissed off and yelled at her, it's pretty coincidental that she'd fall and break her hand without any help from him."

"I don't know. It doesn't make sense, but that's what she said. She swears it was an accident."

"So why wouldn't she tell the doc then?"

"They have to report domestic abuse, even if it's just suspected."

"So? Let the stupid fuckwit spend a night in the Omega lockup."

"Think, Martha. The Camerons would have a field day with that."

"Hey, I can't think. I just want to kill the man. I'm thinking she better press charges, just in case. He's got to be insane."

Susannah pulled into her driveway and turned off the engine. "I wonder if it's a very delayed reaction to losing Penelope. He stayed so calm, you know. He never really let himself fall apart when she died. I've been wondering when the other shoe would drop. Anyway, Lucy insists Joey didn't have anything to do with her broken hand. The last thing she wants is to give any ammunition to the Camerons right now. She kept saying that whatever happened, she doesn't want Tessa to suffer."

"Man, you're both way too full of excuses. The man is completely out of control. And Lucy's a glutton for punishment."

"No, she's thinking of the girls. If Joey were to get pulled out of the house—that would leave them alone with Siobhan. Lucy wants Tessa to get treatment, but she wants Joey to be around to soften the edges."

"What a freaking mess. You must be exhausted."

"No, I'm still on Phoenix time for some reason."

"Susannah, thanks for going—"

"Don't mention it. You'd do the same for me, I know that."

"Still. By the way, I got a call back from my law school friend. She says Sorensen can come see her and they'll try to find a way to confine the terms of the audit to the foundation's official business. Did you bring copies of the paper trail between him and the auditors?"

"Yep. They're on your desk already."

"Thanks."

"Oh, Martha, Lucy looks so forlorn! Go see her tomorrow."

"I will. Sateesh can bring her food. Do you think we should get her a cleaning service?"

Susannah snorted. "I'm afraid she's been doing nothing but clean since the girls and Joey moved out. The house reeks with the smell of Murphy Oil Soap. I've never seen it so immaculate and you know how clean Lucy's clean can be."

Chapter Twenty

The next morning, at five forty-five, Sateesh arrived at Joey's and unlocked the front door. He moved quietly up the stairs to Joey's room and just as quietly opened the door to the master bedroom. Joey was sleeping on his side, legs curled into a fetal curve around a bunched pillow. He was wearing a pair of boxers and a T-shirt, the neck of which Sateesh clenched with one fist.

He used the other to muffle Joey's mouth and his strangled objections, saying, "Get up. We need to talk."

"What the hell are you doing here? Get the hell out of my room."

"Silence. Get dressed. I'll wait for you outside."

"Like hell you will."

"Don't test me, Joey. The girls do not need to hear this. My car's in the drive."

When Joey came out to the car, wearing the tattered khakis he'd worn for days, he opened the door to Sateesh's station wagon and slid into the passenger seat. The door, though, he left wide open. His eyes were fastened tight on the front door of his house, his right hand gripping the overhead strap like it was the stop indicator on a bus he wanted off of in the worst kind of way.

"You broke her painting hand, Joey."

"What?"

"Lucy. Her left hand's broken, you fuck."

"That's not possible!"

"You tremendous fuck! What in God's name has gotten into you?"

Joey relinquished the strap above his head, reached for the door and closed it. The sound coming from his mouth was not human; it was accompanied by a butting motion that brought his forehead into close, personal and bruising contact with the dashboard.

"I can't tell you," Joey groaned.

"Why can't you tell me? Am I not your best friend?"

"I thought you were."

Sateesh pulled a napkin from the console and handed it to Joey. "Wipe your nose. It's bleeding on my leather seats."

"Fuck." Joey's voice was strangled and he tilted his head back to look at the ceiling, pressing the napkin to stanch the flow of blood from his nose. "I couldn't have broken her hand! I didn't even touch her."

"Well, it's hard for me to believe she did this to herself, much as that is what she's claiming. What's gotten into you? And why haven't you called me back?" Sateesh opened a bottle of water and set it into a cup holder before pulling out of the driveway. He said nothing until they'd stopped behind another car in the Bagel Bagel drive-through. "Look, I know you threw a note she'd written at her and then took it away before she could see what it was. Why would you do that? How could you possibly be so upset with her over something so—I cannot understand. I can't."

"Did she tell you what was in the note?"

"Good God, Jo-hee!" Sateesh said with exasperated patience. "Do you really think she did what she did out of malice?"

"Cut the bullshit, Sateesh. I'm so sick of that line of stupidity. She's responsible for her actions. And by the way, I know now."

"You know what?"

"I found out what everyone of you probably knew for years."

"What in God's name are you talking about?"

"Lucy and—I can't even say her name—"

"Lucy and who? Who are you talking about?"

It was Joey's turn to be confused now. "Sateesh, why are you doing this to me? I told you. I *know*."

"Joey, I might just have to hurt you if you say that again. *What* do you know?"

Joey nodded his head as if assenting to the insurgent misery within, then reached into his pocket and retrieved the offending letter, its form a mangled origami whose wings he flattened against the surface of his thigh.

He handed the document to Sateesh, fighting nausea.

When Sateesh was finished reading, he carefully gave it back to Joey. "Where did you get this?"

"In the mail. Last week."

"My God. Who would do this to you?"

"Apparently my wife and her best friend."

"But why—who would send this to you now?"

"I don't know."

"Joey, are you certain it's actually something written by Penelope? What if someone just made this up and sent it out of mischief?"

Joey didn't answer at first. He swallowed and could not help but wish that Sateesh had a point. "No. I can tell Penelope wrote it. She had a distinctive style. And Lucy knew exactly what I was talking about! She even apologized for keeping it from me all this time."

"I didn't know!" Sateesh murmured. "I never knew. I thought you were upset about Tessa. We all did."

"Maybe you did. But Lucy knows. She knew exactly what I was talking about. In fact, she brought a second copy of this letter to the house yesterday, in a box of stuff for Tessa. It's so pathological, I don't even know what to say. I thought I knew her."

"But that's not like Lucy. Why on earth would she want Tessa to know?"

"Exactly! You know, I know nothing at all anymore. Penelope could have been cheating on me all the time. That thing she said about the girls? What if—what if they aren't mine? What if the girls aren't mine?"

Sateesh shook his head. "No, they're yours, Joey. They look just like you."

"No, they look just like their mother."

"Yes, they do. But they also resemble you. Don't even let yourself go there, my friend."

"I feel like I've been hit by a train. You can't tell anyone, Sateesh. Not even Martha."

"That goes without saying. I'm so sorry."

At breakfast that morning, Siobhan served oatmeal, June's least-favorite thing. Because their dad wasn't there, it wasn't even warm, having been dished up without the ceremony of the piping-hot treatment that seemed to coincide with Joey's presence at the table. June tried to cover the soggy texture with cinnamon and sugar but after a spoonful, she found Miss Siobhan's small fingers pressing at her wrist. "That's enough," was all she said, using her eyes to indicate the bowl of blueberries. "If you want something sweet, try some of those. The glycemic index of fruit is much better than sugar."

"Is Daddy taking me to school?"

"No, he's in meetings this morning. I can run you over, though. Tessa, you'll have to come too, of course."

It wasn't until June had gotten to homeroom and unpacked her backpack that she realized she'd forgotten her lunch. Having recently been lectured on responsibility by Mrs. Williams, who kept waking June up when she was supposed to be listening to geography facts, June was loath to ask permission to call home. Instead, she waited until the teacher stepped out to bring the attendance log to the office, which gave her enough time to make a quick call from her cell phone.

This was a forbidden technology. Like her friends, June kept her phone turned off to avoid having it taken away for the full week of "confiscation" time Mrs. Williams imposed as a deterrent. For June, her only form of contact with Lucy was all the more precious for that reason. She was careful to keep her eyes on the door while she powered up, dialed and left a message asking Miss Siobhan to please bring her lunch in and leave it at the office.

Part of the new household regimen meant that June's debit card for the school cafeteria had been cut off, along with all spare change she might use to buy candy or sodas from vending machines. June, having skimped on breakfast, hoped Miss Siobhan listened to her message as soon as she got home.

As a matter of fact, June's voice was just saying, "Bye," when Tessa and Siobhan reentered the kitchen. Tessa hurried to press the Replay button but was intercepted by Siobhan, who silently but significantly wagged her pointer finger at the girl to remind her that the phone was off-limits. Siobhan replayed June's message and then deleted it before settling down at the table with Tessa to sign off on the breakfast she'd consumed.

"Will I have to go back over there with you?" Tessa asked.

"Where?"

"To bring June lunch?"

"No, Tessa, you won't. Sometimes I wonder how you two children have made it as far as you have. Have you not been taught there are consequences to one's actions? Bringing June her lunch would only reward her for being irresponsible. She'll be fine skipping a meal, and it will teach her to remember her belongings the next time she leaves the house. It's not like she's wasting away, for goodness sake."

"But that's like eight hours with no food! She gets a headache and dizzy when she doesn't eat."

"Nonsense. Her relationship with food is complicated, just like yours. Except the compulsion that makes *you* starve yourself makes her overdo things."

"And just how do you know this?" Tessa stammered, so filled with outrage on June's behalf she had trouble not spitting.

"I know this because I too was a child once, Tessa. Believe it or not, I suffered a similar craving for parental attention, for routine, for some sort of structure by which I might feel safe. My mother wasn't out saving the world, she was trying to create the next 'Stairway to Heaven,' but it's all the same in the end. When you're too busy to raise the children you've brought into the world, they invent all sorts of ways to cry for help, whether it's overeating, undereating, or fear of stranger danger."

Tessa didn't know what was harder, not kicking this horrendous bitch in the teeth or counting the minutes until she was excused from the table to go back into her mom's study and begin her homework. Tessa remembered having seen her dad's cell phone on the desk, charging.

Exactly forty minutes later Tessa finally broke away from supervision long enough to compose a brief text message to June.

Bitch wn't brng u lunch. Try Lucy.

Tessa had barely put the phone back onto the charger when Miss Siobhan came waltzing in to ask Tessa to give her a moment of her time.

"What?"

"What do you know about a secret Lucy's been keeping from your father?"

"She told you that?"

"You know?"

"Duh."

"But, Tessa, how in the world did you keep such an awful thing inside, not talking to anyone else? Do you not realize it's part of getting better?"

"Lucy told you? She promised she wouldn't!"

"Has it ever occurred to you that keeping secrets might be related to your problem with food?"

"Duh," Tessa repeated, providing Siobhan with the comfort of believing she'd hit the deductive nail of Lucy's romantic coffin precisely on its properly deserving head. For this reason, she let the child's disrespect slide without further investigation, leaving Tessa to ponder the simplistic tautology of Siobhan's inquiry in all its incredibly idiotic splendor. Geez, not talking about not eating lunch might have something to do with a problem with food? How many college degrees had it taken to put that one together?

• • •

When Lucy got a text from June saying **911! Starving! Can u brng me lunch!** she had no idea what to do. Joey had told her in no uncertain terms not to go near his girls, but Lucy knew how June got when she didn't eat. She hated the thought of her waiting all day for food that wouldn't arrive. Lucy dialed Susannah, whose voice mail answered; then Martha, who was out running with Sateesh; then Clover, who was not home either. Next, Lucy surrendered her self-respect completely and dialed the number she knew so well it might as well have been her own. The phone rang twice before Siobhan picked up and announced the name of her employer with such deference it made Lucy's head swim. Without even making a peep, Lucy used her little finger to press the Off button and only hoped there was no way for Siobhan to see who had just hung up on her.

Because Lucy didn't remember how to send a text, and would have had trouble doing so anyhow with her left hand in a cast, she dialed June's phone. Lucy knew it would be on Silent, but she figured that June could check for messages when she went to the bathroom or when the teacher left the room. "Hon, I can't come!" Lucy was whispering into the phone, before she heard an adult's unmistakably outraged question: "Whose phone just rang in my class?"

Lucy quickly pressed the Off button, wincing at the thought that she'd gotten June in trouble, wishing she'd hadn't wimped out of talking to Siobhan.

Miss Williams squinted at the tiny screen. "June, let's see what you've been doing while we've covered the Erie Canal. Why don't you read the class your text message? Or was it a phone call? I'm sure we'd all like to know why you've chosen to disrupt my class."

June shook her head, swallowing. The teacher, unfamiliar with June's phone, tried pushing buttons haphazardly. She then turned to the class, irritated by June's noncompliance, and scanned the children's faces. "Here, Eric, you're good with technology. Come read us the messages June's found so important."

Eric, the class clown, was only too happy to have a reason to stand up and put his voice into a falsetto, reading first the note from Tessa with its swear word stretched out for full effect, and then June's appeal to Lucy, which he imbued with all the operatic drama of a lovesick and hungry Pavarotti.

By the time the teacher realized what the children were laughing about, or more accurately, *who they were laughing at* it was too late. June was crying and her friend Willow had kicked Eric in the shins. The three of them were sent to the office to sort out their hurt feelings, indignation and aching tibias without regard to the fact that they would all likely miss recess and lunch, the latter a subject that had begun all this trouble in the first place.

Fowles Bunker Jr., attorney at law, was a good old boy from way back, a proud member of the Gator Nation. He'd officially represented Joey's interests when he'd signed the codicil to Penelope's will. Having Joey get his own lawyer had been Martha's idea, part of what had been required to make sure Penelope's document would stand up in court. This made going back to Fowles to find out how to *contest* that very same piece of paper pretty ironic. Recognizing irony and finding it at all amusing, however, were two vastly different things, as Joey had surmised more than once over the past few days.

On top of their brief legal connection, Fowles had also been a poker buddy back when Joey had had time for games. The man knew how to play whatever cards he was dealt. In addition to his strategic skills, Bunker had recently gone through a bad divorce, having been abandoned by his wife for a man she met at Al-Anon. That this romance had made clients in Omega and the surrounding counties think Fowles had a drinking problem, when it was in fact the woman's father who caused her need for meetings—this was one of those painful gifts of divorce that just kept on giving. Much of the God-fearing, liquor-loathing part of the town's population suddenly doubted whether Fowles could be trusted with their assets, much less their trusts.

That Joey was able to throw some business Fowles's way was about the only happy part of this legal errand, made at least slightly less awkward by the fact that Fowles appeared familiar with the volatility of Joey's emotional register. He seemed unfazed by the sordid conclusions Joey had drawn about the contents of his wife's letter, simply nodding somberly at appropriate junctures or waiting patiently during those baleful pauses in the conversation brought about by a breath taken too soon or a swallow gone awry.

"Forget the probate court, Joey. Too many appeals and you don't want this in the public record. Our first goal is to get the rest of the parties to agree to mediation before an arbitrator, who's like a judge in the sense that the decision he makes'll be binding. Second, we've got two options I can think of right away. One, we seek to dissolve the codicil based on your having been talked into signing it under false pretenses. Not an easy sell, but it might fly if we can find more evidence on possible deceptive actions by Penelope. Or another avenue would be to bring a motion to disqualify Lucy Vargas—who is effectively standing as a guardian of the children's interests—on the basis of problems with her character and/or competence. The burden of proof will fall to us either way, but if we get the right arbitrator, it might be worth a try."

"What are the risks?"

"You sure you want to know?"

"No."

"Well, give me a week or two so I can make sure I get 'em all, but the two I can think of right off? One—the probate judge could decide to offload your wife's cousins' complaint to the same mediator, which means they'd be privy to whatever you disclose. Worse is that those boogers could wrest control of the estate *if* the arbitrator decides in their favor. This is real bad because—unlike a court case—you cannot appeal it. Period, end of story. And two, Joey, I gotta tell you, whatever happens, if you duke it out in court or in mediation, this is gonna tear you apart. Trust me on that fact. You think you're after resolution, I know that. The truth is, son, you're only going to stretch out your agony and turn up the tension to intolerable. Also, and this is no small thing, considering these are your best friends and basically family to your kids, there's at least half a chance that by bringing this case forward, you'll not only alienate Lucy Vargas but the rest of your so-called Gang of Four."

"I don't have a choice, Fowles. Otherwise I've handed over my balls on a silver platter for my wife's girlfriends to carve up as they choose. What the fuck was I thinking?"

"You were thinking you loved your wife. And believe me, Joey, I know all the places you're bleeding from, but you should at least consider the idea that, all appearances to the contrary and despite her mistakes, that same wife really loved you too."

Joey shook his head, unable to respond, a slight tightening in his jaw the only sign of Fowles's words having filtered through what Joey had come to think of a constant choke hold on his soul. Just as Fowles offered the opinion that Joey was going to spend a lot of time and money conducting what would end up being a test more of loyalty than justice, the receptionist knocked on the door to say that a Miss Fitzpatrick was on the phone with an urgent call about Mr. Adorno's daughter.

Between the time it took the call to be transferred and Joey to pick up, he'd lost all contact with past or future, so focused was he on the sound of an ocean of blood pulsing in his ears. "Siobhan?"

"I'm sorry to bother you, but June's school called."

"Is she alright?"

"Yes. She's just gotten called in to the principal. Something about a cell phone that rang in class."

"June doesn't have a cell."

"Well, apparently she does now. Not only was there some sort of tussle with a boy and Susannah's little one, but I take it some foul language was used more than once. Please don't repeat this to Susannah, but I wonder if this Willow's a good influence. There's a bit of an attitude problem, and I think it seeps into June's respect for authority. Do you want me to run over there and collect her?"

"No. Just call the school and tell them I'll be there as soon as I can."

When Joey got home, he wouldn't answer Siobhan's tactful inquiries about what had happened. Nor would he say why June had been allowed to come home without being punished beyond what the school had inflicted by calling her father. In Joey's opinion, his daughter had suffered enough. Susannah had been in the principal's office when he got there, and when the kids were sent to fetch their backpacks, the parents were given a brief synopsis of June's crimes and the teacher's very regrettable reaction. If Willow hadn't used physical violence, the principal would have likely forgotten the whole thing. Unfortunately, the school had a zero-tolerance policy for such things, even though, as Susannah would later put it, that Eric made her want to kick him too. As far as Joey was concerned, June had been through enough, even if she had broken the school rules by trying to use her cell phone. That she'd not even told her father about having been given a cell phone might have been a problem in any other context, but the copious tears she'd been shedding since she'd gotten in the car had exempted her from criticism on just about any front.

"Honey, it's okay!" Joey said, pulling her close. "I know you're not a bad kid. Do you want to tell me what happened?"

June only shook her head and continued to cry. Joey patted her leg. "It's okay. You don't have to talk about it if you don't want to, honey. I'm just sorry you feel so bad."

At this, another torrent of tears was released as June came to realize she could not discuss with anyone, not even Lucy, the deep shame of having her hunger mocked so winningly in front of her whole geography class. Worse still was the way she'd seen herself reflected in Eric's pantomime, an act that she knew would already be spreading like wildfire through the whole fifth grade. Just one more crybaby fact on big fat June Adorno, who'd never made it through a sleepover without having to go home and now had proved herself equally ridiculous in the bright white light of day.

"Dad, she's evil," Tessa was saying as soon as Siobhan left for the grocery store. "I can't do this."

"You can, Tessa. I know you hate her. You'd hate anyone right now. It's part of the program. Please, just try and do what you have to, to get better, okay?"

"Look, Dad. Why can't Lucy do it instead? I promise, I'll eat. I will. If we could just go back to Lucy's? Or she could come here?"

"I think you know that's not an option, honey. Look—" Here Joey paused awkwardly before forcing himself to continue. "I've been wanting to talk to you about this. Siobhan thinks maybe Lucy's been part of your problem."

"Lucy?"

"Like maybe she was a little too loose about the rules, that maybe she acted more like a friend than a parent."

"What's wrong with that? She's not my parent. I'd hate her if she acted like she should be my mother all of a sudden."

"I don't know. I just . . . wonder. Something's pulled the rug out from under your appetite. Maybe you've needed more structure."

"No. I'm not—Dad, it's not Lucy's fault! I just, I don't know. I just have trouble eating, that's all. I feel like, I don't know, like it's just—whenever I do eat, it's like I just get really nervous afterward. When I don't eat, I don't have to think so hard, but when I do, I just feel . . . I can't explain. Like something bad's going to happen. I don't know why."

"What does your therapist say?"

"She wants me to think about taking pills," Tessa muttered.

"What do you think?"

"I don't want to." Tessa opened her mouth and closed it just in time. The first thing she'd started to say was that Zoloft made people gain weight. How this side effect had made itself known to her, Tessa couldn't even remember, but it had stuck to her brain, one of those annoyingly unforgettable facts that had taken on an internal power all its own. Still, Tessa knew that if she said this out loud to her dad, it would sound like she was really crazy, since gaining weight was exactly what her treatment plan was in fact designed to do. "By the way, Dad, just for the record, Siobhan is not the answer to my problems. She doesn't make me feel safe, she makes my skin crawl."

Joey crossed the floor and knelt at his daughter's side. He held her hand and said patiently, "She told me you'd hate her. It's okay. Just hang in there."

Tessa inhaled deeply and said, "It's not like I have a real choice, is it?"

Chapter Twenty-one

J oey made no explanation for why he'd chosen to block all visitation between the children and Lucy, or why he'd taken June's cell phone from the principal's office and returned it to Susannah with a stiffly worded request that she ask permission before ever again offering his child so expensive a gift.

Sateesh, around whom Joey had become newly reserved, could still observe the panic in his friend's eyes, that up-against-the-wall sort of fury that just begged you to give him a reason to further entrench his position with nails, a hammer and some perpendicular wooden slabs from Galilee. Though Sateesh would have liked to convince Joey that what happened so long ago shouldn't have had such power to hurt him, he knew it wasn't true. In fact, the length of time Joey hadn't known appeared to have only intensified the betrayal he now felt.

Sateesh resisted the urge to tell Martha what he knew. He was certainly tempted, especially when his wife complained noisily about Joey's excommunication of Lucy. It would have been satisfying to set her to rights on who had actually done more damage to whom. Sateesh told himself his silence was about keeping his friend's confidence, but it actually had more to do with his sense that the more people who knew, the greater would be Joey's humiliation. This was logic from the collective male unconscious that held firm, despite Sateesh's intellectual sophistication.

And Lucy. Lucy had her own worries, starting with how to get up in the morning and ending with how to sleep at night, punctuated by repeated assaults on the territories formerly known as her synapses, wherein all thought had since become a dispirited Ping-Pong game composed entirely of noodle shots into the net. Her girls were gone, she couldn't paint and her MasterCard had been cut off for nonpayment. None of these losses held a candle to the fact that Joey appeared to genuinely despise her.

Still, though she certainly possessed a hyperdeveloped conscience, Lucy had great difficulty seeing how her hesitation to tell Joey about Tessa's lunch problems, even complicated by Tessa's feelings of anger toward her father and guilt about her mother, could have resulted in such a drastic response. It took hours of pacing up and down her hall, scouring her memories, before she came to terms with the fact that explicable or not, Joey blamed her for Tessa's illness. In his mind, Lucy had chosen the path of least resistance by agreeing to keep Tessa's secret. Worse, she'd tucked the matter away, let herself avoid facing its ramifications, employing a form of denial at which she'd long been practiced. The truth, observed in the bitter chill of Joey's overnight freeze, was inescapably transparent. Lucy had neglected Tessa's welfare in the heat of her own selfish passions. She'd been recklessly happy, so thrown by the confusion of being loved by the man she'd wanted for so long, she'd not been able to think in a straight line. She'd taken her eyes off the prize, in this case the sacred trust of his daughter's well-being. And, when she thought about it now, for what? A chance to prove a central axiom of the World According to Penelope, that when it came to infatuation, there were no mistakes too stupid for its practitioners to commit?

Chapter Twenty-two

By Monday morning of the following week, Martha had called to order an emergency meeting of the Gang of Four, whose members trailed into the back room at Sateesh's restaurant with the look of sheep to the slaughter. There was Lucy, her arm in a sling, wearing a loose peasant shirt that Susannah had helped her into, tucked into jeans, the ones Susannah had had to button for her and then hitched up with a belt because of the weight she'd lost.

Susannah's black gauchos and fitted bolero jacket were covered with cat hairs, a reflection of the fact that Lucy's helplessness extended to lint brushes, even when the trauma of looking at such messiness was causing the left side of Lucy's face to blossom into a nascent series of facial tics.

Clover, sitting next to Martha, was too busy trying to surreptitiously read over the attorney's shoulder to notice Lucy's significant eye movements, signals that cast back and forth between Susannah's blighted torso and the roll of masking tape sitting on the canned goods shelf, just waiting for someone like Clover to wrap it inside-out around the flat of her hand and eradicate the damned cat hair from Susannah's clothing, once and for all.

Although Sateesh was not an official member of the Gang of Four, Martha had invited him too. He was the last person to join them, wiping flour on his black-checkered cook's pants, this smear adding to the clamor in Lucy's psyche.

Martha waited until her husband settled and said, "Joey has hired Fowles Bunker Jr., who sent me a memorandum stating their desire to begin arbitration proceedings."

"Why?" Clover asked, still trying to read the print despite the fact that it was obscured by Martha's hands, her fingers interwoven like the lawyer had taken up praying.

Martha set the papers in front of Clover and said, "Be my guest."

Turning to Susannah and Lucy, she repeated what she'd already explained to Sateesh, that Joey wanted them to agree to have certain aspects of his wife's will resolved by a court-appointed arbitrator. If they agreed, his lawyer would schedule their first hearing as soon as the Monday before Thanksgiving. "I think he's going to challenge the terms of the codicil."

"But why?" Susannah asked. "I guess I mean, why now?"

"You've got me. The man's lost his mind. I suspect they're going to try to get us to stand down."

"On what?" Lucy asked.

"What do you think, hon? Deciding whether or not the person he decides to marry is good for his girls."

Clover shook her head and put down the thicket of text she'd been unable to decipher. "No way."

"I agree," Martha said. "We made her a promise and so did he."

"My question remains, why now?" Susannah pressed. "What's the point?"

"Do you really have to know?" Sateesh asked. "I mean, think about it. He's finally coming to terms with Penelope's loss, and suddenly, he's furious. This represents something to him."

"But we promised," Martha insisted.

"But Penelope's gone. And he's here. I say you should think of the living."

"Look, ya'll may be atheistic but I'm not. My sister is still with us. And I'm not going back on my word to her. I'll tell you that."

"It's not about God, Clover, or whether Penelope's spirit lives on," Susannah demurred, fidgeting with the trim on her jacket. "It's about helping Joey heal from his loss."

"Hey, he's not the only one who's lost her, damn it. My nieces could tell you a thing or two about that. And she was the only family I ever had."

Lucy could not keep from asking her next question, however weak and pathetic it made her feel when her voice quavered mid-sentence. "Does he have someone he wants to marry?"

"I have no clue," Martha said. "Sateesh?"

Sateesh shook his head and shrugged. "I know nothing."

Martha stared at her husband, willing him to spill the words she could tell he had been holding on to ever since that morning he'd gone to punch out Joey's lights, only to return hours later, shaken but determinedly mute.

"Look," Martha said. "We've got three options. One, insist this remains in court. He'd have trouble winning there, I think, but it could backfire on us if the judge wants us off his docket and wonders why we won't be reasonable and move it to mediation. Two, we could enter mediation hoping we can reach an agreement that calms Joey down but doesn't abrogate our obligation to Penelope. Three, we could accept an arbitrator, which means we don't get to control anything. It's more like a trial: we each make our case and the arbitrator decides who's right. Whatever he or she decides would be binding."

"Why would we agree to that, then?" Clover asked.

"Because that's what Joey wants. Otherwise he says he's taking the girls and moving them back to Ohio to be near his parents."

"No way!" Clover cried. "He can't do that. Brittany's had enough losses and the girls need—they need us."

"The thing is, as long as he doesn't remarry, he's free to do whatever he wants."

"We have to do it then," Lucy said quietly. "We have to."

"Do what?" Sateesh asked.

"The arbitrator."

"If he's got someone in mind to marry, I don't understand why he doesn't just ask if we'll go ahead and approve her. I, for one, can think of only one person in town he'd even be interested in, and she's already living with them."

Clover's words were nothing Lucy hadn't imagined already. Still, hearing them out loud was enough to send shock waves through her fractured hand, as if it had been picked up and pounded against the surface of the table instead of pressed tightly against her ribs.

Sateesh was asking Clover why she was so intent on enforcing the codicil if she thought Joey wanted to marry Siobhan

"Because it's what Penelope wanted. She wanted us to approve the union."

"But, Clover, if it makes Joey feel better to feel like he's free to make a choice, then why can't you give him that?" Sateesh pressed.

"Because he's not *free*. He's got two daughters and there is no way in hell I'm playing Indian giver on my word."

"Clover!" Susannah scolded. "That's such a regressive view of history, and it's racist too. The Indians didn't know what they were signing, they were just jollying the crazy Pilgrims."

"Exactly. Just as Joey jollied Penelope!" Sateesh said, his tone heated. "I think you're all being quite hypocritical here, holding Joey to something that takes away his right of self-determination, and for what? So Penelope could stop obsessing and move on to something else?"

"You know what?" Susannah mused. "I have to find myself agreeing with Sateesh. It's not fair. If Darryl's best friends had gotten to decide who I was allowed to marry, I'd feel enslaved. It's not right."

Martha threw her head back so violently she hit a can of tomatoes on the shelf behind her. "Ow! Susannah, stop! First off, Darryl doesn't have even one friend, much less four, and two, you wouldn't let yourself get brainwashed by a woman with the body of Barbie and the brains of a chicken."

"She's got a master's degree!" Clover said heatedly at the very same moment Lucy threw her head into her hands and began to bray.

"Is she laughing or crying?" Susannah whispered to Sateesh, before she too was carried along by Lucy's hysterical wails, exacerbated when she pulled her broken hand out of its support with such force that it banged loudly against the table.

"You poor man," Siobhan was saying. "You don't deserve this."

Tessa was at the therapist's, June was at school and Joey had taken the short span of time when both girls were out of the house to conduct a bleary-eyed pacing campaign from his desk to his window and back again. Siobhan could not help but overhear his rhythmic footsteps from her newest domain a floor below, in Penelope's study.

Siobhan had set herself up at the late mother's desk, showing by example that there was nothing sacred about a piece of furniture. It was just an eight-by-five burled-mahogany top, made to be used, not enshrined.

Siobhan had looked forward to the quiet, had looked forward to entering further evidence of progress into her ledgers. Instead, fate had intervened in the form of a disturbance of sound and fury that was simply crying out for her intervention.

First she was standing upstairs at the doorway of her employer's home office; next she was crossing to his path. She took his elbows into her small hands and led him to sit down at his desk.

"When was the last time you slept?" Siobhan scolded gently.

Joey shook his head. He could not remember what day it was, could not remember the last time he'd truly disappeared without dreaming of Lucy and his wife making love to each other, their eyes and hands in places he'd never reach. These images, strung together in some infinite mirrored regression, rippled out against his own ignorance, his invisibility, his insignificance.

Siobhan moved around behind the seated man to work her fingers into his knotted shoulders, to slowly and steadily warm the muscles bunched against bone as a form of survival. Joey leaned forward into his hands, closed his eyes, and Siobhan could not help but feel regret at the suffering she'd inadvertently brought his way.

"You don't deserve this," she repeated, whispering the words. "You're a good man. Come here now. You need to get some sleep, you need to take care of yourself. Your children need you."

The master bedroom was down the hall, at the front of the house. Siobhan led him slowly toward it, coaxing him with soft, murmured assurances. "You're a beautiful man, you're a wonderful father. You're tired and you work too hard and you need to rest. Come here."

By the time Joey had gotten under the covers, Siobhan had divested herself of all her clothing. She stretched herself over Joseph Adorno like a warm cat and began to kiss him gently. She persevered in her comforts until she could feel he was erect.

"I'm going to help you sleep, you beautiful man, and then I'm going to take care of you the way you deserve to be cared for. Wouldn't you like that? Don't you worry now. Don't. I'm here."

When it was time to collect Tessa from the therapist's, Siobhan insisted on driving there herself. "You sleep. Let me take care of you. Let it go."

Joey heard her words, tried them on in his head as this mysterious sylph tiptoed out of his room with her clothing in a bundle.

As the days went by, Siobhan was careful to tread lightly into his room at night, careful to leave before the dawn broke pink between the curtains. She was the soul of rectitude when the girls were near. Her work with them was unaffected by her growing attachment to their father, which would remain for her a point of no small pride. She remained brisk, efficient and rational in her treatment of Tessa, who had grudgingly begun to eat again. Siobhan forgave June her woeful clumsiness, her ungainly paunch, even her never-ending stories about Lucy and her mother, both of whom, unbeknownst to the oblivious child, brought a fresh glint of pain to her father's eyes every time their names were uttered aloud.

When Rocky got into the garbage, or Tessa refrained from ever once thanking her for the food, or Clover called incessantly with suggestions for the dance team's next costume order, Siobhan remained calm and focused on her mission, that of showing Joey just how much better his life might be with her care and devotion.

The father she'd never had, the mother she'd always wanted—Siobhan's aspiration somehow involved cocooning herself inside the latter to attain the former. As she tended nightly to Joey's insatiable appetites, she poured her whole being into his, convinced that Joey's suffering and her own were linked somehow, that her childhood abuse and his conjugal betrayal were both part of the same pattern of neglect.

Siobhan was practiced in timing and tact and she used these strengths to optimize each teachable moment. There was a way of saying without saying, a straying onto subjects that might otherwise raise unnecessary hackles. "I'm here to please you," she'd explain, waving away Joey's apologies for waking her. "I can't imagine being too tired for you. I can't imagine not wanting you to own me. All of me."

Siobhan was a performance artist of submissive persuasion, portraying the woman she knew all men secretly desired and wanted. She would be his geisha; it pleased her to do this. She had no will other than to heal the soul.

She would use this word often, *heal*.

The inference was unmistakable. He was a survivor of trauma brought on by his selfish and domineering wife. When she could, Siobhan would press the envelope, at moments when he seemed capable of hearing her point. "Do you ever wonder why she couldn't trust men?" she'd ask. "I cannot imagine choosing my children's future over my husband's. Did she even make certain you'd have enough to live on?"

"My salary's good. And the girls' allowance is plenty too."

"Well, that's fortunate, given how things have turned out." Siobhan would lay her hand on Joey's shoulder, coaxing him to defend himself against the damage he'd endured. Her eyes would mist up indignantly. "You are so generous and forgiving. Truly, I cannot imagine the suffering your poor wife must have gone through to come out looking at life so fearfully."

At practice for dance team, June and Willow were giggling in a corner when they were supposed to be paying attention. Siobhan cleared her throat, and still, the girls didn't heed her. Irritated, Siobhan clapped her hands in the air and said, "Jack and Mrs. Sprat? Would you like to share the joke?"

Several of the other girls laughed, but Willow and June did not. They hadn't heard the words, having been caught up in the "sillies," as Susannah called them, the infectious laughter that came from nothing but looking at each other when they were in the right mood. Brittany reached over and jostled June's shoulder gently, trying to remember where she'd heard Jack Sprat's name before.

June turned her face up toward the teacher, and so did Willow. Both straightened their backs and proceeded with the steps the rest of the girls were performing to the snapping of the teacher's fingers and the count of her "One and two and three and four and five and six and seven and eight." When they caught sight of each other in the mirror, though, neither girl could help herself. Willow collapsed on the floor in the middle of the routine.

"Willow, you can take a time-out! Now. Go to my office and call your mother to pick you up."

June held up her hand but Miss Siobhan ignored her. Willow left the room and June called out, "Miss Siobhan, it wasn't her fault. I was—"

"Look, June, when you know the dance perfectly, you may speak to me. For now, I want you to concentrate on learning the steps. And hold in your tummy. You look five months pregnant, for God's sake."

June was cowed into silence. She forced herself to try to follow along with the other girls, despite the fact that her vision was blurred by a film of tears. June felt a sharp stab of pain in the back of her throat as she replayed Miss Siobhan's words over and over in her head, their sting having all the greater effect because she hadn't expected them.

That night, when they'd finished eating dinner and Tessa was being forced to sit at the table for an hour and a half, June headed upstairs and carefully closed the door between her bedroom and her sister's. She washed her hands. Then she poked her index and pointer finger at the strip of flesh hanging at the curtain of her throat, where they'd learned in science the gag reflex resided. It wasn't until her third try that June managed to bring up her food, a muddy string of debris held together by a bubbly necklace of spit. The sight of this was so disgusting to June that she vomited again, this time heaving up what seemed like mostly water but which burned the back of her throat and the inside of her nostrils.

When she was done, June breathed deeply and stood up straight, looking in the full-length mirror to see if her stomach had gotten any flatter. She brushed her teeth and headed to her father's study, where she was hoping he'd give her a hug.

She was tempted to tell him about Willow, about how they'd gotten into trouble at Kicks!, but she was also afraid. If she told him what Miss Siobhan had said about her stomach, she'd cry. It was too embarrassing to say what had happened, too awful to think about how all her dance friends had heard. Worst of all, what could Miss Siobhan, with her perfect figure, think of June to say such a thing?

That night, when Lucy finally got home from town, all she wanted was to go to bed with a drink and a Vicodin. Her hand was killing her. Susannah, though, had insisted on cooking her an omelet. "You are losing weight, Lucy."

"Stress diet."

"Listen, Lucy, let me call Amber and then we'll talk." Susannah pulled her cell phone out of her purse and examined the screen.

"Grrr. Battery's down." She reached for Lucy's cordless phone and made her call, stirring the egg mixture slowly. "Lucy?" she asked when she'd finished her conversation with Amber. "You've got that stuttering dial tone. Shall I check your messages?"

Lucy, lying on her couch, her injured hand resting on several pillows, was clenching her teeth, waiting for the Vicodin to kick in. "Sure. The code's the same as my alarm system. But will you please, please make me a gin and tonic?"

"Lucy? Are you sure you can drink when you're taking pain pills? I don't want you to end up in a coma."

"Oh, a coma!" Lucy sighed wistfully. "Just make me a drink and double my dose."

"I will not."

"Susannah. I'm only having half a pill and a weak drink. It's not going to kill me. Remember when Martha put out her back? She never stopped drinking. Hell, she was taking pills and chugging drinks like there was no tomorrow."

"Well, there might *not* be one, a *tomorrow*, that is, if you don't follow the pharmacy's directions."

"Like I said. Please. Bring it on."

"Lucy, it's not like you to drink anyway."

"Susannah, I promise you, I won't die on you, much as the idea compels me."

Susannah nodded, though the drink she made would properly be called a tonic and thimbleful of gin. After pouring herself a glass of white wine and carrying the omelet to Lucy, Susannah sat across from her friend and rang the number for voice mail, pen and message pad in hand.

When she was done, Susannah rose and went to the kitchen, brought back the bottle of gin and held it over Lucy's glass. "Here, Lucy. I shorted you. I don't think you'll want to have this discussion unless you're fortified."

"Susannah? What is it? Is something wrong with the girls!"

"Only indirectly. Give me your glass and let me put my feet up. All I've done is wait on you, and now I want you to be nice back to me. Tell me where you keep your bills and let me take them into work tomorrow."

"I'm fine," Lucy said. "What about the girls?"

"They're fine, Lucy Vargas, but you're not. The electric company wants to know when you're going to pay the past-due on your account and so does MasterCard. And your bank says you owe three hundred dollars in bounce protection and late-payment fees!"

Lucy did that thing she did whenever anyone mentioned money to her, a dismissive wave, except she forgot that her waving hand was also her broken hand. Thus, her "it's nothing" wave, carried out to assure Susannah of her well-being, was sabotaged by her facial expression, half wince, half whimper. Lucy grimaced against the unpleasant electric jolt that illuminated each and every molecule along the fractured fault lines of her knuckles. "Ow!"

"Lucy, where are they?"

"The girls?"

"The bills!"

"Susannah. I'm fine."

"No, you are not. You are going to let me examine your accounts or I'm going to search the house 'til I find them."

Lucy shook her head wanly. "Susannah, don't do this to me."

"Lucy Vargas, I'm serious. Where are your bills and bank statement?"

"Susannah, stop. You told me there was something to do with the girls? What was it?"

"Oh, it's nothing serious. June's teacher called to say she's been falling asleep in class. I take it she doesn't know they've moved back into town?"

Like his youngest daughter, Joey had been having trouble sleeping. Indeed, the shrink he'd begun seeing twice a week was presently handing him a prescription for Ambien.

"Just take it right before you want to go to bed," Dr. Collier said.

Joey shook his head. "I don't do pills."

"Look, if you don't start sleeping, you're going to start decompensating. Seriously. You've got to get your circadian rhythms back on track. I don't want things spiraling down for you."

"I don't think they could get much worse."

"Believe me, they can. So just be a man about this. Overcome your fear of looking weak."

"It's not that. But I read about Ambien. It makes people do crazy stuff."

"Look, every pill has its risks. Aspirin kills people too."

"See?"

"No, aspirin also saves lives and you know it. Those cases in the news about Ambien, they were people who would take the pill before driving home, thinking they'd just let it kick in so they could sleep as soon as they got there. Ambien is a disinhibitor, like all those drugs. That's why it can, if you're predisposed to sleepwalking, make you do things you might not otherwise do. You don't sleepwalk, do you?"

"No, but I might just decide to wake up and eat a gallon of ice cream."

"That's the least of your worries. You need to be strong to help your daughter get well."

"How do you think she's doing?"

"You'd have to ask her therapist."

"But what do you think? I mean, of how we're doing this treatment plan at home instead of in a hospital?"

"Joey, I've told you already. I think the best option might be a hospital, but everyone's different. Also, it looks like your nutritionist has good credentials. She interned at one of the best programs in the country."

"You've heard of it?"

"Everyone's heard of Ridge Mountain, Joey. So listen, let's talk about you. You going to cooperate on the pills or not? I swear, as long as you just make sure you take them right before you want to go to sleep, you'll be fine."

• • •

The Cameron twins had taken British Airways to Phoenix, with a stop in Atlanta. Pasha Sorensen was waiting at arrivals, wearing cowboy boots, a tight white denim skirt and a T-shirt declaring PETS ARE PEOPLE TOO. Nigel had to pinch Peter's biceps to force him toward the woman, for there was something in her stance that made the younger twin fear for the more delicate portions of his anatomy.

They drove in near silence to the Ritz-Carlton, making awkward small talk about the rain, or lack of it, and other obvious truths about the desert climate. Nigel had never seen an uglier city in his life. However, the Ritz, ah, that was entirely different. The Ritz was an oasis of luxury that made him feel nostalgic for Princess Diana and Dodi Fayed, for movie stars and Knightsbridge boutiques. Once they'd installed themselves in the hotel bar and ordered proper drinks, Pasha embarked on a tale she had insisted was too personal to tell over the phone. Much of what she said was irrelevant to the Camerons' purpose, but these were details that, like life's other inconveniences, the Camerons endured with dignity and stoic restraint. Ghastly discussions of vortices in the mountains near Sedona, Wiccan ritual involving placentas and bared breasts, shamans reincarnated from Mormon polygamists— all of these unpleasantries were somehow connected to Pasha's conviction that she must single-handedly rescue the planet from the shameful influences of her ex-husband's libidinous excesses, the full measure of which she appeared to see as part of a vast conspiracy to oppress women in general and herself in particular.

It wasn't until their third Oban scotch, when the twins excused themselves to smoke a cigarette, that Pasha warmed up. "You smoke? Can I bum one?"

Four Dunhills later, the three were fast friends, members of the same persecuted-smokers' rights coalition formed ad hoc on the back patio. Waiters rushed to catch their ashes as though such remnants were offal from untouchables, even as they bowed and scraped with obsequious submission like monkeys at the Taj Mahal.

"God, what hypocrites," Pasha mumbled. "Every one of them with leather shoes." She was so lost in thought she didn't seem to notice that the twins were suddenly swaying forward in the wind, using their commodious bellies to cloak the matching taupe Prada loafers they'd chosen for the visit. "Gabe used to love this place."

"Who?"

"My husband. Gabriel Sorensen. Fucking capitalist trust fund asshole. Spent the first year of our marriage here and a whole lot of his daddy's money drinking his guilt away. That's why I brought you two here."

"Guilt?" Nigel asked, taking Pasha's rough elbow and escorting her back toward the dark bar, all the better to draw attention away from his many calfskin accessories, belt, bolo, briefcase.

"You better believe it. His father's stores made a shitload of money ripping off people in the barrio. Until Gabe got the balls to quit, he used to come in here and drink. Though if he left a big enough tip at the end of the night it would make up for what his daddy did. Anyway, I brought you here to see the place because this is where they met."

"They?"

"Your cousin and her whore friend met Gabriel here."

"Right. Who was that?" Nigel asked, as though she'd already mentioned it but he was simply needing his memory banks refilled.

"You know . . . shit, what's her name? My brain is—some artist bitch. Gabe and I walked in on them in bed together."

Nigel cleared his throat. "How very awkward for you."

"You don't know the half of it. A month or so later, when we were fighting, he finally admitted he'd been involved with the two of them the very night before! Fucking rich bitches think they own everything, including my husband. Thought nothing of inviting him into bed. Fucking sluts."

"How rude!"

"Some people with money—Gabe was like that too—it's like the rules don't apply to them. Like they were born with such privilege they get out of jail free no matter what they do."

"This ménage à trois?" Nigel asked delicately. "This happened when?"

"Oh, you won't believe this! See, Gabe comes home at three in the morning with stars in his eyes. Little did I know at the time what *put* them there. Fucking asshole! He tells me he's met these women with their own foundation and he's spent all night drinking with them at the hotel pool and talking about his neighborhood project. He'd already been hitting up all his dad's friends for money and nobody was biting. Anyhow, he's all excited because the next day he gets up at eight and writes up a proposal and says he's gonna run it over to them. I smelled something fishy right there and then.

"'I'll go with you,' I said, like I just really wanted to meet these nice little old rich ladies. I figured the whole thing was a lie and he'd been out fucking someone and just didn't have the cojones to tell me."

"How terrible for you!" Peter sighed.

"Anyway, I could tell he didn't want me to come but I wasn't getting left at home like some used piece of Kleenex. What a son of a bitch he was to me! I have lived my life in such pain, you just don't know."

"So, you arrived together?"

"Yeah. We knock at the door but there's no answer so Gabe gets his waiter buddy in room service to open it. He says he'll just take the proposal into the living room of the suite and leave it there. Or so he said. The son of a bitch. Anyhow, we tiptoe in and the place is really dark. The doors are all shut except the fucking bedroom door and there they are, twats just *out there*, fucking whores. Bitches. Gabe grabbed my arm and pulled me out of the place, but not before I got a good look."

"So, how did you find out who it was? In the bed with our cousin?"

"It wasn't easy, I'll tell you that. Gabe acted like what we'd seen wasn't anything. Like it was just two friends sleeping together, but I told him no women in the world sleep naked together like *that* unless they're having sex. Fucking liar told me it was none of our business and I should just forget what I saw. Little did I know he'd been fucking their brains out the night before. Fucking liar."

Nigel's brain was already cartwheeling through space and time, giddy with the sheer felicity of this new information. "So he confessed later."

"Right. Son of a bitch. No wonder they funded him. He knew too much."

"So, do you—are you saying he blackmailed them, then?"

"No, that would have been way too practical for Captain Crusader. But I wasn't afraid to let Miss Rich Bitch know what I'd seen. I told her it made me *sick* to see married women cheating on their husbands like that and using mine to get their rocks off. What perverts."

"That was awfully assertive of you."

"No shit! I was so *pissed* when I found out what they did to me, no way I was gonna sit there like Miss Goody Two-Shoes! Fucking bitches."

"So—what in heaven's name did Penelope say?"

"What could she say? She started bawling and telling me she hadn't meant to hurt anyone." Here Pasha put her voice into a falsetto and said, "'I spend every day of my life filled with remorse for what I did and I apologize to you from the bottom of my heart.' Then she said she had no idea that Gabe was married when it happened but that it was still wrong, no matter what. She said if she could make it up to me in any way, I should let her know."

"And?"

"I told her I didn't want her fucking money. Who did she think she was, trying to buy me off? I said I just wanted to call her *girlfriend* so I could ask her how she might feel if I slept with *her* husband."

"Oh my Lord!" Peter whispered. "You were so—badly—used, weren't you? What in the world did she say?"

"The usual. How her friend regretted it too, and so on and blah, blah. 'Talk to the hand,' I said. 'I want her number, or I'm calling your husband.'"

"Heavens!" Nigel exulted. "What on earth did she do?"

"Begged me not to call anyone. Told me the other woman wasn't married, as if that made jack-shit difference! Then she asked me what I valued most in the world. I told her honesty was right up there with apple pie and animal rights and that I wanted an apology from the woman who wronged me."

"And?" Peter was rubbing his hands together delightedly.

"I got a call the next day from the second woman saying she was very sorry she'd slept with my husband, that it had been a terrible drunken mistake, and if it made me feel better, she wasn't married. That blackmailing her would do nothing at all, since this was the twenty-first century, so maybe I should just go seek couples' counseling and leave Penelope alone."

"What did you say?"

"That it wasn't about blackmail but she needed to know people weren't there just for her to exploit when she felt like it. Bitch."

"So how did you figure out who she was then?"

"Process of elimination. One of my friends from the Animal Liberation Front's pretty good with computers. He hacked into the hotel register and got their names. Then a colleague in Jacksonville drove over where they live and asked around. The other three chicks in a suite that weekend were married. Plus, the bitch I talked to said something about being a painter and how in her world, it wasn't a big deal to be—how did she say it?— 'unconventional.'"

"Heavens, what a story!"

"Yeah, one of the many nightmares I've had to go through because I made the mistake of marrying the wrong asshole."

"You poor thing."

"Not so poor anymore. Arizona's community property, so I got half Gabriel's money and I bled Miss Rich Bitch for this and that when I felt like making sure she paid for what she did to me. I donated the money she gave me to the Animal Liberation Front, but still—I wanted her to pay for what she did."

"Do you have copies of the checks she sent you?"

"No. I burned them as part of a healing ceremony after my divorce."

"Ah." Nigel nodded as though such things were to be expected. "I see."

Chapter Twenty-three

Lucy's legs were a sight to behold, spotted with tiny pieces of tissue anchored by blotted dried blood. That was the first thing her friends noticed when she answered the front door. To be fair, however, it was only one of many signs in her appearance hinting that something was amiss. She looked like one of those drawings in which children were asked to point out the blatant mistakes, one by one: the wrinkled frock, left in the dryer too long and buttoned haphazardly; the uneven smoothness of her hair where the brush reached, the matted plaque where it did not.

"Lucy, are you okay?" Clover asked, setting her package of bubble wrap on the table in the foyer before pulling back for a second look.

"Does it look like she's okay?" Martha asked, leaning in to bestow a kiss on Lucy's left cheek. "How did you cut yourself?"

"Shaving. Stupid idea but I looked like Godzilla."

"Why didn't you wait for us to help you, Lucy?" Susannah was carrying a bag of groceries and a casserole dish filled with packing tape. She brushed past the women clogging the hall and set the groceries on the kitchen island. Lucy followed her and opened the fridge before carefully lifting one item at a time with her right hand and placing it awkwardly on the shelves.

"Lucy!" Martha snapped. "Can you relax just a minute and tell me what to do? We want to help you."

"I know. I'm so grateful you brought it but if we leave this up here, the dogs'll get to it."

"So tell us what to do, for Pete's sake!" Clover turned to Lucy and unbuttoned the front of her dress to reveal a faded cotton jog bra that Lucy had been fortunate enough to have wriggled into without needing to fasten clasps. Still, the bra was twisted around her torso, the elastic so worn it puckered out against her ribs.

"Do you know you got this buttoned up wrong? Here, just let me help you now. Honey, why don't you move into town and let me take care of you? You're a mess."

"I like it here," Lucy said, touched by Clover's solicitous tone. "Thanks, though."

"I talked to Sigi today," Susannah said. "He wants you to send your paintings up COD."

"Cash on delivery," Clover explained, ever helpful.

"How did you get Sigi's number, and, more to the point, why would you take it upon yourself to call him?" Lucy slumped down against one of the stools in her kitchen, resting her sling on the countertop.

"Your phone bill. I couldn't help but see the New York area code. Sweetie, the thing is, it'll take time to get your finances in order," Susannah explained, wincing at the look of embarrassment that crossed Lucy's face. "I applied for some reimbursement monies for the extra household costs you've taken on, but Frick and Frack just drag their heels about everything."

"I told you, I don't need—"

"But you do, Lucy. You do need to be reimbursed. And we're pressing them to do the right thing, but the way the trust works, we have to jump through hoops and it'll take us a while—"

"What are ya'll talking about?" Clover was washing fruit in the kitchen sink. "What's this about?"

"Nothing," Lucy warned, glaring at Susannah.

"It's not *nothing*. We need to explain this to Clover because she's got pull with the twins. Here's the problem. While we were all going about our lives again after Penelope was killed, Lucy wasn't taking any guests. Now she's in serious financial trouble. A huge payment comes due this December and if she doesn't pay it, she could lose this house."

"Susannah, I'm—I wish you'd asked me before you called Sigi," Lucy said. "I hope you didn't tell him I broke my hand!"

"For one thing, *you* didn't break your hand," Martha interrupted. "But don't worry, your lurid secret's safe from Sigi and ten thousand of his closest friends. Is that what you were worried about?"

"No. It's that I've still got to finish *The Three Graces* and get it off to the Galbreath competition by next Tuesday. I don't want Sigi freaking out. He's got other artists he could have nominated instead of me."

"How you gonna do that? Finish the painting?" Susannah asked.

"I don't know."

"I can help you, Lucy," Clover offered. "I used to love to do paint by numbers. If you show me where to put the paint, I can totally keep it in the lines. And Martha, how can you say she didn't break her hand! It looks pretty dang broken to me."

"Look, you're all so . . . great," Lucy said. "You've got enough—I don't need help."

"Yes, you do. So shut up and sit still a minute," Martha said. "Like Susannah said, we talked to Joey and we can petition the trustees to cover the extras, but because Joey just withdrew a bunch of money to hire Nurse Bitchette, it'll take time. In the meantime, Sigi's waiting for you to ship the pieces for the new show. He says he's been calling you but you haven't returned his calls."

Lucy shook her head. "What's the point?"

"What's the point? The point is to make some money, sweetheart. We've already called an arts marketing expert on Fire Island that Sigi suggested and he wants to talk to you—"

"But all I've got are paintings of Penelope."

"So?" Clover's voice had a hitch in it. It was one thing for Clover to feel a tad jealous of Lucy's ability to reproduce her sister's image so beautifully, entirely another for anyone *else* to dare question such things.

"Sigi didn't tell you his theory?" Lucy asked Susannah. "He thinks I'm insanely obsessed with Penelope."

"So?" Clover raised her voice this time, repeating the question. "Who wouldn't be?"

"How do I put it delicately? Sigi thinks we were lovers."

"Hah!" Clover said.

"So what would be wrong with that?" Susannah asked. "What century is this?"

"Are you serious?" Clover was incensed. "How dare he say such a thing about my sister?"

"Sigi's as gay as they come," Martha explained. "He wouldn't be dissing her."

"Well, that is totally beside the point!" Clover exploded. "My sister was not a lesbian!"

"I know that," Lucy said. "You know that. But Sigi just thinks it's weird that I keep painting her."

Martha was staring at Lucy with the look of someone who was trying not to pry but was also overcome by curiosity. "Lucy, you and Penelope—you didn't . . . ?"

"Martha!" Clover cried. "I swear, is everyone but me on the urge of a breakdown?"

"Don't you think if Penelope and I were lovers, you might have picked up on it?" Lucy was asking, her eyebrows lifted in such a way as to suggest that she was mildly amused rather than slightly alarmed.

"Look, Lucy, listen to me," Susannah urged. "Let's not get drawn into Sigi's paranoia. The point is, your paintings are lovely. So let's get them packed and off."

"That's what I'm trying to tell you, Susannah. I'm surprised he didn't mention the problem. His clients, the ones who have money. They're all *Social Register* types. Even if they didn't presume she was my secret lover, just the fact that she was murdered is enough to put them off buying the paintings."

"Fuck 'em," Martha said. "I think Susannah's right. They're beautiful."

"Wait, Penelope could have been in the *Social Register* if she wanted! Her family goes back to the queen of England. I don't see what those snobs think they've got over on her," Clover mused as they trooped into the studio. Susannah was in the lead, carrying bubble wrap and packing tape, followed by Martha, who was pulling Lucy along by her elbow.

"They don't like scandal is all," Lucy muttered.

"Says who?" Clover snorted. "If they're anything like my Junior League ladies, there's nothing they like better."

After Clover and Susannah had loaded the Element with Lucy's paintings, Martha stayed behind to clean up the mess in Lucy's studio. "Sateesh is coming out and cooking dinner," she explained. "That way I can drink. Speaking of which—"

"Second shelf in the fridge."

Martha found the bottle, opened it and immediately dialed Sateesh at the restaurant. "Love of mine, will you please bring some wine along with dinner? Lucy's down to the dregs."

Martha made Lucy a gin and tonic and poured herself a large glass of Gallo rosé. "I didn't know they even made this stuff anymore. And weren't we all boycotting Gallo back in the day?"

"I didn't buy it. You'll be glad to know it was a birthday present from your favorite person the night of my party."

"Oh, perfect. So the midget bitch is cheap on top of all her other gifts."

"She doesn't drink. She probably doesn't know. At least she walked in the door carrying something."

Martha shook her head. "Geez, that was how we met her. I forgot. Another Clover moment that keeps on giving."

"Hey, you yourself said Tessa's looking better." Lucy used her right hand to fish her lime from her glass, sucking on its tartness as a means of distracting herself from the torrent of longing unleashed by the concept Martha had raised, the idea that they might never have met Siobhan. "Whatever else, it's—my fault."

"Your fault, my ass. Joey's lost his mind."

"I should have told him about Tessa right away."

"Don't let him off the hook, Lucy. He's—the man is *out there*. Or as Clover so aptly put it, on the urge of a breakdown. Whenever I try to talk to him, it's almost like he's not with me. Like he's a Moonie or something. Do you know what I mean?"

Lucy just stared at Martha. It was too painful to say the words, too masochistic to admit that despite what Joey had done to her, she was flayed by chronic yearning. She envied Martha whatever contact she'd had with him, even if he wasn't all there.

"Maybe we need to hire a deprogrammer," Martha added. "I can't help thinking that all of this started when Nurse Ratched moved in."

"Too simple."

"I don't know. Maybe she's a body snatcher."

"Martha. Repeat after me: Tessa's getting better."

"Physically, as of the last time I saw her. But think about how everyone else is falling apart. Joey. You. June. Even Willow."

"Willow?"

"You heard she kicked some kid in school, right? And she's been suspended from dance for being disrespectful. Again, who's the common denominator in all of this?" Martha double-tied the garbage bag filled with scraps of bubble wrap, twine, sticky tape and cardboard. "It doesn't make sense. Look, let's go upstairs and sit out on the deck. You can call the Fire Island marketing consultant from there."

"No, I can't."

"Stop it. He's eager to hear from you. All you have to do is talk. Tell you what, if you want, we'll do it as a conference call. How's that?"

"Can't you just pretend to be me?" Lucy pleaded.

"As if," Martha said. "That's the last thing you need. We want the guy to *like* you, honey."

• • •

According to Sigi's marketing expert, unless an artist was internationally recognized, either for her art or her celebrity, making money was all about finding a niche and working from there. "Sigi tells me you do very well with the Hamptons crowd, your Centre Island socialites, the Park Avenue and Greenwich, Connecticut, wannabes. And if that's who Sigi says you sell to, believe you me, he knows. They may not be Robert Mapplethorpe connoisseurs, but on the upside, they've got enough money to afford quality work. Sigi showed me your slides. I think they're quite wonderful."

"Oh, thank you! What about Sigi's worry? Did he tell you? That they're all of Penelope?"

"Oh, he told me that. Poor Sigi's gotten a bit paranoid ever since the last two elections. The man sees a homophobe behind every tree. Besides, it's not as if your patron's nude or even suggestively dressed. She's simply a beautiful woman—a female Medici—whose mystique you've managed to transfer to canvas. I think what we'll want to do is get some profiles of her in the *Wall Street Journal*, maybe the *New York Times Magazine*, equating her with sponsorship of the arts, maybe a bit of Andrew Carnegie too, wealth, privilege, luxury. I can see a saga-ish story line about her family going back to the English links to the monarchy. Get the prospective buyers dying to have a chunk of that pedigree in their foyers. Her murder's long enough ago, its power to frighten has worn off. More like a tragic fluke accident, really, more like Princess Diana. We'll play up Penelope's aristocratic roots, hide the left-wing politics in the closet along with Sigi's overactive imagination and see if we can't get the article placed near ads for Cartier and Hermès. Meanwhile, I want to immediately develop a website for your work. People expect that. I'll do the copy but I'll need a digital photo of you, something very Ralph Lauren. Send me the names of your Charleston day schools, how long your family lived in Charleston, whom you've sold to before, that sort of thing. We'll put a link to Sigi's gallery, and I'll coax some of my other clients who sell well in that *Social Register* niche to give you testimonials. I've a friend in Amagansett who owes me a favor."

"I'm so grateful—look, I'm not sure how I'll pay—"

"Don't worry about it right now. Your friends have paid my initial fee. And I'll get most of my money in commissions through Sigi. You know, Miss Vargas, if you could produce a boyfriend, that would be lovely too, just to dispel any whiff of scandal."

"I wish," Lucy said.

"*Pity*. Well, p'raps you can manage to work in the fact that you're straight. If you are, that is."

"How soon do you need the photo?" Lucy asked.

"Yesterday, but if you can get it to me by Tuesday, that should work. Remember, I want you on message. No Putumayo skirts, no ethnic jewelry. You know what I mean, none of that whole world-music, indigenous-roots bohemian thing. No wild frizzy hair. We want you looking like you're ready for lunch at the Colony Club. Clothes need to be subdued. Hair too. Very velvet headbandish, if you know what I mean. Study the Ralph Lauren and Chanel ads. That's the look we're striving for."

By the time Lucy hung up, Martha, who'd been listening on the extension and taking notes, insisted they call Clover. "She's the only one of us who knows anything about fashion. I'll tell her to get out her *Vogues*." Martha dialed her cell phone and explained the situation to Clover. Lucy didn't need to be on the phone to hear Clover's thoughtful sigh, followed by a surprised trill of triumph. "Oh, wait! I know the perfect thing! Penelope's Chanel suit. I haven't gotten around to getting it altered and now I know why. It's a deep emerald green and—oh, my Lord, it will kill with Lucy's hair. She can wear it to the opening too! That way, if they've looked her up online, they'll recognize her. And I can loan her the Cameron pearls Penelope left me."

"What about shoes?" Martha asked. "Clover, I'm putting you on speaker so Lucy can hear."

"I don't know. Pumps, I think, or maybe even some low, flat leather boots. Lucy? What size are you?"

"Seven and a half."

"Me too, baby! This is meant to be. I'll bring everything over—when are we doing this!"

"I'm thinking after the weekend. Maybe Monday?" Lucy said.

"Oh, I am so excited. A makeover! I'm so excited! I'll bring Brittany too. She's really good at hair. And I'll do your makeup, of course. Oh, Lucy, we're gonna make you look just like Isabella Rossellini!"

Clover's gratification at being asked to help dress Lucy was a thing of beauty, causing Lucy to feel some of her first genuine pleasure since the day Joey'd stopped talking to her. She sighed, giving in to the unfamiliar sensation. Meanwhile Martha and Clover continued to discuss "branding," "buzz campaigns" and other exotica. For some reason—maybe it was just the lovely notion of letting someone else take care of her—Lucy hung up the phone and relaxed for the first time in what seemed like ages.

Chapter Twenty-four

Theodore Galbreath—the creator of the fortune and of the charity that endowed the Galbreath Prize each year—had been a terrific romantic when it came to art, a subject in which he'd dabbled for years. Not only did he believe the arts were the single aspect of human activity that distinguished man from animal, he also felt that the apprehension of beauty was in and of itself one of the highest forms of spiritual exploration. Much like the Christian edict "Wherever two or more of you are gathered in my name . . . ," Theo Galbreath's philanthropic theology revolved around a certain *communitas* of worship. Thus, much of the process for selecting the Galbreath Prize recipient was highly ritualized.

First, while the short list of finalists would be based on each artist's cumulative body of accomplishments, the final prize would be based only on one piece of art, one that had never been seen before by any member of the committee—all of whom would only view it while in the company of the others and on the same day as they first saw each of the remaining finalists' work. Second, like a jury, once the deliberations had begun on the four final pieces, the committee would be sequestered on-site at Galbreath House, circling the respective entries until they could unanimously agree on a winner. Their decision, once made, would be written up for posterity and made available to the public as well as commemorated on a wall plaque in the Galbreath Gallery, allowing visitors to view the recipients' work in chronological order and understand the piece within the prize's historical context.

Each year, the selection committee was composed of two artists and one art historian. Its members were, according to the Galbreath's bylaws, not publicly disclosed until the prize had been announced.

This was, at least, the official story, faithfully repeated by the Galbreath program staff. The truth lay elsewhere. Certainly for arts insiders—among whom Sigmund Hartmann was present or accounted for—there existed no such thing as a secret, because virtually no soul appointed to such a prestigious committee appeared capable of letting such a delicious feather go begging simply for lack of a cap.

Keven Auchincloss was the youngest member of the Galbreath selection committee since Robert Smithson had been named to the group back in the seventies. Even if Keven hadn't called Sigi's assistant, Claire Ann (a.k.a. Keven's girlfriend), within seconds of getting the magical phone call, it would have been impossible for keen observers not to remark that the twenty-four-year-old had postponed his installation of card noisemakers on unsuspecting messenger bikes in Lower Manhattan. He'd also cloistered himself at the Museum of Modern Art's library, where he stayed from opening to closing six days a week.

The art historian chosen for the award committee had needed to be released from her semester's teaching duties at one of the nation's land-grant universities. Gloria Fernandez was coming up for full professor that year, allowing her to make a quick and providential amendment to her promotion-and-tenure folder, the contents of which were exposed to the clerical staff at said university, to seven members of the promotion committee, to her program chair and, finally, to the three faculty members the chair had begged to take over her "Material Cultures of the Third World" and "Critical Theory" courses for the fall semester.

The third member of the committee was ostensibly an artist as well, though her selection had had more to do with her teaching than her body of work as a photographer.

Claudia Bigelow had retired from Exeter in 2001 to join the Peace Corps, after a painful divorce from another faculty member had made it impossible for her to continue teaching on the preparatory school's small campus.

Mrs. Bigelow had been a favorite among two successive generations of Galbreath first cousins, one of whom had run into Claudia at the Islip airport and had taken it upon himself to rescue the woman's savaged pride by appointing her to help decide upon America's next visual genius.

Claudia was the only member of the committee to honor her vow of silence. Not for nothing all those years enforcing the honor code. However, such disclosures were, at that point, entirely unnecessary given the number of Galbreath cousins whose lobbying weight had been swung into service on Mrs. Bigelow's behalf.

When the first official meeting of the Galbreath Committee occurred, three weeks of screening had already been conducted and the nominees narrowed down to a group of four finalists. Up until this point, the committee members had relied on slides and photos of each candidate's work, as well as the traditional résumés listing gallery shows, awards and accomplishments.

For the preliminary meeting to discuss the four finalists, Keven was the first to arrive at Galbreath House. He was sporting a flat-top crew cut, shiny saddle shoes and a Buddy Holly–esque suit. Keven took the spot at the head of the table, where he placed his leather Day-Timer exactly two inches from the table's edge. Claudia came in the door shortly after he did, two minutes by the watch he'd set two inches to the left of his calendar. The older woman smiled; she'd come of age in the fifties and found subsequent generations' cultural homage to the "good old days" most perplexing. Kitschy allusions to sock hops and letter sweaters were one thing, but what Claudia recalled were the McCarthy hearings and her father's forced abandonment of his successful screenwriting career to write advertising copy on Madison Avenue.

Claudia's clothes were timeless: white turtleneck, calf-length kilt, navy stockings and a pair of burgundy walking shoes so well made they didn't have a brand. Instead they held the imprint of a dead cobbler whose handiwork was repaired annually by a shoe shop on the Upper West Side. This neighborhood was where Claudia's Wellesley friends had settled after college and where she still stayed whenever she came to New York. Though Claudia's hair had been allowed to go to silver, it was cut in the exact style she'd worn as a girl, a severe geometric bob that set off her sharp cheekbones and inquisitive glass-blue eyes.

Claudia was reaching out to shake Keven's hand and to apologize for being late when Gloria arrived, escorted by the building's security guard, her eyes snapping at the insult. "You should know better, brother. Will one of you two please tell this man I can be trusted not to lift the artwork?"

Keven stood and reached out to shake her hand. "Keven Auchincloss," he said. "You must be Gloria Fernandez."

"Where's the program director?" Claudia asked the security guard.

"Gone down to the loading stage to pick up some deliveries. I'm s'posed to get ID." The heavyset guard was sweating from the exertion of following an incensed committee member up three flights of stairs.

"I had to present mine, if that makes you feel better," Claudia told Gloria.

"Me too," Keven offered.

"Dr. Gloria Fernandez. Here's my card." The tall woman, made even taller by the Frida Kahlo bun atop her head, reached into her jeans and retrieved two business cards. "It says right here who I am!"

By the time the program director had arrived with apologies for missing their arrivals because of a foul-up on the loading dock, Gloria Fernandez had displaced Keven from his seat. "Do you mind? I'm claustrophobic. I need to be able to look out the window. I just know you're not into that whole man-in-charge thing anyhow."

Having pegged Keven as gay, relying on his gentle manner, stylish clothes and niche as a performance artist to determine his sexual orientation, Gloria had already welcomed the young man into her club of the disempowered, whose persecution she made it her business to redress in her work.

Fernandez's political outlook was slightly puzzling to her family, since her father had been a member of the Ecuadorian consulate and her grandparents had all been born in Spain. Gloria had attended private schools and the Sorbonne before winning a highly coveted job at one of the best public universities in the United States on the basis of her last name and keenly emphatic ethnic identity.

"You know what I don't understand?" she said, once the discussion had begun, a prelude to the following Tuesday's undraping of the four works of art. "Why doesn't the artist's background come into play? I can't see making a decision without knowing what obstacles they've had to overcome."

The director was a soft-spoken African-American man in his midsixties. This was a question he'd had to answer almost daily over the past two decades, at the constant circuit of media interviews and cocktail parties that comprised a large part of his job. "It was the founder's will that art should be judged irrespective of background. And if you think about it, at the time he set up the foundation, that was a progressive view to hold. Gender, race— none of that was to be taken into consideration, which was how you ended up with such people as Mary Cassatt and Richard Hunt winning the prize during times of great prejudice."

"Still, it's insane to pretend we don't know who the artists are," Gloria pressed. "We've looked at their portfolios and their histories. It's not like we're not going to recognize their styles, to say nothing of their respective media."

"I don't think it's necessary to pretend that," Claudia said. "But we've signed a contract saying we won't let anything but the art itself affect our choice, so that's what we are bound to do. What do you think, Keven?"

"I think this Theo dude rocks. He's insane!"

Keven's grin was infectious, and his meaning was entirely at odds with his words. Despite how idiotic he sounded, it was clear to everyone but Gloria that he was poking fun at the self-importance and sobriety with which academics like Gloria seemed to judge an activity that was, at heart, rooted in play.

The trouble was, as far as Keven was concerned, all the finalists were incredibly talented. Besides, their work was so different, it was like comparing apples to orangutans. The sculptor's tiny shadowboxes made of bone were breathtakingly beautiful, but so were the video clips that stretched peripheral space past the canvas through a wide-angle view out Bangladesh apartment windows, so that hanging laundry, birds' wings and clouds of smoke from cooking fires became ghostly reminders of all that was omitted from the normal canvas. Lucy Vargas's portraits were, to Keven's mind, slightly conventional but also hauntingly nostalgic, combining eighteenth-century figurative technique with an arresting sense of having stopped time and fast-forwarded to a future of looking back on that moment. It made him want to recapture some element that couldn't be named, some ethereal quality of life that had gone missing. The last contender was a conceptual environmentalist whose installations included sea turtle lifeguard troupes, wildflower sowings in junkyards, intricate worm farm condo complexes complete with solar-paneled display cases, legumed trellises and water-cleansing fountains of brilliant-colored sand and rocks.

How could anyone possibly decide on who should win without throwing a dart blindly and letting it land on whomever the wind favored that day?

"I mean, don't you feel like you're playing God?" he asked, after the director had taken them all to lunch and the three committee members were being driven back to Galbreath House. The limousine they were in was a large Bentley with tiny glass sconces of fresh flowers.

Claudia, who'd poured herself a Perrier, sighed dramatically and smiled. "Absolutely, isn't it glorious?"

"No, I'm serious. How will we decide?"

"I'm sorry, but it's not rocket science," Gloria suggested. "Art is both social construction and *constructor*. Some of it glorifies the status quo and some of it challenges the status quo. Now, if you think the status quo is all *that*, then hey, support Lucy Vargas's objectification of women as *bling*. Or put your money on this century's version of scrimshaw whalebone carving. Even that so-called conceptual artist is more about patting corporate America on the arm and making like it's all okay if we all just try to beautify America 'one community garden at a time.' I mean, where do these people come from?"

Claudia shifted her drink to her other hand and dug for something in her purse. "I'm curious, Gloria. If you felt that way, how did we end up with our list of finalists?"

"Can you spell *token*? I didn't vote for any of them but the video artist. I figured you two must have."

Keven and Claudia exchanged quick sheepish glances. Keven spoke first. "I voted for all of them."

"I did too," Claudia said, taking a cigarette from her purse. "Don't worry. I'm not lighting it. I just like it in my fingers."

"See what I meant? If you two agree, I guess you just cancel me out."

"Except we have to be unanimous when it comes to the prize," Keven added, his expression growing somber as he realized that Gloria's tokenism had now come to a sudden and screeching halt.

"Well, I guess that won't be that much of a problem, since you two both liked the third world artist too."

"Hey, we're not supposed to talk about their backgrounds, right?" Keven murmured.

"That's just buying into the Dead White Man's crap as far as I'm concerned. How's it at all fair when three of the artists had a leg up and one didn't? That's not a level playing field. Shit, the sculptor is head of his department at Cranbrook and the environmental Oreo has a cushy job at Harvard. How do you compare them with a woman whose mother was a street sweeper?"

"Because we're not allowed to consider those factors, that's how," Claudia said mildly. Since Claudia's photography had consisted largely of the human face, Gloria's comment about Lucy's work was particularly galling. "Besides, may I ask you something? What makes you think portraiture objectifies women as bling when it hasn't undermined the powers of kings and popes who paid large sums to be memorialized for posterity?"

"Lucy Vargas is a member of the ruling elite, and she sells to the ruling elite. Shit, that woman hasn't had to work a day in her life."

"Unless you count the painting," Keven murmured soothingly, as though in assent. He shot Claudia a quick naughty wink and, with that, a subtle shift in sympathies was given a large nudge forward, or backward, depending on one's seat and perspective in the luxurious frame of the limo.

Joey had good days and bad. On some, he was fairly successful at burying his pain, numb to the marital reconsiderations and refractions his wife's letter had awakened in him. On others, he was ambushed by sudden bursts of extraordinary anger. These could be triggered by unpredictable stimuli—smells, songs, a chance remark heard on the radio—unleashing a visceral rage against which any high-mindedness was a snowflake in hell. Then, the knowledge that Penelope had loved him was a chill speck on a hot flame, there only to symbolize what he'd lost, what he was incapable of revisiting, souvenir of a place so far removed it might as well have been the North Pole of Santa's workshop for all its bearing on reality.

Even on the worst of days, the intellectual part of Joey's brain struggled to understand, even to forgive. *After all*, he constantly pled with himself, *it may have only happened once with Lucy, it might have been one lapse in an otherwise perfect record of sexual fidelity*. This intellectual reasoning and his anger sat alongside each other like benched members of opposing teams who didn't speak the same language. Joey knew he was irrational. Still, he couldn't seem to control the waves of harsh emotion that swamped his previously stable soul.

When Susannah delivered the travel records to his office, she asked if he'd like her to help him go over them. "I can explain what things mean. There're lots of codes you might not recognize," she said, standing above his desk with a six-inch stack of papers. "It's a lot, I know, but you said you wanted everything."

Joey put his elbows on his desk, his brow in his hands, and summoned the will not to let his voice break. "Tell you what. Let me look first. I'll get back to you."

"Okay, just let me know."

Susannah's voice was gentle, for despite the fact that she couldn't understand the harshness of his response to Lucy's infraction, she also could see the man was suffering. Whether it was Tessa's illness or the final realization that Penelope was gone, it didn't much matter. What was important was giving him support in his time of sorrow. "Are you alright?" she asked. "Is Tessa okay?"

Joey looked up at Susannah. His eyes flickered with an impulse to unload, to ask her what she knew. He knew, though, if he asked the question, he would lose control. He had to leave in a few minutes to collect June at school, which meant holding himself together enough to pass muster as a functional human being. He shook his head, saying, "We'll get better. We will."

"Joey, I have to tell you something," Susannah pressed, putting her hand on his arm. "I should have told you a long time ago."

Joey shook his head. "Susannah. I can't talk right now. I just can't."

"Okay. But when you feel like it, Joey, please know, I'm here."

It was Tessa's report on the 1998 famine in Sudan that led her astray. Tessa entered *starving* into the Google search box. The site that came up first, because it had the most hits, was called *Starving for Fun and Prophet*. This was Tessa's first interaction with the

pro-anorexia or "pro-ana" movement, and it was entirely uninten-
tional. Even once she'd opened it, she didn't understand where
she was. The truth was, the model she was looking at could have
passed for seriously Ethiopian. She had long, dark hair, a nose ring
and a deep tan. Plus, she was wearing an oversize silk hoodie that
could be mistaken for one of those weird head scarves desert people
wore to keep the sand out of their eyes.

There was a link to click, one large pink arrow that took Tessa
to photos of emaciated models wearing sexy bathing suits and an
oversize female backbone where the vertebrae looked like those
topographical maps of mountain ranges. Diet pills and laxatives
were advertised, along with expert advice on powering through
hunger to achieve alertness.

Though Siobhan didn't actively supervise her in the study,
Tessa had been steadfast in following the new rules: no Internet
except for school. The lure of looking at this, however, the lure of
finding a place with other people like her—these links were scary
in a queasy, tantalizing kind of way. Tessa's breath stopped in her
throat. There was a "Hide This Site" button that she could not
help but press, just in case someone came snooping after her. She
had just opened a link titled *Childhood Abuse and Eating Disorders*
when she heard a car in the driveway and immediately closed her
screen. Pulling Google up again, she typed in *famine* and *Sudan*.

The images were stark. A dying child in his dying mother's
arms, their black skin dull and chalky. Shriveled teats lay flat
against the woman's bony chest; the child's hand grazed her still.
"Malnourishment" was what the caption said, but to Tessa it was
so much more than that. This mother was starving herself to feed
her child. The child had sucked the life from her skin, draining
her with its all-consuming thirst. There was something holy in
this sacrifice, something Tessa longed for, strange as that emotion
may have been.

Tessa knew how lucky she was, but that was part of her problem. She knew just how lucky she was to be alive and to live in
a world of plenty, when so many children were starving, when so

many parents had died. Yes, she'd lost her mother, but so had her own mom, when she was only six years old. That must have been so much worse for her, only half the age Tessa had been when she'd assumed nothing bad would ever happen, like the very worst thing that might befall her was the pitiful curse of boredom. Now, all Tessa could feel was a terrible sense of guilt over not being happier when she could have been, over the anger she felt at having lost her mother, over not being able to eat, not being able to make her father feel better, not having done more since her mother had died to make it all worthwhile, to make her mother's life worthwhile.

"Daddy, can I spend the night at Willow's?" June asked.

They had just finished dinner and were in the study, one big happy family if you didn't count the elder daughter's anorexia, the younger child's nightly bouts with paralysis brought on by terror of intruders, their father's obsession with his late wife's betrayal, his subsequent nightly sex with the in-home treatment professional and the dog's newest addiction to the neighbors' harvest wreaths, which he first captured, then toyed with as though they were coiled snakes before ingesting them, until all that remained were skeletons of tortured grapevine lacquered with dog spit.

Joey looked up from his laptop, put up one finger, clicked on the "Advanced Search" button and said, "When?"

"Friday." June looked quickly at Tessa, then back at her father. "Tessa's invited too."

"What's the occasion?"

"Nothing. Just hanging out."

"The thing is, honey, I think you need your sleep. You fell asleep watching *Gilmore Girls* again last night."

Siobhan cleared her throat. "I think it would be good for the children to have some fun," she said briskly. "Susannah called and invited them last night but you were out and I forgot to tell you. Tessa's had a good week and I think she should celebrate her weight gain by doing regular girly things."

"Weight gain? Honey, did you weigh yourself today?"

Joey's eagerness was a thing of beauty, or would have been if it didn't contrast so mightily with the funk he'd been encased in for what felt like an eternity.

"Must be all the Halloween candy," Siobhan said, winking at Tessa, whose expression of passivity was unfazed by jocular announcements regarding chocolate. "Five pounds in two weeks."

"Honey, that's great! I'm so proud!"

"And that's not all," Siobhan added, rising from where she was working at Penelope's desk. She crossed behind the sofa where June was sitting to place a light hand on the younger girl's shoulder. "June's lost three."

"Wow," Joey murmured, unsure of the protocol.

He wasn't aware that June was dieting. For some reason, rather than being pleased, he found himself alarmed. "Honey, maybe that's why you've been so tired; you're not eating enough."

"I think she's just entering puberty," Siobhan explained. "Her body is gearing itself up to change, and that takes a lot of fuel. So that probably explained the sleepiness and the weight loss. That and the fact that she's eating a healthy diet now, without all those empty calories she took in at Luc—uh, before."

"Well, wow, I'm proud of both of you! Of course you can spend the night. If that's what you want."

By ten o'clock Wednesday evening, the Cameron twins, fresh from their trip to Phoenix, were at Tumblers Bar for karaoke night. When Peter returned from the Gents', he was surprised to discover that Clover, who'd picked them up at the airport, had already left. Nigel was motioning to the waitress.

"Where's she run off to?" Peter asked. "How will we get home? We didn't do 'Stand by Your Man'! I've been practicing all week!"

"Two Jamesons, please," Nigel told the waitress, ignoring Peter altogether until she was out of earshot. "She had to pick up that child of hers. We'll take a taxi home. Don't worry about the song; we can do it without her. I can go tenor when I need to. Besides, we might want to start with something more celebratory. 'Wedding Bell Blues,' perhaps? Or 'I'm Getting Married in the Morning'?"

"Those aren't even in the same key, Nigel."

"Calm yourself, Peter. I've just heard more astonishingly good news."

"What?"

"Guess who Clover's Junior League president spotted in the apothecary buying condoms? Together?"

Peter shook his head. "I don't know!"

Nigel smiled and leaned forward as if about to deliver a dirty joke. "None other than our own Miss Fitzpatrick and the merry widower!"

"And so?" Peter asked cautiously.

"The thing is, dear Peter, if he's serious about her, which Clover believes he must be, then think of the possibilities! Other than Clover, there's not a soul on the committee who'd say yes to him marrying Siobhan. You've got Wicked Bitch Martha, Sloppy Susannah and Loosey Lucy Vargas, all of whom will hate this new romance. We already know Wicked Bitch's response; we've heard her moan about the woman ad infinitum. And Lucy—if she's got any feelings left—she'd not be likely to approve it either. That's two. Then there's Sloppy Susannah, who's not got the backbone to buck her friends. Which means, of course, guess who'd eventually be forced to resign his post on the board of trustees?"

"Oh, Nigel, that's brilliant. Except, of course, the fact that the man's shagging the Irish doesn't necessarily lead him to the altar."

"No, it doesn't. *But*—and this is true genius on my part, I must give myself a wee pat on the back about it—I do remember a certain turn of phrase in the legal mumbo jumbo about *cohabitation*. I daresay we could let it slip to the Coven that the man's sleeping with his child's caretaker, p'raps stir up a bit of enmity by dropping a few triumphant remarks regarding the man's excellent taste in stepmothers, and let the catfight begin. Meanwhile, of course, we continue to destabilize Adorno through allegations about his wife's behavior in Phoenix."

"Brilliant! Where are our drinks, Nigel? Oh, miss?" Peter trilled, using his hand to circle a halo in the air above their table.

After the waitress delivered the drinks and the two brothers had drunk to their dead cousin Penelope, Nigel's cell phone rang. "Hurry!" Peter whispered as his brother stood and gestured that he was taking the phone outside. "I can't sing by myself."

Nigel returned from outside with a wide smile on his face, just in time to join his brother onstage. The two men swayed in time back and forth to a heartfelt and truly melodious "Stand by Your Man."

"That was glorious!" Peter said to his brother when the two sat down and mopped their foreheads with the edges of their identical Burberry handkerchiefs.

"Not half-bad, was it? Let's do have another scotch!" Nigel shouted, before he leaned over and explained what their attorney had called so late in the evening to announce.

As usual, Peter was a bit thick about understanding the point of Nigel's news. "Now, wait, Nigel. Why would we want our case moved to arbitration?"

"Because, dear brother, there's no appeal. Whatever the arbitrator decides, that's going to be it. End of story. The beauty of such finality is this: the safest course would be to afford the children the *most* protection, which means we'd stay on here until the youngest comes of age! And can you imagine a better time for this matter to come to trial? Adorno will be trying to prove the Coven's not qualified to judge his choice of brides, while *they'll* be trying to prove the man's in dire need of supervision. They'll do our dirty work for us; all we have to do is sit back and take notes while the warring parties find fault with one another. Either way, we win. If the Coven's dismissed, they'll be more likely to vote against Adorno in board matters. If they win, they'll still be so insulted at his daring to question their authority, they'll seek to punish him, especially for shagging the help without their permission! He won't even have to marry the Irish to have the shite hit the fan!"

"Still, it would be lovely to see him marry her," Peter reflected. "Think of how eager she'd be to keep her email correspondence with us a private matter."

"I hadn't thought of that! Peter, I take back every insult I've ever paid you. You're positively worth your weight in gold. And that's a small fortune."

Chapter Twenty-five

When the red truck pulled into Lucy's driveway, its large magnetic sign was slightly off-center. It read WILL BUY HOUSES FOR CASH: CALL 1-800-FREEDOM.

Lucy answered the door wearing an indigo peasant skirt with a white V-necked T-shirt, her arm bundled against her waist by a champagne-colored cashmere sling Clover had knitted for her.

Standing there, wearing Tommy Bahama resort wear from head to toe, were two young men, one with a yellow goatee and green eyes. The other had a ponytail and Ray-Bans, which he pulled off to shake Lucy's right hand. "Ow!" he said empathetically, gesturing at her injured arm.

Lucy nodded and looked slightly confused. "Are you here about the ad in the paper?"

The goateed man tilted his head back and whistled at the black and white marble foyer. "Wow. This is the bomb. I'm Sandy, this here's Elroy. We're friends of your cousin Clover."

Lucy backed up into the hall, not bothering to contradict their assumption that she and Clover were related. The men followed her, clipboards in hand. "We've got five guest bedrooms on the second floor and three on the third."

"Come again?"

"You're not looking for a place to stay?"

"Well, no, ma'am, we hadn't been, but I tell you! I could get used to this place! Right now we're working out of the Ramada. What do you charge?"

"Would two hundred a night be too much?"

Sandy whistled. "Afraid so. We're only paying eighty-five dollars in town."

"Oh, I meant two hundred for two. And I'd make breakfast too."

"Tell you what. Keep us off the books and you won't have to pay the hotel tax. That way you can charge us ninety each. I'm assuming you got a space we can use for an office."

Lucy gestured with her right hand to a small room past the stairwell. "There's high speed Internet in there."

"Hey, that's great. You got a fax?"

"I do."

"Listen, your cousin, Clover, she said you might be having a little problem with cash flow? If we could just take a few minutes of your time—"

"Do you want some coffee?" Lucy asked. "Come back to the kitchen."

"How'd you hurt your arm?"

Lucy swallowed. "Fell."

"Well, at least it was your left arm."

"Unfortunately, I'm left-handed."

Sandy's voice was soothing, like honey. "That's terrible, hon. How long you gonna be out of commission?" He and Elroy settled at the kitchen island while Lucy fumbled for the coffeepot.

Lucy set mugs down in front of the men and nodded her permission for them to help themselves. "Too long," she said. "But anyway, Clover sent you here?"

"See, we—Clover said you might be wanting to refinance. We can give you a rate that'll lower your payments and give you cash out to pay off some bills."

Lucy looked at them apologetically. "I keep telling Clover this but I *can't* refinance. I haven't had any income in two years. I've got a show of my paintings coming next week but I can't guarantee how much that will bring in."

"No problem," Elroy said. "You're clearly an honest woman. I know if we loan you money, you'll make good on it. I can tell by your eyes. Besides, we know where you live. Right, Sandy?"

"The problem is," Lucy continued, "I can't guarantee I'll make money when my show happens. And I don't know—I just don't know if any bank's going to—"

"Here's the nice thing about us. We *are* the bank. Kind of like a mobile credit union. When we make money in our real estate side, we need a secure place to build interest. We used to work with the banks, but with the interest they pay, you might as well keep your money in a mattress. It's not business-savvy. So we use our networks to find people we're sure we can trust. We lend money at a rate that's cheaper than the bank but a better interest rate than we'd be able to get in a savings account. So that way, we got more latitude. And like Clover told us, this place is worth a lot of money. How much you in for with your other loan?"

"I took out two hundred two years ago. But I've only been making the minimum payments. I'm supposed to pay off the whole note when the balloon comes due at the end of December."

Instead of looking pained at this revelation, the two men simply smiled and nodded. Sandy was writing a column of notes and working a calculator while he gazed up at the crown molding surrounding the edges of the trey ceiling. "So what's it up to now?"

"To tell you the truth, I'm not sure. I've been afraid to look."

"Tell you what. Give us the paperwork. We'll swallow that bitter pill for you."

"Do you really think you might be able to loan me money?"

"Why else would we be here? See, what we do is we negotiate with your lender. We can prob'ly just pay it off and then refi with a new balloon coming due in a couple more years. Or we might be able to push the present balloon back a couple of years. The banks have lost their shirt on so many foreclosures flooding the market, they're trying to be flexible. You will have a higher rate, no doubt about it, but still . . ."

"Wow. Tell me—is this for real? 'Cause I've been told 'no' so many times, I'm not sure I can believe—"

"No, we're the real deal. The only problem is, we gotta get this paperwork in today. It's first come, first served, and there's only so many of these work-outs authorized. With Congress looking at tightening the regs, it's crazy not to go with the bird in the hand we got now. You see what I'm saying, Miss Lucy?"

Lucy swallowed. "No."

"Well, you heard of the whole subprime mess, right?"

"Of course."

"Well, some people are blaming it on loose regulation in the banking industry. Used to be when a bank gave you a mortgage, they held the note. So it was in their interest to make sure you could pay it back. But then some genius on Wall Street figured out a way to bundle the loans together and sell them off to other banks, with everyone and his brother getting a cut along the way. The mortgage brokers were printing money in commissions, but they didn't have to be accountable for any risk. It was like the right hand didn't know what the left hand was doing, and nobody had to look too hard to see if the borrowers could really pay back what they borrowed. So now that people realize this, the pendulum's swung the other way. That's why we need to get you started ASAP. I want to get you in the pipeline before another genius comes into the Fed and says no more home loans or some such other measures. We don't want you getting caught in the middle of it. That's all."

"I don't think I can get everything together right away."

"Don't worry. You just give us a bill; we'll contact your lender and start the process going. Tell them we want to renegotiate. What matters is making sure they don't use this impending balloon as a chance to grab your property and run. You wouldn't believe what these stinkers will do to people."

Elroy was shaking his head and Sandy rose to accompany Lucy into the study, where she squatted in front of a drawer and yanked it open with her right hand.

Inside, each month's neatly folded bills were held together with large metal clips. "I don't have this month's," Lucy said, referring to the most recent stack Susannah had absconded with. "But here's September."

The men were orderly, efficient, kind. They added up her bills, they apologized for the mountains of paperwork their company required and explained why they would need power of attorney to renegotiate terms with her present lender. Besides, as Sandy pointed out, an artist's hands were like a surgeon's, maybe even more important. The last thing Lucy needed was to delay her healing by getting writer's cramp over pages and pages of documents. "Tell you what," he added. "We'll bring it all back tonight and let you look at everything before we submit it in the morning."

Before they left, Sandy shook Lucy's good hand, telling her they had a deal. To prove it, the man wrote out a six-thousand-dollar check to deposit that very day.

That afternoon, after driving into town to deposit the check, Lucy drove to the small park on High Street and pressed Susannah's cell number into her phone.

Susannah answered on the second ring, "Hey, Lucy! You're using your cell phone! I'm so proud of you."

"I just—since you have my bills, I thought I'd tell you my news! I got some cash to deposit."

"Did Sigi sell a painting already?"

"No, but these—I refinanced my mortgage. It's such a relief? They're going to try and renegotiate with my lender and push back the due date for the balloon payment I owe."

"Lucy, that's great. I'm . . . glad . . ." Susannah's voice trailed off worriedly. How could Lucy have convinced a bank to loan her money? Even double-income couples were having trouble getting loans. "Who did you go to?"

"They came to me, if you can believe that! Clover sent them."

"Who is this bank, Lucy?"

"I—they're, like, real estate guys but they do mortgages on

the side. Clover's used them and she knew I needed money."

"Lucy, where are you?"

"Down the street from your office. In the park around the corner."

"Look, why don't you come by? Martha and I can look over the documents to make sure everything's on the up-and-up."

"I can't; I'm afraid I'll run into Joey. Or, God forbid, he'll think I'm trying to see the girls." Lucy's voice cracked on the last word, her loneliness palpable in the crossed octaves.

"Oh. Right. Okay. Listen, let's go get lunch. My treat. I'll bring Martha." Susannah hung up before Lucy could object. Five minutes later she and Martha had walked around the block to the park, where Lucy's car was parked under a large live oak tree. Lucy was leaning against it, staring wistfully at a stretch of vine-covered fence.

"Where do you want to go?" Lucy asked, holding her keys up in the air before hugging her friends. "My treat."

"Anywhere but Sapphire. Peter and Nigel just left for lunch a few minutes ago."

"And Joey?" Lucy's tone was light and completely ineffective in striking a casual note. "Is he . . ."

"Still insane? Yep," Martha said. "In fact, once we decide where we're going to eat, we've got to think about what we're going to do—"

"How about that sandwich shop on Green?" Susannah asked. "I love their hummus. And, Lucy, you are not going to treat us on borrowed money."

"Oh, come on, let me celebrate."

"Lucy, honey, how much did you deposit?" Susannah pressed. "And by the way, listen, those late fees at the bank are from early last month. Apparently you only had fifty bucks in your account but took out two hundred. Do you remember borrowing that?"

"That's impossible. I don't know what they're talking about, Susannah. I didn't do any such thing."

"Well, they're saying you did. And on the one fifty they say you borrowed so you wouldn't bounce, you've accumulated a boatload of fees and penalties. That's where they're getting the three hundred plus."

"Those bastards!" Martha said. "They just take advantage of people."

"But I never took out a loan with them. Look, I'll go over there and straighten this out. But for right now, can you please not bum me out? I've just been granted a temporary stay of execution. Can I please savor the moment?"

"While we're on that topic, Lucy, I'd like to go over what you signed and make sure everything's on the up-and-up. How much did you deposit?"

"Six thousand."

"Here, let me look at the contract," Martha said.

"I don't have a copy with me."

"Well, let's go out to your house then. We can eat at the Crab Shack. Then we can pick up the contract on the way."

Lucy cleared her throat and said, "I'm starving. Let's get going." With that, she got back into the driver's seat and started the car, waiting for Martha and Susannah to buckle in before she pulled out of the lot.

"Lucy, why are you going this way?" Martha asked. "We'll get creamed in traffic."

"I'm going to the hummus place. The Crab Shack'll be crazed, and besides, the thing is, Martha, I don't have the loan documents yet. They're getting me a copy tonight after everything's done."

"What?"

"See, they downloaded the contract from the office and I read it online. But my printer is really slow. They had to be somewhere for a meeting and it was taking forever. So they'll be bringing it all back to me later tonight."

"Lucy, did you read it carefully?" Susannah asked.

"Of course I read it carefully. I just—look, Clover's done business with these people. And it looked like the standard mortgage contract I've always signed. I've signed them before."

Martha forced herself to stay calm, injecting a note of lawyerly dispassion into her words. "So you didn't sign it?"

"I didn't have to. They're gonna sign for me and then I'll approve it all before they turn it in. That's the other good news. They're going to pay me one eighty a night to stay at my house instead of the hotel in town!"

"Oh, Jesus, Lucy. You didn't grant them power of attorney, did you?"

"Just the clause about renegotiating the terms of my mortgage. I'm not a complete idiot, Martha."

"Well, complete or not, you *never* give anybody your power of attorney. What were you thinking?"

"Martha, excuse me? Didn't you just tell me to do that very thing just a few days ago?"

"With Susannah, you nitwit, not some door-to-door jerk-offs Clover sends your way! What the hell were you thinking?"

Whether it was anxiety over Lucy's having signed an unknown contract with two men she'd never met, or the fact that Martha had run ten miles on an empty stomach, she wasn't quite sure. Whatever the cause, by the time they discovered that the hummus place was closed and had driven across town to settle into a booth at Luigi's, the attorney's hands wouldn't keep still. Even after her Chardonnay arrived and she ordered a second before she'd sipped at the first, Martha's jitters were enough to put Susannah into her own miniature tailspin.

"What's wrong with you, Martha?" the accountant asked, running her fingers around the rim of her iced raspberry tea glass, producing a ringing sound that set Lucy's teeth on edge.

"Lots. For one thing, we need to talk about Joey. He's gone off the reservation. I'm thinking we may want to preempt him next week."

"Why?" Lucy asked, gently pressing her hand over Susannah's and pulling it away from the glass.

"I want to invoke the codicil," Martha said. "Then we can get the midget bitch out of there."

"Martha, why would we do that?" Lucy was confused. "Tessa's getting better, isn't she? She is, isn't she?"

"I don't know. Still, I'm thinking there's no reason on earth the woman has to live in the house with Joey and the girls. She could come in the morning, make sure Tessa eats, then pack up and leave when dinner's over."

"Martha," Susannah interrupted. "What she does isn't our concern."

"Yes, it is!" Martha said. "Right now, she's cohabiting. Did you forget that part of the codicil's language? We have control over what happens."

"Now come on, Martha. No matter how much you dislike her, it's not fair to use a technicality to get her out of the house," Susannah scolded. "Besides, Siobhan doesn't have a place to live. She canceled her lease. You know that."

"I couldn't care less. Let her move into the Ramada. And actually, cohabitation is *not* a technicality. According to Nigel Cameron, one of Clover's Junior League ladies saw Siobhan and Joey buying condoms together. He says Clover is pretty sure they're sleeping together."

Lucy, who was stirring sugar into her tea, found the spoon had a mind of its own, knocking the drink into her lap. The ensuing crisis gave her a reason to yelp and rise up as though she'd been attacked.

"How do you know the twins aren't just trying to mess with us?" Susannah whispered, using her napkin to sop up the mess on Lucy's vacated seat.

"Because I called Clover. Her friend, Judy Somebody, saw them at the drugstore."

Lucy shook her head and used a stack of napkins to dab at the wet spot on the table. "That can't be right. For one thing, Joey's got a vasectomy."

"Well, you gotta give him credit for having the sense to think about sexually transmitted diseases," Martha admitted. "Though, still, his taste in women leaves me wondering."

"Maybe the condoms were for her. Not him."

"Why would she be handing them to Joey at the register and having him pick up the tab then?"

"That doesn't sound like Joey," Susannah insisted.

"Nothing sounds like Joey lately. I'll tell you one thing. He can fuck her all he wants, but not in Penelope's bed."

"Come on, Martha," Susannah objected. "She may not be our cup of tea but that doesn't mean she's Penelope's stepmother reincarnated."

"Look," Martha began. "I want to file a motion to invoke the codicil right now and tell Joey either the skank leaves his house *now* or he's got a whole bunch of shit to wade through if he wants to keep his job at the foundation."

"Martha, shouldn't he be free to make his own choice?" Susannah pleaded.

"No. The man obviously can't see past his prick. Come on, this is exactly why Penelope wanted the codicil in the first place! Susannah, please, trust me on this. Imagine it was Willow and Amber who had to live with her."

At this, Susannah's face blanched. She turned to ask Lucy what she thought.

"I can't do it," Lucy whispered, staring off into the middle distance, stunned. "I can't be fair. Not about Joey."

"Fair?" Martha retorted. "Who cares about fair? Jesus, Lucy, if I don't go to the hearing with at least three of us four on board, we won't have a snowball's chance in hell of—"

"Oh, my God, Lucy?" Susannah interrupted, her face contorting. "I can't believe I didn't see it. Oh, honey, I am so sorry!"

"Good God, Susannah," Martha snapped. "Can we please stay on task here? Lucy needs to get her ass in gear or we—"

"Martha Templeton, if you don't shut your mouth, I'm going to have to crawl across the table and put a sock in it. Can you *not* see what Lucy's trying to tell us?"

◆ ◆ ◆

Susannah tried not to worry when she dropped Lucy at her house and discovered the moneylenders had left a note taped to the knocker. *Had personal emergency at home. Sorry! Gone to Mobile. Be back on Tuesday. Left payment inside.* True to their promise, the men had slipped a check under the door for nine hundred dollars, payment for the five nights they'd be gone. Unfortunately, though, they'd not left a copy of the contract, nor a phone number by which to reach them.

When Susannah got back into her car, she dialed Martha at the office and explained the situation. "No contract. But Lucy thinks if she'd been home and the door hadn't been locked, they'd have left her copy. They did leave her a check for five nights, which made her feel they're straight shooters. Did you reach the mortgage company to see if they've been in touch yet?"

"Nobody over there would talk to me without her permission. She gave you her PIN codes when you paid her bills, right? So in the morning you should be able to get past the gatekeepers. I tried getting her on her cell but she wasn't answering and now they're closed for the day. I figure better not to worry her right now, with how she's feeling about Joey."

"Poor Lucy. Did you have any idea how she felt about Joey?"

"Well, Sateesh always thought Joey might have had a thing for her a long time ago. But Lucy—no. Fuck no. It explains a lot, though."

"Well, maybe worrying about her house will distract her. By the way, she's got three days to change her mind on any contract if I remember. Right?"

"Three including today. The problem is, how can she notify the lender if she can't find the contract or remember who they are? And she's cashed their check."

"Can she not simply return the money and claim she's changed her mind?"

"Sure. But didn't you say the bank had debited a few hundred bucks for late fees?"

Susannah shook her head. "She has no clue what they're talking about. But you're right. I've got her power of attorney, so at least I can look into things tomorrow. Hey, what about Clover? If she sent those guys over to Lucy's, maybe she's got a way to get in touch."

"I'll call her right now," Martha said. "Maybe she can show me her contract. That'll give me the name and address of their company."

When Martha reached Clover on her cell phone and asked about the men she'd sent to Lucy's, there was a pregnant pause before Clover told her how cute the men were, how nice, how they had helped a lot of people at her church.

"How about your business dealings with them, Clover?"

Clover yelped defensively. "Who says I had any business, Martha Templeton!"

Martha a took a deep breath. "Clover, I'm not going to give you a hard time. I promise. Just, I'm a little bit worried about Lucy's contract. I'd just feel better if I could look at your paperwork and tell myself these guys haven't absconded to Bermuda with the deed to her property."

"It's nothing to worry about, Martha. They're not like that at all. Don't be so suspicious."

"Can I come look at the paperwork, Clover? I can be there in five minutes."

"The thing is, Martha, I'm not at home. I'm driving back from Jacksonville."

"How soon'll you be back?"

"We're stopping at the outlet mall in just a couple of minutes. It'll be ten by the time we get home, Martha. Plus, I don't even know where I put the dang thing."

Martha weighed the idea of staying at the office and working until ten, or going home and having a glass of wine before Sateesh arrived with dinner. "How about tomorrow morning then? I can stop on my way to work."

"Shoot, I got to be up at the crack of dawn to do the 'Donuts and Dads' at Brit's school. Then I got a bunch of errands over in Southport."

It occurred to Martha that Clover wasn't usually so difficult to pin down.

Was she already anticipating a difficult conversation about her friend Siobhan? When they'd talked that morning, Martha had tried not to show how distressed she'd been by Clover's confirmation of the Camerons' gossip about Siobhan and Joey sleeping together. Clover had been proud of having introduced Joey to his new sweetheart, a sentiment which had, even before Martha knew about Lucy's heartache, irked the attorney so deeply she'd been at a loss for words.

Martha tucked her hair behind her ear and tried to think strategically about getting Clover on their side. "Look, why don't you bring a copy over to Susannah's tomorrow night? She's been trying to get hold of you to see if you and Brittany want to come over. She's having Tessa and June spend the night."

"Well—tomorrow," Clover's voice dropped for a moment, weighing the prospect of being left out against the scolding she was likely to get when she admitted to Martha that she hadn't actually gotten around to picking up the promised copy of her contract. It was something she remembered only at odd moments. Sometimes it was the middle of the night, when she couldn't even call Elroy and Sandy, much less drop by their hotel. Others, she'd be with Brett, on her way to church, and found herself guilty about not having mentioned the refinancing to him, her property or not. Daddy Marcus had always said possession was nine tenths of the law, but he'd also warned his daughter never to sign anything without having a lawyer go over it.

"What time is Susannah's?" Clover asked. It had occurred to her that she could just pick up the contract the next afternoon, on the way to Susannah's. That way she could satisfy her own worried mind as well as Martha's.

"Right after school. Make sure you bring the contract with you. And do you have a number for these people?"

"Not with me, but I'll call them when I get home and ask them to call *you* right back. And I'll bring my contract to Susannah's tomorrow. But hey, I thought Tessa wasn't allowed to see her friends 'til she gained some weight?"

As soon as Martha had hung up, Clover dialed Siobhan's cell. "Hey! I hear congratulations are in order!"

Siobhan, not normally prone to flights of fancy, nevertheless found herself caught up in an instantaneous fantasy plot—a sort of inverse paranoia—wherein Joey had confessed to Clover a passionate desire to marry Siobhan, had asked for her blessing, perhaps even requested a diamond ring of Penelope's to symbolize just how blessed the union was to him.

"You do?" Siobhan asked, speaking as slowly as she could, wanting to prolong her daydream.

"Tessa's weight gain! I'm so proud of you. I knew you could help her. When I think of how we just met by chance and here you are saving the child's life! I'm just—I just thank the Lord Jesus He put you in my path just at the very time we needed help. I knew you could help her!"

"Thank you, Clover. I think you know how challenging it's been for me."

"Look, Siobhan, Brittany's invited to the sleepover at Susannah's, so I thought I'd drop by and pick up June and Tessa after school. That way they can ride out there together and spend some cousin time beforehand. Sometimes Brittany has trouble fitting in when she has to compete with Susannah's girls, so it's nice if she can spend some time alone with her cousins before—"

"I understand. Believe me, if anyone knows what it's like to feel the outsider, it's me."

"Aw, Siobhan. Have you been feeling left out?"

"Not by you, Clover. You've invited me here and there. But I can see that I'm not one of the Omega inner circle."

"Oh, Siobhan, once they get to know you, everyone is going to just love you. But we've all been kind of hibernating lately. Believe me, you haven't missed any big parties or anything. It's like, I don't know, everyone's been trying to respect your rules—so we've left ya'll be. Why don't you come to Susannah's with me? Get to know her and Martha better?"

"No—I—actually . . ." Siobhan lowered her voice to just above a whisper. "I'm hoping Joey will take me out to dinner, p'raps at Sapphire. I've never been there."

"Are you two—are you getting serious?"

"I know I am—"

"You go, girl! That explains a few things."

"What?"

"Well, he's all het up about that codicil in Penelope's will. It made me wonder if there was someone he had his eyes on. That's all."

"What do you mean, het up?"

"Angry like."

"No, sorry. I know what *het up* means but how did you know he was feeling that way?"

"He wants us to go to an arbitrator and duke it out."

"Seriously? I wonder why he'd do such a thing?"

"I don't know, but maybe it's 'cause he's got his eye on marrying somebody, if you know what I'm getting at."

"If he goes to this arbitrator, Clover, what kind of things do you think they'll be looking at?"

Siobhan didn't usually leave Tessa alone during dinner, but she knew she only had an hour to meet with the Camerons before Joey returned from his meeting in Southport.

Taking only a minute to put on lipstick, Siobhan said quickly. "Tessa, you know the rules, right?"

Tessa looked away and nodded.

Siobhan asked June, who was still at the table with Tessa, "Will you keep her company for a while, please? Make sure she doesn't leave the table. And, June, no more sweet potatoes. I'm saving them for your dad."

As soon as the girls heard Siobhan's car start in the driveway, Tessa opened the door to the laundry room to let Rocky into the kitchen. June was thrilled to have the dog with them, thrilled at her sister's disobedience, though she'd not have dared to break the no-dog-in-the-house rule Miss Siobhan's newly discovered allergies had imposed.

When Tessa noticed her sister looking longingly at the sweet potatoes, she offered June the small mound that was still left on her plate. Of all the new foods she'd had to reacquaint herself with, sweet potatoes were hardest to get used to. Though Siobhan's recipe wasn't at all like the marshmallow and brown sugar casserole her mom had made on Thanksgivings, they still made Tessa think of the Pyrex dish sitting on the stovetop waiting to be put in the oven.

All morning long, two years before, each time Tessa had passed the kitchen, on the way from the TV to the phone, she'd dug her finger into the edges to scoop out some of the sweet topping, despite her mother's instructions to leave it alone. "There's raw egg in there, hon," her mom had said on her way out the door. "I'll cook it when I get back."

"Remember the sweet potatoes Mom used to make with marshmallows on top?" Tessa asked her sister, scooping what was left of the whipped potatoes onto June's plate. June picked up her spoon and finished the helping in three quick bites. Then she took a roll and buttered it, sighing. Almost without stopping to breathe, she asked Tessa if she was going to eat her lima beans.

"Since when do you like limas?" Tessa asked, fascinated by the speed with which her sister had used the roll to wipe the sauce from her plate before popping the doughy mess into her mouth and swallowing it whole. "Slow down, you're gonna choke," she said automatically. When she saw the hurt look on her sister's face, she whispered, "I'm just imitating the Warden." Tessa handed her plate to her sister, a form of apology.

Strangely enough, as soon as Tessa had given the beans to June, she wanted them back in the worst way. The very thought of someone *else* wanting her food made Tessa feel reluctant to give it up. Especially lima beans. They were so bland and fibrous, Tessa figured they might be one of those foods that took more calories to digest than they left the body to use as fuel. It was the oddest sensation, this *greed* she suddenly felt. Her sister was using her fingers to savor each one like it was candy corn or Hershey's kisses. Unfortunately, she'd already let June have her beans. It was too late to get them back.

If she snuck some from her father's plate, Siobhan would know. She had all those freaking portions imprinted in her skull, from the deck of cards for a helping of meat (or tofu steak) to the dice for cheese to the fist-sized hills of starchy foods she doled out on each family member's plate.

"Do you remember it? That casserole Mommy made?" Tessa asked, trying to get over the lima beans.

"No," June said, suddenly looking very bleak. "I can't believe I ate all that."

"You had two hours of dance this morning. I think you're in a growth spurt."

"I'm so full . . . I wish I was like you, Tessa. Food doesn't matter to you."

"Don't even think about wishing you were like me. Does it look like I'm having fun? Besides, if you were like me, the Warden would blame me for making you sick."

"Can you—can I—Tessa, can I please be excused? I have to go to the bathroom. Bad."

"I'm not stopping you."

"If Miss Siobhan asks, will you say I stayed?"

"Geez, who died and named her God? Of course I will. We'll both get it if I don't."

"I'll be right back."

There was a look about June, an eager furtiveness that was familiar to Tessa though not something she was accustomed to seeing in her little sister. June was moving toward the back stairs rather than using the powder room off the kitchen. Tessa sat leaning on her elbow, thinking about those sweet potatoes her mom had made.

Did someone throw them away that horrible day, without making them? Or had somebody put the casserole in the oven? Had Tessa eaten some?

She very slowly reached over to the plate Siobhan had set aside for her father and snuck a lima bean. It tasted better than anything she had eaten in a long time. She reached for another and chewed it quickly, wondering what kind of sick person she was to suddenly want what she couldn't have.

Tessa wondered why June was taking so long. She was being pretty quiet too. Did she really have to go or was she using the time Tessa was supposed to be at the table to sneak some of her older sister's new MAC eyeshadow? Or her lip gloss?

By the time Tessa tiptoed up the stairs and quietly opened the bathroom door, June was kneeling over the toilet. One hand was resting over her collapsed head, its telltale pointer and index fingers held together like a wedge, slick with spit. June was heaving, groaning into the bowl, until the torrent of food she'd just consumed was splashing back into the toilet.

"Oh, Juniper," Tessa whispered mournfully. She took a blue washcloth from the pile next to the sink, rinsed it in cold water and wiped her sister's forehead. Next she cleaned June's fingers, the ones she'd used to make herself gag. "Come on, you come on into my room," Tessa murmured, nudging June up from under her armpit. She led her away from the toilet, away from the sink, out toward the open door.

Tessa's bed was made up with soft yellow sheets and a comforter that had been washed so many times its blue flowers had gone to white. Once she'd pulled back the sheets, Tessa patted the space in the middle, motioning for June to lie down. Then she wrapped her frail arms around her sister's sturdy back. "There, now," was all she could think of to say, over and over, like she might be saying something profound, or at least pointing them in some direction. Instead they stayed right where they were and Tessa prayed that the dizzy echo of fear pounding through her pulse would just go away and leave them both be.

Chapter Twenty-six

L ucy, where have you been all morning?" Sigi's voice was hoarse.

"What's wrong? Are you sick?" Lucy asked.

"Only of dialing your number. I wish you'd move to New York, Lucy. Think of how much easier it would be for me. I hate having to dial foreign area codes. Oh, speaking of which, did you make your plane reservation yet?"

"I'm going to—"

"Perfect! That's one of the reasons I'm calling. I had to make a list, Lucy, there was so much new information to give you. Where were you all morning? The buttons on my vest are positively bursting!"

"Sorry. I had a bunch of errands in town. What's up?"

"Your prospects, darling. First, my dear friend Joan Peckingham has offered to host a cocktail party on Tuesday night before your show. She's the headmistress at St. Mark's and her little black book is chock-full of people who owe her or who want to get their babies into her school. You could not *do* any better than that. She's got a teensy nineteen-room cottage in Sag Harbor. You should probably fly into Islip."

"Wow. That's awesome."

"Lucy, expunge that word from your vocabulary, please, the sooner the better. Next, Alvin Chaires called and said he'd been trying to email you for three days about getting him your photo for the website."

"I thought he didn't need it till Tuesday."

"Well, now he does. The *Times Magazine* had to cancel their celebratorial for Sunday because the diva's checked into rehab. Alvin's talked them into a retrospective profile on none other than your dear love object, Penelope Cameron May! Which coverage, of course, we can use to buzz your show. There's no time to send a photographer down, so they've asked for a JPEG of you posthaste."

"A what?"

"It's a digital file with your photo. Note to Lucy, pull head from sand in nineteenth century. Shampoo, blow-dry ostrich feathers. Et cetera, et cetera. The information revolution *will* be televised. Alvin needs a photo by tonight. He says the one I have on file won't do at all. *Capisce?*"

"*Capisce,*" Lucy said, although the idea of having to produce something technical was causing her windpipe to close.

"Once you've got it, just send it to him. Copy it to me too, so Joan can put it on her Evite. The *Times* photographer is here, as we speak, by the by, taking snaps of your Penelope portraits."

"Awesome."

"Lucy!"

"Sorry. Too much time spent in the company of ten-year-olds."

"Now . . . drumroll . . . the best news of all!"

"There's more?"

"Yes. Why do you think it's been driving me insane not to reach you? Remember my assistant, Claire Ann? Her boyfriend Keven is the performance artist?"

"The one who knows everyone who's anyone in the Manhattan art world?"

"Right. Well anyhow, remember how I thought he might get appointed to the Galbreath? I was right!"

"But how is that good news? He's a performance artist, Sigi. They would hate my stuff. That is *so* not good news."

"Well, I haven't gotten to the juicy part yet, my dear. I guess someone in the Galbreath family insisted on recommending an old art teacher of his from Exeter who's profoundly anti-postmodern. She's actually known to be sympathetic to the Stuckists."

"Who?"

"Lucy. Where have you been? They're so *five years ago*. Anyhow, they *hate* conceptual and performance pieces. They're all about a return to figurative art. One of their most famous slogans is 'If you aren't a painter, you're not an artist.'"

"How have I not heard of this group?"

"How have you not heard of a JPEG?"

"Why Stuckist?"

"I guess someone told one of the founders his work was 'stuck, stuck, stuck' and it stuck."

"Funny."

"Anywho—do you see how fabulous this might be for you?"

"Wow."

"Look, while you're getting yourself all dolled up, would you have the photographer do a shot of *The Three Graces*? I want to see where you are with it. And remember, you need to overnight it by Monday, Lucy. Which means the paint has to be dry."

"Monday? Since when?"

"Since forever? I called and left a message reminding you last week. Did you not get it?"

"I—lost some messages," Lucy sighed. "I forgot to pay my bill."

"Shame on you. Not in keeping with Alvin's campaign to portray you as the new darling of the East Coast upper crust. Do you need money, Lucy?"

"Actually, I just got some."

"Alright then. Just make sure you can get to Long Island by Tuesday night. Send me your itinerary with the rest of the stuff once you've made your reservations."

"Is that all, Sigi? Sure you don't need me to solve global warming by Tuesday?"

"Don't be facetious. That's my bailiwick. Just get moving."

✦   ✦   ✦

When Clover's phone rang, Nigel could not help but laugh. Who else would use Dionne Warwick's "One Less Bell to Answer" as her ringtone without even a trace of irony? Clover had asked Nigel to field her calls while she dashed into Brett's office for money. Her car was double-parked. Nigel, whom Clover had collected for lunch, was left in the passenger seat, well primed to play receptionist. Clover had gotten a call from *The New York Times* and was waiting for the reporter to call back, but she was too nervous to talk in front of Brett's secretary and salespeople.

When he saw the 212 area code flashing on the screen, Nigel wanted to fling himself on the ground and worship Mecca, would it not have interrupted his chance to speak personally with the reporter. "My cousin Clover will be right back," Nigel said, after identifying himself as a member of the larger Cameron family. Not only did he wax eloquent about his late cousin's devotion to improving the world, he also had what he hoped was a helpful suggestion. "I think you should interview someone from one of her flagship projects. I imagine you've heard of it. The Phoenix Neighborhood Initiative? Yes, the director's name is Sorensen. Here, let me give you his home phone. His wife Pasha will put you in touch. And she may have lovely memories of her own, as well. Oh, here's Clover now. Just one moment."

While Clover talked to the reporter on her phone, Nigel used his own to text his brother. **w8 4 me @ ur desk.**

After Clover had dropped him back at the office, Nigel opened his brother's door and closed it quietly behind him. "Can you get onto the web for me? This poor reporter doesn't understand why Penelope's husband won't talk to her, poor thing. It's only fair, I think, that we share what little we've heard—but in an anonymous forum—so the poor writer discovers why Cousin Penelope and Lucy's bond has been so very strong."

"I'll look and see what I can do with Wiki."

"Wiki?"

"Wikipedia. You have heard of it?"

"Of course. But how—"

"Because it's open source, Nigel. Anyone and everyone can make a contribution. That's how."

"Clover?" Lucy's voice was strung tighter than a steel banjo by the time she reached a real live person on the phone. "Is there any way we can make the photo shoot today? I just found out they need it tonight. I guess the *Times* is doing a spread—"

"I know! I talked to the reporter this morning! That's beaucoup publicity, honey!"

"Anyway, they need me to send a photo by tonight. So—would there be any way you could come over this afternoon? . . . I could come *there* if it's easier for you."

"No, don't be silly. I'll come there. Let me just rearrange a couple of things and Brittany and I will be there as soon as I fetch her from school."

Clover hung up the phone, dialed another number and waited through the recorded message to say, "Joey, it's Clover. Listen, the *New York Times* is writing a big piece on Penelope and the reporter said she was having trouble getting through—" Clover's melodic suggestion was preempted by an electronic shriek.

"Hello?" Siobhan's voice was low, compensation perhaps for the awful beep she'd caused by picking up the handset midmessage.

"Siobhan? It's Clover."

"Right. Hi."

"Look, I know I offered to drive Tessa and June out to Susannah's this afternoon, and now something's come up. I was thinking—"

Clover heard Siobhan's impatient sigh. It was then that some tender element in Clover—a line of sentiment that was kissing cousins with her very last remaining nerve—snapped in two.

That Siobhan would sigh like that when Clover was only trying to be nice! *Little Miss High Horse had another thing coming!* Maybe Clover had misjudged the dancer. Siobhan seemed pretty ungrateful to treat Clover like that after she'd introduced the girl to Joey in the first place! It hurt Clover's feelings, it truly did. "Actually, never mind, Siobhan. It's nothing I can't do. You're so busy! I'll pick my nieces up right after school. Just make sure they're set to go, okay?"

Clover's trunk was filled with wheat canvas tote bags trimmed in different polka-dotted grosgrain trim. The sky-blue-edged bag, conveying to Clover an image of calm and collectedness, held exfoliants, lotions, aromatic candles, sea salt and kelp rubs for the hair and skin. The lime-green bag, signifying money, was packed with Clover's computer, Brett's digital camera, the Cameron pearls and Penelope's deep green velvet Chanel suit. The pink bag, exuding femininity, was filled with makeup, blow-dryers, curling irons and manicure equipment.

Clover nudged these sacred vessels over to make room for Brittany's Vera Bradley Citrus backpack, a two-liter bottle of Diet Dr Pepper, three shoeboxes and a stack of old *Vogue* and *Town & Country* magazines. She reached into freshly ironed chinos for her cell, pressed number one and then the speaker button. "I'm ready, honey bun. Let's get a move on."

Brittany tumbled out of the front door of her school headfirst, her long blond hair spilling out of a Burberry kerchief that matched the sage green of her Polo top and the creamy dark velour of her low-rise gauchos. It was at moments like this, when she was unaware of being watched, that Brittany most inspired Clover's maternal pride. There was something in her coltish, long-legged loveliness that was so unstudied and all the more affecting precisely because it was so exceedingly innocent.

As soon as Brittany was buckled into the back seat, Clover switched on the CD player and backed out of the driveway, her throat swollen with happiness, her vocal cords keeping perfect pitch with "Brandy." The more often she heard her mom sing this song, the more confused Brittany got. Was Brandy blind? Was that why her mom was singing what a fine world it would be, if only she could see? It made no sense, though. If the chick couldn't see, then how could she serve drinks to sailors? Or watch stuff in her boyfriend's eyes? Any why would the singer be telling Brandy she was his wife, his dove and his baby, if she could only *see*. How mean was that?

At this point, Brittany plugged her ears with her knuckles. Complaining would only set her mom off on how they never had fun like they used to and how they just didn't write songs like they used to or something equally retarded. Bad enough Brittany was being forced to spend the night at Susannah's, where the older girls would ignore her and the younger ones would be annoying and nobody would have any fun at all. The only part Brittany was looking forward to was Lucy's makeover.

When they pulled into the driveway of the High Street house, June was sitting on the front porch with Siobhan. June rose to open the screen door and stuck her head inside, then returned to zip her backpack before she picked it up. Clover turned off the music and hopped out of her car. She danced up the sidewalk, brimming with excitement, then hugged June before Tessa strolled outside. Clover held Tessa's ropy shoulders, kissed both temples and pulled back to survey her again. "You look great, honey pie. Just great.

"Siobhan, you're a miracle worker," Clover exclaimed. She was in that mood toward Siobhan they used to joke about at Auburn, an extreme Southern bitchiness where a girl hugged a friend and shrieked a compliment. "Love your hair!" she'd say, all the while hanging on to the unspoken, whispered "Hate your guts!" This latter sentiment would be all the more enjoyable for having been projected through a toothful, squinty smile. "You have a good night, you hear?"

"Okay, girls," Clover said, herding them into the car. "Let's hurry. We're late already."

"But I just talked to Amber on her cell. They're still at the orthodontist," Tessa said. "So how could we be late?"

"Well, see, I have a little surprise. I hope it's okay with you two.

I'm in kind of a pinch and I couldn't exactly reach your dad to get permission. So I'm wondering if we can keep this a secret."

"This what?" June asked.

"The thing is—well, I've—Lucy's in a real jam and she needs our help."

"Oh, my God!" Martha was crowing loudly into the ear of her running partner. "Are you sure it's them?"

"Ow!" the assistant DA cried, slapping his hand over his offended ear. "Who else would make you think you've gotten drunk watching Elton John on VH1?"

Gary was referring to the twins, who favored a certain type of white suit in the summer, the sort of thing that had made the composer of "Tiny Dancer" so recognizable. "Besides, they had to provide identification to the clerk of the circuit court and she wrote down their passport numbers."

"Wow, I knew they were scumbags, but I didn't think they had it in them to sink that low."

"Yeah. Well, unfortunately, we've not been able to link them directly with the Freedom Loan people. Until we do, they can keep telling us they simply happened on some real estate bargains in foreclosure auctions."

"So wait. I wonder if . . . You know Clover told me the Camerons were the ones who told her about those guys at Freedom Loan. What if she testified to that?"

"That's risky for a couple of reasons. First, I can't guarantee if we set up some kind of sting, we'd be able to prove they conspired to commit fraud. It might be years before it came to trial and until then, your friend Clover is screwed."

"But this has got to be illegal."

"It's kind of a fine line. Buyer beware and all that. We'd have to prove fraud. See, the way this usually works is the Camerons and their buddies, they're just the middlemen. They don't actually hold the property very long. They file the deed at the clerk of court and hold a quickie auction to unload it, offering their own special financing. The highest bidder, whose name we don't get until it's filed with the deed stamp and correlated with the survey, is the one who'll take the heat. Trouble is, this new buyer is getting scammed at the other end so it's pointless to go after him. In fact, he's taken on a bitch of a mortgage without any idea of how bad it's gonna be down the line. The way it starts, the payments are negligible in the first two years. By that time, the property payments go up so high the buyer can't pay, so the lender can foreclose. As long as they can sell it for more than they put into it, which, remember, is small potatoes, they're still ahead of the game. Meanwhile, they've pulled in all those interest and fees while they waited for the over-ripe fruit to fall from the tree."

"Yeah, but I thought real estate was falling apart. Aren't borrowers walking away from their property because they owe more than the place is worth and can't resell when the market's falling?"

"That's where this group has been really canny. They've done a lot of homework and they 'cream the crop.'"

"What's that mean?"

"They concentrate on people who owe little or nothing. Maybe they purchased their houses in the fifties and paid it off a long time ago, but with age they've had medical bills or tax liabilities that worry them. Elroy and Sandy offer them the moon, tell 'em they deserve to enjoy life while they can, and by the time the marks understand they've signed away their property rights, the deeds have been transferred to middlemen, who resell it at these investment seminars. That's where the audience members will end up getting fleeced by borrowing eighty percent of the inflated price at a hundred and twenty percent higher than standard market fees and interest. It's pretty damn golden, really, a candle burning at each end. Especially in this market since legitimate banks aren't lending like they used to. By the time we catch it, the middle has evaporated away with everything else. There's no paperwork linking the lenders and the middlemen, who say they were just honest speculators in a high-risk financial market. 'Caveat emptor' is what Nigel Cameron actually said to me when I interviewed him. Patronizing bastard."

"But can't you find their names in the title documents?"

"That's the really tidy part. We might find names, but we can't prove any collusion between them and the lenders. They claim they were just buying low and selling high."

"Easy to do when you've got a gun to someone's head."

"Right, except with a real gun, it's called armed robbery. With these slimeballs, the guns are so small you need an electron microscope to read which way they're pointed and a particle decelerator to slow things down to the point where you can see who pulled the trigger."

There was something comforting in Aunt Clover's constant chatter. This truth surprised Tessa as much as anything else on this day of days, her first of being out of the Warden's presence in what felt like three lifetimes.

The light looked different against the trees, their leaves hit by the bloody fire of an unexpected freeze, unheard of in North Florida before Thanksgiving. Out of place, out of time. The hibiscus had been decimated, along with young bougainvillea, the fresh banana trees and lemons too tropical for the latitude. Still, the view of the woods was spectacular, the colors garish in the late afternoon sun.

It all felt so weird to Tessa, so out-of-body to be ferried in the back seat of her aunt's PT Cruiser while the countryside whipped past her.

It was still there. All of it. Even while Tessa had disappeared, the forest had remained. Except, of course, it had changed dramatically, snapped by the traumatic frost into a multitude of warm hues.

The look in Aunt Lucy's eyes when she saw her surprise, Tessa and June standing shyly at the screen of her front door, the dogs yowling to the heavens with excitement, peeing on the rough gray wood of the front porch when they rushed out to greet the girls. There was so much to take in, the broken hand that Lucy held inside a knitted sling, wincing as she pressed Tessa and June into her body, tears welling in her eyes.

Clover became all beauty-parlorish in her fever to "fix things right." There was the washing of Lucy's hair, a task she'd not been able to handle by herself. She was propped awkwardly on the edge of the kitchen sink, backward, like she was doing the limbo, eyes closed to the pleasure of the warm spray, small fingers gently pressing lather through her hair while others softly rubbed her face with exfoliating scrub made of almond and honey and coconut. Her skin gleamed in its wake.

Clover briskly blew Lucy's hair dry and set each of the girls to work. They used the curling and flat irons to create a cascade of gently sloping waves, silky russet lit with flashes of auburn and mahogany. Clover applied the makeup so expertly that Lucy ended up looking like she was wearing nothing but what God gave her, those dark-rimmed bright green eyes, the sharp arch of her brows echoed in the rosy rise of Manchurian cheekbones, their lines inverted in the peaked point of her chin, the mischievous V shape of her lips.

By the time they'd brought her out to the deck wearing their mother's fitted suit, there was a flush to Lucy's cheeks that had nothing to do with Clover's makeup. It was the glow of well-being, of being cared for and nurtured by clucking females in varying states of development. Their touch had curative powers.

Lucy was taken out of herself in the same out-of-body way that Tessa had felt earlier. She momentarily forgot her difficulties with Joey, forgot the Galbreath, the upcoming show, the balloon payment, the bills.

There was a hush to the sound of the waves, just lapping, as if the ocean were one more conspirator in this festival of gentle rhythmic care, a rebellion of the children and their aunt against the abrupt strictures of Joey's inexplicable rage.

None of that mattered right that minute. So Clover told herself, turning off her cell phone to guard against interruptions. What mattered was getting Lucy's photo finished. Clover wanted to *wow* the viewers of Lucy's site, to communicate how very lovely she was, she *and* her art.

Clover snapped the shutter like a champion, someone who was practiced at such things. In fact, this was a challenge in which Clover's genius for visual trivia was brought to the fore. There was a staging required, an atmospheric duet that had to be accomplished. Not only would the photo have to seem entirely authentic, it needed also to contain the magic of near perfection, or at least the illusion of such. As it happened, Lucy's joke, that she felt as if she should be posing with the horse and hounds, stimulated Clover's cerebral cortex from so deep within, it was almost like a voice from above.

Out of thin air, Penelope's stepsister produced a set of lime-green sateen ribbons to collar the dogs and tether them lightly to their mistress's elbow, her Napoleonic left hand buried under the right lapel of her open jacket. The dogs were graceful, with sculpted torsos, not a pouf in sight, just the greyhound form of poodles cut short to the scalp. Their rich, velvety coats made Tessa think of medieval paintings. There was a sort of surreal feel to the photo of the dark brown dogs and Lucy's green eyes, silhouetted against the elements of gray sky and cobalt water. It looked like ads in *Vogue* for Dolce & Gabbana, Versace, Prada.

This Florentine influence was an unconscious but serendipitous echo of the pitch Alvin Chaires had already made to the *New York Times* reporter about the Medici-like nature of Penelope's philanthropy.

Later, when it was time to leave, the seconds crumbled in on each other. So much to do and say, to see and hear, but no time for it all. Aunt Clover had checked her voice mail.

Three calls had come in from Susannah: they were back home and eagerly waiting for the girls. Two from Uncle Brett asking who in blazes would have taken his office's digital camera without asking when it was only supposed to be used for insurance purposes per the IRS regulations governing office equipment. Each of these calls might have been something Aunt Clover could ignore, but then she heard the final message. Joey was on his way to Susannah's with a set of healthy snacks that Siobhan had prepared.

This last caused Clover to squeak like a mouse and move like she'd been shot from a cannon. She was a frenzy of efficiency, sweeping everything willy-nilly into bags and air-kissing Lucy while shouting instructions on how to email pictures as attachments.

It was hard to tell if this last was what was making Lucy cry or if it was having to settle for quick stolen hugs and a vacant wave from the porch. All the wind had been pulled from her sails; mascara ran down her cheeks. This despite Clover's careful wizardry and no small amount of warnings about making sure the Chanel suit didn't get stained, as it was a whole lot of trouble to dry-clean.

The strangest part was that Aunt Clover was crying too.

She insisted it was the song on the radio, which she'd turned on only to hear, out of nowhere, something Daddy Marcus had played when she and Penelope were little. It was just so perfect for what they'd been doing at Lucy's.

"Don't you see?" Clover asked. "It's like Penelope is telling us it's all okay, what we've done, sneaking off to Lucy's to help fix her up." All this was gulped out afterward, when the song ended. Until then the three children were treated to a stunned, heartfelt and wobble-throated accompaniment to "Georgy Girl," a makeover ballad if there ever was one, in which the wallflower's rescue is composed of flattering outfits and simply making an effort with her appearance.

Clover belted out this anthem at the top of her vocal range, the windows open, their hair flying every which way. For some reason Tessa felt her lips pulled back into an involuntary grin. She let herself imagine that maybe, just maybe, it was true. Her mom might have laughed at what Aunt Clover said, but she'd have sung along and made her girls do it too.

Back at Lucy's, a different kind of communication was taking place, a whispered review of the directions Clover had given, over and over again. Like an infant's self-soothing, or a form of absolution, or maybe even whistling in the dark, Lucy repeated, "Ruler bar: Insert File Attachment; find My Pictures; double-click. Press Open," over and over so she wouldn't forget, while she waited for her slow behemoth of a computer to respond.

It was almost miraculous, the way it made Lucy feel to complete this task she had dreaded with the sort of panic that different phobics felt at the threshold of an elevator, a bridge, a penthouse balcony. Indeed, Lucy was so filled with confidence (or was it adrenaline?) at having overcome her fear of the machine that once she'd sent the photo to Alvin, Sigi and the Gang of Four, she changed her clothes and went into the studio.

If ever an error might have been feared, it was in finishing *The Three Graces* with her right hand. However, given Sigi's call, it really was now or never. The paint needed to dry, it needed to be shipped on Monday, and there was no time like the present to do what she'd already been putting off for too long.

After mixing the colors, Lucy practiced crosshatching the paint with her right hand on a piece of blank canvas. She found that if she reversed the direction of the strokes and made them much shorter, she could keep better control. From there she moved to the painting itself. All that remained were the final flesh tones for Martha and Susannah, whose fair coloring had meant a different formulary than for Penelope's olive-based skin. When her hand began to ache, Lucy reminded herself that Michelangelo had endured hours of discomfort. When it hurt like hell, she shamed herself by remembering stories of that poor quadriplegic illustrator who'd used her mouth to hold a paintbrush when all else failed.

At midnight, Lucy was finally finished. She stood back and examined the work from a distance. The use of new brushstrokes on the blondes made them stand out from the rest of the painting. She considered applying a matching texture onto Penelope's skin. She even went so far as to mix the colors, but she could not bring herself to ruin what she considered her finest portrait of her lost friend. Climbing the stairs an hour later, she assured herself that the opposing brushstrokes would be undetectable to anyone but the artist. If she'd not known it herself, she'd have liked it just fine. Either way, there was no looking back. The painting needed to go out by Monday or she'd lose her chance at the Galbreath Prize altogether.

When Clover arrived at Susannah's, she was loaded with alibis but found no one to shoot them at. Only Amber and Willow were home.

"Where's your mom?"

"She went somewhere with June's dad," Willow said. "Where were you guys?"

"At Lucy's!" June exulted. "But you can't tell."

"When's your mom coming back?" Clover asked.

The girls shrugged. Clover asked if they'd be alright while she ran the camera back to Brett's office. Everyone but June looked at her like she was crazy. Even June was too delighted to be back at Willow's to do more than wince for a nanosecond and then shrug along with everyone else.

"Ya'll hungry?" Clover said, stalling for a minute, opening the fridge to see if there was something she could whip up quickly before heading into town. Clover was removing the plastic wrap from a nine-by-thirteen glass container and asking if Siobhan had sent the lasagna.

"Mom made that this morning. But we ate already," Amber said. "I was starving. There's a tray in the back of the fridge with zucchini bread and apples."

"Well, here, let's just get ya'll some plates and we'll warm up the lasagna. I bet Tessa could use a break from health food. Okay?"

Clover's words might as well have been in Swahili for all the attention the girls paid. They'd already vacated the premises of the kitchen in that prescient way teenagers had, just in case Clover's conversation might turn to subjects like setting the table or making a salad. Even Brittany, buoyed by the camaraderie of their afternoon, had gone along into the living room to flounce onto beanbag chairs and listen to music with the others.

Clover, left alone in the kitchen, was free to straighten up the counters while the food warmed. She shooed the cats away until the girls came traipsing back in to eat.

After she'd surreptitiously watched Tessa eat most of her serving, Clover tried to reach Susannah on the phone. Instead, she got an immediate response that the customer she was calling could not be found.

"I'll be back as soon as I can!" Clover shouted when she'd decided to risk running the camera back to Brett. "Just tell your momma that!"

By the time Clover drove all the way into town and then headed back to Susannah's, she was more than ready for a wine cooler.

"Hey, girl!" she cried, opening the front door and calling out, eager for the girlfest to begin.

Unfortunately, though, Susannah just wasn't acting right. Something about the look in her eyes.

"You okay, doll?" Clover asked.

Susannah murmured something about her head hurting.

Clover wasn't buying it. "Seriously, what's wrong? Where did you go with Joey?"

"We just took a walk around the lake."

"In that?" Clover, ever the connoisseur of clothing, couldn't help noticing that Susannah was still wearing her work outfit: a long vintage wool skirt and a colorful cardigan with a pair of Dansko clogs.

"These shoes are more comfortable than you think."

"Your phone was turned off, Susannah. Did you know that?"

"I did," Susannah said, not a trace of apology in her tone. "Why? Were you needing something?"

"The girls didn't know where you were." Clover put that out

by itself, not meaning to sound accusatory but sounding that way anyhow. "And I had to run Brett's camera back into town. Oh, hey, you should see the pictures we got of Lucy!"

"Oh, that's where you were? Oh, I'm so glad. So she got to see June and Tessa?"

"Don't tell Joey. I just—I didn't plan it but then Lucy had to have her stuff in by tonight so it was sort of . . . catch as catch can."

"She must have been so happy to get to see them!" Susannah's voice was suddenly full of emotion and she sat heavily at the table, allowing herself to imagine the reunion.

"To the point of tears," Clover sighed. "I can't understand why Joey's gotten a bee in his belfry about her. Do you?"

Susannah opened her mouth to say something, thought better of it and shrugged. "Look, Martha left a message while we were out. She's over in Deep Springs running a marathon tomorrow and it turns out they're supposed to stay there till Sunday. She wants us to fax your contract to her hotel."

"Oh, shoot! I totally forgot it."

"Well, how about if I give you the number and you fax it when you get back home?"

Susannah's cell phone went off, its ring a series of atonal gongs. Not exactly a bell she was saved by, but whatever the sounds, Clover was grateful to be rescued from having to confess that she still hadn't been able to locate Elroy and Sandy, still hadn't picked up her contract. When Susannah carried the phone with her into the other room, Clover cleared their dinner plates and made busy with the dishes, running hot water and pouring soap into the sink. When she couldn't find a clean sponge, it was a perfect excuse to follow Susannah into her office, where she stood with her back to Clover, holding on to her desk like she was bracing for a fall. "We've got to talk," Susannah was saying. "Right away."

Clover knew better than to interrupt her. The urgency in her voice made it clear. This was some serious business and not to be interrupted as housewifely matters. Clover tiptoed back around the jamb of the door and turned the water on to cover her tracks. When Susannah came back into the kitchen, Clover was up to her arms in sudsy water, having substituted a washcloth from the linen closet. She told herself it couldn't be *too* infected with cat cooties, since there wasn't a square inch of shelf space that wasn't already jammed with towels and sheets.

Clover yearned to take the closet apart and sort it into piles. However, having spent too many years scolding Lucy about the way she cleaned up after Susannah, Clover felt sheepish about her sudden desire to do the same.

Maybe it was that Susannah suddenly seemed vulnerable to Clover, in a way she'd not been previously. All that Zen calm she usually projected had flown the coop. In fact, Clover thought she seemed angry, even afraid.

It didn't take a rocket scientist to put Susannah's distress into that category of raw emotionality reserved for ex-husbands. "Darryl?" Clover asked.

"What? Oh, no, not Darryl. Listen, never mind about faxing the contract to Martha. She's driving back after the race tomorrow. She said she'd just stop over at your house and get it sometime this weekend."

"Whoa. Hold the phone. That was Martha? Wait, why're you mad at Martha?"

Chapter Twenty-seven

The next morning, Siobhan was sitting at Penelope's desk, curled intently over the laptop computer. "Come here," she murmured soberly to Joey, who had entered the room carrying a stack of Tessa's books. "You've—you'd better get a look at this."

The screen she revealed to Joey showed a beautiful young woman with long dark hair and skin, a nose ring and what looked like something the Virgin Mother wore in religious paintings.

Like his daughter when she'd looked at it, Joey was reminded of Africa or Asia. Somewhere exotic. "What?" he asked.

"Look at the name of this site. 'Starving for Fun and Prophet.'"

"What?"

Siobhan clicked through a variety of screens showing emaciated young women in alluring poses. "This is called a pro-ana site. Short for *pro-anorexia.*"

"Now I see why you didn't want Tessa online."

"Yes. Well, unfortunately, not only *was* Tessa online, viewing this very page, but she actually went further. See this button?" Siobhan showed him the icon marked "Hide This Site" and proceeded to explain that after Tessa had viewed the page, she'd navigated to a site called *Childhood Abuse and Eating Disorders.* "I hate to say this, Joey, but this makes me wonder if something happened to her."

"Wait a minute. I don't understand. How do you know Tessa did this stuff?"

"eBlaster. It's a program that emails me with every move she makes on the Internet."

Joey aimed to keep his tone light and nonchalant. "You spying on anyone else in the house?"

"Look, Joey, I told you treatment wasn't pleasant. I told you it would go against your instincts. You're the one who didn't want to send her to a hospital. Believe me, they'd be a lot more in-her-face."

"You know, Tessa might have just accidentally ended up on this site."

"She's got you wrapped around her little finger."

"She's my daughter, Siobhan."

"My point exactly. That's why you can't see the forest for the trees."

Joey leaned his head back on the couch and closed his eyes.

When he opened them, Siobhan was still looking at him, thoughtful, patient. "I know this is hard for you. Especially the evidence that she may have been abused."

Joey shook his head. "That's impossible. Whatever else my wife might have lied about, she'd never have hurt either one of our kids."

Siobhan crossed to the couch, sat down, took Joey's hand and stared off into space. "I'm not thinking of your wife. It could have been a family friend, a close relative."

Joey turned to look at Siobhan. "No one we're close to would do such a thing."

"That's the difference between you and other people, Joey. Just because you're such a good person, you can't believe everyone else *isn't*."

Siobhan's words sounded so familiar that Joey's habit of dismissing them kicked in automatically. It took a few seconds for him to realize that it had actually been over two years since Penelope had used almost identical words to chide him for being too trusting.

Déjà vu vied with nausea as Joey considered the possibility that despite everything, despite his resentment about the clause in her will, Penelope may have been right. Maybe he wasn't equipped to judge human nature after all. This new uncertainty, so reminiscent of Penelope's chronic anxiety, roiled in Joey's empty stomach, chipping away at what was left of his orientation.

As soon as Susannah brought the girls back from their sleepover, Siobhan led Tessa into Penelope's study, where Joey was waiting.

"Tessa," Siobhan started, facing off from the opposite love seat. "I want you to talk to your father about why you chose to break the rules and go on the Internet."

Tessa, already bummed at having to return to house arrest, seemed genuinely puzzled. Her head reared back on her neck. "What are you talking about?"

"We know, Tessa."

"Know what?"

Siobhan turned on the computer, pulled up the pro-ana site and tilted the screen back so the family could see it. "What do you have to say for yourself?"

"I—that's not mine!"

"Tessa, before you get trapped in a lie, you need to know that these pages were sent to me from a monitoring program on your computer. I'm concerned that not only were you sneaking online, but now you're making things worse by lying about it."

"Wait, you're spying on me? Dad? Did you—were you?"

"The point is, Tessa," Joey said worriedly, "why would you—what do you find so appealing about this? I'm trying to understand—"

"I didn't mean to. I was researching my famine project."

"That is total hokum and you know it," Siobhan said. "To use genuine starvation as an excuse for your choices is obscene."

"That's not true!" Tessa cried. "I wasn't—"

"Look, let's stop before you say anything else you don't mean," Siobhan insisted. "Lying is part of your disease. Getting better means giving up the deception."

"I'm not—"

"Sweetheart?" Joey said. "It looks like you were reading an ar-ticle online about child abuse. Is that right? Is there something you want to talk about?"

"No! It just was—there, and I clicked on it."

"If something happened to you, it wouldn't be your fault—"

"No, Dad! Nothing—how can you even think that?"

"I just want you to—"

"Joey," Siobhan interrupted. "When she's ready to be honest, she'll talk. Until then, she's—"

"That is such bullshit!" Tessa's voice was raised. She stood up and began to pace, her arms folded across her waist.

"Look here, Tessa, unless you want to go away for treatment, you need to follow the rules. Consequences are part of being ac-countable and honest in your—"

"Dad, can't you see what she's doing?" Tessa asked, looking at her father, who was shaking his head. "She's so . . . fascist!"

"Tessa." Joey's voice was stern. "Name-calling isn't going to get us anywhere."

"What? It's okay for her to tell you I'm a liar and that's not calling names?"

"If the shoe fits . . . ," Siobhan said patiently. "Look, Tessa, we're going to get you well whether you cooperate or not. You can't see the forest for the trees right now, but we can. This illness is a demon, and it makes you do things you wouldn't normally do. It's all part of a piece. The fibs, the cover-ups, the hoarding."

"Hoarding? What have I hoarded?" Tessa asked.

Siobhan stood, held up her forefinger and proceeded to the hall closet. She pulled down the hatbox Lucy had brought, full of soaps and lotions from the hotels Tessa's parents had visited. When Siobhan returned, she'd untied the ribbons at the top of the box and opened the lid. "Do you not think that holding on to these items when there are homeless shelters in need of pre-cisely these sorts of things—how can you *not* see that as anything *but* hoarding?"

* * *

After dinner, June asked her father if they could take the dog for a walk.

"Oh, shoot, baby." Joey had just taken an Ambien, something he'd been doing sooner and sooner after dinner, when the closing dusk made him feel like diving into a dark ditch of sleep. At the look on his daughter's face, however, Joey stood up. "You know what, if you don't mind making it a short one, I'd love to."

Joey followed June through the kitchen to the laundry room, where Rocky was still being held prisoner because of Siobhan's allergies. June took a leash from the hook on the wall. She knelt down to circle the retriever's head with both arms, pausing for a minute to bury her head in his neck. This was a move her father could not help but notice. When they set out, he put his arm around June's shoulder, noting as he did that she looked a little peaked.

"You okay, sweetheart?" he asked.

June nodded, then quickly pressed her forehead into her father's armpit so he couldn't see how much she felt like crying.

Tessa had pulled June aside before dinner and given her instructions.

"I need you to get Daddy out of the house long enough so I can go use his computer real quick. I just want to email Amber without the Warden seeing it."

"Tessa, you aren't going to that website again, are you? Promise me."

"I promise. Cross my heart," Tessa had said. "Hope to die. *Not.*"

"You better not!" June had tried to laugh but it sounded more like a cry.

June was grateful to her older sister, not just for letting her sleep in her bed with her the last few nights, but for saying over and over that she'd take care of her, just like Mommy and Lucy before Tessa had gotten sick. "But you can't throw up, June. You can't."

This last instruction, part of a bargain, was the only thing June had trouble being grateful about.

"I promise I'll eat like I should," Tessa had said. "But you've got to promise you won't do it again. Okay?"

It was this promise that was troubling June. Despite what she knew about how evil it was to make herself vomit, she also knew that for at least a few minutes on either side of the act, there was this deep forgetting, something she'd come to look forward to. Now she'd made the mistake of promising her sister she'd stop, and she missed it, along with all the other things in the world she'd had to get used to doing without.

Clover was on the phone with Lucy, having offered to help her navigate through Priceline, Hotwire and other cheap-travel sites to get last-minute tickets to New York. Clover was on a comfy chaise lounge in her living room, laptop on her knees, reciting directions to Lucy with the soothing cadences of a yoga instructor.

"What time is the opening, sweet pea? Could you fly in that day? That way you wouldn't need a hotel."

"I have to be there on Tuesday for a cocktail party but Sigi says the hostess will put me up."

"Hey, that reminds me, Lucy, did you send the photos I took?"

"Last night. I sent you a copy."

"I tell you, I hate technology sometimes. I've been missing so many emails."

"How do you even know if you miss one?" Lucy asked. She'd checked her mail several times that day to see if Sigi or Alvin had sent the article that would come out in the next morning's *Times*.

"Because Elroy keeps trying to send me an electronic copy of the contract on the farm. He keeps sending it but it's not in my inbox."

"I wonder if they sent me one too?"

"Maybe. By the way, I thought you promised not to tell anybody I mortgaged the farm property!"

"What do you mean?"

"Martha called me with all kinds of questions."

"Oh shoot, I'm sorry, Clover. I didn't think—"

"It's okay. I'm in trouble already because they called Brett and scared the shit out of him."

"Who called? Who's 'they'?"

"Some old busybody over at the clerk of courts. It's got to be some kind of mistake, but he had a conniption fit thinking I'd sold the property without telling him."

"Did you tell him you borrowed money?"

"He'll get over it. The man is just so . . . cautious. He makes me crazy. Oh, Lucy! Oh, my Lord Jesus and *Becky of Sunnybrook Farm*! I just Googled you, Lucy! Your site is up! It's too cute! Here, I'll send you the link."

"The what?"

"Open the mail I just sent you. Click on the line that's underlined in blue. That's called a *link*. Oh, Lucy, your picture looks so great!"

"Wait a minute, Clover, my cell is ringing. I better get it."

"Okay, call me right back; okay? I want you to see how great I made you look!"

Lucy caught her phone on the last ring and in her impatience accidentally pressed the wrong button. "Hello?" she shouted; trying to make up for the fact that she'd put whoever was calling on hold.

"Martha?" Lucy said, but Martha's name had disappeared. The screen was asking her if she wanted to "lock" the call. Lucy began to press buttons haphazardly, trying to somehow connect with her friend. "Martha?" Lucy said again, but another flashing green icon was crossing her screen. Lucy pressed the corresponding button.

"Martha?"

"No, but if she's your lawyer friend, we may soon be needing her services, Lucy. Sit down."

"Sigi? What's wrong?"

"I'm afraid I've got upsetting news."

"What?"

"Well, first, the *Times* pulled the article on Penelope."

"Why?"

"The reporter says they have a policy of not outing people who don't want to come out of the closet. But somebody at the paper leaked some of the piece anyway. Now a gossip site has posted it on their daily blog. There are also new entries about you on Wikipedia! Joan Peckingham, our Sag Harbor hostess, just called to cancel the party because she can't be associated with deviant lifestyles."

"Sigi, what are you talking about?"

"Lucy, can you get online?"

"Yes. I'm on already."

"Okay. Listen very carefully. Do you see that blank space up top, with the http?"

"Yes."

"Alright. I want you to backspace over what's there and type in what I tell you." Sigi proceeded to get Lucy to the site of the gossip blog, where one of the paintings in Lucy's show—a portrait of Penelope in a strapless dress—was featured above the headline.

PENELOPE CAMERON MAY—
MODERN-DAY MEDICI OR MADAME X?

Lucy Luria Vargas is a painter of some renown in upscale social circles, and she will tell you quite candidly that she wouldn't be where she is without the help of a woman she calls her patron, the late Penelope Cameron May.

Heir to the one of England's greatest fortunes, a philanthropist who spent her life giving much of it away, Ms. May, who never took her husband's name, was murdered on Thanksgiving morning two years ago, leaving two young daughters in the care of her husband and Ms. Vargas.

According to sources close to the family and foundation, it now appears that the late Ms. May's generous nature may have extended to certain intimate matters as well as those financial. According to Pasha Sorensen, the former wife of the Phoenix Neighborhood Initiative's executive director, Gabriel Sorensen, at least some of the charities the Cameron Foundation funded were sealed in the bedroom as well as the boardroom. (Ms. Sorensen's charges were corroborated by at least one unnamed source, who was able to provide this reporter with documentary evidence of correspondence between Ms. Cameron May and Ms. Vargas that supports the allegations of an extramarital affair.)

Ms. Vargas denies having ever been anything more than "friends" with Penelope Cameron May (the two met as college roommates at the University of Virginia). However, the painter's canvases, soon to be displayed at Sigmund Hartmann's Hamptons gallery, tell a different story. The overwhelming impression they provide is one of obsession, of a physical familiarity that is at once intimate and otherworldly. These portraits cannot help but bring the beholder to experience loss, love and, most saliently, lust.

How Cameron May's husband felt about sharing his wife with one of her close friends, to say nothing of an alleged affair with at least one of her project directors, remains unknown. Mr. Adorno, who has not remarried, did not respond to repeated requests for an interview. Nor has he returned calls regarding Ms. Vargas's upcoming show or current legal proceedings that appear to challenge certain aspects of his late wife's will.

"Aren't you tired?" Siobhan asked.

She was calling Joey's cell phone from her bedroom, where she'd retreated after following him down the hall, waiting patiently for him to simply turn and notice her. Instead, he'd been oblivious, as though she didn't exist. He'd taken the time to check on his daughters but not Siobhan. And if that wasn't hurtful enough, the man had passed his bedroom, marched into his study and closed his door behind him. The sound of the lock turning in the housing was a rebuke Siobhan could not erase, though she told herself it certainly couldn't be her fault. She'd done nothing wrong. Still, it worried her to see Joey caught up, so unaware of her presence. Was he starting to take her for granted?

"No. I'm just gonna work for a while," Joey murmured back into the phone.

"Why don't you take a sleeping pill?"

"I did. For some reason, it's not working."

Joey figured that his walk with June had somehow interfered with the chemistry of the Ambien, but rather than be subjected to yet another lecture from Siobhan about how he let his daughters' needs override his own, Joey simply told Siobhan he had work to do.

The truth was different. After talking to Susannah the night before, he'd felt a strong desire to be alone, to think things through, to reckon with a growing confusion. Sitting at his desk reading emails seemed the best excuse for that, a chance to zone out, to try to escape the nagging sense that he'd been neglecting something important.

Joey scrolled through his new mail but there was nothing there he wanted to open. Lots of foundation stuff, an old message from the *Times* reporter who couldn't seem to take no for an answer and something from Clover titled "Adorable!"

Deleting Clover's messages before he opened them was a habit Joey had gotten into ever since his sister-in-law had passed along a worm virus embedded in a Heavenly Angels chain letter. Joey's cursor was poised over the subject line. The box was checked. He was ready to delete. As his arrow panned up toward the wrecking ball icon, however, it occurred to him that Clover had been over at Susannah's that weekend with his daughters. Maybe the attachment she was sending was a photo of June or Tessa.

Throwing caution to the wind, he moved back and double-clicked the email. He scrolled down to see her message: "Wait 'til you see how cute!"

Joey navigated down to the bottom, past Clover's Heavenly

Angels signature, and opened the photograph of Lucy with her dogs. It was so unexpected, so lovely, he could not move. *Do you wish to save the file to your computer?* Joey was afraid to say yes, afraid it would cause the photograph to disappear, but he inhaled and followed the instructions.

Then he turned back to Clover's message, hoping for another picture, something to fill him with the same sense of wonder, an emotion he'd not expected himself to feel in conjunction with the subject of Lucy.

Maybe it had to do with having told Susannah about the letter. Maybe talking had loosened something inside. It was almost like an out-of-body experience, like looking down at himself from the ceiling and forgiving himself for feeling so very brokenhearted.

This time, when he reread Clover's message, Joey spotted the link she'd sent under the picture's attachment. Without thinking, Joey double-clicked.

He was in a virtual gallery, the camera sweeping along the floor of Sigmund Hartmann's reception area, panning up from bamboo floors to white plaster walls to land on canvases that were brimming with his late wife's image. There she was, combing her hair in a car window, and there she was, breast-feeding Tessa, and here! It was so beautiful it knocked the air from his lungs. Penelope was laughing, her head pulled back by the centrifugal force of a playground merry-go-round, her hands holding tight on the metal bars, dark hair flying out behind her, her mouth curled around the joy.

This was not the gallon of ice cream Joey had feared. No calories were consumed in his Ambien daydream. No, this was a far more costly greed, a compulsion to own all of these paintings, to retrieve his wife. He still wanted her back in the worst kind of way.

Joey didn't stop to wonder how he'd pay for the bids he was making, nor did he blink at the reserve price set on each one. He was more afraid of losing, so he set his offers well above the asking cost. When he got a reply from the gallery saying his bids had been received and would be evaluated against other offers within the seventy-two-hour auction period, Joey found himself rising from his desk and pacing back and forth until he couldn't stop himself from wanting to look at Lucy's photo and the paintings once again.

Joey pressed an arrow button to activate his screen and found he'd been signed off the server. "Shit!" he whispered, typing "Lucy Vargas" quickly into the Google window. This was the fastest way he could think of to retrieve the website.

Instead he had unlocked Pandora's box. First there was the Madame X tagline, which took him to a page on Wikipedia where John Singer Sargent's portrait of Madame X was accompanied by contributors' discussions of the sex scandal that had rocked the painter's world, his society portrait of a married woman too palpable, too suggestive, a smoking gun. It wasn't the slip of the strap on his subject's delicate white-skinned arm. It was the sensuality of her profile that gave it all away, something beyond words but not beyond the beholders' abilities to imagine.

Already the busy bees who kept this open-source encyclopedia alive had cross-referenced the gossip blog about Lucy's show with this article, as well as another about Lucy and Penelope's alleged "friendship" that someone else had posted.

One click led to another, each tap of the board fueled by Joey's obsessive hunger to find more damning information. Eventually, he landed in territory he'd never thought to imagine: a first-person account by Gabriel Sorensen's ex-wife claiming he'd slept with Penelope and Lucy the night they'd first met at the Ritz. The writing screeched with anger, the sentences rolling over each other, the condemnations wrapped in Pasha's self-pity, the force of her anger carrying the narrative past its glaring need for punctuation and sentence structure.

In her most recent post, titled "FRAUD!" Pasha took Lucy Vargas to task for hiring a model to pose with her dogs, for subjecting her dogs to imprisonment, for trying to disguise herself when everyone knew exactly who the real Lucy Vargas was, knew exactly what she looked like. Did she think she could really get away with torpedoing a marriage and posting someone else's picture on the web to cover it up?

Reading the woman's harangue had a perverse effect on Joey. Pasha's reaction was so over-the-top, so all-encompassing, that Joey wanted only to distance himself from her blistering rage. He immediately felt a desire to protect his wife and Lucy from the woman, even as he could not help but pity the dreadful creature. Anyone who spent so much time hating someone they hardly knew, blaming them for their own unhappiness, what a shell of a woman she must be. There'd be no core left, just a self-fufilling emptiness after a while, the callused husk of a hand used only to hit, a marked hollowness, the wind whirling around inside to keep itself company.

Joey closed the page, returned to the *Times* reporter's leaked article, read it one more time and clicked "Contact the webmaster." Then, just to make certain of reaching the original author, he opened his inbox, found the *Times* reporter's most recent request for information and responded with an informational request of his very own.

As soon as Sateesh had locked Sapphire's doors, he dialed Joey on his cell phone. "Joey? Sorry to call so late, do you have a minute?"

"I'm up anyway. You just getting done with work?"

"Right. Look, there's something I need to discuss. It's a bit delicate."

"Come on over. We'll sit on the front steps and have a beer."

When Sateesh had settled in with his Guinness, Joey asked if he was alright.

"I'm fine. It's just, there are two things we need to discuss, my friend, but I'm actually not supposed to tell you either one. So I'm unsure whether by telling you I'll put you in a spot you'd rather not be. But I think I can't *not* tell you."

"About?"

"You've got to promise me—you cannot fly off the handle or you'll ruin my friendship with at least two of my favorite people."

"Hey, I'm doped up on Ambien, Sateesh. No flying anywhere."

"Tessa sent us an email earlier this evening."

Joey rubbed his forehead. "Us?"

"Martha and I. Actually it went to Susannah and Lucy as well, so they may have already gotten in touch?"

"No."

"Alright. Tessa acknowledged she's not supposed to be using the Internet. She begged us not to say anything about how we'd gotten the information."

"Yet you are."

"Yes. I think it's important. It's about June."

When Sateesh had finished, Joey nodded as if he'd absorbed the information, as if Tessa's worries about her sister were the stuff of fact, as if there was a way to reckon with the fear that was seeping slowly through him without a frame to hang it on. Joey took a long sip of his beer and gathered himself together enough to say, "I'm glad you told me."

"What are you going to do?"

"I don't know. It's hard to know whether Tessa's projecting. Do you know what I mean? I do know she hates Siobhan and wants to get her out of the house, any way, any how."

"Yes," Sateesh said, looking over at Joey, who was staring out into the night.

"Trouble is, how do I know if this is just Tessa finding another reason to resist treatment or whether she's telling the truth?"

"I don't know. But it's better that you be aware. That's why I told you. I know you're . . . involved, which may have made it difficult for Tessa to say anything to you."

"Involved?"

Sateesh lowered his voice. "With Siobhan."

"How did you—did Tessa say something?"

"No. Not at all."

"So—how did you—who told you?"

Sateesh cleared his throat. "It's a small town."

"Shit. Who all knows?"

"I'm not sure. Clover told Martha, and she told Susannah and Lucy and me."

"Lucy! How does—how did they find out?"

Sateesh shook his head. "Don't know."

"Shit."

"Look, no one's criticizing you. You deserve to have sex, for God's sake."

"I don't want the girls to know."

"Of course not. Listen, Joseph. There's more, I'm afraid."

"More."

"Lucy came to see me yesterday morning. She was very upset. Seems she felt it wasn't fair of her to be on Penelope's codicil committee any longer. She asked me to take her place, because she felt she couldn't make a proper choice, not about you."

"What are you talking about?"

"Lucy. She's apparently high-minded enough to be distressed at the idea of preventing you from happiness with Siobhan. She's asked me if I'd take her place on the committee. So *if* that's the reason you were wanting to go to arbitration, simply because you cannot stand the concept of her deciding about your romantic possibilities, you needn't."

"Is she doing this to stop me going to court?"

"No! She wasn't thinking that analytically. She's simply feeling that if she were asked by an arbitrator to make a decision about you and Miss Fitzpatrick, she couldn't be fair. She is, in fact, trying to do the right thing, much as it kills her to do so."

"Can she do that? What did Martha say?"

"I haven't discussed it with my wife. I'm not sure I'm willing to take the hot seat in Lucy's place, much as I'd do anything to help her feel better right now. I said I'd think about it."

"Jesus."

"Call me Sateesh. And by the way, I think you're an ass."

"Look, put yourself in my place, man."

"I try, I do. I can't blame you for being angry. But—I don't know. Why not let some time pass before you make any life-altering decisions? If that's where you're headed. You've certainly got enough on your plate with the children."

"So to speak."

"Glad you've held on to some semblance of a sense of humor," Sateesh murmured, thinking unwillingly of Martha's complaint about Siobhan Fitzpatrick's lack thereof. The truth was, for Sateesh, who'd always thought of the Gang of Four as an archaic, amusing and completely hypothetical legal device, the idea of replacing Lucy on the committee had brought with it all sorts of ruminations. Most of these were unwelcome but persisted nevertheless. Were it up to Sateesh to decide on the children's next mother, how would he evaluate the importance of a sense of humor or a generosity of spirit? These were qualities that Sateesh sensed, without much evidence but with an aching sense of dread, might have gone missing in the dancer-slash-nutritionist. And Lucy? Even if she had slept with Penelope behind Joey's back, Sateesh felt—he *knew*—these same traits were abundant in Lucy Vargas. Most troubling for Sateesh was the question that kept circling back to him: if he had been the child in question and someone had been blessed with the power to keep his father from doing the things he'd done in the name of parental authority, wouldn't Sateesh have prayed for that someone to intervene, individual liberties and self-determination be damned?

Lucy was wakened by the sound of glass breaking, followed by the dogs howling as they catapulted down the stairway toward the front door. She found her phone, awkwardly pressed in a nine, a one, and a final one, waiting only to press the send key. She crouched down the stairs, though why such a posture would protect her from intruders was unclear. The fact that the dogs were now whimpering at the door rather than growling meant they recognized the sound or scent or whatever it was that dogs used to detect danger. Having expected to see the glass surround for her front door in pieces on her floor and a hand reaching in to unlock the deadbolt, Lucy was relieved to see nothing of the sort. She stood up and let her call go unsent.

Still, it took all of her willpower to force herself to edge forward to see who was illuminated by the front porch light.

Martha's T-shirt read DEEP SPRINGS RUNNERS DO IT IN THE ROAD, a motto Lucy had no trouble reading. It was emblazoned across the lawyer's back and getting the full spotlight treatment as she squatted down to pick up what was left of her wine bottle.

"Martha, don't!" Lucy scolded, opening the door just enough to be heard but not enough to let the dogs out. "You'll cut yourself!"

"Shit, Lucy, did I wake you?"

Martha's voice was just slightly slurred; her lips were framed around each word as if trying, unsuccessfully, to keep them from escaping at all.

"Get in here." Lucy whispered. "I'll get a broom. Just come on in."

When Martha stood up she was holding an envelope full of paperwork tight to her chest, which she proffered to Lucy as an excuse for the visit. "I gotta talk to you, Luce."

"What?" Lucy asked, shooing the dogs out of the entryway. She moved to the kitchen to get a broom, paper towels and a folded paper grocery bag. "Look, just come on in."

"Lucy, let me do that," Martha insisted, but Lucy was, even with only one working hand, nearly finished. She swept the glass into a pile, shook out the bag into a boxy nest and scrunched a long sheet of paper towel into a ball. All Martha had to do was take the bag and hold it steady, but even *that* had her teetering over toward Lucy until they bumped heads. "I got it, Martha. Come on, let's go back inside. I'll get you some Gatorade and Cheetos."

By the time they'd settled at the island, Martha had consumed the entire bowl of Cheetos without stopping for air.

Lucy, meanwhile, was trying not to obsess about how Martha

had driven by herself. This was a sin that Lucy, having lost her parents to a drunk driver on the wrong side of the freeway, could not overlook. "Martha, where's Sateesh?"

"Augggh," Martha cried, for the sound of his name was enough to send her running to the small bathroom, where she vomited neatly into the commode. "Auggh," she added without affect and flushed the toilet.

"Here. Drink some water now. Just a sip."

"Oh, Lucy, I feel so bad!"

"I know, honey," Lucy murmured, though she didn't. She had no idea. "Come on up and I'll get you into bed."

She took Martha's elbow and propelled her up to the rightmost bedroom on the second floor. It was the calmest of her guest rooms, its walls a creamy sand, the bedding a bright white matelasse cover and shams. The furniture was art deco maple, and the only painting was a landscape by one of Lucy's friends, a pasture in various shades of purple and green.

Lucy pulled back the covers and dusted the pillow with her right hand. Martha stepped out of her running shorts and fell sloppily across the bed. "We have to talk!" she scolded.

"Tomorrow," Lucy promised, dipping to sweep the shorts off the floor, laying them neatly over a chair back. Then she turned off the light and headed downstairs to dial the phone.

"Sateesh?"

"Lucy? I'm sorry I haven't gotten back to you. I know you're eager for an answer but I haven't actually been able to decide yet."

"Oh, don't worry. I'm not calling about that. I just wanted to let you know that your wife is sleeping over. She wasn't in any shape to drive."

"Martha's in Deep Springs, Lucy."

"She just knocked at my door about half an hour ago."

"She left the race?"

"Apparently."

"Oh, damn it! Shall I come get her?"

"No, she's already asleep. I just didn't want you to worry."

"Too late for that."

"What do you mean?"

"Have you not noticed how very much she's been drinking?"

"No. I mean, yes. Sorry."

"Right. Well, I'm sorry you had to cope with her tonight. I don't understand why. It's not like her to leave a race."

"She has seemed, I don't know, stressed lately." Lucy sighed. "I guess I'd better get back to sleep."

"Of course. Lucy, thank you for taking care of her."

"No problem. Tomorrow I'll give her the lecture about designated drivers."

Chapter Twenty-eight

The next morning, Lucy was making coffee when Martha walked in the back door. She was wearing the same shirt and shorts and shoes she'd had on the night before. They were now soaked in a new layer of sweat, as was her hair and skin. The dogs were licking her legs, something that normally made Martha laugh uncontrollably. Not today.

"Luce?"

"You okay?"

Martha shook her head, as if to say anything more was futile. "I'm just gonna hop in the shower. After I grab a change of clothes from my car."

Lucy took a towel from the laundry room and they proceeded upstairs. "Here. You go ahead. I'll get your bag and put it on the bed. Then we're gonna talk about how you drove drunk last night."

Martha couldn't meet Lucy's eyes. "Just let me get clean."

"There's a new toothbrush in the medicine cabinet."

"I got one in my purse. Where did I leave my purse?"

"Downstairs. Well, actually, you left it on the porch but I brought it in for you."

Lucy started the shower for Martha and eased around the lawyer, who was peeling off her wet clothes as if they were stinging her skin.

Martha's body was taut and muscled, a vision of good health

355

except for the invisible part of her brain about an inch behind her eyes, the exact location of which felt like a cold metal plate digging into her sinuses, all the better to distract Martha from the unpleasant fact that she was rank with the sour aftertaste of a magnum of Chardonnay poured out into sixteen-ounce paper cups until empty.

When she arrived downstairs, she was wearing a pair of jeans with a plain white T-shirt and navy cardigan. Martha sank on the couch where Lucy was sitting and said, "Just so you know, I didn't drive."

"That's not your car out there?"

"It is. But Susannah drove it."

"Where did—"

"She walked back with Amber and Willow along the beach."

"That's a relief! I wish I'd known that last night! I was really worried! Sateesh was too."

"Oh, fuck! You told Sateesh! What did you tell him?"

"That you were sleeping here. That you were safe. He didn't even know you'd left Deep Springs."

"Oh, Lucy. I don't even know where to start." Martha put her head onto her folded arms, and Lucy rubbed her back.

"It can't be that bad, honey."

"Oh, it's worse. But before we get into it, I gotta get your signature on some papers."

"I don't understand."

"It's just a precaution, Lucy, but that loan you signed, I'm pretty sure those guys weren't legitimate. If we don't file a rescission of your power of attorney and any agreements they might have signed in your name, they might be able to steal your property."

Martha let the second part of what she knew go unsaid. If the lenders had filed a transfer of the deed with the clerk already, Lucy might have to spend years in court to prove she was swindled.

"What do you mean?"

"Well, for one thing, my running buddy works at the DA's office and these guys you worked with—Sandy and Elroy, a.k.a. Sam and

Euston, a.k.a. Steve and Edward Jones—have been convicted before on loan fraud. And Susannah called your mortgage company
yesterday. Nobody's contacted them to pay off your other loan,
even though that's what the assholes promised you they'd do."

Martha rose to the desk where Lucy had put her file folder.
She brought it back to the couch and extracted a pen and a small
stapled document flagged with small arrowed SIGN HERE Post-its.

"What are you saying?"

"I'm saying they were scamming you. That paper you signed,
they could have used it to sign a quitclaim on your deed."

"A what?"

"It's something that renounces your rights to ownership of your
property."

"Martha, are you serious? These were people Clover sent
me . . ."

There was a dread that crept into Lucy's sentence as she recognized that trusting Clover to vet her lenders was like asking Rocky
to distinguish between pizza boxes and his chew toys. She'd known
this deep down, perhaps. She'd craved the illusion of safety, even
if it meant believing in a fantasy she should have known was too
good to be true.

Lucy's shoulder joints felt suddenly full of gravel, as if she'd
shoveled rows of soil or swum too long. It would have been funny,
how every single thing was falling apart, except for the bit where
she was homeless and carrying her clothes in a sack at the end of a
stick. This was an image that stories of the Dust Bowl had planted
in Lucy with a panic peculiar to her obsessive-compulsive disorder.
Even as a child, it hadn't been the lack of food or even shelter in
the plight of those poor hobos that so distressed the artist. No, it
was the image of having to carry one's belongings in a manner so
haphazard, so uncylindrical, all mushed fabrics and road dirt, no
running water, much less tidy bureaus or symmetric shelves.

Lucy was brought back to the present when Martha said, "Clover never got a copy of her contract either."

"So what does it mean?"

"I don't know exactly, since it's Sunday. Everything's closed," Martha said, holding the pad for Lucy to make it easier for her to sign one-handed. "Tomorrow, first thing, I'm going to the clerk of courts to file a rescission on your behalf. I'll look and see if anyone's filed for title on Clover's farm too. We got less of a chance to save her, but you've got three business days to change your mind on any loan. Tomorrow's your third."

Again, Martha didn't elaborate on Lucy's peril. While she would certainly be able to wiggle out of the new mortgage she'd entered into with the lenders, it wouldn't necessarily invalidate the transfer of the deed if she'd signed something that appeared legitimate.

"Oh, my God. This can't be happening. I've already spent a lot of the money."

"I know. We'll figure out how to pay it back, but for now, I just gotta get you to sign this. I don't want to forget."

"Martha, this isn't something I'm going to forget. This is my life!"

Martha shook her head. "I know that. I know. I didn't mean it like that. But, honey. I've got something to tell you." Martha took a deep breath and looked up at Lucy. "God, I need a glass of wine."

"No, you don't. Quit procrastinating. Come on, I can take it. It can't be any worse than what you've just laid on me." Lucy set the signed document on top of the folder. She looked at Martha warily.

"You know how we all thought Joey was mad at you because of Tessa? Well, it turns out there's something different."

"What?"

"He thinks you slept with Penelope."

Lucy threw her palms forward as though pushing away something she'd already refused several times. "Who keeps spreading this rumor! It's on the Internet too! I never slept with her. Never. Not only did I not do it, I didn't want to either! Fuck! What is *up* with that?"

"What do you mean, the Internet?"

"Oh, I haven't even gotten to tell you how the rest of my universe is in a freaking nosedive. *The New York Times* canceled their story on Penelope because they have a policy of never outing someone who hasn't already come out. When Sigi tried to tell them I wasn't gay and neither was she, they didn't believe me. So, all those people who might have read about my show and maybe even wandered over to the gallery, they won't even hear about it. For sure, my niche demographic won't be coming because they've all got sticks up their butts. I'm sure by Wednesday night there won't be a single person who's not seen these gossip blogs circulating a lie about Penelope and me sleeping with this Sorensen guy out in Phoenix. Fuck! I'm not even attracted to blond men, for God's sake!"

"Wait a minute. What blogs?"

"Oh, Martha, I'd show you but I'm afraid to see how many times you can Google me and get 'lesbian painter.' Oh, and another penny from heaven? That Sag Harbor cocktail party got canceled too. The headmistress can't be seen as supporting a deviant lifestyle. Jesus, Martha, if I don't sell any paintings, I'm so screwed! Do you think Sateesh will let me work at Sapphire? Maybe I can sleep in the back room."

"What gossip blogs, Lucy?"

"I don't know. A bunch of these stupid—they're like really cheesy newsletters online. I never read them but apparently other people do. Sigi is out of his mind over this. Apparently the reporter talked to this woman in Arizona—weird first name? Anyway, she claims Penelope and I slept with her husband. Together! But, Martha, if I did that—hell, I was really drunk that night, but I'd remember that! Wouldn't I?"

When she responded, Martha's voice was oddly flat. She tucked her hair behind her ear, took a breath and nodded at Lucy. Her manner was that of a doctor telling a patient her cancer had metastasized.

"You would. You wouldn't want to, but you would."

Lucy's head cocked ever so slightly to the right. She narrowed her eyes, trying to understand what Martha had just said.

"Oh, my God!" Lucy stood up and leaned over, unable to contain herself. She was so relieved to find out she hadn't done what everyone said she had, she felt almost giddy. "Martha, it was you?"

"Lucy, it's not funny."

"I cannot believe it! Are you serious?" Lucy sank down on the couch and asked, "You slept with Penelope and that cute guy? How did it . . . when did it . . . oh, Martha! What's wrong? Oh honey, I was just surprised. Don't cry."

Martha was bent over her knees sobbing. Lucy patted her friend's back and made soothing noises. Martha stopped for a moment, then sat up and wailed, "Lucy, not only did Penelope betray Joey, which is why he's been so damn pissed off, but I betrayed Sateesh! Who would never in a million years do that to me!"

"Oh, honey. That was years ago. Or did you—"

"No, never again."

"Oh, my God! You and Penelope! That's so weird."

"It *was* that."

"Well, I'm confused. What happened—or, I don't need to know what happened, but why did . . ."

Martha took a breath. "God. I don't know. We were so stupid. Both of us. So stupid. Remember how I couldn't get pregnant?"

"Whoa," Lucy murmured at the idea that Martha would have passed off another man's child to her husband. "You'd have done that to Sateesh?"

"No, no, of course not. I wouldn't. Not like that. See, Penelope thought I should use Joey's sperm, but Sateesh had this *thing* about artificial insemination. And Penelope thought maybe if I had sex with Joey, well, somehow it would be less—I don't know, threatening to her if she was there too. But she wasn't sure she could share him, nor was she sure she wouldn't be grossed out being—in bed—with another woman. She didn't want to make *me* a promise she couldn't keep, and she didn't want to make *Joey* a promise she couldn't keep. I guess, well, it was kind of like jumping off a cliff."

"So wait, you were practicing for a threesome with Joey?"

"Oh, fuck. Not really. But that's how we found ourselves more . . . open to it than we might have been otherwise. I don't know. See—Penelope thought Joey would get tired of her. She wanted to spice things up by bringing in somebody else. But she didn't want to offer it to him and then have to retract it. Especially if she got jealous as soon as he got into it. Also, she didn't want to tell me that we could have Joey's sperm and then find herself backing out over jealousy. So, I don't know. We were drunk. We smoked pot. Sorensen—who subsequently became the project director for the Neighborhood Initiative, but that's a whole separate ball of wax—came on to us. It was like, one thing led to another, just like they always say in those stupid fucking movies about infidelity. It's all so incredibly lame."

In the eight years since, Martha had found herself looking back on that night through a kaleidoscope of shifting emotions. Often came denial, a survivor's instinct that protected her from an overwhelming remorse that would, if left alone, consume her entirely. This switchback between making believe it didn't happen and utter regret would inevitably be dog-heeled by an awful, ever-present anxiety. If Martha, so practical, so reliable, had it in her to do what she'd done, what would keep Sateesh from betraying her? Worse, what if, in doing so, he fell in love? This dread surrendered itself then to a constant ache of self-hatred, the price Martha paid for this irrevocable intimacy she'd bestowed upon a complete stranger. It was *that* she felt worst about. Somehow, what she and Penelope had done didn't seem to matter nearly so much. She'd always loved her friend, and despite being naked when they embraced, their affection was straightforward and platonic.

The object of their desire, perhaps precisely because they knew so little about him, was the stranger who'd come over to their table with his bottle of Dom Pérignon. "Celebrate with me," he'd insisted, pouring sips in their mouths directly from the bottle. "Celebrate my ruined life."

"Anyone who can afford Dom can't be too ruined," Martha had said, having dribbled most of his pour down her chin. He'd reached over with his left hand and followed the trail down her neck until Penelope had grasped his wrist and set it down on the table. "She's married, darling."

"Of course. The good ones are always taken, the taken ones always good. More doom to commemorate. And what of you? Is your doctor or lawyer or Indian chief waiting up for you in Paradise Valley?"

"We're not from here," Penelope had said, dodging the question.

"Ah, good. I wouldn't want to have to call your husbands to collect you. And I certainly can't drive."

"How refreshing. A man who admits *that* can't be all bad. What are you celebrating?" Penelope laughed.

"In six short hours I've managed to throw away the past four years of my life. My career's over. My father's disowned me. And my company car's been towed from the lot across the street."

"What do you do?"

"I did work for my father's company."

"And?"

"Irreconcilable differences. Let's drink to that. But this time, if I spill, promise I can lick it off."

"You're appallingly drunk, you know."

"That would be the kettle calling the pot black, my dear. I'm not the one who's just spent the evening broadcasting my domestic affairs in stunning detail. It was a great distraction from my imminent execution. Even my father couldn't manage to plug his ears fast enough. Perhaps it made my own offenses seem less—I don't know—offensive."

"Brilliant tautology. What were we talking about?"

"What did you *not* talk about? It's a good thing no one had a tape recorder or I could blackmail you both into that ménage à trois you're not sure you've the courage to try, much as you think it might add pizzazz to your husband's portfolio. Since when did women begin to discuss their love lives as though they were stocks and bonds? Just when I was trying desperately to call it quits in the financial world, there you are, making it sound irresistibly sexy."

"That's mortifying."

"No, not at all. My father doesn't know who you are and I won't tell."

"Who are we?"

"I'm not sure about your lovely blond friend, but you're Penelope Cameron May."

"Have we met?" Penelope asked.

"Not officially. But I know your foundation. I did an internship on Wall Street, trading bonds, before my father convinced me to come back home and work for him."

Penelope nodded, pulling her dark hair behind her ear. "Ah, so the ruined man is actually independently wealthy."

"You say that as if it's a *bad* thing. And again, the pot calling the kettle black. I'm Gabriel Sorensen. I think we met years ago when I was interning in the charitable trusts division at Barclays."

"Sorry, I don't remember."

"Why would you? I was just one of many fawning over your father and his beautiful daughter. Here, have another sip. Open those brilliant pearly whites. That's it. Pull your lip over the rim. Here, Blondie, come sit by me. I can't reach you all the way over there. Don't be afraid, I don't bite."

"Only if you tell me why we're celebrating," Martha said, already moving to the other side of the banquette.

"I'm not sure you want to know." Here Sorensen's bantering tone had changed. He'd combed his fingers back through his hair and whispered. "I've caught something in my conscience and it might be contagious."

Later, when Martha would analyze what she'd done, what she'd allowed herself to do, her attention would snag on the nobility of his decision, how attractive it had made Sorensen seem, as if that single fact might somehow wash her clean, make it all better. It was a boat that wouldn't float, this line of reasoning, no matter how often she set it into the water. It wasn't goodness she'd been after, nor sympathy or kinship. No, it was the way his hand had felt on her throat. He'd had smooth, tapered fingers lit by bright gold hairs, and he'd lingered just long enough to make her wonder what they'd feel like on her breasts. There was a mystery to the man, a troubled darkness that reminded her of all the bad boys she'd ever wanted, knowing their danger and wanting them *because* of that, even as her better judgment had quashed any delusions about who they were, what they wanted. There was a mocking familiarity to Sorensen, as elusive and ephemeral as his attentive presence, which threatened to take flight at any moment. He was the sort of man who glittered risk, the opposite of her loyal, reliable mate. This was what drew her to him, in fact, because if she couldn't have the pregnancy she so desired, she might as well cast herself off the cliff of domestic safety, taking her deluded husband and his stubborn resistance to artificial insemination with her.

The only thing worse than what she'd done that night was what she'd done since, keeping this betrayal from Sateesh. In doing so, without realizing it, Martha had not only deprived Sateesh of the truth, she had also, unintentionally, shut herself down in ways she'd been unable to fully acknowledge, denying herself conjugal pleasures she no longer felt she deserved.

When Martha had finished telling Lucy what had happened, Lucy remained still for a long time. She shook her head and reached over to place her right hand on Martha's shoulder. "Wow. It must have been so hard for you."

"Oh, God, we both felt so terrible, Lucy! And embarrassed! Penelope had to write me a letter, that's how awkward we felt. I think she'd not even have done that if she'd not gotten a phone call from Gabriel's wife. Pasha's the weird name you were trying to remember."

"Shit. That's it!"

"Yeah. This crazy lady had smoke coming out of her ears. She told Penelope if I didn't call her and apologize, she'd call Joey and tell him what happened. So I called her and apologized. I had to."

"Hey, wait a minute. What happened? Did she call Joey?"

"I don't think so."

"So how did Joey find out? And why would he be so mad at *me*?"

"Somebody sent him a copy of this letter Penelope had sent me. If you saw it, you'd see why he assumed it was written to you."

"Like everyone else. What is it? A big L across my forehead?"

"No. See, this is where you are going to hate me, Lucy, but it might be my fault. I, at least as far as the crazy wife went, I let her think I was *you* on purpose."

"Why?"

"Because Penelope thought if she realized I was married too she'd make both of our lives miserable. So Penelope told her I was a painter, didn't have a husband or any money to speak of, and she'd not have any luck trying to get something out of me. When I called, I repeated it. Of course, I didn't realize how it might come back to haunt you later. At the time, Penelope just wanted to keep her from threatening me like she was her, I don't know how Pasha figured out your last name, but somehow she found out you were the fourth person staying at the Ritz, the only one of us who wasn't married. So in her mind, the person she *thought* had been with her husband was Lucy Vargas. She even convinced Gabriel that Lucy was the name of the woman he'd slept with."

"How could he not remember your name?"

"It wasn't like we talked a whole lot, hon. And later, the one time he talked to Penelope about it, he mentioned something that made her realize he thought my name was Lucy too. She didn't correct him. I think he still thinks—I mean, he thinks the blond woman he slept with is a painter, if you know what I mean. And when he's picturing the lawyer who filed his documents, he's thinking it's that gorgeous redhead who wouldn't give him the time of day. Since I don't fly anymore, well, we've never had to run into each other."

"Oh, Martha. You poor thing. This must have just killed you! And then to have that plane almost—oh wait, that was the plane you were on, right?"

"Oh yeah, that was icing on the cake. Jesus, like we weren't flipped out enough? I think we both thought God was giving us a huge wake-up call."

"Wow."

"I'm so sorry, Lucy."

Lucy shook her head. "Why? I mean, why are you apologizing to me?"

"Because Joey has been thinking it was you."

"But—oh, right. I hadn't—" Lucy pondered this. In the shock of hearing Martha's story, it hadn't sunk in that Joey had put her through hell for something she hadn't in fact done. "That's why he was so furious!"

"Look, Lucy, I'm going to go over there right now to tell him the truth. If I'd known what he thought, I'd never have let you take the heat for it. I'd have told him a long time ago. I just wanted this to stay dead and buried. I would have talked to him already but I wanted to explain it to you first. I'm so sorry."

Lucy was quietly trying to piece it all together. Though she'd been pretty certain she hadn't done what she'd been accused of, she couldn't remember the details of that last night in Phoenix except for waking up on the luxurious marble floor, her head next to the toilet. Then she remembered how angry Joey had been the last time she saw him. "But when he came out, he brought that note I'd written Tessa."

"Did you actually confirm that?"

"No, Miss Lawyer. But it was pretty obvious."

"Why couldn't it have been the letter he'd gotten in the mail? The one Penelope had sent to me all those years ago?"

"I suppose. But who—"

"I have no idea. I destroyed my copy the day I got it. Even if Penelope had saved a copy at her end, why would it end up being sent in the mail two years after she died? The only person I can think of who'd have done this is that crazy bitch in Arizona, but how would she have a copy? Susannah and I have been racking our brains."

"So—Susannah knew about this?"

"I had to tell somebody."

"Penelope never told me."

"Oh Jesus, Lucy. Of all the things to be upset about, Lucy, that's the least."

"So say you. I thought she was my best friend. She was. And I thought I was hers, but apparently I wasn't."

"Oh Lucy Loo, she loved you so much. That night, well, after we did what we did, Penelope was pretty drunk. She told me something else I've never mentioned."

Lucy was distracted by a rising anger at how she'd been blamed for what she didn't do, something she didn't know to defend herself against. All the while, she'd been the only one of the four friends who'd not known this enormous secret. She opened her mouth to ask a question but shut it abruptly. She waited instead, letting Martha take her time to articulate whatever point she seemed to be trying to make.

"Penelope had this idea that she, well, that maybe *you'd* always liked Joey. And that, if she was really a good person, she should have been willing to share him, especially since you were her best friend."

"But that's ridiculous! Who'd expect their best friend to share her husband with them?"

"I know. But being ridiculous never stopped her before, did it? Anyhow, I guess, well, let's just put it this way. She was pretty sure Joey would have liked nothing better than for her to bring you into their bed. And as much as she wanted to please him and felt she should give you something you also might have wanted, she couldn't bear to do it. She found herself feeling incredibly guilty but at the same time insanely jealous. Especially *after* we—had that thing in Phoenix."

"But that makes no sense."

"I think we both realized how easy it was to do something impulsive. We got carried away in the heat of the moment, and it scared Penelope. If she could do that and still be so much in love with her husband, what was going to keep *him* from doing that to *her*? Not love, right? Because she'd loved him, and yet she'd done this awful thing. She'd betrayed him. And she couldn't stand the idea he could do that to her!"

"That is sooo fucked up."

"I know. Anyway, all this to say she was your best friend and she wanted to give you everything, but when it came down to it, she didn't have it in her. So she gave you the beach house instead."

"Oh, my God, I think I'm going to vomit."

"Why?"

"Why? One, because she gave me the house for such a pathetic reason, and two, because her husband is such an asshole, and three, because even as I want to kill him, I miss him so much it hurts to breathe."

As soon as Martha left her house, Lucy took her dogs on the beach and walked in the opposite direction from Susannah's. If she could just move fast enough, she might escape the sound of the phone not ringing, the computer left dark since she'd pulled the plug the night before.

No one was calling, no one was buying, her show was a disaster, no one could save her from her own stupidity. Her mistakes were legion, pursuing her no matter how fast she walked.

Why hadn't she tried harder to find out why Joey was so upset with her? How could she have accepted him flipping out like he had, at least without pushing back? Why, after he'd jettisoned her from his life because of false assumptions, why didn't she hate him completely? If she had any spine, she'd never talk to the man again. Was she a complete masochist? He'd even pushed her away so violently she'd broken her hand, and still, her head was pounding with the thrum of hope. She was like those domestic violence victims who kept going back for more. What was wrong with her? Was she just too stupid to know when someone was bad for her? Was that it? As she tried to wrestle with this question, Lucy felt hollowed out, empty. She walked faster, trying to rid her brain of distressing images.

Unfortunately, the hits just kept on coming. Next on her mind was the possibility of having been duped by the mortgage imposters into losing her house. She'd signed a power of attorney form, thinking nobody, not even a stranger in resort wear, would sit in her kitchen, be so nice and then lie to her face.

She should have known better, she really should have, but even after suffering the loss of Penelope, Lucy had somehow refused to learn from the experience. Instead, she'd almost felt protected. Having weathered such grief, she subconsciously presumed a just God would be careful about meting out any additional punishment. He'd make sure Lucy Vargas didn't get more than she could handle. Certainly, after having her friend *stolen*, it wouldn't be in the odds for another thief to come and take what little she had left, right?

How could she have been so gullible? Did it all just come down to this in the end, a dog-eat-dog contest for the scraps? This was a game she'd forfeited before it had even begun, continuing to believe in people's inherent goodness, despite abundant evidence to the contrary.

There was a gray cast to the ocean that day, a bleak absence of color, a sickening tinge of brown dreck and plastic washed up on the sand. The water had a rainbowed look of meat gone bad in the shallow wake of surf, the mess so listless it couldn't get brought back to the sea.

The dogs were snapping at a bloated fish. Lucy couldn't summon the voice to keep them away from danger. She watched them in the surf and felt helpless to keep them away from the possibility of being poisoned, just one more inevitable heartache to come in on the tide.

And Joey, the thought of him was intolerable. She felt stalled, stuck, unable to move, and yet she was shaking uncontrollably. Lucy sat in the low surf while the dogs tugged the dead fish into nothing but a string of bones that rained clods of flesh and silvery skin onto the shell-pocked sand.

She couldn't allow herself to think of Tessa and June right then; it was too painful to absorb them into that greedy landscape. Nothing was as it seemed, only this colorless all-consuming vacuum that was pulling her into its deep black center.

When Lucy started walking again, she reached a point on the beach where the sand was swallowed into a fast eddy of moving water. Precious and Bijou nipped at her heels, trying to herd her back onto dry land. Without forethought of any kind, Lucy stopped and turned out to face the water. She then pulled her small black cell phone from her pocket. Without opening it or turning it on, Lucy threw the obelisk as far as she could, watching as it hit the slate-colored water and disappeared. Next, feeling a tiny release, she tucked her head toward her feet and made for home.

Of all she would miss when they took her house, this churning border of sand and spray and salt and sound, it would be this lovely mirage she'd miss the most.

Joey was on the phone with the *New York Times* reporter when Martha knocked at his door. The attorney seated herself while he spoke into the handset.

"Look, my wife's privacy is beside the point now. I'm not even trying to dispute the story, but I'm curious. How did you get your hands on this so-called documentary evidence? As far as I know, there were only two copies of that letter my wife wrote and I'm in possession of both."

Martha waited while Joey explained that he understood about sources being confidential. "It's just, in this case, the person who outed my wife was also trying to out Lucy Vargas. Has it occurred to you to wonder why this evidence is all coming out right now? Did you know Lucy's work is up for the Galbreath Prize?"

Martha was quiet while Joey listened to the reporter's reply, waited while she heard him say, "From what I hear, the competition in the arts world is pretty cutthroat. It's worth checking out, that's all I think. I'd just hate to see you get used like that."

When Joey hung up, the first thing Martha asked was "How did you know?"

"What are you talking about?"

"How did you find out? That it wasn't Lucy. I'm assuming that's why you're trying to change the writer's mind."

"What are you talking about?" Joey's head was tilted slightly to the right. He looked as though he hadn't slept or shaved in days.

"That letter you got in the mail, Joey. When did you realize it wasn't for Lucy?"

Joey reared back a bit in his chair, adjusting to what he'd just heard. He shook his head as though trying to rid himself of a dissonant concept. "Wait, did Sateesh say something, Martha?"

Martha swallowed hard and asked, her voice cracking, "Sateesh?"

"Who told you about the letter?"

"Susannah did. She had to, Joey. What does Sateesh have to do with it? Anyway, the thing is, Joey, I've got something awful to tell you."

Martha inhaled, pulling her breath in, pulling her back up. She wouldn't let herself cry. "The letter you showed Susannah? It wasn't to Lucy. Penelope wrote it to me."

Joey looked only puzzled at first. Her words made no sense. He shook his head, not getting it. She must have been saying something else. "That makes no sense, Martha. Are you trying to cover up for Lucy? Because if you are—"

"No. I wish I were. Believe me. But it's not—it wasn't how you think."

"Martha, I don't understand what you're saying. What are you saying?"

"I don't know where to start, except to say that, believe it or not, Penelope was trying to help me."

"Look, whatever you say, do *not* give me that bullshit!"

"Do you want to know the truth or not?"

Joey looked at Martha and nodded up and down. It wasn't an affirmation. It was a sarcastic biding of time. The look said *I don't believe a word you're saying.* It was almost like she wasn't really sitting there, not a real person he knew, but more like she was a talking head on TV.

Martha bowed her head, knowing that this was just the beginning of the punishment she certainly deserved, a warm-up for confessing what she'd done to Sateesh.

Joey stood and just as abruptly sat back down. He tried to get his breathing under control. "Martha? What the fuck?"

"Promise me you'll hear me out."

"I'm not making any promises to you."

"Fair enough."

"Look, did you and my wife sleep with that asshole in Phoenix? Yes or no?"

"Yes."

Martha was stumped for words, an unusual experience. It was hard to explain how any of it had happened without sounding self-serving. The way she felt, the way Penelope had felt, what did it really matter? What mattered was that they'd betrayed their husbands. How in God's name was there any explanation for that?

"It wasn't fun, Joey. Just so you know."

"I just can't understand this. Why, Martha? Why did she do it to me?"

"Oh, Joey, it was just a complete fuckup. She felt worse about it than anything else she'd ever done. And so did I. We both just hated ourselves afterward."

"Explain to me. I don't understand."

"I don't know where to start. Remember how Marcus had died that fall? And Sateesh and I couldn't get pregnant? Remember that movie—*The Big Chill?*"

Joey shook his head. Of course he'd seen the movie, but what did that have to do with anything? It was a movie.

"There was something wrong with Sateesh's sperm. So Penelope said maybe we could use yours. But given the way my husband felt about artificial insemination, she thought—it was so stupid, Joey, but she was really trying to help me."

"That is such bullshit!"

"I know. I know. But you said you wanted to know what happened. It's the truth."

Martha proceeded to explain how her friend Astrid's child had died of a genetic deformity, how she and Sateesh were worried the plastic in the instruments might leach into the DNA, how Joey fathering Martha's child might kill two birds with one stone, her desire for a baby and what Penelope perceived as Joey's resentment over not having had as much experience as his wife.

"Did it ever even occur to you that you might have consulted your husbands?"

"Oh God, Joey. I know! We weren't really thinking straight."

"So that's what she was talking about in the letter. About my kids wondering if they were mine?"

Martha nodded. "She thought they'd be jealous if they knew, well, that you were technically the father of another child."

"Why she didn't tell me any of this? I might have wanted to be asked."

"Believe it or not, there's even more stupidity in this story, if you want to hear it." By the time she arrived at what Penelope had told her about Lucy, how Penelope felt she ought to be *big enough* to share her husband with Lucy and vice versa, Joey stood up and abruptly snatched his keys and wallet from the desktop.

"Oh Jesus, Martha! I can't believe it! Lucy!"

The dogs saw Joey first, loping toward him as though they hadn't run for several miles already. They ignored Lucy's commands, skittering through the sand on the path to her house, paws on Joey's shoulders. They licked his face, giving Lucy time to steel herself against any inclination to forgive.

Joey crouched down, rubbing the poodles' brown coats, looking steadfastly at Lucy as she moved slowly toward him, her face averted, focusing on the ground two feet ahead, no more.

"Lucy, Martha just came and told me what happened. I'm so sorry!" he said, as soon as she was close enough to hear. "Can you ever forgive me?"

"Of course. It's all fine. I forgive you. Now go away."

Lucy was still scrutinizing the countless flecks of dun-colored sand. Each was the same, each was different, but none distinguished itself in any meaningful way.

"Lucy."

"You know what? We are no longer on a first-name basis. So stop calling me that."

"I can't stop—"

"You see, it brings back too many difficult memories," Lucy said, holding up a hand to her forehead. "I really thought I loved you."

"I loved you too. I do love you."

"Right. That's why you came out here, threw accusations at me and broke my hand."

Joey rubbed his eyes. He shook his head. "I'm a complete fuck. I know that. Just, for what it's worth, and this will make no sense to you, one reason I was so *lost* is *because* it was you. Or at least I thought it was."

Lucy nodded at Joey with every element of suspicion and incredulity she could muster while simultaneously tamping down the desire flooding through her system, impervious to the cognitive demands of her recently reconstructed self. "That's the crux of the problem, Joey. When you love someone, you give them the benefit of the doubt. You didn't even offer me a chance to defend myself. You convicted me and sentenced me to solitary confinement on the basis of some letter you got in the mail? That's the part I can't forgive."

"I didn't just get a copy in the mail, Lucy. I—there was another in that box of soaps you brought to Tessa that day. I still don't understand how or why it got there, but at the time, I just thought—"

"You just thought what? Why would I bring her a copy of a letter I never even knew about?"

"I know. I know that now." Any explanation Joey could offer Lucy would sound ridiculous, conspiratorial, self-serving. He couldn't move, couldn't think. If remorse were a tradable commodity he'd have had no need of his late wife's money, no peer when it came to the regret that was burning a hole in the three feet between the woman he had lost and the lesser man he'd now become.

"At the time—oh Lucy, there's nothing I can say, is there?"

"Other than good-bye? No. There's nothing you can say. I'm tired of being a doormat. Go sleep with your fucking girlfriend."

"Lucy, she's—she's nothing to me."

"Right."

"Lucy, I've always loved you. Even the first time we met, I remember thinking how fucking beautiful you were."

"Stop it. You chose Penelope. And I chose to cede you to my friend. Just so you know? If I'd have betrayed anybody, it would certainly have been *her*, not *you*. Did you not understand that*?*"

"Is that true? You never acted like you were—I don't know—interested in me."

"Of course I didn't. Penelope was my best friend. Much as I might have wanted you, I'd never have hurt her. And maybe now, what happened to us, it's for the best. I still feel like I've stolen her life out from under her."

"Oh Lucy. She's gone."

"I told you. Stop calling me that. And the thing is, she's gone, but really, she's not. You're still in love with her, and I'm never going to feel right about taking you away."

"Look—can we just—can we try to talk this through?"

"No. We are *not* friends, Joey Adorno. I'll act all sweet when the girls are around but we're done. You know I wanted you. But we both loved Penelope, and that mattered more to both of us than anything else. Now that's she's gone, I won't dance on her grave."

"But you're alive, Lucy."

"Oh stop it! You sound like one of Clover's dipshit posters. If I look alive, Joey, it's only all those years of acting practice I've had, pretending to everyone and his brother that I didn't want the one person in the world I couldn't fucking have."

When Claire Ann divulged Keven's latest news, that Gloria Fernandez was up in arms over the fact that Lucy had posed for a website photo wearing a Chanel suit and looking like some kind of Italian monarch with her poodles, Sigi had to force himself to count to ten.

"We are so screwed," he sighed. "Get me my friend Joan on the line, will you, Claire Ann? Make that my *ex*-friend Joan."

When Claire Ann transferred the call, Sigi was already in full-tilt hissy fit, gunning for the hurdles ahead. "I cannot believe you're doing this to me! What century is this?"

"Sigi, I feel terrible."

"Show some backbone, why don't you? It's all just speculation."

"Look, if I were in any other line of work, it wouldn't matter. I just can't be associated with her."

"But she's not even gay!"

"Sigi."

"I think I'd know."

"You might have gaydar for men, honey, but it doesn't work with lesbians."

"Says the pot to the kettle!"

"Look, Sigi. That's exactly my point. If I were married, or even widowed, I could take this sort of stand, but my kids' parents don't look past the label. If I'm gay, I might as well be a child molester too. If you think I've not thought about this already—"

"What about Alice? What does she say?"

"She'll get over it."

"Joan, please don't do this to Lucy. Or to hell with Lucy! Don't do this to me!"

Joan sighed. "I hate myself but I know where my bread's buttered, Sigi, and it's not in SoHo. I'm really, really sorry."

"Look, sorry is as sorry does. Let me speak to Alice."

"There's nothing she can do."

"Yes, there is. If you're going to abandon Lucy because she's gay, then we might as well enlist some closet troops on her behalf, don't you think?"

Chapter Twenty-nine

At five o'clock on Monday morning, Martha knocked at Susannah's office door. The accountant was already sitting at her desk, using her calculator to go back and forth between the computer screen and a batch of budget pages.

"Have you seen Lucy?" Martha asked, her voice hoarse. "Joey just called from her house, frantic. She's not answering the phone and there's no one in the house."

"No, I've been trying to reach her too. I've called her cell and house three times and she hasn't called me back. But, honey, how did it go yesterday? With Lucy and Joey?"

"On a scale of one to ten, I'd say a two."

"Ow. I'm sorry, Martha. Is there anything I can do?"

"Well, you want to talk to Sateesh for me?"

Susannah's expression softened. "Would that I could."

"I can't bear to do this to him. I don't know what to say."

"I'm so sorry. Let me sign off and we'll—" Susannah's face, which had been moving back and forth between her friend and the computer screen, wrinkled into a puzzled frown. "What is this?"

"What are you doing?"

"Joey put bids on some of Lucy's paintings Saturday night. He wanted me to scare up the funds but—I don't believe this. I'm on Lucy's site and—"

Martha crossed the room, groaning at the thought of what had happened to Lucy in the blogosphere, all because Martha and Penelope had used her as cover. "She told me what happened. I'd like to sue those bloggers for defaming her and Penelope—"

"Well, you might want to change your mind. Look at this! I'm on Sigmund Hartmann's gallery page for Lucy. Joey sent it to me this morning—but I just refreshed it. Oh, this is awesome! Get over here! Look at this."

Susannah pointed to a section of the screen titled "Bid History." "Joey tried to buy a bunch of stuff. And the prices have doubled in less than forty-eight hours!"

"How did that happen?"

"I don't know! All I know is Joey sent me the links Saturday night and told me to try to scare up the money to cover his bids. I just checked his initial offers against where they are now. The way it looks now, Lucy won't even have anything left to sell by the time Wednesday's opening starts."

"That is so great! She must be so happy!"

"*If* she even knows. Where is she? How was she when you left yesterday?"

"At that point, she was really worried about how she was going to sell her work with all of the stuff being canceled. She was planning for the show to be a disaster. Just a sec, Susannah, let me try Joey again." Martha dialed Joey's number. "Hey. Susannah's been trying to reach her too. Were the dogs there?"

Martha listened to Joey's response and then said, "Okay. Well, when you find her, tell her Susannah's got great news."

Martha hung up the phone. "The dogs aren't there, and neither is her car."

"Where could she be?"

"Hey, don't you have the PIN number for her MasterCard? See if you can look online. Maybe she bought airline tickets."

Susannah typed some numbers into the keyboard, squinted at the screen and shook her head. "No, but she dropped the dogs at the kennel and paid for gas on Interstate 95 north of Jacksonville. What do you bet she's driving to New York?"

"In a forty-year-old car? Come on. Let's just hope she rented one."

"Not with her MasterCard she didn't."

At nine AM, Martha was the first person in line at the clerk of courts, armed with Lucy's signed notice of rescission. She stood at the window, holding on to the ledge while the clerk gave her the bad news, all delivered in what Martha had come to call Slow-Motion Southern.

According to Doris Hayes, who'd worked this desk for thirteen years, two English fellows had come in Friday morning, accompanied by lawyers. They had provided all the required papers to transfer the deeds of several town properties. Their contracts had included valid signatures, which the clerk had taken the trouble to check against the previous transfers of title. That morning, possibly for the first time in Martha's legal practice in North Florida, she didn't mind the slow delivery of the news. In fact, once she'd finished listening the first time, she had to ask the woman to repeat the whole sorry story a second time. Then Martha presented the clerk with the necessary proxies and asked to see if Lucy's and Clover's properties were among the deeds the Camerons had transferred.

After she had fled into the ladies' room and dialed her pal at the district attorney's office, Martha was struck by the air of unreality in the whole narrative, especially the part where Doris recounted that after she'd stamped each of the transfers with her official instrument, Peter had taken Nigel's photograph with her and then Nigel had taken Peter's.

"What the hell do I do now?" Martha asked. When she hung up, that question, asked in a voice she almost didn't recognize, the syllables drawn out like they were someone else's voice, seemed to reverberate back at her in the harsh fluorescent restroom lights.

◆ ◆ ◆

By noon, Joey had called an emergency session of the Cameron Foundation's board of directors. Joey and Susannah were explaining to Martha, Clover and the Cameron brothers why they needed to take three million dollars from the real estate trust and put it into a new investment fund.

Joey was terse but urgent in his reasoning, pacing up and down the conference room floor as a means of working off some of the intense emotional energy of not being able to reach Lucy, of not knowing how to begin to explain himself, of knowing she was most likely driving herself and her painting to New York in an unreliable car he should have replaced if he'd only been thinking clearly.

"I don't think we need to talk too much more about how local real estate's tanked. With the subprime meltdown and the announcement tomorrow that all three of the only companies still insuring Florida beach properties are doubling their rates, we've got to unload whatever we can, as fast as we can."

"How did you hear this?" Nigel Cameron was asking, straightening his tie. "About the beach properties?"

"Brett's company is one of the three insurers," Clover whispered conspiratorially. All her life, Clover had liked nothing more than a good skit. If only Penelope could see her now, maybe she'd forgive her for signing away her daddy's farm papers.

"Oh geez, poor Lucy," Martha sighed. "She's never going to be able to sell that white elephant."

"What do you mean?" Peter asked. "Why, I'd think a business opportunity like that would interest all sorts of buyers."

Martha opined briskly that Lucy had let the place go without proper maintenance, that the house would cost more to renovate than it could fetch in the market. "Now that she's not been renting out rooms, she's let her commercial license expire. Besides, who's going to buy a commercial property that can't show a single customer receipt for two years?"

"Look, can we please get back to our own portfolio?" Joey said, his voice tight and low. "We don't have time to worry about that woman!"

"But surely we can put Susannah's mind at ease," Nigel murmured. "Can she not just renew her bed-and-breakfast license?"

This was a point of some concern. It would be difficult for the twins to sell the house in the present market, so they'd planned to either rent it out as a bed-and-breakfast or put it on the market as a commercial entity.

"Not in this part of the coast. The rule is twenty months fallow and you're out, unless you're zoned commercial. Which Lucy's not. She was grandfathered in based on the prior ownership. Which is what made her place so special and private. No other hotels in sight."

"I can't believe she let my daddy's license expire," Clover said. "Isn't it just like Lucy to completely space out on something like that!"

"Look, can we please get back to the business at hand?" Joey sat down and began to drum his fingers on the table, impatient, snappish. "We need to sign off on selling the apartment complex on South Orange and Ocean Drive before five o'clock. The buyer's offer expires at that time, and if we don't take it, I don't need to tell you, we are *screwed*. All aye?"

Everyone around the table but Nigel raised a hand.

"Nigel?" Susannah asked. "Do you abstain?"

"I object. And, Peter, I don't think you meant to raise your hand, did you?"

Peter looked at Nigel uncertainly and quickly lowered his hand to his lap.

"Three to two, the resolution passes."

Nigel interrupted, raising his hand, his voice as smooth as he could make it while simultaneously trying to will his sweat glands to cease and desist their blitz of his forehead.

"Look now, we need to consider how unloading a lot of property at once could flood the market. It could bring all the prices in town down!" Nigel picked up a pencil and let its eraser tilt toward the large portrait of Penelope hanging behind Clover. "We don't want to make the same mistake twice."

His tablemates nodded. They were familiar enough with how he felt about Penelope's catastrophic sell-off of Payday Lending Pals, with how it had dragged down the price of the Camerons' shares right along with everyone else's. In fact, the other trustees had counted on this very traumatic experience to motivate the twins.

Susannah leaned forward and offered Nigel a list of figures she'd printed out. "I've run the numbers and we'll do alright. We've owned most of these places for so long, we'll still make a tidy profit. Only the speculators in town will get hurt, and they deserve it."

"Why would they get hurt?" Peter asked nervously.

"Look," Joey interceded. "Let's talk economics later. Right now, if we don't get surety for those bids, we're going to miss out on getting two of those paintings. I don't need to remind you the prices are only going up while we wait."

"You're buying art?" Nigel said. "That's terribly risky."

"Fine art's appreciated faster than any other sector of the marketplace," Susannah reminded them. "With more super-rich skewing the demographics, plus Russian and Chinese entrepreneurs shopping at auction, it's more bidders for the same pieces. And these paintings we're looking at!" Susannah continued. "They've already doubled in price since they went to auction over the weekend."

"I heard from Lucy's gallery owner that her work's gone up much faster than the rest of her competitors for the Galbreath Prize. I wonder if they think she's going to win," Martha said. "Wouldn't that be incredible?"

"Apparently, everyone wants the next *Madame* X," Susannah added.

"I told you those society ladies love their scandals!" Clover put in.

"What *are* you talking about?" Peter asked. "Who's Madame X?"

"I'm surprised you didn't learn about John Singer Sargent in college," Joey said.

"Oh, that Madame X. I'm just not certain I see the connection."

Joey took a deep breath and buried his fists in his knees, try-

ing not to show the stress he was being caused by staying in the
same room with the architects of his misery and not punching
his fist through the wall. The private investigator Martha had
called had traced the edits on Wikipedia back to Peter's Internet
address. He'd also determined that the CONFIDENTIAL stamp on
the envelope holding Penelope's letter was in a font sold only at
very expensive British stationers. These and other bits of evidence
tying the Camerons to Lucy's troubles were documented in Martha's brief, which she planned to present to the probate arbitrator
in that afternoon's hearing. Such notations would be accompanied by a sheaf of copies showing that properties in Clover's and
Lucy's names had, without their knowledge, much less consent,
been transferred over to Peter and Nigel Cameron. In a twist of
irony Lucy would have appreciated, Martha had been forced to
forge her name on an affidavit testifying that Lucy had been asked
to sign a power of attorney solely for the purpose of delaying her
balloon payment, not the quitclaim and deed transfer presently on
file at the clerk of courts. Because the courts would be slow and
unpredictable, however, Martha's first priority, and the purpose of
this emergency session, was to manipulate the twins into dumping
the deeds at the lowest possible price. If they decided to bid on a
painting or two, so much the better.

"Could someone please respond to my brother's question about
Madame X?" Nigel said.

"Well, see, it's a long story, but somebody's been spreading ru-
mors that Lucy and my sister were lovers. Only, instead of hurting
Lucy's reputation as an artist, the gossip just fanned the flames.
Now it's like *everyone's* bidding on her work. They know *Madame
X* is one of the most valuable paintings of all time!" Clover was
proud of having memorized her lines so perfectly.

"It doesn't hurt that Rosie O'Donnell bid on the one of Penelope breast-feeding and put it on her blog," Susannah sighed.

"How much are they fetching? Her paintings?" Nigel asked.

"The last I heard, one of them is already at three hundred thousand."

"At least she'll have enough to pay off her loan," Clover chimed in.

"What loan?" Joey asked bitterly, pouring his anger and self-reproach into the question. "Why would Lucy have a loan? Penelope gave her that land free and clear."

"See, the thing is, she needed cash and didn't want to ask for help. So she borrowed some and then got another loan from these guys, Elroy and Sandy, friends of Nigel's. Or is it Peter? Which one of you introduced us?" Clover asked.

Nigel cleared his throat and shook his head at Clover. "Ahem—actually, Clover, that's—I barely know these men. Did I put you on to them?"

"Of course you did, silly. Remember? I've got emails from both of them thanking you and Peter for introducing us."

"Goodness, I—it slipped my mind."

"Well, anyhow, do you know how to reach them? Lucy wants to pay off her note and I want to borrow more on the farm so I can bid on one of the paintings. She told me any of Penelope's family could get one at the asking price, which is like way low. Not that I want to sell my farm, but with land values the way they are, it makes more sense to put the money into something else. Besides, if this auction goes any higher, it'll be my last chance to own a Lucy Vargas."

"But do you really think you'll be able to borrow more, Clover?" Susannah cautioned. "With your land value as low as it is?"

Clover gave Martha a look of reproach and used her hand like a dainty knife cutting across her neck. This bit of theater was aimed at arousing the twins' curiosity. "Look, legally, until the word is out officially, we don't know squat about the insurance crisis. Brett will kill me if he finds out I mentioned it."

"But your property's not on the beach," Nigel interjected. "So why would its insurance go up?"

"Oh, see, that's what is so dang unfair about the insurance company's new rules! I've got two hundred and thirty-five acres and only thirty feet fronts the Intracoastal Waterway, but the whole shebang counts as oceanfront because it can't be subdivided."

"What?" Peter asked. "Nigel, it can't be subdivided!"

"No, honey, it's part of the historic land trust. I thought you knew that."

"Nigel! Did you know that?"

"Quiet, Peter. Let Clover finish." Nigel's upper lip had turned a whitish gray, the hue a fish's underbelly turns when it has been deboned. Martha thought it was a joy to behold, maybe an even more precious sight than Lucy's beautiful paintings.

From that point on, the Camerons were quick to request a short recess before approving any more purchases from the auction. When they returned, they were beaming and bearing a fax from Freedom Loan. "Here is the paperwork for your mortgage, Clover. They can't grant you cash out at this time, but if you'd like to pay back everything you owe today, they're willing to waive any penalties for early payment."

"I don't know, Clover," Martha objected. "I don't think Nigel's deputized to act as the lenders' proxy."

"I've got that paperwork too. See, we're on the articles of incorporation." Nigel smiled, handing Martha the missing link that would prove collusion between the predatory lenders and the names now listed on the deeds to Lucy and Clover's properties.

Were this meeting with the arbitrator on any other day, Martha would have laughed at the absurdity of being forced to sit in a circle of child-sized chairs in a church basement. The court-appointed mediator, whose day job as a clinical social worker brought him up close and personal with human frailty, was going on at length about the importance of mutual respect and consensus-building. "What we're seeking here is a common solution to each of the disputing parties' challenges and concerns."

The normal Martha would have enjoyed the sight of the Camerons' elephantine butt cheeks hanging like saddlebags on either side of their small wooden seats. Meanwhile, the brothers grimaced mightily, as if they were actually listening, as if the therapist's words weren't spilling in one ear and out the other, like mercury from a broken tube, glistening, weightless, repellent.

Joey had turned his chair around and was hunched over its back with his thighs pulled tight against the welt of his corduroy trousers, frowning in concentration at the paper Martha had handed him on the way into the proceeding, reading to the last line. He tilted his head just slightly toward Martha, then shook it back and forth in vehement objection.

Martha shrugged, as if she'd not just thrown herself under the professional bus. The sworn affidavit she'd handed Joey would impel the arbitrator to report her to the local bar association for exercising undue influence with a client. It would also kill another bird by invalidating the codicil she'd drafted for said client. Joey would be free to marry whomever he wished.

"Excuse me, sir," Joey interrupted. "Could I please have a minute alone with my lawyer?"

"Mr. Bunker, Mr. Adorno? Can you make it quick? My time is expensive, as you know, and the meter's ticking."

"Actually, I meant Ms. Templeton."

"She's representing the other side in this issue, is she not?"

"Actually, not anymore."

"What do you mean?"

"I mean I no longer want to contest the codicil to my wife's will. Let it stand."

"Joey?" Fowles Bunker was asking.

"You can come too. This will just take a minute."

Joey took Martha's hand and led her out, followed by Fowles Bunker. They closed the door tightly behind them, all the better to begin hissing loudly in several directions.

"I know what I'm doing, Joey," Martha began.

"Actually, you don't."

"What is he talking about?" Fowles directed his question at Martha.

"Telling the truth. I shouldn't have drafted the codicil. I'm just stipulating to that."

"Martha, get off your fucking high horse a minute and use that million-dollar brain we pay you for."

"Actually, I think it's more like a billion," Martha said. "Give or take a dollar."

"I don't know why I didn't see it before," Joey said. He then proceeded to explain the epiphany that had arrived in the middle of the arbitrator's introduction. Penelope's codicil provided her children with the exact protection the Camerons were claiming the original will required. By agreeing to its revocation, Martha would only strengthen the twins' case that their oversight was necessary to complying with their ancestors' intentions. When Joey finished, Martha nodded slowly. She looked to Bunker for confirmation.

"He's right. Though damned if it doesn't put me out of work."

"Actually," Martha said, smiling, "I think we need you for a little while longer. Ready to strap on your poker balls? Let's make the Tweedles think they're about to hand us ours on a platter."

When Martha opened the door, her color was high, as it might be if she were suddenly overcome with a fit of pique. "Sir," she apologized. "It turns out we've not been able to come to an agreement after all. We wish to continue the proceedings. With your help, of course. The only thing is, since one of our members, Lucy Vargas, is out of town, we'd like to reverse the order of inquiry and begin with the Cameron brothers' pleadings."

"Actually, Ms. Templeton, you needn't be so formal. This isn't a courtroom. As long as all those here have agreed to abide by my decision, we can proceed any way we want. I prefer we avoid legal hoopla and speak to each other just like we would in any other conversation.

"Sirs," the arbitrator continued, turning toward the Cameron brothers. "Why don't you tell me in your own words why you think you're needed to protect the interests of Mr. Adorno's little girls."

Nigel glared at his attorney, who had failed to object to this surprising turn of events. "Just a moment, Your Honor," the lawyer was stammering, digging among the papers in his briefcase. "Or

Doctor. Or whatever it is you wish to be called. My clients' case relies on several major precedents in civil jurisprudence stemming back to the Magna Carta."

The arbitrator held up a palm and murmured, "Plain English, please."

"The Cameron fortune is of such magnitude that it requires injunctive—"

"Stop. Please. You know, maybe your case would be best served if you let the clients speak for themselves."

"Look," Martha interrupted. "If they can't state their case, maybe they'd prefer to move it back to probate court. We'd be fine with that, right, Joey? In fact, we'd prefer it."

"You would?" the Camerons' lawyer asked warily, blinking as if he'd only recently woken.

"Oh no," Nigel insisted. "We've all agreed to be bound by this arbitration in writing! What's good for the goose is good for the gander!"

If the Wicked Bitch wanted them out of the proceeding, then that was reason enough for the Camerons to remain. What was it she feared?

Nigel looked back and forth between his adversaries, trying to determine what precisely it was that they'd been fighting over. He took a deep breath and held up one hand. "Oh no, sir. I don't think we'll agree to that. Mr. Adorno moves to revoke his signature to the codicil, and Ms. Templeton objects? Might it be because our late cousin, in her infinite wisdom, knew that her daughters' interests should be protected against the impulsive—lest we say reckless— behavior of their father? It's almost as though dear Cousin Penelope intuited the very same possibility that caused her forefathers to insist that in the unfortunate event of her death, her husband might, for any number of reasons, lose his way and require the guidance of less-muddled minds."

"That's a really good point," Fowles Bunker said enthusiastically, as if he'd just now spotted it. "But if her husband agreed to the help of his wife's best friends, who also happen to have professional training in accounting and law, why would the children need such a very expensive and downright redundant protection from strangers? In fact, my client will gladly stipulate to the desirability of the protection offered by the codicil, which was drafted at the request of the children's mother and agreed to by their father. He just feels that, at this point, based on some of their recent behaviors, the Camerons clearly don't have the skills or the moral fiber to act in their nieces' interests."

"That's ridiculous," Nigel said. "We are far better suited to make fiduciary judgments precisely because we've nothing to gain from the estate."

"Except your sizable executors' percentage," Martha interjected before turning to the arbitrator and saying that she had no problem with Fowles Bunker's suggestion. "We're fine having you decide which of the groups is best equipped to protect the children's interests, their aunt and three godmothers, whom they've known all their lives, or the Cameron brothers, whom their mother never met and whom the children have yet to meet outside of a courtroom."

Nigel could not believe his good fortune.

Was Wicked Bitch really bringing this down to a battle over the cousins' impartial, detached perspectives versus the infinite series of incestuous entanglements the Camerons' private investigator had identified among the Coven? Nigel stood so quickly his chair came off the floor with him before falling back to the floor with a thump. "Your Honor, it may interest you to know that one of the members of this so-called protective group that's entrusted with protecting my nieces' interests was involved in a sexual relationship with Mr. Adorno while keeping quiet about her prior lesbian affair with his wife. This is the same woman who forgot to fetch the younger child after a dance lesson, who had sex in a public park with Mr. Adorno, from whose care the eldest daughter was removed to protect her health and who has mismanaged her own finances to the point of losing her house to foreclosure."

At this, Joey moved so quickly across the room that the only thing Martha could think of to do was extend her foot at the knee. "Ow!" she screamed, taking the arbitrator's attention off Joey's sprawled body and onto her insulted right foot. "How did that happen? Sir, could we please have a very short recess while I talk to my client?"

Siobhan had just fed the girls when she got the phone call from Joey. "Now?" she asked.

"It shouldn't take long."

"I hate to leave Tessa alone right after she eats."

"She'll be alright."

"I don't know. Besides, what would this arbitrator guy want from me? Isn't probate, like, to do with wills and such?"

"Right. I think he just wants to ask you how you think Tessa's coming along."

As soon as Siobhan's car left the driveway, the girls moved into gear.

June opened the door for Rocky and welcomed him with a hug. "Sorry, boy," she whispered. His exclusion to the prison of the laundry room struck June as deeply unfair. After giving him a piece of cheese, June ran up to her dad's study to email Willow with the steps she'd missed at practice, redressing another injustice. Siobhan had said that Willow would have to try out for the dance team all over again if she wanted to come back. At the same time, she'd forbidden any of the girls to help her learn what she'd missed during her suspension.

Tessa, meanwhile, tiptoed upstairs and into Siobhan's bedroom, where she hoped to find a book that might explain bulimia. She was afraid her email to Lucy and the others might not be believed by her father, and she needed to know what it was she should do to prevent June from getting any worse. Instead, all Tessa found were some back issues of *Cosmopolitan*, a couple of reference books with nutritional measurements and a long row of large green ledgers like the one Siobhan usually wrote in after meals. In Tessa's haste to get back upstairs to check on June, the teen left the door slightly ajar, not thinking of how much trouble she would get into for having snuck into Siobhan's bedroom without permission. All she wanted to do was figure out how to make her sister stop, to make it up to June for having passed along her own craziness without realizing she was even freaking contagious.

While they were waiting for Siobhan to show up, Martha pulled the Camerons aside. "It's time to fess up, Nigel. We know you conspired to steal Lucy's and Clover's property." She proceeded to offer them a deal. If they would sign quitclaims and transfer the titles back to Lucy, Clover and the five other local property owners whose land they'd appropriated, Martha would refrain from bringing her evidence to the district attorney. "I'll keep it in my safe."

"What's to keep you from turning it in once we've done what you asked?" Peter inquired.

Nigel shook his head. "We didn't do anything wrong. We had to pay dearly for the titles Elroy and Sandy sold us. We can't afford to simply give them away."

"So you're saying you were scammed?"

"Right."

Martha nodded her head slowly and said, "Alright. I'm sure you can prove that to the district attorney. But if I were you, I'd get a sharper lawyer than the one you have now, 'cause by the time we're done, I will definitely tear you a new one. Which your new cellmates in the state prison will greatly appreciate, I can promise you that."

Siobhan was wearing a white mohair sweater dress with white tights and navy pumps. Her hair was scooped into an elegant French twist. She appeared nervous when she entered the basement door, all the more so because Joey hadn't met her eyes from the minute she walked into the room. Meanwhile, the Cameron brothers were boring holes into her skull with significant eye movements that she could not begin to understand.

"Ms. Fitzpatrick, can you tell us how you came into possession of this?" Fowles Bunker asked. He handed Siobhan a copy of Penelope's letter, which the twins had presented as part of their evidence that Lucy Vargas's conduct was inconsistent with the strong moral character state law would require of a child's guardian.

"I don't—what do you mean?"

"Nigel Cameron told us you sent the original to him."

"That's true. It was—I—when I was hired, they told me I had to keep them informed."

"Did you mention that condition to your employer, Mr. Adorno?"

"No. I was instructed not to."

"Ms. Fitzpatrick, where did you find this letter?"

"On the laptop I was using."

"And whose computer was that?"

"The children's mother."

"You just found it!"

"The Camerons instructed me to look in her deleted files."

"Excuse me, sir," Martha interrupted. "May I ask Ms. Fitzpatrick what made her do such a thing?"

"They told me it was part of my job—"

"To spy on the family you were hired to help?" Martha pressed.

"It wasn't like that. I was—I felt sorry for those girls. I knew they were—they had unrealistic ideas about their mom and—I don't know. I just thought it was better that everything be out in the open. That's all."

When Martha asked Siobhan if she'd considered the possibility that she might have contributed to the family's stress rather than improving its emotional fortitude, Siobhan looked genuinely stunned. "No. I just thought, if I was married to someone and they'd cheated on me, I'd want to know."

"Have you ever been married, Ms. Fitzpatrick?" Martha asked.

"No. Not yet," Siobhan said, faltering. She tried to catch Joey's gaze and then wished she hadn't.

As soon as Joey called, Clover drove to the house to collect the girls. "I'm taking you to the mall, children. Let's run upstairs and get all pretty."

Tessa was lying back on her bed, watching as her aunt deftly braided her sister's hair. From time to time, they heard the sound of Rocky barking, a constant, yet somehow unconvincing, complaint.

"Does he need to go out?" Clover had asked absently, pointing her hairbrush in the direction of the sound.

"No, he just hates being in the laundry room," June said. "Miss Siobhan's allergic."

"Poor thing," Clover said. "Let's hurry up. I promised your dad we'd be *vamanos* by the time they get home."

In their rush to vacate, it didn't occur to any one of the three to go check behind the laundry room door for Rocky, who'd stopped his barking. They certainly never thought to go search for him in Siobhan's bedroom, where he'd been stranded after following Tessa in her search for a book on bulimia. Although Tessa had left the door slightly ajar, it opened in toward the room. Therefore, when Rocky had backed up playfully after pulling his prey into the center of the floor, his wagging tail had pushed the door tight against the frame.

By the time Siobhan, followed by Joey, pulled her car into the driveway, the girls were long gone, captive audience to their aunt's concert à la Nancy Sinatra whose fabled boots had a way of rescuing a woman's vanquished pride.

The house was quiet when Joey opened the front door. Rocky, for his part, was silent, knowing the sound of his master's footsteps on the porch. Besides, the 1990s were a grand distraction, a movable feast rendered in newsprint, wheat paste, forest-green vellum and the glorious smell of indelible ink. The dog was both too far away and too far gone to notice the sound of the other shoe dropping in the foyer below.

Joey had never in his life had to fire an employee, saved from such unpleasantness by his wife's propensity to hire her friends instead of the more easily expendable stranger. Even now, angry as he felt about Siobhan's invasion of his family's privacy, Joey wished he could simply blink an eye and have her disappear, rather than have to face the colossal failure of judgment she represented in his recent pantheon of mistakes.

"Can I please explain?" Siobhan entreated. "I know it seemed—I know the way it seemed like—you know, it wasn't—I couldn't explain the context for why I did what I did."

"It won't help. You've—you can't work here anymore."

"What about Tessa?"

"We'll see the doctor, find our way from there."

"But, Joey, I care about you."

"Notwithstanding all appearances to the contrary? You might have warned me about the Camerons. You might have told me what you'd done."

"I know. I know that now. But when I was hired, I didn't know who I was supposed to trust."

"So you used my wife's computer, files she'd tried to destroy, to turn me against her, to make me doubt everything I ever knew about her? How could you think you were doing me any kind of favor!"

"I guess I thought if you knew, then you'd be able to see the forest for the trees."

"Siobhan, you keep using that metaphor. How can you think to judge my wife by one letter on her computer? That's just one tree. Why would you think it was the forest? Her life was full of things you'll never see or know."

"Joey, please, I know you're upset. But don't shoot the messenger. Your wife treated you terribly. The fact is, you've got every right to be angry at her, and with Lucy too. Or don't you want the truth from the people you love?"

"Of course I do. Even the ones I don't love," Joey remarked pointedly. "I can't fathom, though, why you felt it was okay for you to lie about Lucy. Why would you have told me you found another copy of that letter in the box she'd brought to Tessa? You had to be the one who put it there. You basically framed an innocent person! Why would you do that?"

Siobhan shook her head. "I—didn't intend . . . I'm sorry about that part. I couldn't think of a way to tell you how I knew about your wife's affair. So I thought, well, since Lucy clearly came over here to talk to Tessa, it must have been what she had in mind. Besides, it's not like she didn't do the things your wife wrote about."

"Well, actually, you stupid bitch, it turns out she didn't. But you know what? I don't have time to even explain how wrong you've gotten everything. You're young. Maybe you'll figure out, if you ever fall in love, what the word *love* means. Until then, take it from me. You don't have a clue." Joey shook his head. "Look, here's the bottom line. I need you to pack your things now. You can stop around back on the way out and settle accounts with Susannah."

Siobhan turned on her heel, still graceful, even then. She hurried up the stairs. Joey counted the seconds, wishing her gone. When he heard her screaming, he took the steps two at a time.

Siobhan's bedroom door was wide open. Rocky was cowering in the corner by the bed, cringing at the curling iron brandished by the dancer in white wool as she lowered herself to the floor among the crumpled, bite-size chunks of sodden pulp, the ragged green spines scattered amid the tattered mulch, the gray mounds of debris that Rocky had made of her beloved ledger domain.

"Come on, boy," Joey called softly while Siobhan fingered through the confettilike remains of her life story. "How did this happen!" she cried, feeling, as she sifted through the mess, that all the king's horses and all the king's men couldn't put her carefully wrought life back together again.

"Some people," Joey would say later that night, trying to explain to June and Tessa why he'd had to dismiss Siobhan, "they take all that's bad in the world and use it as a reason to shut themselves down. They harden into a shell, thinking that's going to keep them safe. Their world gets smaller and smaller. What's left of their heart shrinks instead of grows. It's like a plant without water. Eventually there's nothing left but the crust of anger they've built to convince themselves that other people can't be trusted. That's just *not* how your mom wanted you to live. When bad things happened to her, she'd take it on the chin and open herself up even more the next time. Knowing how it had felt to hurt, she'd bring that understanding to the way she connected with other people. She was so brave, choosing to see the best in everyone. It helped her grow inside. What's more, it brought out the best in the people she loved. That's really heroic, when you think about it."

"Scary heroic," Tessa said. "I could never be as brave as Mom."

"Sure you could. It's all about understanding that no one's perfect. You can forgive someone else for not being perfect, but the good thing about that is if you accept imperfection in them, you can let yourself off the hook when you fail. Everyone falls down once in a while. I certainly do. Nothing's foolproof. But this connection we've got to each other, it's what makes life worth living. The more you put yourself out there for other people, the more they'll do the same for you. It's a win-win, girls. Maybe that's what they mean by the Golden Rule, love others as you love yourself. Maybe loving others is what allows you to love yourself and loving yourself allows you to better love others."

"So we're s'posed to love Siobhan?" June asked, trying to reconcile what her father was saying with the deep relief she'd felt at hearing of the dance teacher's abrupt departure.

"I guess the Bible would say that. But there's a difference between trying to forgive somebody their faults, which is what I think that line means, and feeling like you have to be their best friend. If you see what I'm saying."

"No," Tessa laughed. "You're making no sense at all. But that's okay. Now can you please go pick up our pizza?"

Chapter Thirty

Two hours after Martha had presented her last piece of evidence proving the Cameron brothers had been involved in stealing the titles to Lucy's and Clover's property, the arbitrator announced several decisions pertinent to *Cameron and Cameron v. Adorno*. Calling the twins in first, he began by warning them that the documents Martha had provided were overwhelmingly suggestive of criminal activities. As such, said documents would be forwarded to the proper law enforcement authorities for immediate investigation. Second, he was prohibiting them from all further participation in the management of the Cameron Foundation. Third, he removed them as coexecutors, cutting off their remuneration retroactive to the date they'd hired Siobhan Fitzpatrick with the express intent of invading Mr. Adorno's privacy and that of his deceased wife.

It might have been Susannah's calculation of the back pay the Camerons owed the foundation or perhaps their panic about the impending insurance hike's effect on coastal real estate that put them in the mood to bargain. Perhaps it was Martha's kind offer of anal reconstruction. Whatever the cause, the Cameron brothers signed quitclaims and transferred the real estate titles back to their prior owners in exchange for the principal each person had borrowed from Freedom Loan.

Susannah was able to use money approved by the remaining

members of the Cameron board to pay off the six thousand Lucy had borrowed. She was also able to prepay her mortgage balloon based on assurances from Sigi Hartmann. Apparently, the gallery's online auction had been so successful that the collection, now dispersed, was already being immortalized by art investors and bloggers as the Penelope Series. Lucy's paintings, which Sigi had to hire extra staff to protect from possible hate groups, had already fetched several times their initial asking prices and would be un-available for sale by the time the public was allowed to see them when the opening took place on Wednesday evening.

That the mischief perpetrated by the Camerons with no small help from Siobhan had restored Lucy's financial house to the same immaculate condition as her beautiful bed-and-breakfast on the beach was an irony Lucy would have appreciated if only she could have been reached.

If only her callers would stop being told that the customer they were calling could not be found, over and over and over again. Each of her friends—Joey, Martha, Susannah and Clover—kept dialing Lucy's phone. They knew full well that her AT&T voice mail was completely full, that her dogs were still in the kennel and that the beach house remained unoccupied. Still, they couldn't keep themselves from trying.

Sigi Hartmann was worried too when Susannah tracked him down to find out if Lucy had gotten to New York. "I promise I'll put her in touch as soon as she arrives. *If* I can manage to keep from killing her first! What *is* that girl thinking?"

Lucy knew if she'd told a soul she was planning on driving *The Three Graces* to New York, thus saving the three hundred dollars FedEx was asking for shipping, plus the cost of the airline tickets she'd left on Priceline without ever buying, they'd have given her a raft of reasons, to say nothing of a boatload of other organic mate-rial, why it was a stupid, even reckless, thing to do.

The truth was, there was something about being on the road,

protected from the sort of bad news that could be delivered in any number of formats—high-speed cable, wireless satellites, even drunken attorney house calls—that Lucy had hoped would provide her with some kind of escape. No matter how fast she drove, alas, there were these awful thoughts she could not outrun.

Even as she believed that Joey was sorry for what he'd done, even as she replayed the words he'd said over and over, especially the part about loving her, she could not stop thinking about how he'd been *sleeping* with Siobhan. He'd given that part of himself to someone he hardly knew. It was astonishing that, given her precarious financial condition, her broken hand, her possible loss of the beach property, it would be the images of Siobhan and Joey that pulled Lucy into a leaden numbness, a physical state somewhere between vertigo and paralysis.

Indeed, Lucy was happiest when she could distract herself with less visceral torments. The foreclosure possibility, one week ago the source of such anxiety, was now an obsession she positively courted.

She drove with her right hand on the wheel, her left on her lap, no music, unless you counted the beat of a very different drummer, this one bent on staying awake without getting bogged down in tears and self-pity. As she headed into the Battery Tunnel, she was thinking about Clover, how she too had been gullible enough, like Lucy, to assume Elroy and Sandy were as nice as they seemed to be. *Poor Clover*, Lucy thought, *she'll feel terrible at having to give up her daddy's farm. It's a fine mess we've made of things*, Lucy thought, remembering Penelope's clear instructions the night they'd signed the codicil. *You have to take care of her*, she'd insisted, passing to Lucy the mantle of caring she'd been so bent on spreading over family and friends. For her, the safety net was a real thing, dynamic and self-perpetuating, defying laws of scarcity or finitude, more like Rumpelstiltskin's bounty, or the miracle of the loaves and the fishes, or even a mother's love. It was this fabled substance that had illuminated Lucy's painting of Penelope breast-feeding, inspired by her joy on the night of June's birth. *I was so afraid I couldn't love another baby the way I did Tessa!* She'd been so blissed out, her rapture a postpartum rush of hormones. Or maybe, Lucy thought as she looked back on it, it was as Penelope had insisted at the time, a tiny hole opening up to heaven in the aperture between finite selfishness and expansive delight, an experience that could make you forget yourself completely.

At seventy miles an hour, Lucy's 1966 Volvo sedan got the shakes, a condition she was well accustomed to. Automatic transmissions weren't what they once were. *And this is a good thing,* Lucy's friends were always scolding her. Even Joey, who had a soft spot for antique cars, had often said she really needed to think about getting a newer car.

Still, even then, in that instant midnight of the Battery Tunnel, just miles from her destination, as her body was thrown to the right along with the rest of the car's contents, Lucy wouldn't have said she'd made a mistake by driving to New York. Well, perhaps, given time to think, maybe she'd have admitted that replacing her tires would have been prudent. The left front had appeared a little bare when she'd filled it with air at the gas station a week before, part of the routine she'd developed to persuade herself that stopping for another quart of oil every two days wasn't such a bad thing.

The worst aspect of having a broken left hand was that it limited one's options. The most pressing of these, at least at that very moment, was the priority of controlling the steering wheel. In a dizzying series of seconds, as the tire unraveled, the car continued to slide into the adjacent lane.

One thing was certain. Lucy's worries disappeared in the oblivion of adrenaline. Her car briefly sideswiped a yellow Grand Prix before being slung back across her lane and over into the next. As she was spinning around and facing a terrifying horde of headlights, Lucy had just enough time to wonder if this was how Penelope had felt right before she passed.

Then the first car hit her, and then the next, their screeching brakes followed by the sound of breaking glass, followed by what seemed like deafening silence. Lucy closed her eyes against a déjà vu image from her final walk on the beach, that same colorless, all-consuming vacuum pulling her into the empty heart of its lost black center. She was alone. It was dark and quiet. She was all alone but for a small whispering scold of indeterminate origin. *Lucy, honey, I never meant for you not to take care of yourself.*

When the phone rang, Martha was trying to summon the words to begin to explain herself. She sat facing Sateesh across the table, feeling worse than she thought possible. Later, though, if she could have chosen to undo it, getting that phone call, hearing the words from the New York officer's unfamiliar voice, she would have given anything not to have answered. She'd much rather have been forced to admit what she'd done to her husband than hear from a stranger what could only be called some very bad news.

Sateesh was a dream, a man among men. He shushed her quiet and told her that whatever argument she'd planned to begin, it would just have to wait. They must leave for Joey's; they couldn't tell him what had happened on the phone. "Get in the car," he said. "We'll make our flights on the way."

Chapter Thirty-one

Lucy Luria Vargas did not win the Galbreath Prize, despite Gloria Fernandez's complete change of heart regarding the artist's need for attention. Ms. Fernandez, after a word with Claire Ann's Keven the night before the unveiling, had quickly Googled Lucy to discover the outcry on her behalf. Gloria declared herself more than a little disposed to vote for Lucy, and perhaps Keven and Claudia would have felt similarly, were they to have an opportunity.

Alas, the Galbreath rules were very clear. Old-fashioned that way. No amount of sympathy, even after hearing of her car accident, would have allowed the committee to vote on a piece that didn't arrive at the loading dock in time for the unveiling. Even if they could extend the deadline by a day, they couldn't help Lucy.

The Three Graces had been flattened inside a wrecked 1966 Volvo that had shut down northbound traffic in the Battery Tunnel for several hours that morning.

The first car to reach Lucy's was a large chauffeur-driven limousine registered to Michael Brantley, one of Wall Street's most successful brokers. Mr. Brantley had, most unfortunately, been crippled in a motorcycle accident some three years before, only to be slammed from behind that day by a large Econoline van with OPERATION RESCUE stenciled on its side. As luck would have it, this time Brantley sustained no greater damage than a slight frisson of post-traumatic stress at the sights and sounds so similar to those of his own undoing.

Mr. Brantley's chauffeur was also a trained nurse and paramedic who traveled with a battery of medical paraphernalia. They carried these supplies not because his employer needed them, but to honor a vow made while the billionaire nearly bled to death waiting for an ambulance in his earlier accident. On any Manhattan thoroughfare, much less in a tunnel like the Battery, traffic locked in on itself and no one could move, not even the emergency vehicles that everyone but the most unrecovered assholes would gladly have moved out of the way to bid Godspeed.

Onlookers would later report that moments after the car caught fire, they witnessed something extremely unusual. A well-dressed man in a wheelchair holding an injured woman in his lap, one hand gripping her waist, the other a bag of plasma attached like an oversize bauble to her wrist, as the woman's head lolled back as though seeking warmth from her burning car. The wheelchair was flying along, being pushed rapidly forward by a burly chauffeur who, after tossing an extinguisher to the Operation Rescue driver, dodged between the stranded cars until the unwieldy triad had reached the flashing lights at the end of the tunnel. There, the ambulance was waiting to take Lucy to Bellevue, summoned by the toll attendant at the very first sound of impact.

Sixteen hours later, Lucy was still unconscious. By that time the doctors had set her broken right hand and left ankle, stanched the blood from the wounds on her face. They had performed two MRIs to determine that her head injury didn't appear to have caused swelling or edema. Her internal organs seemed intact as well.

"It's possible her brain just doesn't want to wake up. Pain can do that to a person," the young resident offered, in lieu of a more scientific explanation. Tessa, June and Joey, having been flown in earlier on the Good Samaritan Brantley's corporate jet, were drained from a night of telling Lucy how much they loved her, of rubbing her one unmarked limb with all the need their fear and adrenaline had ignited. They hung on everything the doctor said, they asked her to repeat herself, to tell them more.

"We had to shave some spots on her head to do some tests. Don't worry, honey, it'll grow back," the resident added, patting June's hand.

"Right away?" Tessa asked, thinking of the last time they saw her, when they'd washed and curled her hair.

"Oh, sure. It'll look a little funny, so she may have to cut it, but it will all grow back."

June repeated this last bit of information to Clover, who called from the airport and again from her taxi on the way in. When she arrived at the room, their aunt was carrying a bouquet of flowers and a pink plaid carrying case, which she lifted toward the children. "I made the driver stop on the way in from Queens."

Then, watching Clover sweep into the room as she extracted one after the next redheaded wig, Joey and the children found themselves unable to utter a word.

Clover stood at Lucy's side, singing, "Lucy Loo-wie," her own cheerfully and soulfully improvised "Louie Louie," followed by "Lucy in the Sky with Diamonds" and "Wake Up Little Lucy," this last performed with a panache that would have done the Everly Brothers proud.

Her need to serenade satisfied, Clover proceeded to hold up the wigs, providing commentary about flattering styles for women with wide cheekbones and entreating her comatose friend to just look and admire.

Who knows, maybe it was the tickle of synthetic hair on her cheek, maybe it was the smell of June and Tessa's hospital cafeteria turkey dinner, or maybe, just maybe, it was the faraway pull of a familiar voice telling her that this was a Clover Moment just way too good to be true. Whatever it was, and she would never know for sure, Lucy Luria Vargas opened her eyes to a world so full of color and life, she was brought to wonder if maybe she'd gotten it wrong. Maybe she'd died and gone to the other side. She had not passed Go, she had not collected her two hundred dollars, but here she was, as close to heaven as you could get and still wonder if that angel you heard singing might not have gotten the lyrics both extremely wrong and satisfyingly right at the very same time.

Epilogue

O n January 6, the day Catholics call Epiphany, Joey was crouched over the back of Lucy's car, which he'd personally towed back to Omega on a rented flatbed truck. *The Three Graces* was still trapped beneath several layers of blackened steel, each of which needed careful removal to determine whether anything but ashes remained of the painting.

The car was up on blocks in front of Lucy's house, where Joey and the girls had moved. They had been nursing her back to health, taking on physical therapy, feeding, washing and housekeeping à la OCD, or, as Clover called it when she came by to help, AC/DC.

Such activities accomplished several ends at once. For Lucy, they were critical to her physical recovery and to her future as a painter.

For the girls, the process was slightly more complex. In addition to following a continued eating plan that Sateesh cooked and Clover delivered, the girls were the ones who cut Lucy's meat, held her spoon and fed her soup. They brought the water to her lips, chatted her up and tempted her with the glorious pleasures and satisfactions of eating. This caretaking role seemed to have had a mysterious healing power for Penelope's daughters, much like what addicts experience in the twelve steps, when helping others so often amounts to the miracle of helping oneself at the very same time.

For Joey, everything he did was an expression of his constant, unrequited desire to undo his descent into the land of the literal and unloving. He had constructed a small padded scaffolding that allowed him to kneel over the trunk and carefully apply the sharp rotating edge of a power saw to one after another thin metal sheath of the crushed trunk's remains. The process was painstaking, noisy, uncomfortable. Assuming *The Three Graces* hadn't been burned in the accident, all it would take to combust it now would be a spark tossed from the molten steel. Moreover, it was impossible to know whether each sheet Joey was cutting would be the last between him and the painting. Thus his caution.

The kneeling was accidental, or coincidental, for it truly was the best means for Joey to control his saw. This was what Lucy told herself whenever she looked out the window to see her love bent on recovering a painting that she couldn't be certain still existed, kneeling on a handmade frame suspiciously akin to a prie-dieu.

Lucy was acutely aware of Joey's desire to do penance but also to forgive Penelope. It took time, all of this, something Lucy wished weren't true. She would have loved to snap her fingers and rid Joey of his sorrows, but then again, though her bones had knitted back together, neither of her broken hands would ever be quite the same.

Lucy was not at the window when Joey finally hit an open pocket of darkness, when he peeled back the metal with such haste that its edge sliced the folds of his fingers right through his canvas gloves. She did not see as he eased the cylindrical roll from its nesting place and ran toward the house, shouting her name.

She was in her studio with the girls, where they were sitting for her, still as bandits, their arms linked. Tessa's hair had regained its sheen; her arms and legs were finely muscled. June was basking in her sister's attentive closeness, in Lucy's rapt expression. The strokes of umber charcoal against rough canvas were the only sound but for their father's cry of delight as he opened this gift, his wife, her friends, rising from a wave they'd ridden, united, unknowing, aloft.

Acknowledgments

To the first readers of this novel, for their insights and encouragement: Mary Ann Hudnall; Cathy Dorfman; Jane Ulrich; Paul Shepherd; Jane Mcpherson; Julianna Baggott; Tere, Tasha and Casey Clarkson; Celia and Ranger Curran Sr.; Dede Curran; Ranger Curran Jr.; Karen Curran; Mary Bush; Ellen O'Daniell; Pat Brewster; Carolyn Stafford; Lynne Bush; Ranger Curran III; Leigh Ann Curran; Jack Hudnall and Ariana Hornsby. A special thanks to John Corrigan and our children, Curran and Helen, each of whom helped me wrestle with plot and character as this story took shape.

To Rita and Linda Spears, and Bobbi and Kristi Holcomb, who so generously shared their stories of the loss and rebuilding; and to my new favorite reader, Duncan Postma, M.D., whose recent vigilance on my behalf might just save my life.

To Gil Hudnall, Esq., for his insights on mortgages; Dr. Thomas Joiner, Celia and Ranger Curran for information on anorexia; Shirley Faist and John Curran for help with estates and Megan Garriga for the drying time on acrylic paints. If I got details wrong, the fault is entirely my own.

To those who helped bring *Diana Lively Is Falling Down* into the world, throwing parties, sending postcards or just buzzing it to your friends, I cannot thank you enough. In Tallahassee: Jane Mcpherson; Julianna Baggott; Dave Scott; Paul and Lois Shepherd; Tracy

Sumner; Meg Baldwin; Chris Dreps; Anne Davis; Graciela Marquina; Amanda Porterfield and Aline Kalbian. In Atlanta: Jack and Stephen Hudnall; their parents, Mac and Gil; Larry, Cathy and Stephanie Dorfman; Mom and Dad; Beth and Mike Curran; Carolyn, Frank and Amy; Kevin Finnegan and Mary and Lynne Bush; Joan and Martin Blank; Adam; Laura; Scott; Susie; Hi, Patti and Mindy Dorfman; Dana and Norm; Joel and Charlotte; Joann and Dick. In New Hampshire: Tere and Robert Clarkson; Ranger and Karen Curran; Steve Bragdon and all the rest of my siblings' wonderful friends. In Washington, DC: the inimitable Murphy family, especially Barb, Ken, Katie, Charlotte and Danno. In Chicago: Susan Estes, Andrew Rojecki, Myrtis Meyer, Marty Cohen, Mimi Meyer, Celeste Wroblewski and Nancy Deuchler. In Guilford: Jane Ulrich and Carlos Eire. In Amelia Island: all the organizers of the book festival. In Charlottesville: Nancy Damon; Meg Klosko; Maruta and Ben Ray; Becky Richardson; Dorothy and Jackie Webber and Gordon Walker. In Phoenix: Julia Patterson; Judy Oksner; Carolyn Scarborough; Michele Scheiner; David Raskin; Cindy Dach; Emily and Tom Cutrer; Charlotte and Mike Morrissey; Tracy Fessenden; Deborah Susser; Debbie Sloan; Candace Smith; Chris Thomas; Doreen Zannis; Paige Lewis; Janeen Bury and Beth Gaughan. In San Francisco: Rhian Miller and Patrice O'Neil. In places as far-flung as England and Dublin and Pittsburgh and the Ozarks: Barbara Mead, Anne Macfarlane, Orla Kennedy, Neal Newman; Mary Crossley and Myra Slocum. To the Corrigans, the Currans, the Perlins, the Gaughans, the Millers, the Kowalskis. To dear friends I have omitted out of pure absentmindedness: forgive me. To Karen Abbott, Joshilyn Jackson, Jon Jefferson, Andi Buchannan, Masha Hamilton, Karin Gillespie, Barbara Hamby, Diane Roberts, Elizabeth Stuckey-French, Umi Desphande and all the other writers I've come to know: you are my peeps. To the readers who've contacted me: you have no idea how much I loved hearing from you.

Laura Gross, I still think we knew each other in a past life. I must have done something spectacular to win your representation in this one. Thank you for nurturing *Diana* and *Everyone She Loved* and listening so patiently to my blathering about new ideas. Oh, yes, and, of course, for getting Lucy's story into the hands of the divine Emily Bestler. Emily is a true editor, the kind that is not supposed to exist anymore, with superb vision, a surgical eye for extraneous information and the creative imagination to pick a perfect title. The fact that these two accomplished women are also extravagantly pretty and great fun to be with—well, it just makes you wonder again about what they must have done prior to this reincarnation. Thanks as well to all the people at Atria Books: Judith Curr, Laura Stern, Aja Pollock, Nalani Kopp, Jeanne Lee, and the staff I haven't yet met whose work will go into the book.

A nod especially to the unsung sales reps who will get the book into stores. Finally, to booksellers far and wide, none of this would exist without your dedication to the magic of the written word. Bless you.

Everyone She Loved
Sheila Curran
A Readers Club Guide

Introduction

Penelope Cameron has convinced her husband and four friends to sign an unusual pact. If Penelope should die before her daughters turn eighteen, her husband, Joey, cannot remarry without the consent of her sister and three best friends. Then, the unthinkable happens, and Penelope's family and friends must struggle to live life without her.

Penelope's young daughters, husband, and friends are slowly rebuilding new lives when the fragile serenity they have gained is suddenly threatened. Penelope's distant cousins are eager to gain control of the family money, and ruthlessly plant seeds of doubt and distrust among the friends. They must pull together and trust each other, as more than their friendships is now at stake.

A Conversation with Sheila Curran

How did you get the idea for this novel?
Everyone She Loved was conceived in the front seat of my friend's car. We were discussing an article I'd written about two young girls in Arizona whose parents had died within months of each other. From there we talked about how difficult it would be to choose which couple among one's siblings and friends would best be suited for the job of raising our children. (Where did one couple's permissiveness slide into overindulgence, another's consistency into unbearable strictness?) The idea of dying was hard enough, but figuring out which couple would most love your kids in your absence? Intolerable.

We paused in our conversation just long enough for my brain to settle on yet another catastrophic possibility. "You know what would be worse?" I asked. "What if I died and John [my husband] married someone awful? I'd have no control at all!"

Another pause. "Unless," I continued, "I could get him to agree that if he remarried, my sisters and friends would check out the bride. Make sure she wasn't some kind of wicked stepmother in hiding."

Did you know at the start that you wanted to address particular issues?
Not really. I just had this character in mind: a lovable, charming, and funny woman who could talk people into seeing things her way, even when her way is slightly over-the-top and outrageous.

You grew up for a time in the South, but ended up moving around a lot. Do you consider yourself a Southerner?
Because we moved so often, I never feel like an insider, no matter where I live. Technically, I've lived in the South long enough to say I belong, but I have a feeling a *real* Southerner can count her granddaddy's granddaddy's people having come from the same place so far back there are quill marks naming the town in the family bible.

Would you ever create or sign a codicil like the one Penelope draws up for her husband?
That is the $64,000 question. What intrigues me about this codicil is it's so *wrong* and yet, so *right*. If you're thinking about young children, who could you imagine to better protect them than your most trusted girlfriend? And yet, how would I feel if my husband asked me to sign a similar document but where the committee was made up of his best friends? Suddenly

I can imagine feeling just the slightest bit uncomfortable. Insulted even!

One of the driving issues of the novel is Tessa's eating disorder. What kind of research did you do to understand this illness, and what would you like your readers to take from Tessa's plight?

I've known three teenage anorexics, all children of close friends. One of those girls has grown up to earn a master's degree in nutrition from Tufts University. She's been extremely generous in sharing her story and her insights with me. I also read scores of books and articles on eating disorders and consulted a psychologist friend at Florida State University when I had questions I couldn't answer on my own. What's most important to understand is that anorexia is very complicated. It's not so simple as "thin people thinking they're fat." There's a whole system of cues and triggers that become obsessive and oppressive. Clearly it has something to do with control, but it's not easy to decipher or to treat.

Siobhan is one of the most complex characters in the book. What were your feelings for her as you were writing the book? Ultimately, how would you like your readers to judge Siobhan?

Siobhan is limited by her need to create a perfectly controlled universe. Everything bad that's happened to her has been used as justification for not trusting anyone else, and for putting up defenses. She's bent on being perfect, on not breaking rules, but what she doesn't understand is that by shutting herself off from compassion, she's ultimately the loser. Without empathy and humility, it's impossible to grow, to experience grace, much less wonder. I just keep thinking of bark on a plant that's gotten so thick, nothing can make its way through, not even sunlight or water.

You grew up in a family of ten kids. How did that affect the way you wrote about Tessa and June's relationship?
It just seems natural to me, to re-create the bond between sisters.

Do you have a close sibling relationship like they do?
Absolutely. We're all close in different ways, but there is a certain protectiveness I feel for my siblings, and they for me. We also suffered through my brother Tommy's death, and I think that made us tighter as a group and more likely to treasure our time together.

What kind of research did you do for the financial fraud plotline in the book?
When I was thinking about the South, and my characters, I was driving back and forth from Tallahassee to Atlanta quite a bit. Every small town I went through seemed to have the same oversized billboards or banners across storefronts: huge, boldly colored, and often the only sign of life on the street: TITLE LOANS! PAYDAY LOANS! When I began researching these "industries" on the web, I found out how pernicious the loan terms were, and how trapped the customer becomes in a cycle of debt. From there I became fascinated by "fine print" and how it can represent all these obligations that have become woven together over time.

Was this a part of the book when you initially began writing?
Yes. I finished the novel in June 2007, well before the subprime crisis was a household word.

Did the current economic crisis influence you at all?
Well, when I used to talk about the research I was doing, I think people thought I was exaggerating the extent to which people could be duped into signing documents they couldn't understand. Most signers assumed that these contracts wouldn't be standard unless they'd been vetted by lots of consumers before them. It turns out the terms were being ratcheted up over time without anyone making a fuss about them. I do remember Alan Greenspan saying fairly recently that, even with his knowledge, he found mortgages almost impenetrably difficult to understand.

How do you see Lucy's character evolving through the story?
Lucy is intuitive and empathetic to a fault. When Penelope was killed, she was so busy worrying about the girls and Joey that she put her own needs on the back burner. She took out a mortgage so that she could shut down her bed-and-breakfast, and at that time, in her state of shock and grief, it was impossible to imagine time going by and that balloon amount about to be due. On top of that, Lucy didn't really think of her house as belonging to her. It was really Penelope's. It seemed appropriate to Lucy that she draw upon its value when Penelope's kids needed her. Still, Lucy wasn't a complete martyr. She loved her work; she considered painting the center of her life. She loved nurturing Penelope's kids, and was so accustomed to repressing her attraction to Joey, she could continue to do so indefinitely.

Do you relate to her on any level?
Yes. I am similarly passionate about my need to write, and I am very intuitive in my responses to things like

parenting. I can't say *why* I'm doing what I do, but I have a deep-seated gut instinct that, for the most part, we should apply the golden rule to raising children. In other words, we should treat children as we ourselves would like to be treated. This is a somewhat unorthodox view of parenting and you can easily imagine how—in times of uncertainty—it could be displaced by someone like Siobhan, who's so confident about her more authoritarian approach.

A major theme of this novel is friendship and sacrifice. Do you think friendship comes with certain loyalties and requirements?
Absolutely.

Would you do anything to help a friend?
Not anything, but my friends know they can count on me for a lot. I think one of the glorious things about friends is that they tend to judge you far more kindly than you do yourself.

If you could choose to be best friends with any character in the novel, who would you choose and why?
Tough choice, but I think I'd choose Penelope. She is so attractive, accomplished, complicated, and charming. (And of course she's gone, which makes her immediately the most desirable.) Plus, what would it be like to be taken under her wing? Actually, it's interesting to me that Penelope is sort of the übermother of them all. Not only does she see her friends' greatest qualities, but she's more than willing to use her connections and money to help them achieve their dreams. What's not to love about that?